TAINTED JEWEL

S.M. HOPE

Published in 2017 by:
Britain's Next Bestseller
An imprint of Live It Ventures LTD
www.bnbsbooks.co.uk

All enquiries should be addressed to Live It Ventures LTD, 126 Kirkleatham Lane, Redcar. Cleveland. TS10 5DD

Cover design by Margo Wiessman and Graeme Wilkinson

ISBN: 978-1-9997882-1-6

With special thanks to you for supporting *Tainted Jewel*

Amanda Corbitt, Lindsey Barnes, Gloria Harding, Vicky Judson, Lyndsey Barton Torr, Becky, Abby Henderson, Terrie Flannery-Clarke, Lesley Dixon, Felix Rosenberger, Nadine Rose Sturgill, Susan Playle, Cheryl, Helen Tiernan, Thea Brown, Emma Aljoe, Geraldine Hall, Hayley Mason, Rachel Weir, Claire, Lyndsey Hall, Glen Blackwood, Abby Henderson, Jacquie Jones, June Wake, Cheryl, Kelly McCaffrey, Nila Brown, Lorraine Wrightson, Paul Stobbart, Darren Moore, S. J. Weir, Janet Monks-Falconer, Corrie, Toni, Jane, Simone Shenton, Susan Bell, Hylke, Helen Richardson, Kathleen Swan, Stephen Westwood, Lisa Clark, Samantha, Vicki Oman, Kathryn Cochran, Jackie, Amy Clarke, Siobhan Heath, Karina, Sarah Dawson, Dianne Goudie, Denise Ross, Anita Waller, Karen Chilvers, Julie Bell, Sarah Lee, Gemma Henderson, Francesca Form, Evelyn Dawson, Suzanne Callaghan, Kirsty, Dawn Hill, Nicola Harvey, Michelle Heaviside, Stuart Bruce, Susan Forster, Kelly Ferguson, Anne Hall, Helena Peck, Katherine, Sam Smallwood, Darren Simpson, Dean Burles, Kirsty Jay, Billy Wilkie, Joan Paxton, Rob Enright, Paul Bone, Lynne, Steph Bell, Charlotte Teece, Tony Fox, Michael Edwards, Jessica Cadorath, Sarah Louise Hall, Kevin Gardner, John Convery.

Thank you for being
part of this

S.M. Hope

Chapter 1 – Meeting Mike

Richard Of York Gave Battle In Vain – red, orange, yellow, green, blue, indigo and violet. They're the colours of the rainbow, and that's exactly how Mrs Woods taught us to remember the colours.

No matter how you look at it, they're the colours; they never change no matter how much you want them to. See, even God had a system. Imagine you looked up one day and saw black in the rainbow, it would shock you, wouldn't it? Well, that's exactly how I feel when someone messes with my system. I have a colour system and everything needs to stay in the right order or I will surely die.

The carrots are with the peaches because they're both orange, the red grapes are with the cherries because they're both red, and the green grapes, well … well, they're in the bin. You can't eat anything with the same initial as the colour, can you? You would surely die if you did. I only use normal colours, like blacks, blues, reds, yellows. I don't go for the funny colours like maroon. That's brownish-red – what does that even mean? Is it brown or red? That would totally confuse things. I could never cope with that, my system works just fine the way it is. Imagine me using all those funny colours, like if the colours of the rainbow were maroon, beige, gold, ivory, amber, grey, and platinum. How on earth would you ever remember that one? *My Back Garden Is A Gangsters' Paradise?*

It's always been just me and my mum, Julie Reilly. Well, I say me and my mum, but also whichever man seemed to be on the menu that week; my mum likes her men. My name is Kathryn Reilly, but everyone calls me Kate. We live in a little town called Bridgeborough, in England. It's the kind of town where everyone knows everyone and we're all related to each other, one way or another. Well, everyone else is, not me and my mum. We just have each other. My mum was fourteen years old when I was born. I always felt like she blamed me for stealing her childhood. Her parents died when she was young and she was raised in care. I don't know who my father is. I have asked on numerous occasions, but I was told that she was so drunk she can't remember. How nice. She has a way of making me feel so special. Normally when she brings back her men, I can hear her giggling and talking through the wall. In the morning, there's the famous bang on the wall, which is my cue to make tea and toast. I'm like a modern-day Cinderella, always cleaning up after her or entertaining her guests. She's not a bad person, just a bad mum. It's not always her fault, I suppose; it's like a child bringing up a child. I feel more grown-up than her most of the time. She's always either working or hungover. She works in one of those clubs where all the pretty girls work and wear outfits meant for the beach. These clubs always seem to be owned by a man in a suit who everyone respects.

She's gorgeous, my mum – lovely figure, blonde hair. The men go wild for her. She always has full make-up on, even if she was to open the door to the milkman she'd have her full face on. Her clothes are always the newest fashion in town. Men seem to fall in love with her at the drop of a hat. They seem to fall out of love with her as well, normally just after the hat's been picked up, which is usually on their way out of the door.

I'm just as pretty, mind, and everyone at school likes me. I have this lovely head of hair. My mum ties my hair in pigtails, neatly, with the prettiest of bobbles every morning and walks me to school, making sure I have all the right books with me and look smart in my school uniform. Oh no, actually, hang on, that's Jennifer Hart, not me. I'm always straight out of bed, hair thrown back, normally messy. I have brown hair and me being ten years old, my hair is still in the wispy stage where it never knows what it wants to do – stay in a bobble or try to escape. I have to do it myself most mornings as my mum's always working late or drinking, so she throws me out of the door, biscuit in hand, and on my way.

It's a cold October morning in 1990 and there she is, Jennie Hart. She's one of those lucky girls blessed with everything: a mum who actually walks her to school every day and a dad who has a good job. She has lovely blonde hair, which has always been brushed neatly and put into pigtails. She always wears frilly socks with colourful bows on.

As we walk down the road, she skips on ahead so I try to quicken up my pace so I'm only a few feet away from Jennie's mum. She's smartly dressed with black trousers, kitten-heel shoes, a blouse and a scarf neatly tied around her neck. Everything is perfect, even her make-up and perfume. She smells just like a mum should smell and her brown hair is neatly tied into a bun so it keeps out of her face.

It's the same routine every morning and I imagine for a little while that I'm Jennie and Jennie's mum is my mum. As I walk through the leaves, which are starting to scatter, I can hear the crunching beneath my feet. My mind is completely lost in the idea of Jennie's mum holding my hand really tight. I feel so loved and protected. Out of nowhere some girls go running past me, shouting, 'Jennie, Jennie, wait up!' My lovely daydream didn't last too long, did it?

They never notice me. In fact, no one ever seems to notice me. Well, apart from Jennie, that is. She notices everything about me, from my messy hair to my saggy socks, and she makes sure the other girls notice it as well. She always has something unpleasant to say to me.

I'm finally inside the school gate and this is when my stomach starts to squeeze itself together so tightly that it hurts, and my eyes scan the school yard anxiously looking for her... Rebecca Bradshaw. Thankfully I spot her, standing on her own, already lined up, so I stand beside her. Rebecca has short brown perfectly straight hair in a bob. You'd think her mum had put a basin on her head and chopped around it. She's quite a big girl for a ten-year-old. She has these dangly arms and her cardigans are always too short for her. I don't think they do cardigans in enormous sizes. Yet she's someone

I get really excited about, but for all the wrong reasons. I know if the girls are picking on her they're leaving me alone; it's almost like I get excited to see her standing in the queue because I know she'll have a worse day than me. My stomach muscles relax the minute I see her.

It's so silly that my security blanket in life is a ten-year-old girl who dresses in clothes one size too small for her. Really, is *this* my protective shield? If I had any sense about me, I would make friends with Rebecca and together we could conquer the girls in our class and pick them off one by one. She could grab them all in her dangly arms and dump them into the nearest puddle. But, for now, my thoughts and plans go as far as pretending Jennie's mum is my mum – and praying Rebecca never gets ill.

The bell rings and all the kids run up to the line, all pushing and shoving each other. Somehow, I started this school day at the beginning of the line behind Rebecca and I've ended up at the back of the line listening to the other kids chat about their weekend and how great it's been. I wonder what their reactions would be if I say I got to make toast again and I rearranged the cupboard because my mum accidently mixed all the tins up so they were no longer ordered alphabetically by colour.

I hate it when she does that. I'm thinking about the cupboard and worried that she has taken the jam out and put it in the first place she can find because the tinned pears are at the front because they're white. My stomach is squeezing itself together so tightly that I can hardly breathe. That also happens when I think of the tins being mixed up.

I come back to earth with a bang as I overhear that another girl is having a party and, yet again, I'm not invited. I wonder if I actually exist in this life or if I'm a dead girl haunting the streets. I bet I'd have more fun, if that was the truth, than the way things are now. I could stand on the school roof singing 'Kum Ba Yah, My Lord' and I believe everyone would still just go about their business.

As we start to make our way into class I check the time and

count down; only six hours left and I'm free. We all put our coats and bags on our pegs. We know which peg is ours because we have a pretty sticker with our name on. Everyone's sticker is about pretty things, like rainbows and flowers for the girls. Jennie's sticker is a heart, which is totally appropriate with her surname being Hart. The boys have trains or cars. And me? Well, the girl unnoticed has an elephant as her sticker. I mean really, an elephant. Even the teachers have it in for me in this life. As we make our way to the mat to sing our 'good morning' song and have story time, all the girls race each other to sit next to Jennie. As usual, I have to sit next to Rebecca and Anthony. Anthony has it worse than me and Rebecca; he always has a snotty nose and, for some strange reason, he eats his pencils. I say to the teacher, 'I'm not sitting next to Anthony Morrison, miss. He eats his pencils and I think he has lead poisoning. He'll start to go grey soon and I'll go grey.'

'Oh be quiet, Kate, you're such a silly girl,' Mrs Woods scolds me.

Imagine me going grey? I'd be a grey girl and I can't be that because that's a colour starting with G, and girl starts with G. I would die, I'm sure I would.

I put my head down and sit there listening to the story, hoping that I don't turn grey or, worse, green with the amount of snot currently dripping down his face. Either way, grey or green, I'll be a goner.

Finally, my six-hour countdown is over. My day didn't go too badly, which is more than I can say for Rebecca. She got thrown into a puddle. I felt sorry for her but, on the other hand, I'm glad it wasn't me. I don't know what it is but I can't seem to stick up for myself. My mum drums it into me that if someone hits me, I hit them back twice as hard. That's really difficult when you run to the toilets crying or trying to find the nearest teacher. It's not in my nature to hit back. But it *is* in my nature to thank God above that Rebecca is a bigger geek than me, so for now I'm settling for that.

I finally get home – after having made it through another week of Rebecca not coming down with some mystery illness – where I can relax and not worry about every little thing. Well, apart from the cupboard.

Our house is a semi-detached house. As you walk in the front door, the hallway is decorated with cream walls and a red carpet. Halfway up the hallway, to your right, is the living room; there isn't much in there, just a TV on top of a stand with our video recorder underneath and a sofa with two chairs. We don't have any ornaments. 'The less ornaments the less cleaning,' my mum always says. As you come out of the living room back into the hallway you face the kitchen. This is where I spend most of my time: the cupboard in the corner is where we keep the tins and that's my safe haven. We do have a kitchen table, but we never use it to eat at. It's normally just for my mum to gossip round. Why eat at a table when you can have it on your lap watching TV?

There are two bedrooms upstairs and a bathroom. Our house can get cluttered from time to time. As long as the kitchen cupboard is in order I don't care how out of order the rest of the house is.

It's Friday night. As usual, my mum's in the kitchen with her wine, getting ready for work. She's dressed up to the nines. I have to get ready to go over to Mr and Mrs Richards. They live round the corner and I spend a lot of time with them. Mr Richards says I remind him of his son, as he had 'systems' as well. Not that I've ever told anyone about my systems, but he seems to just know. Maybe it's him, maybe he infects us with the need to have a system. Their son George no longer lives with them. He moved to London years ago and is a doctor. I think they have a little bit of a soft spot for my mum, with her being so young when she had a baby. Mr Richards used to own the corner shop that my mum had a Saturday job in when she was younger. Mr and Mrs Richards are both in their sixties and you can tell they totally adore each other. They have their routines every week. Monday is shopping day, Tuesday is rent day, Wednesday is bingo, Thursday they never leave the house and Friday they pay their bills. No matter how bad they are or what has happened in their lives that week, that's the way their week goes. I think they're grateful that I visit most Fridays and Saturdays, and at 10am sharp every Sunday, I'm round there. Mr Richards likes to take me to the car boot sales in Bridgeborough town while Mrs Richards cooks Sunday lunch. It's always my best day. I love the car boot sales and he always gives me one pound to spend and I try to find the best stall, which normally means I've dragged him round a few times to make sure I'm not getting ripped off and can't buy my chosen purchase cheaper on another stall. I sometimes spend my money on Mrs Richards too. I love the look on her face when I walk in with her present.

So off I go running round there for the evening, waiting for my mum to finish work.

'So, Kate, tell me about your day at school,' Mr Richards always asks. I give him a blow-by-blow account of all the work I've done, yet I never mention the fact that I hide behind someone as I'm so frightened of the other girls. I pretend I'm like any other ten-year-old enjoying life.

It's 2am and here she comes, laughing, down the path. I can always hear her before she knocks. I can hear several voices; great – it's a party now.

'Hello love, get your coat, it's time for home.' These are the times when she does notice me, she wants to show me off to her friends. We finally get back into the house and I really want my bed. 'Go on, get your magic set out to show us some tricks. She's fabulous. My daughter takes after me, don't you? Come here, give your mum a hug.' She tries to cuddle me, and kiss me on the cheek but I can smell the alcohol so strongly on her breath. I don't want to be kissed and cuddled by her when she's like this. Why can't she say it: 'Oh look, here she comes, the one who ruined my life. I'd have *been* something if it wasn't for her.' But, for now, we'll put on our show and let everyone think you're the perfect mum and I'm the perfect daughter.

I got a magic set when I was about four and I'm really good at it. I think it comes from spending a lot of time on my own, so I got to master these things. I bring down my box of tricks.

In the room, there's my mum, who seems to have another man attached to her. 'Lawrence, this is my daughter.'

'Hello,' he says in the usual friendly voice of 'I better be nice to you so I can get what I want out of your mum.'

Her best friend, Shelly Mason, also works in the club. Shelly is equally as pretty as my mum. Well, you have to be to work in the club. She has brown hair and it's normally tied up. She also has the cutest laugh. Shelly and my mum are more like sisters than friends. Shelly is a little younger than my mum, but I think my mum tries to relive her youth a little and Shelly helps her do that. Shelly seems to have found herself a gentleman friend for the evening too. He's quite tall and thin and not bad looking for an older man. He has a friendly smile and says, 'Hello young 'un, and what do they call you?'

'Kate,' I say and he giggles, mimicking a posh voice. 'Well, good evening, Miss Kate, please sit down and join us.' He noticed me and I never even had to show him any of my magic tricks, and he's not with my mum. Maybe he is a genuinely nice man, who knows? Mind, he's also noticed Shelly a little bit more than me, so maybe not so genuine. Shelly introduces him to me. 'Kate, this is Mike, please show him your tricks. You have got to watch this, Mike, she's so clever,' she drunkenly slurs.

I show him the disappearing sponge ball and he laughs his head off. 'Wow! That's amazing, that is,' he says in a voice which, to be honest, I can never work out if it means they actually are amazed or they know it's just a trick from a silly kid's box. I show him a few card tricks and by this time he's amazed. It starts to excite me a bit, that I'm getting attention from someone, and I make the most of it as you never know when it will happen again.

'What do you get if you cross some ants and some tics?'

'I don't know, Miss Kate, what do you get if you cross some ants and some tics?' says Mike.

'Allsorts of antics. Knock Knock.'

'Who's there?' they all shout.

'Lettuce.'

'Lettuce who?'

'Well lettuce come in and you'll soon find out.'

They all laugh at me and Shelly says, 'If you're not on the stage when you grow up, I'll eat my hat.'

'What did Mummy toilet paper say to baby toilet paper?'

'I don't know,' says Mike.

'Watch out, here comes Papa.'

That's my favourite joke. Whenever I feel sad I think of that joke and it cheers me right up. The conversation soon changes to keeping fit and Lawrence says, 'Hey, we should go on a bike ride – that would help us keep in shape.'

'Well, we can't, can we? You locked up your bike in the shed and forgot the code for your bike lock,' Mike drunkenly reminds him.

'Oh yeah,' Lawrence drunkenly remembers.

Mike mutters to himself, 'I wouldn't care, it's not even worth anything.'

My mum quickly tells them, 'Oh, our Kate can sort that for you. She can open bike locks and things like that, can't you, Kate?'

'No way,' says Mike, 'she can't open that. It's got a code lock on it. We'll have to chainsaw it off.'

'No, she can,' my mum tells him eagerly. 'Show them, Kate, go get the bike lock out of the cupboard under the stairs.' I go to get the bike lock reluctantly as it's nearly 3am and I really want everyone to leave and let me get some sleep tonight. I come back into the living room with the lock and tell Lawrence to change the code to anything he likes. He changes the code and passes the lock back to me. I play with the lock and try out the codes. There's a knack for doing it; if you look at the size of the gap between the numbers you can normally tell. I can also open it by listening closely and the clicks sound different, but that's pretty hard with the noise of my mum asking me to be quicker. I finally get the code and open the lock. Lawrence and Mike are totally stunned.

'No way, it must be a fake lock, it has to be. Give me a try.' Mike changes the code and after a few attempts the lock is open. Shelly laughs. 'See, I told you she was amazing. She's going to be a magician when she grows up.'

'Well, not a magician,' I say. 'That's a boy's job. I'll have to be the assistant and tell the magician what to do.'

Shelly gestures over for Mike to walk her home. 'Come on, you can walk me home, there could be all kinds out there this time of night and I'd hate to be stolen. I need a knight in shining armour just in case.' They start to laugh and off they go.

My mum's pouring more drinks for her new friend. I'll be seeing Lawrence again in the morning, no doubt. But, for now, my duties are done and my entertaining is over until tomorrow.

Next morning, there it is – that familiar knock on the wall. I go to the kitchen to put the kettle on and the usual round of toast. The kitchen is a mess, empty bottles and glasses all over the place. I start to clean it up and take my mum her breakfast in bed for her and her new-found prince.

Later that day, Shelly pops in and she and my mum are laughing about the antics they got up to last night. My mum asks how her knight in shining armour went.

'Not too bad, he wants to take me out tonight. He walked me home and went straight home himself, a true gent that's what he is.' My mum gives Shelly a funny look and says, 'You do know who that is, don't you?'

'Yeah, his name is Michael Taylor.'

'Yes, Michael Taylor,' my mum says, 'as in, Mike Taylor, Mr Simpson's sidekick. They're the Taylor brothers. That was Lawrence I was with last night.'

Shelly can't believe it. 'No way, he was such a gent, how could he be Mike Taylor? Are you sure?'

My mum comes back with, 'Hey, I know my Mikes from my Ikes, girl. That's him in the flesh. Look, they're OK for a bit of fun but don't be getting messed up with him, he'll break your heart or end up in prison and you'll be left on your own with a couple of kids, mark my words.'

'Well, maybe one more date with him then I'll tell him I'm not interested in him.' Shelly says this like she means it.

'Shelly, a girl like you can't say no. Hopefully he'll get bored of you before long and save you any hassle,' my mum says while shaking her head.

I don't know who the Taylor brothers are, or who this Mr

Simpson man is, or even what kind of hassle Shelly could get into, but it's not like my mum to put anyone off going out with a man.

On Sunday night Shelly comes round and she's grinning from ear to ear. My mum gives her that look and the words, 'Oo. Looks like someone enjoyed their date last night.'

'Yes, and my breakfast this morning. He's such a gent. He took me to that new restaurant in town. He never booked but they turned two people away who had booked to fit us in,' Shelly states excitedly.

'Well, you don't turn Mike Taylor away, do you?' my mum says. Shelly is still too excited to listen to what my mum has to say about Mike Taylor and the Taylor brothers. She's still dreamily thinking about her date.

'We had wine and the most delicious food ever, he bought me a rose and everything off one of those street sellers. I tell you, Julie, everyone who walked into that restaurant knew who he was and shook his hand.'

'Don't go there, Shelly. It's what he does best, he charms the birds from the trees to get what he wants. He'll use and abuse you, just like he does everyone else.'

'What about you and Lawrence? Mike tells me you two are going out next week.'

'Yes, but I can handle men like them, I've been doing it my whole life. It's about staying in control, Shelly, and never letting your feelings get in the way. Don't get involved, don't get hurt. That's my motto. They'll wine and dine us two this week and it'll be two other women by next week. You mark my words, love.'

Chapter 2 – Jennie Fart

A few weeks go by and things seem to still be going on with my mum and Lawrence and Shelly and Mike. Maybe my mum isn't right all the time after all.

My mum comes into my room with my list of commands for tonight. 'Right you, the boys are coming over tonight. I want you in your room all night, no excuses to come down. Don't be seen or heard tonight, you.'

It's funny, I do that on a daily basis at school without even trying.

I'm in my room and I can hear them all laughing downstairs and I'm desperate for a drink. I'm thinking of ways I can get one without being seen or heard. Mind you, I can manage this quite easily every other day. I'm the girl who's never noticed. I make my way down the staircase like a Russian spy and go to the kitchen. I pour myself a drink. I'm really good at this, mission nearly accomplished – just as I switch the tap off, in comes that friendly face.

'Ah look, it's the magician. Have you got any more of those tricks?' says Mike, the worst of the Taylor brothers in my mother's humble opinion.

'Oh no, I have to go to bed,' I say as quietly as possible before I get caught. Too late, in walks my mum.

'Hey, who are you talking to, Mike?' She takes one look at me and gives me that look of 'What are you doing down here. I warned you.'

'Oh, let her stay here for a little while,' says Mike.

'OK, for a little while,' she reluctantly says. It gives my mum a chance to show off as the doting parent in front of her new boyfriend.

I like Mike. I show him a few more tricks from my magic box and out of ears' way he teaches me a trick. He lays four cards on the table and says, 'We'll get Shelly to pick a card, you turn your back and when she says "ready" come back and place your hand over each card separately. Tell her you know which card is hers because of the heat coming off the card. When you have your hand over the correct card, I'll take a drink. We'll charge them all 10p for every time you get it right.'

First we try the game on Shelly. She loves it. Lawrence has a turn, even my mum has a turn. It's not long before I get really tired and say, 'I'm heading off to bed.' Before I go Mike asks if I'm OK to open the lock on Lawrence's bike. He reminds me that I was showing them that trick last time they were here.

'Yes, of course I can. I'll go tomorrow, pick me up,' I sleepily say as I walk up the stairs.

The following day I wake up and get my mum her usual round of tea and toast. Lawrence stays the night but I don't mind him staying – he's OK, for a boy, I guess. Mike turns up with his van. 'Come on, you two, are you ready?' he eagerly says.

'Oh, great, a lift home,' Lawrence says. I'd forgotten all about me opening the bike lock for them today.

We make our way to their house. It's a nice little house and as you walk in there are photographs covering the whole of the passage wall. There are some of them boxing, they must have both been in a club when they were younger.

'Ha! Look, Lawrence! There's you in your shorts, look at how skinny you were,' I mock.

'Hey, cheeky, that's what you call the lean mean fighting machine.' He giggles and starts to pretend box. Mike says, 'Yes, but that was before I came on the scene.' He starts to pretend box as well. They start to have a play boxing match in the hallway. We all laugh. I quite like these two.

'Who are you two talking to?' comes a voice from the living room.

'Hello, Dad,' says Mike. 'This is Miss Kate, she's come to help us do something in the back yard.'

We make our way into the yard and there's a shed at the bottom of it. It looks like it was red at one point, but it's an old rickety thing now. Lawrence opens the door and says, 'There, that's it,' and points to a bike which is full of cobwebs. The bike lock looks older than these two put together and I'm not sure if I'll be able to open such an old lock, but I'll try. If not, we could always go with Mike's original thought of the chainsaw. I fiddle with the lock for a while and you can definitely hear the clicking is different. Within minutes it's open and they both look at each other in astonishment.

'Look at that, eh. Have you ever seen anything like it, Lawrence?' Mike is grinning from ear to ear, like it's his bike that's been released. 'Come on, little 'un, I'll get you home,' he says.

As we walk back in the house there's a woman there. She looks like she's been shopping.

'Hello, Mum,' says Lawrence and they both kiss her on the cheek. She looks in my direction and asks the question with a hint of a giggle, 'Who's the angel, then? Not one of yours, is she?'

'No, miss, I'm Julie Reilly's daughter, I don't belong to either of these. My mum got drunk at a party and she doesn't know who my dad is.'

Mike laughs and says, 'Miss Kate, I'm sure that's not true.' His mum gives him a grin as if to say, Bless that little girl, everyone should know who their father is.

'I'm about to stick the kettle on, do join us for tea and biscuits, er, Miss Kate, is it? Daughter of Mrs or Miss – as the case may be – Reilly.'

I get myself comfortable on the sofa while she brings over some biscuits and asks if I like chocolate. I say, 'Yes,' and she hands over the bourbons. 'Oo, I can't eat bourbons, Mrs Taylor.'

'Why not? I thought you liked chocolate.'

'Have you any digestives? I'm safe eating them.'

'What do you mean, safe? Has there been an attack of the killer bourbon someone's not telling me about?' I take a digestive. I dare not tell these people about my eating habits. I eat my biscuit and drink my tea. I don't know what it is about this house but I feel so comfortable in it and would like to spend a lot of time in here. The Taylor brothers indeed. My mum never really knows what she's talking about. Mike says, 'Come on then, you, it's time for home.' He drives me home and thanks me for helping Lawrence out with his bike.

On Monday morning, as I enter the school gate, there's no sign of Rebecca. My stomach cramps up more than it normally does. This can only mean one thing: it's my turn to be picked on all day by Jennie and the other girls. It's started already and they're playing passy with my bag and won't give me it back, great. The bell finally goes and I can't see my bag for all the kids pushing and shoving. Oh, I see it in that muddy puddle. As I pick my wet bag up, I wonder what I have possibly done in a past life for this to happen to me. Maybe my mum has mixed up the tins while I've been out. I mean, it's been a whole ten minutes, anything could have happened in that cupboard by now. If the tins are muddled up with other colours something bad will happen. It just has to. It's messing with the system. As I think of the tins being all messed up my stomach starts to cramp up again. I really wish it didn't do that, but it has always cramped up when I get a little worried about things. I don't know why.

It's the day of the spelling test, which means every child has to stand up on their own and spell out a word that the teacher tells us to. Everyone has a go and eventually it's my turn. It doesn't bother me as I'm really good at spelling. In fact, I'm pretty good at all my school subjects. My mum says I have an overactive mind, that's how I can open up bike locks and do magic tricks. I'm standing up waiting for my word and suddenly I hear Jennie say, 'Oh look, it's Flakey Katie's turn to spell a word, wonder if she'll get "hairbrush".' And all the other girls laugh.

The teacher says, 'Right, Kate, your word is "design".'

I know this word, it's so easy, yet I can still feel the girls giggling at me and how I would love to have the guts to smack Jennie right on the nose and DESIGN a bloodstained picture from her little 'accident'...

'D-I-' Everyone starts to laugh.

'Wrong, Miss Reilly, try again,' states Mrs Woods in her condescending voice.

I can't, I simply can't. I can feel them, the tears are rolling down my face and the whole class is laughing. There's only one thing left to do. I run out of the classroom and up the yard as quick as I can. Oh no, where will I go at this time? I don't have anyone to run to. I suppose I could go home, my mum probably won't notice me anyway. I run up the road near the local shops and tears are still streaming down my face. I bump into a very big figure and he pulls me away as I look up to see him. It's him, Mike Taylor.

'Hey, it's you,' he says. 'And where are you going in such a hurry, little girl?' I don't know why, but I cuddle into him and cry like a baby. I can't stop, yet in a funny way I realise it's probably the first time I've ever been held in a way where I feel safe. No one can get me now that Mike's taking care of me. He ushers me towards his van.

'Hey, you, it's not like you to be upset. Tell your uncle Mike all about it, what's happened then?' It takes me a while to compose myself and I'm a little embarrassed to say that everyone ignores me and that he's the only person ever to notice me.

'It's Jennie Hart, I hate her and everyone loves her and if Rebecca was in today then none of this would have happened.'

'Well, who's Rebecca? Your friend?'

'No, she's the girl everyone picks on but if she's not in then *I'm* the girl everyone picks on. Because Jennie tells them to.'

'I take it Jennie is the class bully?' Mike asks. 'Well, why don't you teach that Jennie a lesson?'

'Well, I can't, can I? I don't know what to do.'

'Did you say her surname was Hart?'

'Yes.'

'Well, it's simple. You should use your tricks to get to her. Surely you could think of something with your brains.'

'No, I can't think of anything. The best I can come up with is to hide behind Rebecca but I can't do that if Rebecca's not in. I did think about hiding behind Anthony but he eats his pencils and might give me lead poisoning.'

Mike giggles at me. 'Well, if she's called Jennie Hart, you know what that rhymes with, don't you?'

'No, what?'

'Well, fart, Kate – come on, everyone knows that. We need to think of something so we can have everyone call her Jennie Fart. Trust me, by the time we've finished with her everyone will call her Jennie Fart and Miss Farty-pants will be begging you to be her friend by the end. Let's see...' Mike thinks for a while. 'Why don't you boil an egg tonight and peel the shell off it and leave it in a box overnight. By the time you get to school tomorrow that egg will be stinking. You can plant it in her pocket when she's not looking. I know you can do it, you're the magician's assistant. By the end of the day she will smell so bad everyone will be calling her Jennie Fart.' I laugh. 'If Jennie Fart starts any more trouble, you punch her square on the nose like this. Hold up your fists and cover your face a bit, this is called holding your guard. You punch like this, a quick jab should do it.' He starts to jab the air and says, 'Now you try, hold your guard.'

I put my fists together so they're practically touching my nose. 'No, not there, a little lower down. Jab my hands.' As I start to punch his hands, which he is holding up for me, he says, 'Wow! You've got some jab on you there, kid.'

'Thanks, Mike.' I hug him again to say goodbye. He pulls me back and says, 'You know how you opened our Lawrence's bike lock? I've got another friend who's forgot his code. Could you open it for him?'

'Yeah, I suppose so. When?'

'Well, now, if you can.'

He drives me to this house and tells me to climb over the fence and open the gate for him. He reassures me that it's OK, it's his friend who is at work and we're going to surprise him by taking the bike round to him.

I eventually get over and open the gate. Mike joins me in the garden and points to the bike. 'That one there, yes, that's the one.' I fiddle with the lock and it soon opens. Mike is smiling from ear to ear. 'God, you're an absolute gem you, aren't you? Let's take it round to him. There might be a plate of chips in it for you.'

Mike puts the bike into the back of the van and we drive off. He pulls up outside a car garage and gets out to speak to the man working on a car. I can't hear what they're saying but he is nodding towards the van. The two of them come over to the van and he opens the back doors. They don't speak but I can see the man has nodded and Mike pulls the bike out of the van. As Mike gets into the van he hands me over a five pound note and says his friend was really happy that I got his bike back for him and he wanted to pay me for it. 'Let's get you those chips I promised you.'

We go into the cafe and he sits me at the table. The man behind the counter shakes Mike's hand and smiles at him saying, 'Mike, what can I get you? Who's the pretty lady? Is she yours?'

'Nah, she's not mine but she would like some of the best chips in town with the plate piled high.'

'No problem, Mike,' says the man. When the chips come out I've never seen a mountain of chips that size before. I start to eat them and in comes another man.

'Hello, Mike, how's things?' He also shakes Mike's hand. 'Is she yours, then?'

'Nah, she's not mine. I'm looking after her for the day.' They start whispering and Mike pulls out some money from his pocket and hands it over. 'I'll give it you back next Tuesday, I promise,' says the man. Mike says, 'Yeah, you know how much interest I charge and don't be late.'

I'm halfway through my chips and another man comes in and sees Mike. He tries to leave quickly and Mike follows him. They go round the corner and I'm not really sure what has happened but when Mike comes back his fist is all red. I ask him what happened and he says he fell over when he went to see his friend outside. I don't question it or even think it's not true. I just love spending time with Mike. I wonder what it would be like if he was my dad. I'd love a dad like Mike.

'Are you finished with those chips yet, Gem? I better get you home.'

'Gem? I'm not called Gem. I'm called Kate.'

'I know you're called Kate, but you're my little gem, so that's your new name.'

As we drive towards my estate he tells me not to let anyone pick on me. He says he'll teach me boxing if I like.

'But I thought boxing was for men who have black faces on the TV, like Chris Eubanks and Frank Bruno.' Mike laughs and says, 'No way, anyone can be a boxer, that's just what you see on the TV. My dad was a boxer for years. It's how we were brought up, round a ring, fighting each other or watching others fight.'

'Maybe I'll leave the boxing, if you don't mind, Mike.'

'That's fine, Gem, it's up to you,' Mike says while smiling at me sweetly. He seems to have adopted the nickname for me. I love that, it makes me feel even more special.

That night I boil an egg, like Mike says. I put it in a container and hide it under my bed. I wake up in the morning and the first thing on my mind is the egg under the bed. I pull up the container and take a sniff. Phwoar, that stinks, that does. I start to get ready for school and feel a little excited, hoping I can pull this off, or it's a case of waiting until Rebecca gets well again. She may have even died for all I know, which means I'll always be picked on. Imagine that, being picked on forever.

As I leave the house I see her, Jennie Farty-pants and her mother, walking to school, like the perfect scene as always. I still quickly catch them up to pretend Jennie's mum is my mum. We finally get into school and there's still no sign of Rebecca, so I'm definitely on for the whole stinky-egg challenge. This is starting to feel real and I'm a little frightened. Maybe I'll leave it for another day. I start to think about Mike and what he taught me. I know he'll be asking me about it and what will he think if I said no, I chickened out. He'd probably come back with some joke about an egg and a chicken. I have to do this. All the kids are pushing and shoving as usual and Jennie Hart is right near me. She pushes me and says, 'You don't belong here, get back to the back of the queue.'

I'm so sad, yet I still get to the back of the queue. We make our way to the cloakroom and she's right beside me. It's like this was meant to happen because she's so close, her pocket is in full view and easy to reach. I can see it on her pinafore. I get the egg out of the container. I can smell it already. I get as close as I can to her and by some miracle her pocket is wide open. My heart is racing but I place it in as gently as I can and make my way to class. Nothing is said for the first half an hour and I've forgotten about it as I'm painting and have managed to get my hands on the red paint; all the girls seem to go for pink paint. But imagine me using pink paint. As I paint my picture, making sure to stay as neat as I can, I hear someone say, 'Urh, what is that smell?'

Before long, the whole class is questioning the smell and I walk towards Jennie and scream, 'Ee, miss, it's Jennie Fart – look, she has an egg in her pocket and it stinks.' The whole class is in uproar, all on their feet, and I never prepared myself for what happened next. Jennie gets up and tries to hit me. I don't know why but I find the courage to put my fist together and punch her right on the nose, just like Mike showed me. She starts to cry and Mrs Woods jumps up and shouts, 'Jennie Fart, do sit down!'

As soon as the words come out of her mouth she realises what she's said and me and the rest of the class can hardly control ourselves. I'm marched down to the headmaster's office. I'm not even bothered about what the headmaster says, it was totally worth it. I can't wait to tell Mike about this. It worked out a lot better than I'd planned. For the whole day Jennie has been called Jennie Fart and sat crying for most of it. Now she knows how me and Rebecca feel. I almost wish Rebecca was here so she can revel in our win against the bully.

The next day, as I walk out of the house, Jennie is there with her mum and, as usual, I expect Jennie will run ahead and I'll pretend to walk with her mum like she's mine, but that doesn't happen. Jennie shouts me over and asks if I want to walk with her, so I do. We soon start skipping up the road together singing 'We Are The Orange Girls' and giggling away. We end up sitting together all day long, she even chooses the same food as me at dinner time. For the first time ever, I've actually got a friend – and it's all down to Mike Taylor.

Chapter 3 – Setting The Bikes Free

Mike and Shelly are still going out together. So Mike and Lawrence are very much part of my life, as Lawrence seems to still be taken with my mum. Why anyone would want to go out with her is beyond me.

Jennie and I are inseparable these days. I think my mum's pleased I finally have a friend. I'm going over to play at her house today. When I get there she's sitting at the table with all of her craft things out. 'What are you doing?'

'I'm making my dad a card for Father's Day.'

Jennie has loads of lovely things to make a card. I get a little upset at seeing how happy she is and how happy I know her dad will be when he opens it on Sunday morning. I forgot all about Father's Day on Sunday as it never really means anything to me. How I would love to be able to hand a card over to my dad. 'Can I make one?'

'Yes, of course you can, who would you give it to, Lawrence?'

'No, I'm thinking if I go home and show my mum the hard work I've done making a card she might tell me who my dad is.'

'That's a great idea. I'll help you.'

I start to fold the card and spot a red pom-pom that would make a great clown nose. I draw a clown shape around the pom-pom and write the words: To Dad, I would love to clown around with you one day. Love Kate xx

I'm so excited to take the card home and finally have my mum tell me who my dad is. Hopefully he lives close by so I can hand deliver the card. I imagine myself knocking on his door and him telling me that he's been searching for me my whole life but never found me. Then giving me the biggest hug and kiss I've ever had. He might even take me to the circus when he sees how great the card is.

I run home as quickly as I can. I'm so excited to finally find out the truth. I head straight into the kitchen where my mum and Shelly are and grab my mum's arm, tugging on it excitedly. 'Mum, it's Father's Day on Sunday. I was thinking it would be nice if I could hand deliver this card to my dad. He might be so happy that he takes me to the circus. Can I? Pleeeeease, just tell me who he is. I'll go straight over and I promise to come straight back.' I push the card right into her face.

My mum pushes the card away from her face and says the same thing she does every time I ask. 'Kate, please stop asking me. I've told you a million times I don't know who he is. Give the card to Lawrence, he's a better father to you than anyone else could ever be.'

My heart drops when she says that. Of course she wasn't going to tell me. She never tells me. Why I thought a stupid card would make a difference I don't know.

It's Saturday morning. Mike and Shelly come over to see my mum and they ask if we want to go on a fishing trip. Mike and Lawrence have a cousin called Mark, and his son Liam wants to come so at least it's company for me. But I don't really need the company of a smelly boy so I ask if Jennie can come as well. Mike says, 'Who, Jennie Fart?' We giggle together and Shelly asks, 'What do you mean?' Mike says, 'Oh, nothing,' and gives me a wink as it's our little secret. As we get on the boat, we all grab a fishing rod.

'Right, little 'un,' says Mike, 'get your rod ready. I'll show you how to hook on your bait.' I assume he means bread or something. He puts his hand in a tub and pulls out a worm. I scream, 'Oh, no way am I touching that!'

Liam and Jennie laugh at me and Liam pulls out a worm and sticks it on to his hook. Jennie does the same.

'Come on scaredy-cat, get one,' teases Mike.

'No way, it's disgusting!'

'What, you're not scared of that ragworm, are you? They can't hurt you, look,' he says while holding up a worm, practically wiggling it in my face. Then he bites its head off.

'Ugh, that's disgusting.' I'm not sure what I'm more horrified at, the fact he's just eaten a worm or the fact the worm is white. He'll surely die now. He opens his mouth to show us that he has actually swallowed the worm.

'You're disgusting!' Shelly screams and smacks him playfully on the bum. He says, 'Oo, that's nice, gis a kiss, go on,' and he chases her round the boat trying to get her to kiss him. My mum and Lawrence start laughing at them. It's a really good day so far – well, apart from the fishing, I suppose. I settle for sandwiches, crisps and pop while Jennie and Liam do the fishing. Lawrence scolds me for playing with my food and picking the sandwiches apart.

'Oh, leave her,' says my mum. 'She's always doing it. No matter what I say she has to pull her food apart. You're wasting your breath even saying anything.'

I'm not sure why, but I feel a little jealous as Mike is standing with Jennie; she's caught something and he's excited and helps her reel it in. 'Look at that,' he says. 'She's the winner of today's fishing trip!' As they reel in the big fish even Lawrence is on his feet to check out her prize catch. I'm wishing I'd never even met Jennie Fart. Lawrence and Mike are *my* friends, not hers. Lawrence helps Jennie unhook the fish and Mike comes over to me and whispers in my ear. 'My friend has locked his bike up and he can't remember the code. Is there any chance you could help him out?'

'Yes, of course I can, let me know when.'

'You really are my little gem, aren't you?' he says and smiles.

As we moor the boat, it's time for home. I'm exhausted. My mum takes Jennie and me straight home with Lawrence, while Shelly and Mike go off with Liam. Jennie runs straight into her house to tell her mum about her day. I'm still not best pleased about it, but never mind. Mike still thinks I'm his favourite as he still called me his 'little gem'.

I lie in bed that night thinking of the day's events. I remember Mike eating the worm. A thought pops into my head about when the teacher told us that if you chop a worm in half it can grow back again. Oh no, what if it's still alive in Mike's belly and it's hungry? It will eat his belly, he will wake up screaming in agony and have no belly left. Surely he'll die with no belly. I quickly get out of bed, thinking if he starts screaming at least I can be there to help and call the ambulance to tell them exactly what is wrong with him. I get my clothes on, rush downstairs and, as quick as I can, I go to Shelly's. I use Mum's spare key. I open the door very quietly and hide in the cupboard under the stairs. My heart is beating so fast. I'm not sure if it's in the hope I don't get caught or in the hope that Mike doesn't scream in pain, dying. What will I say if I do get caught? I know, I'll say I dropped food all over the floor and wanted to borrow the hoover. If they question why I need Shelly's, I'll tell them ours is broken. While I'm thinking of reasons why our hoover is broken, I hear the phone ringing. Oh no, the phone sits on a table at the bottom of the stairs. What if I breathe so heavily they can hear me in the cupboard? Hopefully they won't hear the phone because they will be asleep. My mind starts to wonder about them both being dead, as the phone has been ringing a really long time.

I hear someone coming down the stairs and Mike says in a sleepy tone, 'All right, all right, I'm coming!' Great, Mike is still alive. I'm so pleased. I hear him pick up the phone.

'Hello. Jesus, what do you want at this time? Can't it wait?' Mike goes quiet while the other person speaks. I hear him say in reply, 'What, and it can't wait till tomorrow? It's just gone past midnight, I've been away for the day.' Again he goes quiet while the other person speaks. 'Give me ten minutes.' I hear Shelly come down and say to Mike, 'You're not going anywhere, Mike, it's late.'

Mike says, 'I'll be an hour, tops.'

'Why do you have to jump every time he says jump?' Shelly snaps.

'Don't start, Shelly.' Mike goes back up the stairs and I hear

Shelly say, 'I'm getting sick of this.'

I wonder who it was on the phone and who tells Mike to jump? Mike comes back down the stairs. 'I promise, I'll make it up to you when I get back.'

Shelly says, 'That's if you get back.'

Mike leaves the house and I sit in that cupboard all night long still wondering who it was that rang Mike.

Eventually Mike returns and I hear Shelly say, 'Some hour.'

Mike in return says, 'Don't start. I'm tired, I'm going to bed.'

They both go up the stairs and I make that my getaway. At least Mike is not dead. I make my way back home and climb into my own bed so it looks like I've been there all night long.

My favourite day has finally arrived: Sunday! I rush round to Mr and Mrs Richards. It doesn't matter how many car boot sales I've been to I always find something different there.

Mr Richards parks the car, it's been raining most of the weekend so the grass is so muddy I sink into it as soon as I step out of the car. 'Come here, Kate, I'll help you walk. We should find you some wellies with weather like this.' Mr Richards grabs me by the arm to stop me sinking any further.

'Wellies, that's a great idea! I've never had a pair of wellies before.'

We go searching for a pair of wellies and finally find some green ones with eyes sticking out of them to show they're frogs. I remember Jennie had a pair of those one day at school. That makes me want them even more. We buy the wellies and a new ornament for Mrs Richards, as Mr Richards smashed her favourite one last week. 'Hopefully, Elizabeth will like this one as much as the other one. It might get me out of the bad books,' he says with a cheeky grin on his face.

'Mr Richards, I don't think you could be in anyone's bad books. But hopefully she'll like it.'

When we arrive back at the Richards' house, Mrs Richards is so happy with her ornament and she loves my wellies. We've decided to name them Freddie and Fiona the frogs. I've never had them on my feet since I got them, I'm just holding them and making pretend conversation between the two of them. I even jokingly make the frogs kiss, which makes Mr Richards laugh so much he nearly chokes on a sprout. I don't think Mrs Richards is too keen on me having second-hand wellies at the table. But she doesn't say anything. All she can do is laugh at Mr Richards because he's so red in the face from coughing. 'That'll teach you to chew your food properly, Graham. I'm sick of telling you about that.'

I rush home, my mum is working tonight so it's just me and Lawrence. He's hired a movie from the shop and bought some popcorn. I love nights in with Lawrence.

We snuggle on the sofa with a blanket. I even manage to squeeze Freddie and Fiona in. 'Kate, get those wellies off the sofa, you don't even know where they've been.'

'No, I can't put them down they would be upset. Meet Freddie and Fiona. Look.' I make them kiss again, which makes Lawrence laugh. 'Be careful there, Kate, we don't want any tadpoles.'

'What do you mean, tadpoles?'

'Well tadpoles, they come from frogspawn and turn into frogs when two frogs mate.'

Just as he says that the door goes and it's Mum. 'Work was quiet today, so Ronnie has let me come home. What are you two up to?'

'Nothing. Lawrence was just telling me about frogs mating.'

Lawrence nearly jumps out of his skin. 'Not really, Julie, we were just joking.' My mum gives him a really funny look, and then walks out of the room and into the kitchen. Lawrence follows her. I can't quite hear what is being said, but they are whispering about something.

The following weekend Mike comes over and asks if I'm OK to help out his friend. Off I go in the van. He tells me that he's been talking to other friends and they all have bikes locked up but they have forgotten the codes. He pulls out a list with all the addresses on and off we go. I collect three bikes and when we get to the fourth bike I notice that the bike lock is black.

'Oh no, I can't pick that one.'

'Why not?' he asks.

'I just can't. It's black.'

'What difference does that make?'

I'm embarrassed to say that I can't open it because it's a black bike lock. He would think I was crazy. So I tell him that the black ones are special and I can't work them.

'That's strange, surely they work the same way as the others? I'll have to tell my friend that I can't get his bike for him.'

I do a couple more bikes and the next bike lock is blue.

'I can't open that one either.'

Mike asks, 'Why not?'

'Because it's blue and it's the same as the black ones and I can't work them out yet.'

I work out that there were ten bikes picked up that day.

He tells me how clever I am for the billionth time and gives me ten pounds and says, 'You can't tell anyone about this. It's our secret, OK? I've been winding my friends up that it's me who can open these locks and I've been betting them a pound each bike. But it's only fair that I give the pounds to you so that's why I've given you that tenner.'

'You don't have to give me money, it's fine. But you may want to change your friends. They're really forgetful.'

Mike laughs and takes me home. 'Can I pick you up if any of my friends get forgetful again?'

'Yes, of course you can.'

I really hope his friends do get forgetful so I get to spend time with Mike, just me and him, without Shelly or Jennie being there.

Lucky for me over the past couple of years Mike has had some really forgetful friends and my weekends are full of me and Mike opening bike locks. Even today we've been out most of the day collecting bikes.

When I get back home my mum and Shelly are at the kitchen table trying to sort out changing shifts with another one of the girls because they're not working the same night and they always like to work the same shift. Shelly holds her belly and says, 'Got terrible cramp today, Julie, it's time of the month. It's not doing my hangover any favours.'

My mum says, 'Shelly, don't talk about time of the month in front of Kate.'

'Don't be so silly, she's nearly a woman herself. You can't keep her a baby forever, you know.'

My mum really snaps back at her. 'Don't you dare tell me what I can and can't do with my daughter. You're not even a mother so what the hell would you know?'

I've never heard my mum and Shelly fall out. 'Mum, what's wrong? Please don't shout at Shelly like that.'

My mum holds my face. 'Sorry, Kate, I don't know what got into me there. You get yourself off to see Mr and Mrs Richards, here take a biscuit with you.' She passes me a biscuit from the tin and I head towards the door. As I get there I hear Shelly say, 'You have to stop this, she's not a baby, even when you sent her away you gave her a biscuit, she's not a toddler she's nearly a teenager.'

'Don't get involved in mine and Kate's relationship. I want to keep her as a baby as long as I can.'

I walk out of the door and head towards Mr and Mrs Richards. 'Hello Kate, sweetheart,' Mrs Richards says. Mr Richards then pops his head round the corner. 'Sunday already?'

'No, Mr Richards, my mum sent me round here to see you. I think her and Shelly are having words and don't want me to hear them.'

'Oh well, never mind, lucky us getting to spend the afternoon with you.'

Mrs Richards then says, 'I'll get the teapot and the biscuits out.'

I'm wondering if I should even get a biscuit now I know they are for toddlers and not teenagers. Mind you, I don't care how old I get, this tea-soaked ginger snap is the best. I think about what Shelly meant when she said 'time of the month'. What time of the month?

Mike wants me to open some more bike locks today, away from Bridgeborough. I have a sneaky feeling that they're not his friends, but I love spending time with him so I try not to think too much about it. I've half-heartedly explained why the black and blue ones can't be opened as they have been coming in thick and fast. It's a Saturday, so it's our usual, free-the-bikes day. We go to the first address and the bike lock is black. There's no way I'm opening that, I can tell you that for nothing. But Mike is still trying to get me to do it.

'No, I can't, I just can't.'

'You can, please just do it.'

'No, Mike, it's black.'

'This is so silly. I've told you nothing is going to happen to you if you open the locks with the colours beginning with B. We've been through this a thousand times.'

'I don't care, we can go through it a thousand more. I'm not opening it.'

'OK, I'll go find another one.'

I hate it when Mike forces me to do stuff I don't want to do. Plus, I'm sick of helping out his friends. I bet I've helped everyone in the UK out by now. As I go to the next shed, I see it: it's like Jennie's. I can't stop looking at it. That girl must be really spoilt, like Jennie, to have a bike like that. Mike is coming over, but I'm too busy inspecting that bike to notice.

'Hey, what you looking at? That bike? Do you want it? Cos my friend says if you get his bike you can have the pink one. I forgot to tell you.'

I really would like that bike. I've never had a bike before.

'If you get that bike for me you can have the pink bike. I'll even take you to the park for an hour afterwards so you can ride it round there.'

'I've never ridden a bike before.'

'What, you've never ridden a bike? Impossible, everyone's ridden a bike, open that lock and I'll teach you.'

'I don't think I even want to ride a bike. I'm not that bothered really.' I say this as I don't want Mike thinking I'm bothered, even though I am a little.

'Oh, go on, please. Do it for me.'

I really do want that bike. 'OK then, I'll try.'

'Good girl,' Mike says while hugging me. This gives me a funny feeling in my belly but not the kind of feeling I get when I'm worried. I go over to the black lock and my palms are so sweaty that I'm turning it and nothing is happening. I'm going to open this lock and it will be the last thing I do. I'm going to die, I'm 100 per cent sure I'm going to die. But I *really* want that pink bike. I finally get the lock open. Mike hugs me again.

'See, nothing happened, you grab that pink bike I promised you and I'll take this one to the van. We'll head off to the park and I'll show you how to ride it.'

We finally get to the park and he gets me to sit on the bike. I'm really unsteady, he lets me go and I wobble all over the place. Mike points out a girl who looks about eight riding her bike. 'Oh look, the baby is better than you,' he teases.

'Hey, stop it, or I'm taking that bike back and locking it back up as well.'

We giggle and I finally get the hang of the bike. I'm going fast down the bank, I can feel the wind in my hair. I love it when me and Mike do things like this. It makes me think again that I wish Mike was my dad.

'That's enough, Gem. I've got things to do tonight, but I've got time to take you for ice cream.'

'Oh, can't we stay a little longer? This is fun!' I beg Mike to stay with me. Riding a bike is so much fun.

'No, we'll come out again tomorrow.'

We go for an ice cream. I choose strawberry and Mike chooses chocolate. We always swap halfway through, unless one of us chooses vanilla. We then spend our time teasing the other one that their ice cream is boring.

I go to the toilets and as I pull down my knickers I notice the blood. I realise that opening that black bike lock was such a mistake and this is my punishment. It's killing me. I'm dying. I run back to the table to tell Mike about it.

'Oh my God, Mike, it's eating me!'

'What?' Mike says in astonishment.

I start to panic. 'The bike, it's eating me.'

'Don't be stupid, bikes don't have teeth. What do you mean?'

'I went to the toilet and I'm bleeding, it's eating me alive, I told you the black ones can't be opened.'

'What?' Mike says with a sigh as he raises his head. 'How old are you?'

'I'm twelve.'

'Has your mother not told you about the birds and the bees yet?'

'The what and the whees?'

'Well, you know...' Mike nervously says, 'Well, like, what a man and a woman do when they love each other, and how you get a baby.'

'No, she's told me about vodka – oo, and Bloody Marys. Hey, cos of that bike I've got a bloody Mary now.'

'Listen, Kate, you're getting older and girls have a thing called a period. You'll get one every month and it means that when you have sex you can fall pregnant. It happens to every girl and it's totally normal.'

'Yeah, I kind of know about sex. Jennie says that a boy two years older than us had that much sex his willy fell off.'

Mike giggles sweetly. 'I don't think someone's willy could fall off. It's like saying you wrote so much at school today that your fingers fell off. So you're having a period, it's not because you're being eaten alive by a bike. Jesus, if I had a human-eating bike I'd be a millionaire by now. I'll take you to the chemist and get you something.'

He drives me to the chemist and tells me to wait in the van, which I'm pleased about. I don't want people thinking they're allowed to get me pregnant. Mike gets back into the van with a packet of sanitary towels and says, 'I got these for you. They were expensive because they have these wing thingies.'

'Wing thingies, what am I supposed to do with them?'

I'm thinking in my head that they fly. He opens up the sanitary pad. 'You open it like this, take the paper off those wings and the back of it and stick that part to your knickers, fold those wings around the gusset of your knickers.'

'Gusset, what's a gusset?'

'Well, it's kind of the bit that lies on your, erm, I don't know what word I should use … fanny.'

'Fanny! Ugh, Mike, it's not my fanny, it's my fuff-fuff.'

'I'm not calling it a fuff-fuff. Anyway, that's enough education for one day. I'll take you home.'

When I get home Jennie is there to invite me out tonight, her mum and dad want to take her out for a meal and she wants me to go along. We even get a taxi into town. Jennie's dad has a good job so there's never really any expense spared. She's a little bit spoilt if I'm honest. As we sit having the meal, I spot Lawrence with two women. They look a bit on the tarty side, short skirts and belly tops, and they're all giggling away at the table. I wonder who they are. He's not spotted me yet, maybe I should go over to him and say hello. I'm sure there's a logical explanation as to why he's with two women. Maybe they're his sisters … no, they can't be, he doesn't have any sisters. To my horror, out he comes from the toilet: it's Mike.

'What we talking about then, you lot?' he says in his charming voice. 'Better not be about me but, then again, if it is, I bet it's all good.' They're all giggling away, having such a good time. I'm going to go over there right now and say, 'Who are these women and why are you with them? I want answers.'

He better not call any of them Gem, I mean it. I feel so angry yet I don't know why. Lawrence has spotted me and his face drops. He gets out of his chair and walks over towards us.

'Hello, Kate, what you doing here?'

'I'm with Jennie and her mum and dad.'

'Oh, hello, you must be Mr Hart,' he says and shakes Jennie's dad's hand. Jennie's dad doesn't look best pleased. I don't think he's quite sure what to say. Mike looks over at us and says, 'Who's he talking to?' Then he spots me. He comes straight over.

'Hello, Gem, I never knew you were coming here tonight.' He looks over at the girls on the table and says, 'Erm, I'm with my cousins over there, they're here on holiday with my uncle Billy, so me and Lawrence promised to take them out. What food you ordered, then?'

'Just food,' I snap back at him.

'Not bolognese, I hope,' and with that he winks because we both know I would never order bolognese, not with it being brown.

'No, pizza, so I'm quite safe.'

He gives me that laugh and says, 'I think it's best we don't mention our cousins to your mum and Shelly, it's our little secret.'

Another one, I think to myself. 'OK, then.'

'Come on, Lawrence, it's getting cold,' he says, nodding over at the table where they came from.

I can heave a sigh of relief. That's good, I knew there would be some logical explanation. It's their cousins, of course.

Jennie's mum then leans in towards Jennie's dad and says, 'David, you do know who that is, don't you?'

'Yes, Brenda, I do. Kate, how do you know the Taylor brothers?'

'Oh, Lawrence is going out with my mum and me and Mike are best friends,' I say very excitedly. They look at each other with a panicked look on their faces. I don't know why because Mike and Lawrence are great fun. In fact, David Hart could do with hanging around with someone like that for a while, it may stop him from being so stuck up. He always has a miserable face. He's not like the Taylor brothers.

Chapter 4 – I'll Be Safe

I'm sleeping at Jennie's tonight because it's the school holidays. Her mum has said we can have a sleepover. We're going shopping in town first, then to the cinema. As we walk up the road I see two girls coming out of the make-up shop on the corner. I can't take my eyes off one of the girls, it's been so long since I've seen her. Part of me wants to even say thank you. It's her! It's Rebecca Bradshaw, the one person in life I was grateful for being around. Before I can say anything Jennie says, 'Oh my God, can you see who that is? It's what's her face from our primary school. Let's go and wind her up, see if we can steal that make-up off her. Look at her stupid little friend. How can she even have a friend? I remember when I pulled her trousers down in primary when the boys were there and she had frilly knickers on like a baby, and we called her baby-knickers all day.' Jennie storms over to the two girls.

'Oh no, Jennie, let's leave them alone and go shopping like we said we would.'

I can't pick on her, she saved me so many times when I was younger, when no one liked me. I never liked Jennie back then and I don't want her thinking I'm a baby or anything, what do I do here? Go along with it or be my own person? 'Hey, you two,' she says and shoves Rebecca. 'What are you two doing here and what's in the bag?'

I'm cringing inside and I really don't want to pick on them. I feel sorry for Rebecca. I give her a little smile and say, 'Jennie, we're going to be late for the movie if we don't hurry.'

The girl who is with Rebecca looks even more frightened than her and Jennie pokes fun at her. 'Oh look, she's going to cry, do you want your mummy?'

'Let's go.' I tug at her arm. She finally starts to walk away from them shouting, 'You little tramps!' and giggles. I don't like her when she's like that, it reminds me of when I used to walk to school pretending her mum was my mum. That was before I realised how stuck up she was, mind.

We finally settle into the cinema but I can't stop thinking of Rebecca. I'm pleased she has a friend. I wonder if she still gets picked on and what my life would have been like if I'd not done the whole Jennie Fart thing. I'm glad we're friends now. I couldn't imagine my life without her in it. Afterwards we go home on the bus and back to Jennie's. Her mum is buying pizza, pop and sweets. We brag we're going to pull an all-nighter but we're both flat out by 10pm. We wake the next day to her mum knocking on the door with milk and some funny little pastry things on a plate. I look at them and say to Jennie, 'What on earth are they?' She laughs and says, 'Croissants, of course, everyone in France eats them.'

It's like she has them all the time. I feel silly for not knowing what they are, but if it's not toast in a morning that I'm handing over to a hungover mum then I don't quite know what it is. I thought that's all breakfast entailed.

Three weeks later and it's my birthday, a teenager at last. Mike comes over at 9am. I've only just opened my eyes and he and Shelly have brought me a present in a big box. Wow, what could this be? I wonder as I open the box.

'It's one of the newest thingy games, like a computer thing, that's what it is,' says Mike. I smile to myself. He has no idea what it is, he's asked someone in the store what a thirteen-year-old would be into, but I don't care. It's a Sega Mega drive and only a handful of kids have these, normally the spoilt ones, but I have one now.

'Help me hook it up,' I say to Mike. I watch him as he plugs it into the TV and tunes it in and it impresses me that you can tune a box into a TV. I grab the controls off him as I want to do it. This kind of thing always gets me excited. Within minutes I have it working and I'm whizzing round the screen with a little blue hedgehog. They go into the kitchen to fix some food and I'm excited Jennie's coming over tonight. My mum has promised that she can sleep over, she'll get us some sweets and pop like Jennie's mum did. As always, my mind starts to work overtime thinking, surely you can crack into this game somehow as I've been stuck on this bridge for ages and I keep getting shot by a crab that's shooting fireballs. There must be a way, there has to be.

I put the menu back to the start and begin playing with the buttons. Before I know it, I try a little thing and that's it, I've cracked it! I'm into the internal mainframe of the game and I can choose any level I want to play. Who wants to start at the beginning anyway, that's what boring people do. Mike walks in and he can't believe what he sees.

'I knew you'd crack it eventually, but seriously, in half an hour? Have you any idea how much of a genius you are?' But it's not being a genius really, it's normal that someone should be intrigued at how their new present works.

Shelly says to my mum, 'Oo, are we still going out tonight then?'

'Ah no, Mum, you promised Jennie could sleep over, you said she could,' I whine. I'm so disappointed she's done this to me.

'Well, she can still stay over, but I can still go out, can't I? Don't be spiteful, I've spent all morning with you. You could at least let me have some time for myself and my friends,' my mum says in an equally whiney voice.

'OK then, you can go out, sorry, Mum.' I start to feel a little guilty, but I know I shouldn't, me and Jennie will still have a good night. Jennie turns up with my present. She's got me some false nails. She's always been a bit girlier than me. They have sticky-back plastic on them. You peel them off and they stick straight to your nails, they are a very girly pink colour. I'm not sure if they would even suit me, but I pretend to be excited as I don't want to hurt her feelings. 'Oo, we can put these on tonight when my mum goes out. You're still OK to stay, aren't you? Your mum will be OK with that, won't she? My mum normally goes out on a Saturday. She says she'll be back early though.'

Mike says, 'We'll come back early and we'll have some music on and a bit of a party for you.'

'Will you?' I say excitedly. 'I've never had a party before.'

Jennie comes back over around 5pm. My mum and Shelly are in the kitchen drinking wine. Mike and Lawrence are sitting with us in the sitting room mocking the girls for how long it takes them to get ready. I hang around Mike, asking what time he'll be back for the party and he says, 'I promise if I can drag them two away from their wine, it will be as soon as possible, honest.'

I know if Mike is saying he'll be back early, he will be. If it was my mum, on the other hand, I wouldn't expect her back at all. I go into the kitchen to get a drink and I spot my mum with my nails on that Jennie brought me.

'Look at these, love, don't I look great with them on?' she says annoyingly as she wiggles her nails in front of me. 'You don't mind, do you darling? It's just, well, you're not even a girly girl are you?'

I'm really upset about this, but I won't show her. She's got them on now, so what's the point in being upset? It shows her that I'm even the slightest bit bothered that she thinks of nothing but herself, her men and her wine. I'm just an inconvenience that came along at the wrong time. As soon as I'm old enough, I'm out of here and never ever will I treat my daughter the way she's treated me, and I'll buy her a different pack of nails every day of the week. I can't believe she's used my birthday present. Why does she always do that? Like the Santa soap Jennie got me for Christmas, my mum used that Christmas morning. I think she does it deliberately to annoy me. It's not that she wanted to wash in that soap or even have girly pink nails tonight, it's just that they were there. She even made up some excuse about me not liking the smell of the soap. I never liked the smell and I never really wanted to use it. I also never really wanted girly pink nails, but she never knew that.

My mum gets up from her seat and gently places her hand on

my stomach exactly where I get the stomach cramps. In fact now I come to think about it, I got them as soon as I opened Jennie's present. She then holds my face and kisses me on the head saying, 'You're a good girl. Jennie will understand.' I don't even know what she means by that.

'Mike, will you be back for 10.30pm, at the latest, pleeeeaaaase?' I beg him. 'I don't want to be here just me and Jennie, I want you here as well.' He kisses me on the head and says, 'I promise I'll be back.' They all go out and it's just me and Jennie left.

'What shall we do then? What have we got to eat?'

'Not much,' I say. 'Let's have a look.'

There's nothing in the cupboards or the fridge and I'm a little embarrassed; her mum had allsorts, even things the French eat.

'Oo, look,' she says, 'there's some rosé wine, let's drink it.'

'What?' I'm totally shocked by this. 'Do you want to end up like my mum?'

She laughs, saying, 'Ah come on, your mum's well cool.'

I shake my head. 'Is she? Since when?'

'Don't be a spoilsport, let's drink it.' She pours us both a glass and I reluctantly take it. She takes a sip and says, 'Your turn, don't be a baby.' I really don't want to drink the wine but I don't want her to think I'm a baby either. I pick up the glass and slowly place it on my lips, I close my eyes then take a big mouthful while imagining it's a glass of lemonade. I can't even describe the taste that's going on in my mouth right now, it's like vinegar. Yak. I swallow it and say, 'That's disgusting.'

Jennie comes up with a great idea. 'Let's phone a Chinese and have it delivered to Mrs Wilson at the corner house. We can watch out of the window when the driver turns up.'

We dial the Chinese and Jennie speaks to them as she has a posh voice compared to me. 'I'll have chicken chow mein with chips and prawn crackers.' She hangs up the phone and we laugh our heads off and can't wait until the driver turns up in forty-five minutes, but what can we do until then?

'Oo, let's throw some eggs at Mr Smith's window,' she suggests excitedly. Before I know it, we're outside throwing eggs against Mr Smith's window. His front door opens and we run as quickly as we can back to my house and hide under the windowsill looking over at Mr Smith's house. He is going crazy looking around to see who it was. We start giggling till our bellies hurt. I'm having so much fun tonight. We keep on drinking the wine and my head feels completely fuzzy.

'You know what? I've been thinking.'

'What have you been thinking?'

'I think Mike's my dad, I can tell.'

'Don't be silly,' says Jennie. 'What makes you think that?'

It seems totally logical yet he's younger than my mum by five years which would mean he was nine when I was conceived.

'I'm going to ask him.' I'm sure it's the wine making me think these thoughts, but nope, that's it: my mind has been made up. I'm asking him as soon as he walks in the door, I have to know. A few more drinks of wine and this notion of Mike being my dad is getting stronger and stronger to the point where he has already been to the courts to gain full custody and I'm going to live with him – tomorrow.

'Why wait till tomorrow? I'll pack my bags now,' I say as I rush to my room to pack every stitch of clothing I have into carrier bags ready for the off. We continue to drink the wine with the great idea that if you close your eyes and pinch your nose it goes down a lot quicker and easier. Jennie says that sugar makes alcohol even stronger so we tip the sugar bowl into the remainder of the bottle. There's sugar all over the bench and floor so we get straws to suck it up. Well, we can't let it go to waste, can we? Especially now we have something to celebrate. My dad has come to claim me back. Jennie is completely rolling with this notion, and more wine makes us think we're sisters and Mike is dad to both of us.

The wine is a really thick, syrupy texture and tastes even worse. The door starts to open and I don't know what it is, the fright or excitement that Daddy is home, but in walks my mum and I take one look at them all and before I know it there's projectile vomit coming from my mouth and nose. I swear it's coming from my eyes as well, but I'm drunk so I could be exaggerating there a little.

My mum rushes straight over. 'Kate, are you OK? You stink of drink. Have you been drinking?'

'Oh my goodness, what have you two been doing?' Mike asks.

'Mmmmike, are you my—'

Blugh... Sick comes out before I can even say the rest, not that it's even coming out clearly anyway.

'Jesus, looks like you started the party without us. Let's get you sorted. What on earth have you been drinking?' says Mike, in a worrying way.

'Sugar,' I say.

He says, 'Yes, pull the other one, sugar doesn't get you in this state.'

'Hey, they've been at my good bloody wine!' my mother shouts. I look over at Jennie and she's really pale in colour and vomits all over as well.

'Not you as well?' says Lawrence. 'Better get them two off to bed.'

I wake up in the morning and Jennie's foot is stuck to my face. I shake her. 'Wake up, Jennie, wake up. What on earth happened last night? Look at my room, there are carrier bags full of clothes all over the place, what's going on?'

Jennie reminds me that I thought Mike was my dad and we were running away together. That he's been to the courts and everything. I'm mortified, what on earth would make me think that? That was my first ever experience with alcohol and I have a feeling it's going to get a hell of a lot worse.

That's it, the famous bang on the wall from her majesty for her toast. I don't know why, maybe it's the alcohol still in my system, but I bang back. It's about time *she* got *me* some toast. In fact, forget that, the thought of eating or drinking anything today is making me run straight to the toilet to be sick again.

'You have a hallway to clean as well, young lady,' Mum shouts from the other room.

Oh no, I can't even face the hallway. If she'd been Jennie's mum there would have been pop, sweets and little French things, not wine. What on earth must Jennie think of this lot – drunk on wine and sugar, a mother who uses my birthday presents before me, and me packing up all my belongings to live with a Taylor brother. If Jennie's mum even thought she was in the same house as a Taylor brother she would have a fit.

I finally finish being sick and slink back into the bedroom. I feel I have some explaining to do to Jennie.

'Jennie, I'm so sorry, I know I promised a bit of a party but—' And before I finish she says, 'Are you kidding? I had the best night ever. Remember Mrs Wilson shouting at that delivery driver with the Chinese order? And Mr Smith will be cleaning those windows for a week. You're my best friend, I love spending time with you and I love you.'

We smile at each other and I'm so pleased she enjoyed herself. I still wish we had some of those silly French things though. Never mind, maybe next birthday.

A few months have gone by and the smell of sick has finally left the hall carpet. Which is lucky for me as my mum kept complaining and spraying it with a lavender perfume she got from Mr and Mrs Richards for Christmas about three years ago. The smell of lavender mixed with vomit is enough to make someone vomit all over the carpet again. Mike turns up at my house with a grey square box and a dial on it. He asks, 'Do you know what this is?'

I shake my head. It's like nothing I've seen before. 'Well, it's called a safe. It holds all your possessions in it and should be able to be opened like the bike locks can.'

He has put a special present inside the safe for me, but the only way I can get it is if I can get the code to open the box.

'OK, great. I'll try later,' I say as I push the safe to one side.

'No, not later, do it now please. I want to see your face when you get your present.'

I look at the dials and listen very carefully to see if any of the numbers sound different and there *is* a slight difference. As I turn the dial the lock seems looser with certain numbers so I start to write them down. I have six digits written down and try them all in sequence and, hey presto, the safe opens. Inside is a little box with a ring in it. Inscribed on the ring is the word 'Gem'.

'That's cos you're my little gem and always will be.'

I'm really happy with my little present and I put it on my finger. I say to Mike I'll keep this forever. Mike says he has to go, but he'll come and see me again soon.

The following month Mike comes round and asks me if I can still remember how I opened the safe. 'Of course I do, it's only been a month. I'm not a goldfish with an eleven-second memory, you know.' He laughs at me. 'How do you know they only have eleven seconds of memory?'

'What? Who are you? I need to go for a swim.' I move my arms as if I'm swimming. Mike then tells me his friend has gone on holiday and left him looking after his house. He has asked him to see if he can get his safe open as he has forgotten the code.

'Not another one! How can people keep forgetting the codes all the time? Maybe they should start writing them down somewhere.'

'Yeah, that's what I said, but please don't forget it's our little secret.' He winks at me and we walk out of the door. We drive to a really posh estate. 'I'm going to park the van here cos it can be a nightmare getting parked near his house. It's a little walk, but you're all right with that, aren't you?'

'Yeah, course I am.'

We head towards the house and when we get there Mike passes me some gloves and says, 'The house is normally really cold so you should wear these gloves and not take them off, ever.' He realises that he has left the key in his house.

'Well, it's OK, we can go back and get it and come back.'

'No, I don't have time. Will you climb round the back and see if any windows are open?'

I'm reluctant, but I'll do anything to please Mike. I climb round the back and see a window open. I open the gate and point it out to him.

‘Go on then, climb in. I’ll give you a hand.’ He lifts me up and puts me through the window. I’m quite scared and say, ‘Oh no, Mike, please let’s just go back and get the key.’

‘I can’t, we don’t have time. I thought you and me were friends? If you loved me you would.’

Well, I do love him and I want to make him happy. So I climb down into the house and he shouts, ‘Right, go back round the front and open the door for me.’

He walks into the house and says, ‘Right, where did he say the safe was? You stay here while I have a look.’ A few minutes go by before he comes back. ‘I’ve found it, this way.’

I get to the safe and start playing with the dial. It takes me a while to figure it out, but I finally get there. The safe opens and it’s full of bundles of money and jewellery. His friend must be really rich with all of this stuff. I’m surprised he forgot the code, this stuff looks like it would be important. Before I know it, Mike is filling a bag with all the money. I look at him and he says, ‘It’s OK, I’m meeting him on holiday and giving him it.’

We leave the house and walk to the van. Mike holds my hand on the way back and says, ‘You know what, Gem, I’ll take care of you forever. If you ever get in any trouble, no matter what it is, you can always come to me. I’ll always sort it out for you.’

I’m starting to feel closer and closer to Mike. I wish it was my mum he was going out with and not Shelly and they would get married and he would adopt me and let me be called Kate Taylor. I like that, it sounds much better than Kate Reilly.

‘Fancy some pizza, Gem?’

‘Yeah OK.’

We go to a little Italian near the cafe where we went the day I helped his friend get his bike back. As soon as we walk in Mike is greeted at the door.

‘Ah, Mr Taylor, a table for two, is it? And who might she be? Is this your beautiful wife?’ The waiter winks over at me and it makes me giggle.

‘Hey, Rusco, if I was to marry anyone this would be the girl for me, she's a total gem.' Mike gives me a wink and a nod which makes me smile.

We sit down and he passes me the menu. There's allsorts to choose from. I don't really understand the jargon so I ask Mike to help me out. He's having king prawn butterfly to start with, but I'm not having any of that, it makes me think of the fishing trip with the worm. I get slightly uncomfortable with the thought of me hiding in the cupboard making sure the worm doesn't eat him from the inside out. I giggle at myself for my stupidity. But, come to think of it, I never did find out who was on the phone that day...

He asks, 'What you laughing at?' I quickly make something up on the spot. How can I tell him that the worm he ate somehow grew another part of its own body in six hours and turned into the killer worm, so I hid in the cupboard all night ready to perform surgery?

'Oh, I'm imagining a prawn flying, with it being called a butterfly.'

'Ha ha, yeah, that's very funny. What do you fancy?'

'I'm not sure, nothing fishy and definitely nothing wormy.'

'Wormy? What do you mean? You're funny at times, you.'

'What's this bruschetty thingy?' I ask.

'It's bruschetta, it's toast topped with garlic and tomatoes.'

'I'll have that then and chicken pizza, please.'

As I eat my bruschetta Mike asks what I'm doing as I dissect my meal. 'Why are you eating the parsley first? You should slice your toast like this and eat it all in one go.' Mike takes my knife and fork and mixes everything up.

'No, no, I can't do that, I like to eat it like this, there's a system,' I snap at him. 'I eat the parsley, then the tomatoes, then the toast.'

Mike shakes his head. 'Why do you always play with your food?'

'I don't play with it. I work to a system.'

'What system? Tell me.'

'No, you'll think I'm stupid.'

'Hey, there's nothing stupid about you, that I do know. Go on, tell me please. I'll tell *you* a secret...'

'Well, you tell me first, and then I will.'

'OK then, when me and Lawrence were younger he thought his rabbit ran away to find a carrot, but the truth of it was I left the cage open and a fox got in and ate it. But you can't tell him that, he loved Snowy.'

'Oh no, Mike, that's awful and a really big secret. OK, I'll tell you. Well, you know how I couldn't eat those bourbons at your mum's house and I can't eat oranges and I can't open a black, blue or brown bike lock... Well, I can't eat or do things with the same initial as the colour. Like grapes begin with a G and they're green and that begins with a G. I have to eat my food in alphabetical order of colour. So the parsley is green and tomatoes are red and G comes before R in the alphabet.'

'So where does the toast come into it then?'

'Well, that's white.'

'But it's not, it's brown because it's been grilled.'

'Yes, but its original colour is white.'

'That makes no sense. What about a tomato? That's green before it goes red.'

'Oh, I never thought of that. Hmm, maybe I should rethink my system.'

'Also, did you know that beans are white? It's the tomato sauce that dyes them orange.'

'Oh no, please don't tell me that! I'd have to eat my beans before my tomatoes because they're red. My sweetcorn is always last, they're yellow and I don't think there's any colour out there beginning with Z.'

'What about zebra colour?' Mike teases me but he doesn't seem overly bothered by my revelation. That's what I love about him, he never judges me.

I notice Mike is wearing a band on his wrist, it's brown and the material is all plaited. 'What's that? You always wear it.' I point to the band.

'This is what's called a friendship band. I got it for my best friend years ago and he died, so I wear it to remind me of him all the time.'

'Your best friend died? That's awful, I would hate it if Jennie died. I'll be your best friend if you like.'

'Thanks, that's really sweet. You can have this friendship band when I die.'

'Yak, no thanks. It's a really nice idea but by the time you die that thing will stink. It already looks old.'

Mike starts to giggle at me. 'Kate, you really are funny sometimes. I'll try and get you a new friendship band one day, I promise.'

I finish my pizza. Well, most of it, I can't manage the rest. Rusco asks me if I want to take it home and I say, 'No, but could you put it in a box anyway?'

Mike asks me why I want to put it in a box if I don't want it. I tell him I see a tramp round the corner from my house and I'd like to give it to him.

'Why would you do that? He's probably got more money than us, all the begging he does.' I take my pizza and Mike pays the bill. He shakes Rusco's hand and gives him ten pounds. 'Get your wife a nice bunch of flowers with that,' he says.

'That's a nice thing to do, Mike,' I say. As we're driving Mike gives me forty pounds and says, 'That's for helping my friend out today, he's really pleased and wanted to pay you.'

I never really wanted any money. Spending time with Mike was enough. I spot the old tramp. 'There he is. Stop the van, I won't be long.'

I get out of the van and head towards the old tramp. He has long tatty hair and hardly any teeth, he has blue fingerless gloves on and they have holes in them. I can't see the point in wearing any gloves really. I remember the gloves Mike gave me. I pull them from my pocket. I hand them over to the old tramp and say, 'I have a pizza, here you can have it, although it might be a little cold.'

He doesn't say anything to me, just looks at me strangely. I take out the forty pounds and hand him twenty, that's exactly half, and say, 'Get your wife a nice bunch of flowers with that.'

He still has that strange look on his face. Mike asks me what

I've done. I was just being nice. 'You can't give your money away like that, you earned that. He needs to earn his own money. You know he'll spend that on booze, don't you?'

'Well, I would only spend it on food or sweets and I never had it in the first place so I'm no worse off really.'

'You're crazy, you. Come on, let's get you home.'

Chapter 5 – Meeting Mr Simpson

I wake up and wonder what I'm going to do today. Mike's here, I can hear him laughing in the kitchen. I quickly make my way downstairs as my mum makes her way up the stairs to tell Lawrence to get up. Mike asks me if I can open another one of his friends' safes.

'Yeah course, when?'

'Tonight, as it gets dark. I'll pick you up. Oh and remember it's our little secret.' He points to his nose and taps it twice.

Later that night, just like the last time, we make our way over towards the estate and park the van away from the house and he hands me some more gloves.

'Another cold house, then?'

It's the same as last time. I climb in and open the door for him and he makes his way in to find the safe and tells me to stand perfectly still. I spot a snow globe on the side and pick it up to give it a shake, just as Mike comes back. He sees me and I jump with fright.

'I'm sorry, Mike, I know you said not to touch anything apart from the safe. I'm really sorry.'

'It's OK, do you want that?'

I nervously say, 'Erm, no. Well, erm, I don't know really.'

'Look, my friend's going to be well happy when I return his things from the safe. I'm sure he won't mind you taking that.'

I make my way to the safe. I pop it open with ease. Mike swings open the safe door then swears and his face is like thunder. 'What's wrong, Mike?'

'Nothing.' I look in the safe and there's nothing there, just some old photographs. He says, 'Right, we'll have to take some other stuff.'

'What? What do you mean, take stuff?'

'Ah no, it's OK. My friend wants to buy his daughter a computer thingy, like what you have, so I said I would get the money from the safe. But he said if there's nothing there then I could sell some of his things and he can surprise her. It's OK, he knows all about it. I'm going to get the van and back it straight on to the drive. You grab anything you can think of to sell.'

I start to make my way around the house picking things up, but I don't really know what you can sell. I look around and spot a fruit bowl. I saw one once when I went to the car boot sale with Mr Richards, someone was selling one. Oh, that's a good idea, think of things for a car boot sale. There are normally loads of ornaments, so they will do. TV remote – someone had that on their stall once. Kids' games… Oo, there's a Tamagotchi. I would totally buy one of those. As I pile all this stuff in the middle of the floor Mike comes back and screams, 'What the bloody hell is all this shit?'

'Well, it's stuff we can sell at a car boot sale that Mr Richards takes me to.'

'Goodness, we'd need an artic truck full of stuff to make any money out of this lot – and sell it at a week-long car boot sale. Look, this is what I mean.'

He takes me round the house. 'That TV will be worth one hundred quid. This necklace, I could get twenty quid for that…'

This goes on for a while, we finally load up the van and off we go.

'Where shall we go now? Shall we go for food again?' Mike doesn't listen to me when I say that as he's too busy fumbling in his pocket. He pulls out a black box with numbers on it. He presses a few numbers and starts to talk into the box. I question what it is and he says, 'Well, it's a mobile phone, all businessmen have them. It's a phone you can take anywhere with you and call people from it. It's a thing of the future, everyone will have one soon.'

'A phone you can talk on and it doesn't even have a wire, that's amazing! So you mean I could ring Jennie while we're driving in the van and speak to her.'

'Yeah, I'll give you a try later on and you can call her and I'll get you one soon, I promise.'

He makes a few phone calls to people, telling them what he has.

'Come with me, I want you to meet somebody.'

We go to a bar. The sign above the door says 'Jimmeez'. We're greeted by a barmaid who's wearing a bikini. She has a big smile on her face when she sees us.

'Hello, gorgeous,' she says to Mike. 'This your kid, then?'

'Erm, yeah, yeah she is.' I get the feeling this is someone Mike wants to impress. I've noticed I'm always his daughter when he talks to good-looking women. I think he wants them to think what a perfect man he is who looks after his daughter all the time. 'Is he in, then, saucy-knickers?'

'Yeah, he's in there.'

As we head over towards the office Mike grabs my hand and says, 'Stay with me, don't talk to anyone at all. Don't even look at them unless I tap you on the shoulder to say that they're OK to talk to.'

We enter the office and a man is sitting behind the desk. Mike goes over and shakes his hand.

'Hello, Mr Simpson.' He must be really important if Mike is calling him Mr Simpson. 'I've got some stuff you might be interested in. I've got this lovely necklace for your missus.' He holds up the necklace and Mr Simpson looks at it and says, 'How much then?'

'For you, Mr Simpson, nothing. You can have it, little present.' Then he says to Mr Simpson, 'Hey, this is my gem I've been telling you about,' and nods his head towards me.

'Oh yeah, that one,' says Mr Simpson. He gets up from his seat and heads towards me. It's almost like his whole personality has taken over the room he has such a large frame, I think I gulp down a huge mouthful of saliva as he stares at me with his big brown eyes. He has shaven brown hair. He looks pretty scary to be honest, now he's close up. But I'll be OK with Mike being here. He's always looked after me. He'd never let anything happen.

Mr Simpson bends right down so we're face-to-face. I grab Mike's hand a little tighter to let him know I'm really uncomfortable. Mike comes down to my level and taps me on the shoulder. I remember that Mike would tap me on the shoulder if they're OK to speak to, so he must be OK.

'It's OK, this is Mr Simpson, he's my friend. His safe is stuck closed. Completely forgot the code, could you open it for him?' Mr Simpson takes a picture from the wall and the safe is hidden behind it. I pull on Mike's arm to walk over with me and he does. 'It's OK, I'm here.'

I instantly feel better and start to open the safe. As it opens I get a peek inside before Mr Simpson quickly closes it again. I saw more money in there than I have ever seen before. There were also some tablets and white powder in there. I'm not sure why anyone would keep talc and headache tablets in a safe, especially when they're stupid enough to forget the code. You'd be in a sorry state if you ever get a headache. Mr Simpson is really pleased that I opened his safe and shakes Mike's hand again.

'Bloody hell, Mike, you're right, she is a gem, ain't she?' He opens the door and shouts to another barmaid, 'Caroline, get some drinks in here and get one for the kid as well, a special one.'

Caroline enters the room, the first thing I notice about her is the colour of her skin, it has an orange tinge to it. She must go on the sunbed to make it look that colour. I only know that because there's a woman in our street who pretends she goes on holiday a lot, my mum and Shelly laugh at her as they know it's a sunbed. Apparently they can tell because of the blue light coming from her bedroom window every night. Caroline is thin, with light brown long hair right down her back, and really pretty. She has lovely brown eyes that have a twinkle in them when she sees Mr Simpson and Mike, like she loves to be in their company. Almost like those two are something special. Especially Mr Simpson. She comes in with two glasses of what looks like whisky for them, and a tall glass of a drinks mixture for me, and it has a lit sparkler in it. Wow, this is fantastic! I must have a big smile on my face because Mr Simpson says, 'Like that do you, little one? Tell me your name.'

'My name is Kate Reilly, I'm thirteen, sir, and I live with my mum.'

Mike starts to laugh and tries to quieten me down. 'Kids, eh?' He gives Mr Simpson the raised eyebrow look.

'Well, Miss Reilly who is thirteen and lives with her mum, you can have one of those drinks every time you come in my club. You saved my life today. I have a friend who has also forgotten the code to his safe. Could you open that one?'

I look at him and say a little shyly, 'Yeah, I suppose so.'

'Good girl.' Then he looks at Mike and says, 'Are you hanging around? There's a party later on. I'll get one of the lads to drop little legs off for you.'

I look at Mike as if to say, You can't leave me with a stranger, please. You brought me here, you should take me home.

'You'll be all right. His driver will take you home.' Mr Simpson leaves the room and brings back another man to take me home. I get into his car and I'm not really happy about it, but it's the only way I can get home. As we're driving down the road the man introduces himself as Roger and asks me, 'Is Mike your boyfriend?'

'No. Mike's my dad.'

I say that because I figure if Mike can say it when it suits him, I can too. He moves the gear stick and his hand slips off and ends up on my knee. I brush his hand away. I'm not sure if he noticed that it even happened.

'You're a pretty girl, you know, you should have a boyfriend. If I was your age, I'd like to be your boyfriend.'

I'm really uncomfortable with this conversation so I ignore him. We finally get to my house and I can't get out of the car quick enough. I'm a little scared of this strange man and totally angry with Mike. How could he leave me?

The next morning I wake up and Mike is on my mind. I'm still angry with him. I've not heard from him all day. How does he even know I got home safe? Every time I've helped his friends out he's always taken me for food or something, but to leave me with that creepy man...

Mike eventually comes round and it's 6.30pm.

'Hello, Gem, you OK?' he says excitedly.

I give him a blank stare and say in my annoyed voice, 'Not really, no. Why did you stay at that club?'

He holds out his arms and says, 'Oh come on, it was a party.'

'Well, could I have not stayed for the party?'

'No, it was only for adults and it was boring anyway, you would have only wanted to come home. If Jennie had turned up and asked you to stay for a party would you, and leave me?'

'Well, I suppose so, I would, yes.'

'Well then, Mr Simpson is my friend and I never wanted to leave him.'

'If he's your friend, how come you have to call him Mr Simpson?'

'He likes people to call him Mr Simpson, that's all.'

'You know you promised to help Mr Simpson's friend, you're still OK with that, aren't you?'

'Yeah, OK.' I quickly forgive Mike. I can never really stay angry with him, he's my best friend.

It's Monday and the school day has finally finished. Jennie and I start to make our way home when a car pulls over. It's Roger, Mr Simpson's creepy driver.

'Hello, love,' he shouts over. 'I thought it was you. Do you want a lift home?'

'No thanks, I'm walking with my friend.'

'Well, I'll take your friend home as well.'

'No, we're fine, thanks.' I turn my back on him. It gives me such a horrible feeling.

'Who on earth was that?' Jennie asks.

'No one. Just someone Mike knows.'

'Ugh, he was strange.'

'Yeah, I know. Let's forget about him.'

We start to hurry home. I really didn't like that. I wonder if he really was just passing.

The next morning Jennie turns up for us to walk to school

together. As we get round the corner I spot Roger's car. He opens his window. 'Hey, twice in two days, are you following me?' he shouts over.

'No, you're following us, you weirdo,' Jennie yells back at him. He drives off. I'm a little worried about him. I better mention this to Mike when I see him, maybe he can have a word.

After school Mike comes round to see me. 'Hey, you know Mr Simpson's friend? Well, it's tonight, are you coming?'

'Yeah, OK.'

We make our way over to a club. The sign above the door says 'Ocean Club' and there are lots of people there. Mike takes me to a back room and tells me to stay there until he comes back for me. 'I'll get someone to stay with you.' And in walks Roger. Mike leaves the room and Roger is staring at me. I really wish Mike would hurry up, he seems to be taking ages and Roger scares me.

'Hello, love. Look I never meant to scare you the other day. I was driving past. I like you… I'd like us to be friends.'

Mike opens the door which gives me such a fright. I jump up and say, 'I'm not staying with him.' I grab Mike close to me and Mike can tell I'm anxious.

'What the hell is wrong, Kate?'

I say, 'I'm not, that's all. Take me home right now. I'm not helping Mr Simpson. I want to go home.'

'Has he done something to you?' Mike turns angry. I've never seen him like that before. 'What have you done to her?' Mike shouts at Roger.

I'm a bit taken aback with the way Mike is and start to panic a bit while saying, 'Nothing. He just touched my leg and asked me if I had a boyfriend, he said he wanted to be my boyfriend, that's all really. I think he's been following me to and from school, he kept pulling over asking if I wanted a lift somewhere.'

'What?' Mike's face has a really furious look on it. 'What the fuck have you been saying and doing to her, you perverted little bastard?'

I get such a shock when Mike loses his temper, I'm really

frightened. Before I know it, he's punching him and Roger is screaming, 'No, Mike, no, she has it wrong!'

'You calling her a liar, you sick bastard?'

He starts to kick him as he is lying on the floor and there's a pool of blood around him now. Mike doesn't seem to be stopping and I can't even scream, I'm so scared of him.

Mr Simpson walks in and shouts, 'What the hell is going on in here?'

'Nothing, your pervert driver is touching up my Kate. I'll kill him Jimmy, I will.'

There was no 'Mr Simpson' this time, so I know Mike is furious. He grabs me and says, 'If anyone ever touches you or scares you again, you come to me, OK?'

'OK, can we go home please? I'm scared.'

Roger is on the floor and he's not moving.

'Look, can we all just calm down in here?' Mr Simpson says in a very stern voice, but I can see he is trying to calm the situation down. 'I've got things to do, we're ready.' He never even mentioned the fact that Roger is lying on the floor or that Mike has just attacked him. Surely he's noticed that his driver's on the floor covered in blood. I hope he doesn't think it was me. I would never hit anyone, ever.

'Kate please go and open the safe and I'll take you straight home, I promise.' Mike is shaking as he is saying this.

'I can't do that now, please don't make me.'

Mr Simpson is heading towards Mike, not looking very happy.

Mike nervously comes down to my level and says, 'You have to do it, you promised. Please do it for me.'

'OK, but I want to go straight home after that.'

As we make our way into another room there's blood all over and a man is lying on the floor, not looking much different from Roger. I've never seen Mike be like this before. I've never seen *anyone* be like this before. I'm wondering if being around these people is such a good idea. I want to go home. I don't want to be

Mike's friend any more, or Roger's or Mr Simpson's. I just like Jennie being my friend. I'll open this safe and tell Mike that I've forgotten how to do it next time he asks or, better still, chop my fingers off then I *can't* do it. As I'm trying to open the safe, I'm feeling a little hazy and my eyes are blurry from the tears.

'I can't, Mike. I want to go home, please take me home. I don't like this.'

'No, please open it. I'll take you straight home after that, I promise.'

I manage to get the safe open and, just like Mr Simpson's, it's full of headache tablets, money and talc. Mr Simpson is laughing.

'That'll teach them bastards to mess with me and my club.' He has a black bag and he's pouring all the contents from the safe into it.

Mike shouts over. 'Jimmy, I'm going to get off. Can I have Roger's car? I need to get her home.'

Mr Simpson throws him the keys and says, 'Yeah, keep it.' He also throws two big wads of cash, which Mike catches then he throws me one. I don't catch it as I wasn't ready. Mike bends down and picks it up for me.

'Let's go.' He takes me by the hand and leads me to Roger's car – well, not Roger's any more, it's his. He gives me the money when we get into the car. 'Take that, you've earned it.'

'No, it's OK, I don't want it, thanks.' I don't want the money. Right now I never want to see Mike again.

'Take it, sweetheart. Listen, things happen in this world that aren't nice and I know that scared you back there, but it should never scare you, nothing should. I'm here and I'll always take care of you.'

'OK,' I say in an unconvincing way. I take the money and put it in my pocket. When I finally get home, I count the money and there's exactly one thousand pounds. My goodness, that's a lot of money, but what on earth can I buy with that? I remember when I got the forty pounds, I gave half to that tramp in the street. This money seems so easy to get a hold of and so easy to lose if you want to. Maybe I could keep some for myself and give the other half to the tramp again, then I won't feel so bad. Because I did something nice, which counteracts the bad. I split the wad in half; that's two piles of five hundred pounds. I run to the train station where the tramp will be. I hand him over one of the piles. He stands up and flicks through the money, takes one look at me and runs off. I wonder if he thought I was going to take it back. I instantly feel better. I even feel better about Mike, thinking, really he only did that to help me because he thought Roger was going to hurt me and, to be fair Roger, did scare me a bit.

The following morning I hear nothing from Mike. Maybe he's annoyed with me for being such a baby last night. I'm sure he will be round after school. I think about last night's events all day at school. I can't concentrate on anything. I wonder what Roger will be thinking. What if he drives to the school tonight when I finish to beat me up? Well, I suppose he can't, he doesn't have a car now, so how can he? Maybe he'll get the bus.

School has finally finished and I can't even wait for Jennie in case Roger is about, so I run all the way home. I hope Mike is there when I get back. I still feel like I need to explain myself. I run in the front door and straight for the kitchen as that's where he would normally be, having a cup of tea with Lawrence. There's a note stuck on the fridge from my mum: *Gone to Shelly's*. I'm so disheartened to find an empty house. I don't even want to fix myself any tea. My stomach is cramping so tight I couldn't eat a thing anyway. My mum eventually gets home.

'Kate, have you not eaten yet?'

'Yes, I went to Jennie's for tea. Where is Shelly? Where is Mike?'

'Never mind about that for now. I'm going back over to Shelly's tonight, I've just came back for a bottle of wine. Don't wait up.' My mum gets the wine from the fridge and walks straight back out of the door.

The night is long and boring. I take myself off to bed still thinking of last night's events. Maybe Mike has told my mum what a baby I was and they no longer want to sit in our house babysitting any more. That's why my mum's been to Shelly's tonight.

Every night this week I've run home in the hope that Mike will be there. Everyday it's the same feeling when the house is empty. I'm totally worried as he's never left it for a full week before seeing me, ever. Even if it's just to pop in for a cup of tea with Lawrence, he always comes round. Come to think of it, I've hardly seen Lawrence. He's been round at Shelly's most of the week.

I'm worried that because I cried when opening that safe Mike thinks I'm a baby and not big enough for him to take around any more. Sometimes I forget that I'm not that cutesy ten-year-old he took around with him. I'm a thirteen-year-old girl with boobs and crazy hormones.

I remember the mobile phone Mike had and that he gave me the number so I can contact him any time. I bite the bullet and try calling him. I'll explain, say I'm sorry and he'll be fine, of course he will. I dial his number and the woman announces, 'This phone may be switched off.' Maybe these stupid mobile phones don't work after all. I mean, a phone without a wire connected to it, that really is stupid. It's 1993 not 2033. Mike has these silly ideas about the future sometimes. He even thinks cars won't need petrol soon and run off power from the sun.

I'll go round to Shelly's house to find out where he is. I won't actually say I'm there for him. I'll say I'm there for something else. She's always leaving her stuff around here. What can I take back? I start to look around the house for something. Oo, I know, there's her handbag. I'll say my mum has asked me to return this. I make my way round there and I knock on the door and Shelly looks dreadful, no make-up on which is really strange for her.

'Hey, Shelly, my mum has asked me to return this to you.' As I walk in the door my mum's sitting in the living room. Oops, maybe I should have checked on my plan before going ahead with it. She gives me that look as if to say, Why are you always hanging around, you're such a pain.

'What's happened? Where's Mike?' I ask as I walk in there.

'Never mind where he is. What are you even doing here, madam?'

scolds my mum. Lawrence looks over at me and almost gives me a look of pity. Oh no, I'm thinking, Mike is dead. Maybe Roger came back and killed him in the night. Maybe Mr Simpson was angry he had to get a taxi from that club. Surely I would have heard something by now. I look at Lawrence and say, 'Is Mike dead, has he been killed?'

'Killed? Of course not, he's been arrested.'

'Arrested? What for?' Oh no, I think, Roger must have told the police about him.

'Burglary. He's been breaking into people's houses. He was caught with a TV and some other stuff from a house in Palmer Street.'

I think to myself for a minute. Palmer Street … oh no, that's where his friend lived. It's dawning on me that it wasn't his friend's house at all. I was there, I was burgling a house. I thought we were helping people out. I have a snow globe from that house. If I get caught with that… Will he tell them? Will he tell the police that it was me who opened the safe? Oh no, I won't see him again.

'How long will he be in prison for? Life?' I ask.

Lawrence laughs. 'Nah, he'll only get a few months.'

A few months! I can't wait that long before I see him again, please no. Someone has to help get him out of there.

'It's probably a good thing as well if you ask me, especially with this turf war going on,' Lawrence says.

What turf war? 'What's a turf war?' I ask.

'Hey, nosey, no one is talking to you,' my mum snaps.

'Kate, love, go to the kitchen and make everyone a nice cup of tea,' says Shelly.

'OK then.'

They must want rid of me so I can't hear what they're saying, but I'm listening at the door anyway. I overhear Lawrence saying to my mum and Shelly, 'Jimmy's lads are having a turf war with Keith's lads and they reckon our Mike was at the Ocean Club last week. Two men were killed. Jimmy's driver, Roger, was one of them. Jimmy took all of Keith's drugs and he's not best pleased about it, as you can imagine. Our Mike's better off where he is till it all blows over. You know what he can be like when that lot are all at war.'

Drugs! I never realised it was drugs. It was me, I stole all that man's drugs and money! And of course Mr Simpson must be Jimmy. Mike did call him Jimmy that night. I need to speak to Mike to try to find out, maybe they have it wrong ... yeah, Roger was pretty hurt, but not that bad. Mike would never do that, would he? Maybe someone else went in after us and killed Roger. I take in the tea. Shelly looks really upset.

'Why does he get involved in this stuff, Lawrence? Aren't I enough for him?'

'Shelly, don't think that, you are enough for him, he just gets hisself excited, that's all. He'll grow out of it soon. You know what him and Jimmy are like.'

Chapter 6 – The Ugly Shoes

There's no school today because it's Saturday. I don't have to get up for anything but I can hear the phone ringing downstairs and I really can't be bothered to get out of bed. I'm having a lie-in. Just as I'm nodding off, I hear it ringing again. It must be really important, whatever it is. I better get up, I suppose.

'Hello. Gem, is that you?'

It's that familiar voice. 'Mike, is that you?'

'Yeah, it is, how have you been? I'm missing you.'

Wow, he's missing me. I'm pleased he's missing me.

'I'm missing you too, what happened? Lawrence said you went to prison because those bike locks I opened and those safes weren't even your friends'. That we've been stealing from people. Am I going to go to prison? Are you going to tell the police about me?'

'No, of course not, I'd never tell anyone you were involved. You've not told Lawrence I got you involved, have you?'

'No, I've not said anything, they don't even know that I know. I was listening at the door. They also said Roger was dead. Did you kill him?'

'Never mind about that, I'll tell you later as I don't have much time. I would like to see you. Will you come and visit me?'

'Yeah, I will. I would love to come and visit you.'

'OK, then. I'll get Mr Simpson to bring you.'

'Yeah, I've been meaning to talk to you about him. Is he called Jimmy? Was it drugs in that safe, was it a turf war?'

Mike laughs at me. 'A turf war? Drugs? What are you on about?

You've been reading too many books, you have. Who's been saying that?'

'It doesn't matter, I overheard two people talking on a bus.' I don't want to get Lawrence into trouble for saying things maybe he shouldn't.

'I need you to go back to Mr Simpson. He is going to give you a mobile phone, it means I can contact you any time and won't get caught calling you on this phone. Mr Simpson will drive you to the prison. You will need a visiting order so I'm going to send you one to his house. Remember: no one is to know, it's our little secret. You'll have to miss school for the day though – it's Tuesday, visiting day.'

'I'm caught up with all my schoolwork and way ahead of the others anyway.' I say this in case he changes his mind with it being a school day, I'm just so pleased to hear from Mike that I don't even care about school.

'What shoe size are you?'

'Me? A three, why?'

'Nothing, I've missed you and thought I'd like to treat you to a new pair of shoes. I'm going to get Mr Simpson to pick them for you. When you come to visit me will you wear the shoes, so I can see them?'

'Yeah, OK.' Again, this is not something I question, yet the trouble we're in I should really…

'They might search you when you come in but it'll be worth it to see me.'

'That's fine. I don't mind.'

'Great, I have to go, but you know I love you, don't you?'

'Yeah, I love you too.'

The phone call ends. I'm so pleased he rang, he even said he loved me. That aching feeling in my belly has gone. I've thought of him every day.

Tuesday comes and I'm excited to see Mike, I can't wait. It's been three weeks and I was so worried he never wanted to see me again with me being such a baby last time we saw each other. I'm going to show him that I'm a grown-up and I can be trusted. I get to Mr Simpson's club and a man is there to meet me.

'Hey, I'm Kate, is Mr Simpson there please?'

'Yeah, he's inside,' he says in a very unfriendly voice. 'Mr Simpson, some tart is here to see you,' he says to Mr Simpson, who doesn't even look in my direction, just walks towards his office.

'Some tart? Hey, I'm not some tart, I'm Mike Taylor's daughter, I'll have you know.' He laughs at me and shakes his head. 'Poor you, then.'

I make my way to Mr Simpson's office and look back at the man who is trying to direct me and say, 'It's OK, I know the way. I don't need an escort, thanks.'

'You're definitely Mike's, you've his same cheeky attitude.'

I bet he wouldn't be saying these things if Mike was here, he'd teach him a lesson like he taught Roger a lesson. What am I thinking, for goodness' sake, why am I even thinking like this? I must have had some 'act really hard' pills for my breakfast or something. Either that or it's about to be ladies' week; I can get a bit stroppy like that at times. Mind you, my periods are always up and down so, thankfully, I don't get stroppy too often.

I walk straight into his office. 'Hi, Mr Simpson.' He looks up at me as if to say, Who the hell are you? Either that or he's annoyed about Roger. If Roger was his driver, they must have been friends.

He gets up out of his seat and says, 'In future, can you knock on my door before walking in? Come on, then.' He gestures that it's time to go. We walk through the club and out of the door. We go towards the car, it's a really posh car with a private reg of: JIMMY S. We drive towards the prison and I'm thinking of Mike and all the things we've done together, like helping his 'friends' get their bikes back. I now know they weren't his friends and I've been an accomplice to probably the biggest bike heist of the 90s. I'm so clever at times yet how could I have been so stupid, to not realise what I was doing? I suppose it's because I really like Mike and wanted him to like me.

The car journey is a bit strange. Mr Simpson is really quiet, he comes across as quite moody. Maybe it's ladies' week for him too. He tries to talk to me but seems a little uncomfortable.

'So, do you go to school?'

'Erm, yeah, I go to James Cook High School.'

'Oh yeah, I know that one, my wife went to that school years ago.'

It's small talk really. They say he's a gangster – well, that's what Lawrence says, but he seems pretty scared to be in a car with me on his own. Maybe my new-found attitude is scaring everyone, even Mr Gangster. See, I can be scary. We pull up near the prison and Mr Simpson remembers my new shoes.

'Oh, I nearly forgot. Mike got you a present, here they are.'

He pulls out some horrible black shoes with a big chunky heel. Not really pretty; in fact, they're pretty ugly. I look at Mr Simpson and say, 'Is he kidding me? Jennie's mother wouldn't even wear shoes like that.'

'Yeah, Mike's never been a one for taste. Just put them on.'

I don't know Mr Simpson very well but I do get the feeling that if he tells you to do something you just do it and don't question it.

So I put the new big chunky platform shoes on and make my way over to the prison. I'm a little bit nervous, not for the guards or anything, more to see Mike. I hope he doesn't mention about me getting upset over Roger. I make my way up to the desk and say, 'Hi, I'm Kate Reilly, here to see Mike Taylor.'

The man behind the desk looks quite friendly. I thought they would all look like headmasters, but he doesn't. 'Do you have a visiting order?' he says. I nervously say, 'No, I don't, sorry.'

'Well, sorry then, missy, you can't come in,' is his reply.

'Oh, hang on a minute, what is that behind your ear?'

And out of a fake thumb I pull a tightly folded visiting order. 'I'm training to be a magician, is that a good trick?'

'Oh yes, dear, very good indeed,' he says sarcastically. 'This way.'

We walk into another room, a woman is standing there. She starts to feel my left leg, then the other, and up my body. 'Open your mouth,' she says. I open my mouth. 'Tongue up, tongue down, let me check your ears.'

'My ears?' I say. 'Why? Do they have to be clean?' She pulls back my hair and checks each ear. I don't know why but I get so nervous my jokes start to spill out.

'Why did the belt get arrested?'

The man in the queue next to me grins while saying, 'I don't know, why did the belt get arrested?'

'Because he held up a pair of trousers.'

She pushes me to one side and shouts, 'Next!' and ushers the person behind me in the queue to come next.

Why can't I just walk in and see Mike? I must have signed half a dozen forms. I don't really like being here to be honest. The sooner Mike gets out the better. Then a man heads towards me and he looks me up and down like I'm a prisoner. Then nods over to the woman who checked my ears and she nods back to him. I hope they don't stop me from seeing Mike. I've come all this way. But he's looking at me like he doesn't want me to go any further.

'A man walks into a bar and he says, "Ouch."'

I hold my head like I've just banged it on a bar. They look at each other again and both start laughing and I think to myself, Gotcha here – and I'm back to that lovable performing monkey that turns everyone into putty in my hands. 'What do you call a Mexican with a rubber toe?'

'I don't know, what do you call a Mexican with a rubber toe?'

'Roberto, silly, ha ha! Want to see a trick?'

'No, missy, I have work to do. Go on, go through there, your prisoner will be in soon.'

I sit down at the seat and wait for Mike. I hope he's pleased to see me.

A buzzer goes and a voice comes over. 'Can all prisoners make their way to the visitor suite.' He's on his way here. It feels like hours before the doors open and a few prisoners come in. One man is covered head to foot in tattoos, you can't see any skin on his body at all. He looks pretty scary and I worry about Mike living with people who look like that. I can't imagine Mike being friendly with people who look like axe murderers and I wonder if he gets picked on a bit by them. Mike walks in and I stand up. He has a grin on his face, he looks straight at my shoes and his grin widens. I wonder if he's grinning because he's glad I wore them or if, secretly, he is laughing at the state of them.

'Gem, you came to see me, I missed you.'

He hugs me really tightly like he really has missed me and kisses me on the cheek. The guard who I made laugh walks over to us and gives Mike a look.

'What's wrong?'

'It's just we're not really allowed to touch each other.'

'We can't touch each other, why?'

'Well, they might think you're passing things to me.'

'Like what, sweets or something?'

'Yeah, sweets, that's it. You're wearing the shoes, then.'

'What were you thinking? They're not the prettiest of shoes.'

'Don't worry, when I get out of here the first thing I'm going to do is get you the prettiest shoes you've ever seen, I promise you. What have you been up to then?'

I tell him about school, but he stops me short saying, 'When you came in did they search you?'

'Yeah, they did, why?'

'I'm just checking. Listen, when you leave here Mr Simpson is going to give you some money and we'll make arrangements for you to keep coming here. Would you like that?'

'Yeah, course I would.'

'I need you to do something for me. I'm going to get us both a drink. I want you to start talking and move your hands about knocking the cups on the floor. When I go under the table to clear it up, you put your left foot towards me.'

'What do you mean?'

'I've hidden some sweets in your heel, you know I like my sweets.'

'What? I don't understand, there's a vending machine over there.

I would have brought some money to get you some sweets if I'd have known.'

'Nah, these are special sweets, my favourite. Just stick your left foot towards me and I'll do the rest.'

He goes to get the drinks. It's tea from the vending machine. He says, 'When you spill it, put your hand in it. It will hurt a little bit, but scream "ouch", like it's *really* hurting you and the guards will come running over to help you. Don't forget to stick your left foot out though.'

'OK then,' I say without any further questions.

I start to talk, waving my arms about and, just as he says, I spill the tea all over the table, making sure that the cups fall on the floor and scream like I've burnt myself. Mike bends down to pick up the cups and I stick my foot out. I'm not sure what he did but it felt like he pulled on the heel. The guards come rushing over and the one I told the jokes to asks me if I'm OK.

I say, 'Yes I am, but I've burnt my hand on the tea.' Mike comes up from under the table with the cups and says, 'Hey, are you OK? The tea shouldn't be that hot in the machine, you know. You should sort that, my kid could be scarred for life.'

'You know what? I think I want to go.' I look at the guard and say, 'Will you take me out, please?'

The guard pulls me back saying, 'Can you sign the accident book before you go, and are you sure you're OK?'

'Yeah, I'm fine thanks. I've got a joke about tea. Do you want to hear it?' I don't even wait for an answer before the joke is rolling off my tongue. 'What's under Mr Teapot's cosy? His box earls.' I start to giggle and the guard gives a little smile. 'No, what is under his cosy? His tea-string.' The guard is laughing his head off at me. 'No, really, do you know what it is? His teanis.' He's now really laughing. 'You're such a funny girl.'

'I hope you mean funny as in "ha ha" and not funny as in strange. Do I need to be searched again?' He's still laughing. 'No, I don't think you're a mastermind criminal just yet. Off you go.' And he leads me to the door.

I want to turn back around and say, 'Hey you, not a mastermind criminal? I'll have you know I can steal every bike in the UK and break into any safe. I've been doing it since I was ten years old.' But, for now, I'll settle with the fact that I got to see Mike and now I get to go home. I head towards Mr Simpson's car and he's reading a newspaper waiting for me.

'Hello, did you see him and get everything sorted?'

'Yes, sorted.' Then a mobile phone rings and Mr Simpson picks it up.

'Hello, Mike.' Mr Simpson must know two Mikes because it can't be my Mike. 'Yeah, she's told me that everything went to plan.' It *is* my Mike. How on earth is he calling? 'Yes, I'll put her on now.' He hands the phone over to me and it really is Mike on the other end. 'You did well there, really well. Could you do it again next time maybe?'

'Well, maybe not *that* way again, Mike, we'll have to think of another way. I can drop the cups on the floor but not burn myself.'

'Why, did it hurt?'

'No, it's not that, it's just they wrote my name in the accident book.'

'Well, what's wrong with that?' Mike asks.

'Well, if I do the same thing next time and they go to the accident book and see my name in it they will start to get suspicious.' Mr Simpson starts to laugh.

'OK, we'll think of something. You take this mobile with you so I can ring you whenever I like. Get yourself something nice to wear with the money off Mr Simpson. I'll see you next time.'

'OK, Mike.'

Mike hangs up the phone. Mr Simpson says, 'Well, get you, madam. Well done.' We start driving home and we've gone back to that awkward silence again.

The weeks are flying by and it's Tuesday already which means visiting day at the prison. This is a fornightly event for me. My relationship with Mr Simpson is no better. In fact, I think it's getting worse. He never talks to me. I sometimes wonder if I'm even in the same car as him. He won't even give me the time of day.

'Mr Simpson, do you have the time please?' I say in a shy voice because, to be honest, around him I don't have any other voice.

'There's a clock there,' he says while nodding to the clock. See what I mean, what can you do with that? I finally get into the prison. I don't really care about the way Mr Simpson is because at least I get to see Mike. It's my favourite day. In he comes.

'Hello, Kate, good to see you again today. I know it's nearly your birthday and I can't be there but I promise when I get out, I'll tell everyone I'm getting out a day later and me and you will do something really nice.'

'Really, like what?'

'I don't know, anything you want. What about Edinburgh Zoo? You ever been to Scotland?'

'No, I've not been past Bridgeborough.'

'Well, that's settled then. Let's do it.'

It's the end of visiting time and this hour has flown. I can't believe the hour is up already. I kiss Mike goodbye and make my way back over to Mr Miserable in the car. Why is he so miserable, surely nothing is that bad?

I get back into the car and Mr Simpson is on the phone and I hear him say, 'Nah, it's got an alarm panel and without the code we'd never get in. I'll tell you what, though, if I don't get my hands on some money soon my club is not going to last much longer. I'm really struggling. Anyway, I better go, we'll talk later but get your thinking head on.'

He doesn't even look in my direction or acknowledge me, he just drives. I really want to turn round to him and say, 'Who on earth do you think you are?' But I think this is one time Kate Reilly knows when to be quiet.

Chapter 7 – Half A Million Pounds

It's Monday night and Jennie has come over.

'Hey, look what I have to celebrate your fourteenth birthday.' She pulls out a bottle of cider. 'Let's drink this and go to the park. There are a few people from our class going over.'

I'm pleased to say our drinking has come along since the rosé wine incident. We still don't really like the taste, but girls and boys drinking in the park ... I can't think of anything better to do.

'Hey, Lee from the year above us is coming. I'm going to try and kiss him, he's gorgeous,' Jennie says excitedly. I'm not sure what it is about Jennie, whether it's because her parents are so stuck up that she wants to rebel, or whether it's just her hormones, but she has boys on the brain all the time.

'You're terrible, you're not going to leave me with his friends, are you? You know I can't be bothered with boys.'

'Why can't you be bothered with boys? Are you a lesbian?'

'What? No way, I don't like immature boys. I prefer men.'

'What, like Mike?'

'Yes, actually, when he gets out me and him are going to have a day away together.'

'You're so in love with Mike, I really don't see what it is you like about him.'

'No, I'm not, don't be so silly. What on earth would make you think I'm in love with Mike?'

'Nothing, I was just kidding.' Jennie shrugs off the comment. She often does that if she thinks she's hit a nerve with me.

It's funny, as I get older my feelings towards Mike are changing. I'm not sure if I want him to be my dad or I want to marry him. The more I think about him getting out of prison and looking forward to seeing Shelly, the more jealous I get. Which is funny because I've never been jealous of Shelly, but when I think of her having Mike in the way I want him now I really dislike her. I wonder what made Jennie talk about me being in love with him. It's not like I've ever told her.

That night we get so drunk on the cider we stumble back to my house and vomit all night and all day, totally missing school. Never again are we drinking, I say to myself for the thousandth time. She finally goes home at 4pm. I'm lounging in bed thinking about last night's events and how funny it was. I can't believe Jennie let Lee put his finger in her. I wonder what it would be like if Mike put his finger in me. Oh no, Mike, I forgot – today is visiting day, he'll kill me. It's my birthday today as well, he wanted to see me. I better call him. I go to my wardrobe and pick up the mobile phone. There are fifteen missed calls from Mike and Mr Simpson. I call Mike quickly.

'Oh, Mike, I'm so sorry. I got drunk last night and I've spent most of the day being sick, I'm so sorry.'

'Mr Simpson, isn't happy, he was waiting for you.'

'Well, it wasn't my fault, it was Jennie's. She let Lee from the year above poke her last night. Have you ever poked anyone?'

'Jesus, Kate, are you listening to me? Are you not even bothered? You better get over and see Mr Simpson quickly and don't tell him you were drinking or that you've been knocking around with boys and that's why you couldn't make it. Whatever you do. Just say you've not been very well.'

I'm so angry with Mike. It's my birthday and if I don't want to go, I don't have to. I think I'll tell Mr Simpson that as well. I'm not sure why I'm feeling so annoyed but I'm furious. I get in his car every fortnight, he never even speaks to me or looks in my direction and he's angry because I never showed up today. Well, I'll soon tell him. He doesn't scare me.

I burst into the club and into Mr Simpson's office. I don't even knock, I'm in that much of a rage.

'So you're not happy, are you? Well, let me tell you, I'm not happy either and don't think I don't know it's not sweets being smuggled into that prison, Jimmy.'

He looks up at me with the angriest look I've ever seen anyone give.

'Hey, it's Mr Simpson round here, not Jimmy. I say who calls me Jimmy, madam, and don't you know how to fucking knock?'

'Oh really, like you think that "Mr Simpson" gives you some kind of respect, does it? I enter a building every day and every adult in that building is a Mr or a Mrs, so don't you go thinking you're anything special. Another thing, I may as well tell you this while I'm on, your family is a cartoon on the TV and you're all bloody yellow, and you MR SIMPSON are the stupidest and fattest in your whole family. You know what, Mr Simpson, or whatever your stupid name is, I'm not going back to the prison ever, that's me finished. You want stuff taken in, take it your bloody self. You know what else? I asked you the time once, I did it to trick you, to see if you would actually give me the time of day and you just nodded to the clock, saying, "There's a clock there". You know what you can do with your clock? Stick it up your big fat arse.'

Oh my God, I think I went a bit too far with that one, his face is like thunder. He stands up and it looks like he's going to come around the desk and give me what for. He slowly walks towards me and with one big slap, he has hit me across the face and knocked me off my feet. I've never been hit before, ever. Maybe Mike was right about him. He's not the type of person you upset and if he tells you to call him Mr Simpson, I suggest you call him Mr Simpson.

I eventually get up on my feet and he's staring at me, looking like he wants to slap me again. I don't say anything to him, I walk out as slowly as I can. I want to cry, really cry, like the type of crying when you put your head in the pillow and you think it's never going to stop. But I'm not giving him the satisfaction of seeing me cry, no way.

I finally get home and slink to my bedroom before my mum spots the red mark on my face. This is the worst birthday I've ever had. I'm missing Mike like crazy, all Jennie's interested in is boys, my mother doesn't care about me, I still don't know who my dad is and, to top it all off, I got slapped.

My phone is ringing and it's Mike. 'Hey, Kate, how's your birthday been?'

'Oh, fine.'

'Did you go and see Mr Simpson?'

'Yeah, I went, I said I wasn't feeling very well. He was fine and said we can make it next week.'

'Did he? Thank God for that. Listen, he gets a bit tense at times, you're lucky you caught him in a good mood. I've been a bit worried about you.'

'I'm fine, honestly. I'm going to go, I still feel a little sickly.'

'OK. Happy birthday.'

Happy bloody birthday indeed, and you think Mr Simpson gets tense – is that what you call it? Slapping fourteen-year-old girls to the floor is a little bit more than feeling tense in my book. I have to face him next week. What if he slaps me again?

I can't believe how quickly this week has gone. The more you dread something, the quicker the time flies. Yet if I was looking forward to something, a week would feel like a year.

It's time. I've got to go and see Mr Simpson. I enter the club and Caroline is there sorting out the bottles.

'Is Mr Simpson in?' I sheepishly ask.

'Yes, darling, he's in his office, go in.'

As I walk towards the door my heart is thumping so loud, there's probably no need to knock as he'll hear my heartbeat before the tapping. I knock gently on the door and hear his heavy voice.

'Come in.'

As I open the door I feel I could run away but I don't want another slap. I slowly open the door and say, 'Hello, Mr Simpson,

I'm here for you to take me to see Mike.'

'Wait in the bar, I won't be long.'

He still never gave me any eye contact. Maybe he's forgotten the things I said. I called him Homer Simpson and called him fat. I smile at myself thinking of how mad I was and how I felt even worse when I got home and realised I'd had my period that day. Hence the fact I was so moody. I wish I was like other girls and regular, then I would know when it's coming so if I ever do feel angry I can lock myself in a cupboard till it's over. Instead, I end up some have-a-go hero, shouting and bawling at gangsters and getting slapped.

Mr Simpson is coming out of his office and I find myself sitting up straight in the seat, not moving a muscle, with my hands neatly folded on my knee. I think I'll stay here until Mr Simpson dismisses me. I've gone from trying to trick someone into speaking to me to praying to God he never speaks to me again. Mike should be out soon, then I never have to see Mr Simpson again.

'Come on then you, let's go,' comes that stern voice that shocks me to the core. I jump out of my seat really quickly. I feel like a frightened rabbit. We get into his car and I wonder if he'll speak to me. I wonder if I should ask him the time – hmm, maybe not, especially now he knows I was trying to trick him. Maybe I could say, 'Oh Mr Simpson, you look nice, have you been losing weight?' That could get me out of the whole 'fatso' comment. We're driving to the prison and no one has spoken for at least half an hour. It's killing me to the point where I'm sitting on my hands and looking like I have ants in my trousers and out of nowhere a joke pops into my head. I can't contain myself any longer, I'm going to burst if I don't tell him a joke. The only thing I can think of is what I do best.

'A man walks into a bar and there's a sign saying: cheese sandwiches one pound, chicken sandwiches one pound fifty and a handjob two pounds. The man says to the pretty bar maid, "Excuse me, darling, do you carry out the handjobs?" She says, "Yes, gorgeous, I do." Man says, "Well wash ya friggin hands, I want a chicken sandwich."'

The next thing I know, Mr Simpson starts to laugh and not just a slight giggle, he has a full-blown belly laugh in front of me, with tears rolling down his eyes. His uncontrollable laughing sets me off to uncontrollable laughing and it takes us around ten minutes to compose ourselves.

He finally composes himself and says, 'Listen here, young 'un, let me tell you something. I know what happened last week was very unpleasant and I mean that for both of us. I was angry. I probably shouldn't have lashed out and I definitely shouldn't have hit you and I'm sorry for that. I have come across some extremely hard and brave people in my lifetime, but I have never come across anyone who would ever dare to speak to me the way you did. That takes guts – guts or stupidity, I'm not sure which.'

'I'm sorry that I spoke to you the way I did, Mr Simpson, but it was my period, it does that to me and I know you have problems at the minute, I know your club is in trouble with money. I heard you tell that man on the phone. But you know the alarm panel can be bypassed. I could teach you if you wanted.'

'Sweetheart, it's very kind of you and I know you can open safes but this is something totally different. It's the post office on Alderson Road and to get in there you would need the alarm code which is digital, not like a safe lock at all.'

'No, I know that. What you need is an ultraviolet torch. You shine it on the alarm panel where the number codes are and the fingerprints will show up. It's obvious that will be the code, as they get used all the time.'

'Yes, but to work out four digits you would probably lock the system.'

'Yeah, but it would be worth a try. You could work it out really. Like if the numbers were 1, 3, 7 and 9 you would automatically try 1-9-7-3 or 1-9-3-7 as you're guaranteed it would be a birth year if there's a 1 and 9 in it. It would always be something that they would remember. If not, the numbers may go straight up and down like 2, 5 and 8, and then you could try either one after that – 2-5-8-5 would be my first guess.'

'Do you have one of these pens, then?'

'Well no, I don't, but I bet we could get one. If you took me to the high street we could go and find one.'

'You know what, I think we should. We'll leave the prison for another day. This is very important.'

Before I know it, me and Mr Simpson – after having never spoken to each other in months, having shouted at each other, a slap, one joke and, hey presto – we're shopping together.

I spot the pen and he buys it. People on the high street seem to be looking at him funny and crossing to the other side when they see us. Maybe they know he slaps kids so they're making sure their kids stay well away.

He drives me home and says, 'I'll pick you up around seven-ish. Make sure you bring the pen with you.'

It's just after seven and there he is pulling over in his car. I climb in and he asks, 'Are you nervous?'

'No, Mr Simpson, why would I be nervous?'

'In case you can't get in or get caught.'

'Well, if I can't get in we're no worse off than we are now, are we? And if we get caught, I'll say I lost my way and I'm looking for my friend Jennie.'

Mr Simpson laughs at me. I think he thinks it's another one of my jokes, but it's not.

We get to the post office and he says, 'That's it, there, that's the one. Can you climb through the window? The alarm panel will be near the front door. As soon as you get in, get straight on to the floor and crawl to the door. Then have a look, see if you can do it. If you can't and you lock the system, you run as quick as you can to the window and get out. I'll be waiting for you.' He puts his head down and mutters under his breath, 'What the hell am I doing letting a kid take charge of something? This is bloody stupid.'

'I'm only trying to help, Mr Simpson,' is my short reply. This man doesn't have any gratitude in him whatsoever. I think he was shocked I heard him.

I finally get into the post office and do as he said, get straight to the floor. I can feel the carpet under my hands, it feels dirty and the dirt is now sticking to me with the sweat from my palms. I feel like it's taking ages. Walking would be much quicker. Mind you it's a good job he said get to the floor. I would have been walking around setting all the sensors off. I finally spot the alarm panel so I stand up in the hope the alarms don't go off. I shine the torch on the control box and, bingo, it has a 1 and a 9 in it. First try, 1-9-6-2. I'm in. I unlatch the front door.

'Do come in, Mr Simpson, help yourself to stamps.'

Mr Simpson laughs at me, three times in one day. Who said this girl isn't funny? He holds my hand the same way Mike used to when we did things like this, and for the first time I'm not scared of him. I feel if anyone were to come in he would protect me before himself.

He leads me to the safe and says, 'Can you open that, then?'

I go over and open the safe. There's more money in there than I have ever seen. I never knew there was that much money in the world. Mr Simpson loads it into black bags and tells me to carry one. We load them into his boot and climb in the car. He starts to laugh again, I must be infectious to him.

We drive away from the Post Office and Mr Simpson seems so much more relaxed he even wants me to tell him another joke.

'A gangster and his girlfriend were walking down the road, she spots a diamond ring in the shop window and says, "Wow, I'd love to have that." The gangster says, "No problem, baby," and throws a brick through the window and gets her the diamond ring. They walk further down the road and she spots a leather jacket in another window, "Wow, I'd love that jacket." The gangster throws a brick through the window and gets the leather jacket for her. Further down the road they walk past a Mercedes car dealership and she says, "Wow, I'd love one of those." The gangster screams at her, "What the bloody hell do you think I am, made of bricks or something?"'

Mr Simpson is laughing his head off again.

'You're a funny little thing, aren't you? You know, you should probably stay away from men like me and Mike, we're not always good company to be around. Where's your dad? What would he think of all of this?'

'I don't have a dad. I've never had a dad. Mike's the closest thing to a dad I have.'

Mr Simpson says, 'Well, I'll tell you what, princess, because I like you so much how about I'll be your uncle. That's as good as a dad sometimes, and if you ever get into any trouble you come and see me and I'll sort it out for you.'

'Uncle Mr Simpson? That's weirder than Mr Simpson. I think I'll just stick to Mr Simpson, thanks.'

He giggles. 'Well, not Uncle Mr Simpson. It'll be Uncle Jimmy.'

'Jimmy, I'm allowed to call you Jimmy?'

'Yes, you can. How about I call you "Treasure", cos you have been a total treasure for me today.'

'What with Mike calling me Gem and you calling me Treasure, if they were to place me on a desert island and put a red cross on my head everyone would be trying to find me.'

He looks at me and smiles and says, 'Oh, and by the way, it's 8.30pm.'

We both smile at each other.

We travel a little further and he says, 'You must be starving, do you fancy food?'

'OK then.'

We pull into this little cafe and he orders himself a burger and chips and says, 'You fancy a beef burger?'

'Oh no, not a beef burger, I'll have a chicken burger.' With all this going on I would never bamboozle him with the whole colour business.

'Mr Simpson, oh I mean, Uncle Jimmy. Why do you want to save your club so much? I mean, I'm not being funny but it's dark and dingy and it smells. Why would you even want to work there? The only nice thing about it is your office and surely it would be cheaper for you to buy an office.'

'Ah no, you just see it through the day. Wait until you're old enough and you go in of a night-time and see it in all its glory. There's a real buzz in the air in my club of a weekend.'

'What, like a bee kind of buzz?'

'No, a buzz as in atmosphere. I walk around my club on Friday night and all my staff are there wanting to shake my hand or talk to me, the lights are on, the music is pounding, pretty girls are dancing everywhere, people are meeting each other, chatting. It's sometimes mentioned in wedding speeches. Remember when we met in Jimmeez bar.'

'I find that really strange, you know.'

'What?'

'Well, people have to call you Mr Simpson, yet your bar is Jimmeez. So when people say, "We went to Jimmeez last night," they're calling you Jimmy. You should have thought it through and called it Mr Simpson's, or Moe's – that's the bar from the Simpsons TV show.'

'Yes, you're probably right. What do you want to be when you grow up?'

'I wanted to be a magician's assistant for ages, I thought I'd be really good at it.'

'You would be good at that.'

'But now, I don't know. Maybe I'll work in your club.'

'What, an intelligent girl like you working in a club for a man like me? You're better than that.'

'What's wrong, am I not pretty enough to work in your club, is that it?'

'No, not at all, you're a very pretty girl, but let me tell you about girls who work in my bars, and remember this if ever you need a job, this is one reason why never to work in a bar: girls who work in my bar wear next to no clothes – they're pretty, don't get me wrong, but they're only good-time girls, girls you want to have fun with. You'd never marry a girl who works in a bar like mine. A lot of men have sex with them and they pay them money for it. That's how they have to pay their bills sometimes, and they take drugs. Don't you ever take drugs, ever. It's not big or clever and it's for idiots, and I'm telling you that as someone who knows exactly how stupid people who buy and take drugs are. The girls in my bar, they can't find husbands, see, so they have to sell their bodies because they have no one paying the bills. A girl with your skills will never need to sell her body and you'll always find a way of making money. Like today, when we get back in the car I have money for you and all you've done is get into somewhere, in the space of ten minutes. You tell me how much you want and it's yours. The girls in my bar are lucky if they make that in a year.'

We eat our meal and drive home. He takes me as far as he can before he says, 'I better not be seen with you by your mother, she may not like it. So then, how much of this money do you want?'

'Well, I know that this might sound really cheeky but me and my friends are all going to the park at the weekend and I'd like a fiver for some cider and things please. But if I take a fiver for me, I need another one.'

'Another one? Why?'

'Well, I have this whole deal going on and if I do something bad and get money from somewhere I have to halve it with the tramp on the corner near my house. The good then counteracts the bad.'

'That's a really nice way to look at it. You're very young at the moment so I'm going to give you two fivers but I'm going to put some away for you for when you get older, deal?'

'Yeah, whatever.'

He hands me over the money and, just like the last time, I find the tramp and hand him half. 'Buy your wife some flowers,' I say and walk away thinking about what a great day I've had.

The following morning it's breaking news. The post office on Alderson Road has been broken into. It's thought more than half a million pounds was taken in the raid, which happened between midnight and dawn. Police have reason to believe that it was a very intelligent, organised raid with sophisticated tools by a highly intelligent gang.

Organised, gang, tools! It was me and Uncle Jimmy, he pushed me through the window and it only got organised in the afternoon and the sophisticated tool was a £34.99 torch. It was 7.30pm as well, they've got it all wrong. Half a million pounds... I should have asked him for three fivers, Jennie could have had one too.

Chapter 8 – The Suicide Note

It's finally here! The day Mike gets out. Well, the day he *really* gets out. Everyone thinks it's tomorrow, but I'm so special he wants to spend the day with me. Mike got Uncle Jimmy to give me some money and he pre-ordered our Edinburgh Zoo tickets over the phone so we just need to collect them when we get there. I can't wait to see Mike. I jump in a taxi and go straight to the prison. There are lots of women there waiting for their men. Out comes the first lot and in front is the guy with all the tattoos. Mike is walking right beside him and, as they both come out of the gate, Mike shakes his hand and says, 'Hey, keep yourself out of trouble, don't forget.'

'I will, Mike, I will.' He gives Mike a smile and I still can't really see them as friends but they must be if Mike is shaking his hand. Mind you, a lot of people shake Mike's hand.

'Hey, Gem, it's you. You're here, have you got money for our train tickets?'

'Yeah, I've got an envelope for you.'

'Good girl, let's go.'

We walk to the train station and I'm talking non-stop, telling him about school and Jennie with all her boyfriends.

'Let's have some fun, just you and me kidda, yeah?'

We go for some breakfast first. I've been awake most of the night as the prison is quite far away and I knew I would be travelling in the taxi for a while. Mike says he's been awake most of the night with excitement. We finally get on the train and I'm thinking of all the things we can go and see. They say there's penguins at the zoo and they do a penguin parade.

'Will you buy me one, Mike?'

'What?'

'A penguin.'

'Where would you keep a penguin, silly? They need ice and they eat fish and you'd never cope with fishing for it to eat.'

'Ha ha, yeah, I never thought about that, maybe just a teddy one then. I could cope with that.'

'I'll get you the biggest penguin teddy there is.'

'What do you call a penguin in the desert?'

'I don't know.'

'Lost.'

We're sitting on the train and we know we'll be travelling for a while so we get comfortable. Before I know it, I'm being shaken quite violently.

'Get up, Kate, get up. We fell asleep and missed our stop. We've ended up in Glasgow, what's even in Glasgow?'

I can't believe we've fallen asleep. We get off the train and walk outside the station.

'Right, the next train back to Edinburgh is in three hours, which means we'll miss most of the day at the zoo, so why don't we skip the zoo and I'll take you shopping here for those shoes I promised you.'

'OK then.'

Mike takes me to nearly every shoe shop in Glasgow and we come across a big shop with a man in a suit with a tall hat on standing outside. He opens the door for us and I feel like royalty.

'Let's get you some shoes from here, this is a proper shoe shop, this one.'

We take a look around and the assistant is looking at us a little funny. She comes over and says, 'Good afternoon, sir, can I help you?'

'Yes,' says Mike. 'I would like to buy my daughter some shoes.'

Oh no, I'm his daughter again which must mean he fancies her. 'I've been away fighting in the army and I told her I would spoil her today.'

Ha! Fighting in the war … fighting in prison more like, and guess why he was in prison? Because he conned a thirteen-year-old girl, who isn't even his daughter by the way, into breaking into a few houses for him.

I give Mike that look as if to say, This is our day, don't spoil it. He stops flirting with the assistant, but she's come over all giggly. Why does he have that effect on women? I choose some shoes, purple with a diamanté bow on the front, really pretty.

We get to the checkout and the girl says, 'That's three hundred and fifty pounds, sir.'

What, three hundred and fifty pounds for a pair of shoes? I probably won't even wear them, ever. Mind, Jennie will love them. I might give her them for her birthday, we'll see. They get placed in a big bag and I say, 'Oh, look, it's Uncle Jimmy.'

'What did you say?' Mike snaps.

'Uncle Jimmy, written on the bag.' The words 'Jimmy Choo' are written on the bag.

'Did Jimmy tell you to call him that?' Mike seems a little uneasy.

'Yeah, he said I could and if I ever needed anything I could go and see him and he would help me.'

'Don't you ever go to see him without asking me first, OK? I know I've not been around much but me and you, well, we're best friends, aren't we? We understand each other.'

'Yeah, yeah, we do.'

'Have you seen much of Jimmy?'

'No, just when he took me to the prison sometimes.'

'Did he ask you to open any safes?'

'No, no, he never.'

I feel like I'm getting a bit upset as Mike is really not happy. Then he changes his tune and says he's sorry and hugs me.

'I'm sorry, I just don't want anyone taking advantage of you.

Remember Roger?'

I put my head down as I really don't want to talk about Roger or that whole night. I want to forget it. I get nervous so my usual jokes start pouring out.

'Oo, a mother says to her little boy, "Hey, honey, you have your shoes on the wrong feet." Little boy says, "Don't be silly, Mummy, these are the only feet I got."'

Mike smiles and we go on with our day. That's the last time I ever call Jimmy 'Uncle' in front of Mike and I better not tell Mike about the post office.

We end up at a posh hotel with a twin room. There's a huge bath.

'Look at that, I've dreamt of that.'

'You sit down there and relax then and I'll run a bath for you.'

I run him a bath. I like looking after him. He finally comes out of the bath, after what seems like hours.

'Shall I run you one?'

'Yeah, please.'

'Do you want bubbles?' I look at Mike with raised eyebrows. 'What, you can't wash with blue bubble bath? God, Kate, you really need to talk to someone about this.'

As I lie in the bath. I think about what Mike said to me about needing to talk to someone about this. What did he mean? Talk to who and about what? He must be tired or something and not know what he's talking about. I get out of the bath as quickly as I can. I don't want him to fall asleep by the time I get out. I want us to stay awake as long as we can so I'll suggest a few card games.

'Let's play cards or something.'

We play a few rounds of blackjack. Mike says, 'I was thinking about when I snapped at you over Jimmy and it was wrong of me, I shouldn't have done that. It's just, I like you as my friend and I don't want someone like him taking advantage of you. It's like if we were at school and he's nicked one of my toys. Not that I think you're a toy but, well, you know what I mean.'

It starts to dawn on me that Mike thinks of me like a security blanket, like I used to think about Rebecca in the school yard years ago. I realise Mike and I are not so different after all.

'It's OK. I'm sorry that I upset you calling Jimmy uncle. I won't do it again. I've never had an uncle before, that's all.'

'So it looks like we're both sorry then.'

I start to yawn as it's been such a long day, even though I want to stay up I don't think I can. 'I'm so tired, Mike.'

'Me too, let's go to bed.'

As I'm lying in bed, I keep thinking of Mike and how I would like to climb into bed next to him. I start to think of him and Shelly together tomorrow night. This uncontrollable anger has come over me. I'm starting to dislike Shelly more and more. I hope when she sees him tomorrow she decides she no longer wants to be with him and has enjoyed her time on her own. Jennie was right, after all; I am in love with Mike.

Mike has settled back into Bridgeborough pretty easily over the last few months. I'm fifteen today. My mum bursts into my room. She's more excited for my birthday than me. Probably because I'll be grown up and off her hands soon.

'Come on, big girl, what's your plans today?'

'I'm popping in to see Mr and Mrs Richards this morning, then Jennie and I are going shopping, then we're going to the park to meet people from school.'

'Well get up then, you don't want to waste the day lying in bed.' I make my way downstairs but there's only Lawrence there which is unusual. Mike is normally here by now. I can't wait to see what he's bought me. He bursts in the door and says, 'Happy birthday, Gem! You're nearly growing into a diamond. I got you this.'

It's a necklace, it's in the shape of a heart and encrusted in diamonds. I bet it was pretty pricey as well. He seems a little more excited than usual and says to Lawrence, 'Hey, Lawrence, you won't believe this when I tell you. I'm the happiest man alive today.' I wonder what it could be. 'Me and Shelly are getting wed.'

As the words come out of his mouth my heart breaks in two. No, I can't be hearing this. I know the tears are going to come any second now – no stop, don't let them see you cry.

'Wow, congratulations,' I say with a heavy heart.

'She's pregnant, can you believe it? I'm going to be a dad and you're going to be an uncle. It's going to be the best-loved kid in England.'

Pregnant! No, this is the worst thing ever. I have to get out of here.

'Well, I must go, Jennie is waiting. Congratulations again,' I say as quickly as I can and run out the door. I keep on running, completely forgetting about the Richards and that I have plans. I run to the local park and cry under a tree for what seems like hours. How can he do this to me after all this time? When I'm finally nearly old enough to be with him, he decides to marry Shelly and have her baby. God, I hate her. I'm not sure why. I've always loved Shelly, but I hate her today. What can I think of that's going to make her seem the worst person in the world right now? Oh I know, there was a girl she went to school with and I overheard Shelly telling my mum once how she'd slept with her boyfriend. Yes, what a terrible person she is for that, that's it. I should tell Mike about that, does he know what a tart he's marrying? I cry some more and think he'll laugh at me for that, as it was years before those two even met.

Even though they've been together years, I was so not expecting a marriage and a baby. I go over to Jennie's and she sees my face.

'What is it? I can tell something is wrong.'

'Oh, Jennie, it's awful. Mike and Shelly are getting married and going to have a baby, can you believe it?'

'Look, Kate,' Jennie says, 'I know how you feel about him, but Mike doesn't feel the same about you, he loves Shelly. I think he loves you as well, but in a different kind of way. Why would you want to be with him anyway, he's older and his life is practically over, ours is just starting. It's your birthday, let's enjoy it.'

'Can I stay here tonight? I can't face going home, they're all excited over at mine and I just want to cry about it.'

Jennie holds me in her arms telling me that it'll be OK, but I don't know how it will be OK. I've lost him now. He'll love the baby much more than me, I know he will. I spend my entire birthday crying. He has spoilt my day, I can't believe it. Why would he choose today, of all days, to announce his good news?

Jennie and I spend all day together sitting in her room discussing things. She suggests I go out and find someone my own age. She's been kissing a boy called Tony. I find it hard to keep up with Jennie and which boys she fancies from one week to the next.

'I'll tell Tony to meet us tonight and to bring a friend,' Jennie says.

'I'm not really in the mood, this is the worst day ever.'

'Can't you just forget about Mike for one day? It's your birthday. We've been looking forward to it.'

I get ready at her house. I can't bear to go home right now. I bet Shelly is round there celebrating with my mum and I feel like I could kill her. Jennie and I get to the park and she points over at Tony.

'Oh look, there he is, he has a friend with him, Mark.' We get chatting and he's OK but the more I have to drink the more I tell him about Mike, only I make it out like Mike and I are boyfriend and girlfriend and he's been cheating with another girl and got her pregnant.

'Oh, a baby at fifteen?' He's assuming Mike and I are the same age but, of course, he would. Why would any fifteen-year-old girl fancy a man who is twenty-four years old? The more I drink, the worse I'm feeling.

I say to Jennie, 'I'm going home but you stay here if you like.' As I walk in my front door I can hear them all laughing and talking. Oh no, it's the dreaded wedding talk. I sneak into the house and into my bedroom. Thank God for that, they never heard me, I can cry on my own without being disturbed.

I wake up the next morning and I'm not feeling any better. In fact, right now, I'm really disliking Mike. Yet he's not done anything wrong really, it's not like we were together and he doesn't even know my feelings towards him. Maybe I should tell him, maybe I could stop him from marrying Shelly if I told him my feelings. Yes, that's a great idea. No, don't be silly, he was pleased as punch yesterday when he walked in. If I told him it would spoil everything. I'll have to grin and bear it. As I make my way downstairs, my mum's sitting in the living room with Shelly. Oh great, just what I need. Mind, I have laid in bed most of the morning trying to avoid the world.

'Hello you, you must have been late last night, or crept in quietly because you were too drunk, madam. I never heard you coming back, how was your night?'

'Yeah, OK, I guess.' I shrug my shoulders, still in a huff with myself and the world.

'Oo, Kate, I have something to ask you,' says Shelly in a really excited manner. I think to myself, Oh, what can this be? Does my ass look big in this? Yes, it does, you big fat pregnant fat person who's pregnanty-fatty ... er, I'm not even making any sense.

'What? Shelly, what is it?'

'Well, you've heard my news, Mike and I are getting married and it has to be quick because there's a baby on the way. Will you be my bridesmaid?'

I'm standing there open-mouthed. Are you crazy, you stupid woman, I'm going to be the bride at this wedding when I snatch him away from you so, no, I won't be your bridesmaid.

'Oh, Shelly, I would love to be your bridesmaid, I can't believe you've asked me. Thanks!' Have I just said that?

'Great, us three can all go shopping next Saturday. Mike says there's no budget, we can have what we want.'

'Oh, does he now,' I mutter. Great. I've not only got to *attend* this wedding from hell, I have to help with the arrangements and be part of it.

Today is the day we have to go wedding-dress shopping. God, I could be sick, like I don't have anything better to do. Shelly tries on every dress in the shop and she does look gorgeous in them all, which makes me even angrier. She tries one on saying, 'Wow, Julie, this is it. This is my dress.'

My mum has tears in her eyes. 'Wow, Shelly, you look like a princess. Doesn't she, Kate?'

I snap back at my mum, 'No, I think she looks like a watermelon.'

My mum tuts and says, 'Kate, don't be rude. Don't listen to her, what does she know.'

Shelly doesn't even listen to me and goes to the till to buy the dress. She also buys mine and guess what. I hate it. It's huge and yellow. I look like one of those flowers in the garden that everyone used to call wetty beds when I was younger. Someone would grab one and chase everyone round and whoever got touched by a wetty bed was, well that, a wetty bed. So that's it, Mike is marrying Shelly and I have to go dressed as a wetty bed. Great!

It's the big wedding tomorrow and I don't know how I'm going to get out of it. What can I possibly do? Oh, I know, I'll commit suicide. Yeah, that's a great idea. I make my way downstairs and open the fridge. Orange juice, that will do it. I gulp that stuff like there's no tomorrow. There's a punnet of green grapes there as well. I eat every single one of those grapes, this is definitely going to work. But how will I die? Will they start to eat me alive like I thought that bike had? Will my mum come in to blood all over my bed? Maybe I should take the bleach upstairs with me so she can clean up. I get back in my bedroom and write out my note.

Dear Mum,

I know you will probably be happy when you find me, it means you can get your life back like you had it before I was born. I'm sorry I've eaten all of your grapes and drunk your orange juice, but trust me it's for the best. Please tell Jennie I am sorry, and she can have my Jimmy Choos as I won't need them in heaven. They're under my bed. I've left a bottle of bleach by my bedside so you can clean up because trust me the killer grapes normally leave a right mess.

Yours truly, Kate x

I wake up the next morning and there's no sign of any blood. So it's official then, I have to go to this stupid wedding. I better take the bleach downstairs and bin the note.

After the wedding Mike is all excited. I wonder if he'll be that excited when we get married. I feel like a lemon meringue in this stupid dress.

'Hello, Gem, look at you all dressed up. I've hardly had a proper chance to see you with everything going on. You look great.'

'Do I? Not really sure what to say to that, Mike – thanks, I suppose.' I know I don't look great, but I do like how he says it. 'Well, you did it then, you're married. No going back now, you know.'

'What makes you think I want to go back? I can't wait for Shelly to have the baby. You can babysit for us. It'll be like a brother or sister to you.' I feel like saying I was hoping for a child with you, more than a sibling. 'I've got to go over there and mingle with Shelly, but I'll see you later, OK?'

'OK, will you dance with me later, Mike?'

'Yeah, course I will.'

I spot Jimmy, so I make my way over there.

'Treasure, look at you all dressed up, don't you look smart?'

'No, I don't. I look like a lemon meringue and I feel stupid.'

'Don't be silly, you look more like a pineapple melba to me.' Me and Jimmy laugh at each other. 'Who on earth chose that dress for you?'

'That stupid Shelly, that's who, and stop laughing at me or I'll tell everyone you broke into the post office on Alderson Road and stole half a million pounds.'

'Hey, don't even joke about it. I could do years for that, my wife Helen is here and I don't want her knowing things like that. Come over here and I'll introduce you two.' Jimmy shouts over, 'Helen, this is my little treas I've been telling you about.'

Jimmy leads me over to the prettiest woman I have ever seen in my life. She's like something you see in a magazine. She has blonde hair, perfectly straight, which lies just below her shoulders, with blue eyes. Wow, she's even outshining the bride, she's that pretty. She has the most stunning figure-hugging blue dress on, with a fascinator in her hair to match. She really could be a supermodel with a figure like that. I've never really looked at Jimmy properly before, he's normally just Jimmy, but he and Helen standing next to each other are both absolutely stunning. It's almost like their great looks bounce off each other and the way they look into each other's eyes … it's exactly how I want Mike to look at me.

'Hello, sweetheart, how are you? Jimmy tells me you sometimes help him out in that club of his. I hope he pays you and it's not child labour. He's obsessed with that club. I wish he took as much of an interest in me as he does that club.'

Jimmy looks at Helen and says, 'Hey, cheeky, it's for you I work so hard at that club, so you can have the house you live in, not to mention how much that dress cost me for today.'

I should really say, Actually, Jimmy, it was me who paid for that house and Helen's dress with my burglary skills. Then I should say, By rights, Helen, that dress belongs to me. Please keep it for me, when I get older I'll look gorgeous in that dress.

Helen giggles to Jimmy, 'Yes, handsome, but you said I was gorgeous this morning and that the dress was worth every penny.'

They grin at each other while kissing each other sweetly on the lips. Wow, I've never seen Jimmy like that before, it's like he's turned all soft around her. It's really quite nice seeing him like that. Helen looks at me. 'Speaking of gorgeous, don't you look lovely being a bridesmaid.'

'Do I? Jimmy said I look like a stupid cake.'

'Oh Jimmy, you never?' She looks at Jimmy as if to say, Jimmy she's a child. Helen looks at me and smiles to try and reassure me that I don't and says, 'You don't, honestly.'

'Yes, I do, we're taking a bet on it, to see if I look like a lemon meringue or a pineapple melba. What's your thoughts? Promise me if I ever get married and my bridesmaids look like this, you'll shoot me at the altar.' We all giggle at each other.

'Oh, Kate, you do look a little like a lemony thing.'

I grin and cheekily say, 'The only way my bridemaids will look like this is if Jimmy and Mike are my bridesmaids.' Helen and Jimmy start laughing at me again.

'You're right, Jimmy, she is a funny little thing, isn't she?'

'Yeah, she is. What you drinking, Treas?'

'Oo, go on then, if I must, I'll have a lemonade. Don't bother going to the bar, you can just squeeze me.' We start laughing again. 'Can I sit with you two, please? I can't bear anyone looking at me in this dress.'

'Yes, of course you can,' says Helen. 'To be honest, I don't even know anyone here – just Mike, Lawrence and their parents. So I'll be grateful of the company.'

'Helen, what you drinking?'

'I'll have a lemonade as well. If you can't beat them, join them, only I'll have a drop of vodka in mine, thanks.' Jimmy goes off and gets the drinks.

'Why don't you work in the club, Helen?'

'Spend all day with Jimmy? No thanks, we'd be divorced in a month.'

'Why? Does he not listen to you either?'

'Jimmy Simpson listens to no one. I'm glad you've caught on quick, sweetheart.'

Me and Helen have a great day together. I really like her. I want to look like her when I grow up, she really is stunning.

The wedding isn't too bad. It would've been better if Jennie had been there. Jimmy and Mike did make a fuss of me.

I'm sitting doing my homework in my room when my mum comes in.

'Shelly has gone into labour! How exciting! As soon as Mike calls to say that the baby is born we can go to hospital and see them.'

Oh no, the baby is on its way. Mike will be all over that baby, and I'll lose him. I hope it's not a girl. I like being the only girl in his life. He might even call it Gemma. Gem for short, I'd hate that. It will all change soon. Mind you, I thought things would change after the wedding but they haven't really. Things are pretty much the same as they always were, only Shelly is now a Taylor. Just then the phone goes so my mum picks it up.

'Oh, congratulations! How is Shelly doing? We're on our way. Kate, it's a boy! Shelly had a boy. Hurry up, get your coat on.'

Thank goodness for that, it's not a girl. I'm still not happy about it, but it's better than him having a Gem. As we make our way to the hospital Mike is there with a huge bunch of flowers for Shelly. I wish he'd got me some flowers. He looks really happy to see me.

'Gem, you're here, come on in and see the baby.' I peer into the crib where the baby is and Mike says, 'We've called him Billy, isn't he a little bruiser, look.'

Ha! Billy, I think, what a stupid name. And he looks like a Cabbage Patch doll, so he looks like a stupid doll and has a stupid name. I'm two up on him already. Imagine his nickname, Bill ... it's something you ask for at the end of a meal. You're not a diamond like me.

'Can I hold him please, Shelly?'

'Yeah, sit down, I'll get Mike to put him on your lap.' Mike brings him over and places him on my lap and says, 'Keep a hold of his head, mind. Julie, take a picture of me, Kate and Billy – my two favourite people.'

Shelly shouts over, 'Hey, what about me?' They grin at each other. Billy is kind of cute. I think he likes me. He smiled at me, well, my mum said it was wind as babies don't smile that early, but I think he takes after me and catches on quick.

Billy is a few weeks old and I'm still Mike's little gem so nothing has changed in that way. I went straight to the club after school tonight. Jimmy lets me help out so I can get my fiver for my cider on a Saturday. I like helping Jimmy. He says I can take whatever I want out of the club. He gave me this bottle of lemonade. The date on it was running out anyway so it's not like he could sell it next week.

As I make my way into the house I can hear my mum and Lawrence arguing. What on earth is wrong? Lawrence shouts, 'You're a fucking slag, Julie, you've always been a fucking slag. Everyone knows it.'

My mum screams, 'Oh, like you've never cheated? Lawrence fucking Taylor who never does anything wrong? Don't think I don't know about you and Marie from the club. I can see it every time you two look at each other.'

Lawrence is packing his things up. I grab a hold of his arm to stop him.

'What's happened, where are you going?'

'I'm leaving but it's nothing for you to worry about, honestly. Me and you can still see each other, but me and your mum ... well, it's over.'

'No, don't leave, please. I like you being here. Has my mum cheated on you?'

'Don't worry about it, honestly, it's not something I want you getting involved in. Could you give me half an hour with your mum?'

'Please don't leave, maybe you have it wrong.'

Lawrence kisses me tenderly on the forehead and says, 'I'll keep in touch, I promise.'

Oh no, I can't believe he's leaving. What if Mike no longer wants to be my friend? I know we're not really friends because of him but Mike might be so angry with my mum he might get angry with me. I make my way over to Jennie's and I tell her what's happened.

'Wow, your mum has cheated? Who with, do you know?'

'I'm not sure, could be anyone, but she seems to think Lawrence has cheated as well. Why are adults so confusing? Why would you want to cheat on your boyfriend? I don't get it. Surely sex is not that good, surely it's the same with someone else.'

'Well, I've got something to tell you. Don't tell anyone but I had sex last night.'

'What? Where? When? What was it like? Who with?'

Jennie grins at me. 'Last night in the park with Chris, one of the lads. It was really good.'

'How did that happen?'

'Well, you weren't there so I was hanging around with the lads. The girls were being boring, just wanted to listen to music all night, so I sat next to Chris. He's Damien's cousin – you know Damien, he's in our music class. Well, he's here for the weekend, he's two years older than me so he really knew what he was doing. We started kissing and he took me into the bushes and we had sex.'

'Oo, you had sex in the bushes?'

'Yeah, wait till you do it, honestly you'll love it.'

'I'll have to wait until I'm sixteen. Mike will never have sex with me underage.'

'Yuk, he's far too old for you.'

'No, he's not, he's only nine years older than me and that's nothing when you're an adult. Jimmy is too old for me. He's eleven years older than me and that's really old. I think he'll be dead soon, he's that old. I bet Mike's really good at sex, he's had loads of practice compared to Chris.'

'Nah, Chris says he's had sex with six different girls.'

'Really? That's a lot. I think Mike's only had sex with Shelly – well, I hope he has. I better go home anyway to make sure my mum's all right. I'll see you later.'

As I walk into the house my mum's sitting on the sofa looking upset. I sit next to her and put my arm around her. 'Are you OK, Mum?'

'Yes, darling, I'm fine. Promise me when you get older, never let a man break your heart, make sure you break his first.'

I'll never break Mike's heart and I'll never cheat on him either. 'OK, Mum, I will, do you want me to sleep in your bed tonight?'

'Would you? I'd really like that. I know you think I hate you, but I don't, you're my baby, I could never hate you. I love you with all my heart.'

I want to say 'I love you' back, but I can't, I don't even know why I feel I don't love her, she's my mum; I should love her, everyone should always love their mum. If I had Jennie's mum I think I would love her. Maybe I'm angry because she won't tell me who my dad is. I don't know.

I just look at her blankly and say, 'I know you do. I'll make you a hot chocolate, we'll take it to bed with us. I'll even put marshmallows on it for you if you like.'

My mum has a tear down her face so I wipe it off which makes her smile. 'I would love marshmallows, Kate, I really would, thank you.'

'Well, you go upstairs and put your pyjamas on ready and I'll bring them up.'

'Thanks Kate.'

As she makes her way to the bedroom I head to the kitchen to make the drinks. I grab the marshmallows from the cupboard and spot a box of chocolates. I open up the box and see there is a caramel heart one there so I place it perfectly on top of my mum's drink and take them upstairs. I get to the room and she's already snuggled in the blankets looking really sorry for herself. 'Look, I put a heart on yours for you.'

This makes my mum cry even more. 'You're such a sweetheart. Thank you for taking care of me.'

I hold her really tightly to try to make her stop crying. I sometimes worry about us two. Sometimes I really dislike her, yet, I'm not sure why, but when she's upset like that, I want to protect her. Why did Lawrence not try talking to her? She just likes attention more than anything, I don't think she did it to hurt him.

The following day I make my way over to Mike's. I must go and see him to make sure that we're still friends.

As I walk in the door Mike is finishing off his breakfast and is more interested in soaking up the bean juice with his toast than Lawrence and my mum breaking up. I was expecting him to have all my gifts I've given him piled up ready to hand over to me with a note attached with all the reasons why we should no longer be friends.

'Hello, Mike, are you OK?'

'Yeah, I'm great, are you?'

'I'm a little worried.'

'What are you worried about? Is everything OK?'

'Just with what happened to my mum and Lawrence, them breaking up.'

'Why would you be worried about that? Lawrence did say to you that he would still see you and, to be honest with you, I could see it coming for a long time. I think they were having problems well before they broke up, it's probably for the best.'

As Mike gets up to put his plate in the sink I follow him. 'It doesn't affect us, does it?'

'What do you mean, affect us?'

'I hope you're not angry with me. I never did anything.'

'Kate, don't be stupid. Come here, you silly thing.' Mike hugs me and giggles. 'Why would I be angry with you? I've told you before, we're best friends. I like spending time with you.' I get as close to Mike's body as I can to take in his scent. I'm so pleased we're still friends. My eyes scan up his chest and on to his lips. I really wish I could kiss those lips.

'Mike.'

'Yes, Gem.'

'Jennie had sex in the bushes with someone.' Mike pulls away from me and gives me a serious look. 'What? I hope you're not doing things like that?'

'Oh no, not me. I'd never do that. I'm waiting for someone special.'

'Oh, got your eye on someone, have you?'

I giggle and say, 'Yeah, I might have, none of your business.'

I didn't dare tell him it's him I have my eye on.

'Yes, well, don't even think of going out with him till I've checked him out first. Seriously, I hope you don't think she's cool for doing things like that with boys? Please don't you be having sex in the bushes. I'm wondering if you should stay away from her if she's starting to do things like that. I know people your age will think Jennie is cool but, seriously, as she gets older she won't be so cool, trust me.'

'All the girls at school are doing things like that. Not me, though. I don't want to do things like that. Not with stupid boys in bushes anyway.'

'Good girl, keep it that way and, whatever you do, don't mention that to Jimmy because he really won't want you knocking around with Jennie any more, he'll hit the roof.'

'Why, does he not like things like that?'

'He's a little old-fashioned when it comes to things like that. I think it's all the club-working he does and the girls acting the way they do around him. He sees the girls as a little desperate and it turns his stomach a bit.'

'No one is as perfect as his Helen, mind.'

'Yeah, she is Little Miss Perfect, isn't she?'

'Not as perfect as me though.' Mike sweeps my hair away from my face and tucks it behind my ear.

'Nah, nowhere near as perfect as you, and you're miles prettier than her.'

'Really?'

'Yeah, really. Now go on, scram – I'm busy, and you keep away from those bushes.' Wow! Mike said I was prettier than Helen.

It's getting easier around the house without Lawrence. It's just so quiet since him and my mum split up. It feels like months not weeks. Jennie has finally stopped talking about having sex in the bushes. Mind you, that's because she's done it with someone else now.

Lawrence is coming come over to see me today. I'm looking forward to it.

'Hello, Kate darling, are you OK?'

'Yeah, I'm great, thanks. I miss you, it's funny you not being round ours. I get a bit bored. I have no one to watch the TV with now. My mum says all the stuff I watch is boring, but we used to love watching the TV together.'

'Nah, she was the boring one, she only ever wanted to watch them stupid soaps all the time. I need to talk to you about something. I've been offered a job in London as a builder and it's too good an opportunity to give up, so I'm moving to London.'

'What? When?'

'Next weekend.'

'Will you be living near the queen? Will you get her autograph for me?'

'Yeah, course I will, and you can come and visit any time you like.'

'How on earth would I get to London? That's like going abroad, isn't it?'

'Nah, it's only three hours on the train.'

'Three hours? That's ages. I would be bored on a train that long.'

'I'll write to you all the time.'

'I'll miss you. I really thought you and my mum would get married and you would have become my dad.'

'You don't need a dad, you've got our Mike and Jimmy Simpson looking after you. Trust me, anyone who has Jimmy looking out for them is going to be OK. Them two have taken quite a shine to you.'

Little does he know it's because I stole half a million pounds for him. I kiss Lawrence on the cheek. It really is a shame about him and my mum, but never mind. Mike did say it was for the best anyway.

Chapter 9 – Let's Go To Jimmeez

It's Friday night and Jennie really wants to go to Jimmeez. She's begged me for weeks to ask Mike if we can go. She walks into my bedroom all dressed up and looks much older than she normally does.

'Kate, I've got you a dress as well. I'll do your hair and make-up.' Once she's finished I look in the mirror and I look way older than fifteen. I bet Mike and Jimmy don't even know it's me. Well here's hoping anyway, I'm not convinced they'll let me in.

'I'm not even sure if we'll get in, Jennie.'

Mike can be a bit funny at times with me with certain things and I have a funny feeling this might be one of them. Even Jimmy has told me he doesn't want me hanging around the club when it's open to the public and I'm definitely not to knock around with any men from the club. 'Men who go to my club are looking for good-time girls, not a wife, Treas,' he says on almost a daily basis.

We finally get to the club and Dave's on the door. I walk straight up to him thinking he'll let me in and once we're in we could hide so Jimmy and Mike don't see us. He lets all the girls in but he's a bit more picky with the boys. There's this group of men and they're getting a bit rowdy, pushing and shoving. Dave tries to stop them entering the club.

'Let us in, we won't be any trouble,' says one of them.

'No, you lot have had far too much to drink. Do yourself a favour, lads, and have an early night,' says Dave.

The men aren't budging. Next thing I know, Dave is on the

walkie-talkie to someone and the doors open. Out comes Mike. Ah, great, he'll definitely see me now.

'All right lads, you heard the man, everybody home,' Mike says in a really stern voice and without question every one of them walks away. Why would they walk away because Mike said that? Dave pulls Mike back and points me out. Even in all that commotion Dave still has his eye on the ball. I suppose that's why he works the doors, so he knows the riff-raff in the queue – and the underage drinkers.

Mike comes straight over to me and says, 'Gem, what are you doing here?'

'It's Jennie, she really wants to come to the club, please let us in.'

'No way, you're only fifteen, you're not getting in. Jimmy would kill me.'

'Oh please, we have fake IDs. I made them myself. Please go ask Jimmy if we can come in.'

'No, why can't you go somewhere else? It's not the kind of place I want you knocking around.'

'Please, I promised her,' I start to whine while grabbing Mike by the arm.

'Hey, Kate, we getting in then?' Jennie is tugging on my arm and I give Mike that 'please don't embarrass me in front of Jennie' look.

'Come with me, I'll have a word.'

Mike leads us up the stairs. There are half-dressed women and good-looking men everywhere. The atmosphere is brilliant. I hope Jimmy lets me in now I'm here. I'll look really clever saying to Jennie, 'Well, I did get you as far as the bar.' She'll think I'm a liar. Mike goes over to Jimmy and I can see him looking over at us and they're talking. Jennie tugs on my arm and says, 'Oh my God, Kate.'

'What?'

'Look, it's him.'

'Who?'

'It's only like, the hardest man in, well, probably the world.'

'Who?'

'Him, over there.' She looks in the direction of Mike and Jimmy. Who is she talking about?

'Who? Where? Do you think Mike and Jimmy know he's the hardest man in the world? Actually, are you sure it's the world. I mean, that's going a bit far, isn't it?'

Jennie does tend to over exaggerate a lot of things. I mean, what on earth would the hardest man in the world be doing in Jimmy's club?

'Well, you know what I mean. He really is hard and no one messes with him. In fact, I've heard you must call him Mr Simpson at all times and if you don't he blows your head off with a shotgun.'

'What are you talking about?' Jimmy is heading towards us.

Jennie all of a sudden goes into panic mode, grabbing my arm even tighter.

'Oh no, he's coming over, what if he blows our heads off for trying to come in here?'

I shake Jennie's arm off me. 'Will you calm down, no one is getting their heads blown off.'

'Treas, what are you doing in my club?' Jimmy says this in a total Jimmy way with no eye contact.

'Jimmy, I know what you're going to say, but it's Jennie's birthday and I promised her. Please, we'll just have a few drinks, we won't be any trouble at all.'

I had to say it was her birthday, I never knew what to say. I notice everyone is staring at us. Jimmy gives me the Jimmy stare and says, 'You're only fifteen, there's no way you can come into the nightclub at fifteen. You only have a few more years to wait. How about I give you two a fiver for your cider instead?'

I'm so disappointed in Jimmy. I really thought he would say yes. What on earth will Jennie say?

'Oh Jimmy, please let me stay, I'll hide in the corner, I promise I will. Please, I helped you when you needed help, remember?' I wink over at Jimmy. I better not mention the post office robbery in front of Jennie.

'I don't know about this, if I get caught and lose my licence for serving underage drinkers...' he says while rubbing his forehead. I think I must be breaking him, I'm sure I am.

'Oh please, look we have these fake IDs so if we get caught we can say that you stopped us at the door and we had these.' I pull out my fake ID and shove it under his nose to make sure he looks at it.

He inspects the ID and pulls a face like he's impressed with it and can't even tell the difference between that and a real one.

'Look, if' – and he points in my face – 'I let you stay, there are rules.'

'What rules?'

'First rule: no talking to men, these men are after good-time girls, like I keep telling you. Second rule: when it's time to go you don't leave with everyone else; it gets a bit chaotic outside and I don't want you caught up in it. You come to get me and I'll get someone to take you home. Third rule: two drinks each, max.'

'What? Two drinks? Ah come on, we can handle at least five.'

'You're not having five, no way.'

'Well, four then, please. It's Jennie's birthday.'

'You'll be the death of me, you.'

Jimmy shouts over at Caroline. 'These two girls are allowed four drinks on the house and they're not to be served any more after that.'

'You're a gent, Jimmy,' I say while I kiss him on the cheek. As I walk away I look at Mike who seems to have women draping themselves over him. He winks at me and shakes his head as if to say, I don't know how you pulled that off.

Jennie pulls me towards her and says, 'Oh my God, how do you know Mr Simpson?'

'What, Jimmy? I've known him a while.'

'That's Jimmy? As in, the one you talk about a lot? All this time you've spoken about a Jimmy ... I never realised it was Mr Simpson you meant. This is brilliant, I'm so chuffed, I can't believe you not only got us into the best club in town but you scored us free drinks off Mr Simpson and you kissed him on the cheek. Did you see everyone looking at us?' Jennie is totally excited about Jimmy for some reason, yet I don't know why, he's just Jimmy.

We make our way to the bar and Caroline says, 'OK girls, what do you want?' Jimmy is walking past at that point and shouts, 'Nothing with gin in it. Last thing I need is two weeping teens on my hands.' Weeping? I wonder what he means.

'What do you recommend, Caroline?'

'Well, I know how you girls like your cider, and I hope you two realise how lucky you are.' I like Caroline, she's always been really nice to me. She's worked for Jimmy for a long time. We take our drinks and soak in the atmosphere of the club. I think I've fallen in love with it. I totally get what Jimmy meant when he said it has a real buzz about it.

Me and Jennie take our drinks on to the dance floor. We really know how to move. If there's one thing me and Jennie are good at it's dancing and having a good time.

Jimmy comes over to see me. 'You enjoying yourself?'

'Yeah, it's OK. I'm not sure what all the fuss is about, though, but Jennie's loving it.'

I've never been a one to say what I really think. What I should be saying is, 'Jimmy, you were right! I love this club, it's totally different when the lights are on and the DJ's playing.'

'Hey, cheeky, not sure what all the fuss is about – I'll have you know people queue around the block to get into my club.'

'But I'm here every week though. It looks different with the lights and music on to when it's during the day. It looks so much bigger.'

As me and Jimmy are talking, I glance up and see my mum and Shelly. Panic sets in as I'm not even sure if my mum will be angry that I'm in a nightclub. They make a beeline straight for Mike.

Jimmy looks over at them and says to me, 'Don't you ever end up like that.'

'What do you mean?'

'Well, that's one of those good-time girls I've told you about, the blonde one, everyone in here knows what she is. I wouldn't go near that with a bargepole.'

Good God, Jimmy has pointed out my mother. Surely he knows it's my mother, she was at Mike's wedding. Then again, Jimmy never really takes much notice of anyone around him. Maybe I should tell him she's my mum. But I'm so embarrassed and a little hurt. I don't want him saying bad things about my mum so I just look at him and say, 'Speaking of which, a blonde wants to fly to America, but she doesn't want to be in the air for too long in case her fake boobs explode. She calls the airline. "Good morning, British Airways," says the operator. "Oh, hello there," says the blonde woman. "I want to fly to America from the UK and need to know how long the flight is." "One minute," says the operator and puts the phone down while she checks. Blonde woman says, "Oh great, my boobs shouldn't explode in one minute," and hangs up the phone.'

Me and Jimmy look at each other and giggle in unison. He loves my jokes, plus, it got me out of that awkward moment with my mum. Until I hear it, that voice of, 'Excuse me, Mr Simpson, what do you think you're doing?'

Oh no, it's her, she's stormed across the bar.

'What did you say to me?' Jimmy has that look on his face, like he used to with me when I first used to get into the car to go to the prison.

'Look, this is my daughter and she's underage. I want to know what you're saying to her.'

Can you believe what she's just said to Jimmy? And Jimmy has given me this look of, well, it's a cross between 'I'm so sorry I insulted your mum, I'm totally embarrassed' and 'You poor thing, having this drag you up.'

'Hey, Caroline!' he shouts. 'This beautiful blonde can drink anything she likes all night.'

'Wow, thank you, Mr Simpson, carry on,' and off she goes. Fancy leaving your fifteen-year-old daughter talking to the hardest man in the world in a nightclub because you were offered a few free drinks. That woman knows no bounds. I look at Jimmy and say, 'You do realise that your profits will be down by tomorrow, don't you? Oh and I'll never end up like her and I don't see what it is she's having a good time about.'

He holds my chin and says, 'Make the most of tonight because you won't be getting back in this club until you're legal. Even then, you'll be watched like a hawk and you'll never meet a bloke from here either.'

I hold his hand, which is still on my chin, and give it a squeeze. 'I'll never be a good-time girl, I promise. I better go, my friend seems to have lost herself on the dance floor.'

I make my way back over to Jennie, who is still loving the entire experience. Mike takes us both home that night and I can't sleep for thinking of the club. I truly am in love with it.

I wake up the following morning and make my way downstairs where my mum's sitting at the table. She turns to me and says, 'Erm, what were you doing in Jimmeez last night? You're far too young and what on earth was that Mr Simpson talking to you about?'

'Who? Jimmy? Nothing, we were just talking and telling jokes as usual. Why?'

'What do you mean, talking as usual? And how come you can call him Jimmy? I hope you never called him Jimmy to his face.'

'Well, of course I called him Jimmy to his face, what else would I call him?'

'How on earth do you know him? Is this because you sat next to him and his wife at the wedding? I knew I should have insisted you sat with me but, as usual, you never listen. Of all the people Mike could have sat you with and he chooses him. I mean it, I'll stop you seeing Mike if he's introducing you to people like that. I told him years ago he's never to introduce you to that man.'

'People like what? There's nothing wrong with him. You never thought there was anything wrong with him when you were getting free drinks last night.'

I storm upstairs. I'm so angry. How dare she say she'll stop me from seeing Mike, who on earth does she think she is? And as for her thinking Jimmy is something bad, what about her? Jimmy knows what she is, he says everyone knows what she is. I sometimes wonder *what* she is. What did Jimmy mean?

The club's open again tonight. I had such a great time last night,

I want to go back. Jimmy said yesterday I wasn't allowed back in but if I go before the doors open he won't tell me to leave, surely?

Jennie comes over. 'How amazing was the club last night? Do you think we can go again next week?'

'I don't think so. Jimmy was really funny about it and told me I'm not allowed back until I'm eighteen.'

'But it was so cool, wait till I tell everyone at school you know Mr Simpson and can call him Jimmy. They won't believe me. Fancy going to the park tonight? A few people from school are getting drunk.'

I can't stop thinking of the club. Who wants to go to the park to get drunk when I can go to Jimmeez and hang around with the hardest man in the world, so to speak – well, that's what Jennie says – and get free drinks. 'Jennie, I'm not feeling very well, you go to the park, though, and I'll see you tomorrow.'

'Really, what's wrong with you?'

'I'm all headachy. I think I have a head cold coming on.'

'Well, I'll stay in with you.'

'Oh no, you don't want to catch it.' I do feel a little guilty but there's no way he'll let us both in again. Jennie leaves and I quickly get my dress and my make-up on and head towards the club.

As I get there Caroline is sorting the bar out. 'Hello, Kate, what you doing here on a Saturday? Shouldn't you be hanging around a street corner getting drunk somewhere and causing trouble? Don't you find it boring here?'

'I wanted to see Jimmy, is he in?'

'Yes, go in, he's in his office.' I knock on the door and make my way in.

Jimmy is looking at some papers on his desk but raises his head and smiles when he sees me, which is a sign he's in a good mood at least.

'Hello, Treasure, what you doing here?'

'I don't know. I was bored I guess.'

He laughs at me. 'Bored were you, and can I ask why you have a dress on and your face is caked in make-up then?' Oh no, he's cottoned on.

'Yeah, I'm going out tonight with Jennie. I wanted to come here first to see you. What you doing?'

'Nothing, I'm just looking at my stocks so I know what to order.'

'Can I help?'

'Have you not got anything better to do?'

'Not really, no.'

'OK, sit down, I'll show you.'

As he shows me the order books I notice that he gets charged five pounds for every order he places.

'Why do you place so many orders? You do know you get charged a fiver each delivery, don't you?'

'It's only five pounds, Treas, it's hardly going to send us into bankruptcy.'

'Yes, but you had four deliveries last week, that's twenty pounds. That could be another two bottles of spirit, that.'

'Yes, but if I need the stock, I need it.'

'But surely by now you know what you need each week. Why don't you get each member of staff to mark on a chart when they use the last bottle of something, and then you'll know in a few weeks how long each bottle of spirit is lasting and how much you should be ordering each week. You could even make it monthly before long and save yourself a fortune.'

'Listen to you. You'll own a club like this one day, you, I can tell.'

'Yes, then I'll be your direct competition and everyone will want to come to *my* club, not yours. I'll call it Kate's Klub and everyone will say, let's go to Kate's Klub, not Jimmeez.'

'I'm sure they will. Right, that's enough for one day, the doors are opening in half an hour, so you'll have to go.' He starts to collect all his papers in a pile ready to start clearing the desk so he can go into the bar area for the night. Now is my chance to ask him.

'Oh no, please let me stay. I'm here now.'

'No way, and don't think I didn't know you were planning this, coming in all dressed up like that.'

'Please, Jimmy,' I beg and pull on his arm as he goes to the filing cabinet.

'No, I've told you. If I get caught with an underage drinker in here they'll take my licence straight off me.'

'But I've got fake ID. Peter out of my English class uses his brother's student ID all the time. I copied off that and it's exactly the same. I'm really clever with that kind of stuff. Please, if you let me, I'll come round every Monday after school and help out at the club. I'll place your orders for you. I'll even give you the fiver for the delivery charges. Oh, please. I'll tell everyone you broke into the post office on Alderson Road and stole half a million pounds if you don't let me.'

'Hey, that was you, not me.'

'What, a little innocent kid? Who on earth would believe that? We'd stand in court and the jury would have to decide if a fifteen-year-old girl did it, or a club owner, and who do you think they would believe?'

'Hey, madam, I can still clip you across the ear, you know,' he says while laughing. 'Anyway, you said you never knew what all the fuss was about with the club so why would you want to come here?'

'Please, Jimmy, pleaaaasssse.'

'Treas, honestly, you'll give me a heart attack one of these days. No.'

'OK then, forget it. I'll go to the park. There's a boy two years older than me, Jennie says he wants to kiss me. I might let him if I have enough to drink.'

'Hey, don't you dare, who is he anyway? Plus, if he's two years older than you he shouldn't be kissing fifteen-year-old girls. I mean it.'

I only said that because he is quite overprotective of me and doesn't want me to turn into a good-time girl so I'm not supposed to knock around with boys. He says I've got years for that.

'Right, you can stay, but you must carry that fake ID with you and any comeback and it's on your toes and, whatever you do, stop mentioning that bloody post office. Another thing as well, you tell that boy he goes anywhere near you and Mr Simpson will cut his dick off.'

Dear Kate,

Finally got settled in London, flat's not the best, especially for the price they charge but I've found someone to share with so at least I can split the rent. Work is really busy at the moment. I can't wait for you to visit me. I'm going to show you all the great things our country has to offer. I have to walk past Big Ben every day, it's nowhere near as big as it looks on the television. Still haven't seen the queen yet. I think one of her guards warns her when I'm out and about so she hides.

Be good for your mum and look after her.

Love Lawrence x x

Fantastic, another letter off Lawrence. I'm so pleased he keeps writing to me. I get so excited to see a letter on the doormat with my name on. Unless it's from the dentist that is. I hate those letters.

Dear Lawrence,

I'm glad you have someone to share your flat with, at least you don't have to watch the television alone at night. I still can't believe you're in London. Have you seen any celebrities yet? I might write to the prime minister and tell him what you said about Big Ben to see if they can change the name to Little Ben. I know about the queen hiding from you, I keep in touch with Prince Charles on a daily basis. I can't wait to visit you in London. Jennie said there is a shop called Harrods and on the very top floor they have a pet shop which sells the cutest puppies. I'd love to go there and see them. I've never had a puppy before. Come to think of it, I've never had a pet before.

Love Kate xx

I've finished school and passed all my exams. I've started college to do my A levels ready for my management degree at university.

What's even better about college is that Jennie is in the next block along learning hair and beauty. It's great we still get to have lunch together. I'm in the club every week getting free drinks off Mr Simpson and everyone knows who I am.

The atmosphere in the club is great tonight. I can't see Mike anywhere, though.

'Hello, Treas, you having a good time?'

'Yeah, great as always. I can't wait to open my own club. Kate's Klub. I wonder if I should start handing flyers out now getting ready for launch night?'

'You'd never do that to me, you'd miss me too much.'

'Nah, you'd come to work for me. Like I keep saying, who wants to come to Jimmeez when you can come to Kate's? You'll have to close this place once my club opens. But don't worry, I'll let you do the ordering if you're a good boy.' We giggle at each other.

'The funny thing is though, madam, I'm never sure if you're joking or not.'

'We'll have to rob the post office again to fund it, mind. So keep yourself free just after my eighteenth.' Dave, the head doorman, comes rushing over to Jimmy.

'Mr Simpson, trouble on the fire escape.'

'Oo, can I come?' I say to Jimmy.

'No, you can't, stay here,' he says as he gently pushes me towards the wall. No way am I staying here if there's a fight. I want to be there to make sure Jimmy's OK. I follow Jimmy and Dave out and as we get to the fire escape Mike is there with his shirt hanging out of his trousers and Shelly is screaming at him.

'Are you fucking kidding me? With that slag, Mike? You're shagging some tart in the doorway when I'm at home with Billy, our baby, you remember him, do you?'

'Hey, I'm no tart!' shouts this woman whose dress is all twisted, with one shoulder strap hanging down her arm. She has short blonde hair, shaven at the back. It's not a natural blonde and she's caked in make-up. She's pretty, but does have a certain tarty look about her. Who is this woman and why is Shelly angry with her?

Has Mike been having sex with her? I'm angry, crazy angry. Mike is mine, if he is going to cheat on Shelly with anyone it should be with me. Who is this woman just coming in and taking him?

'Mike, what on earth are you thinking?' I scream at him.

'Piss off, Kate, it's none of your business!' he screams at me. He's never shouted at me before and I'm quite shocked that he has.

Jimmy snaps back, 'Oi, Mike, that's enough, it's not Kate's fault. Kate, go inside.' He looks at Dave the doorman and says, 'Will you take her home?'

I shout back, 'No, I'm not going anywhere, I want to know what's going on here. Who is she?' I point to the woman. I don't think I've ever been this angry, ever. I scream over at Mike, 'Why are her clothes all twisted? What have you been doing? Have you been doing what Jennie did in the bushes?'

Mike shouts, 'Grow up, Kate, and stop acting like a fucking baby all the time.'

Mike called me a baby. I'm so upset that he called me a baby. I've never seen Mike act like this before.

Shelly screams, 'Don't you think it's you who's acting like a baby? Speaking of which, should you not be at home with your baby? You're a selfish prick, you always have been. Come on, Kate, I'll come with you. Billy is at yours anyway. I'm staying at Julie's tonight, Mike. And, I mean it, don't you come anywhere near me.'

Dave takes me and Shelly to her house to pick up their things. Shelly is totally inconsolable. As we step into my house, my mum's there to hug Shelly.

'Come here, babe, forget him. I always told you what he was like, I told you for years to stay away from him.'

'Oh, Julie, do we have to do the whole I told you so thing? Not tonight, please.'

My mum turns to me and says, 'Kate, get Shelly a cup of tea.' As I make the tea, I can hear my mum saying, 'With that bloody Diane Thompson, of all people... She's a slag. He'll be back tomorrow with his tail between his legs. He's making a mistake going off with that tart, she's crazy, honest, she always has been.'

I've never even seen Diane before. How does Mike know her and does he know that she's a crazy slag? I feel like I could cry. I honestly think I'm more hurt than Shelly right now. My Mike's gone off with some crazy slag. I don't even want to look at him again.

We all head off to bed and first thing in the morning I can hear Mike's voice. He's come round to see Shelly. I don't want to go downstairs so I listen with my ear to the floor.

'How could you, Mike, what is wrong with you? I really thought after Billy you would have settled down, and it's not the first time, I know it's not, and I know for a fact that it wasn't the first time with *her*. I've thought about it for weeks now.'

'Shelly, please, babe, listen to me, she was a mistake. It's you I want, you and Billy, you know I love you.'

'No, you don't. You're at that fucking club every weekend. I'm sick of you being there, you and Jimmy thinking you're something special all the time.'

'No, we don't. Let's go home, we'll talk properly there.'

'No, I want you out. I mean it, there's no way I'm staying married to you now. I have Billy to think about. If you're not out by the time I get back round there, I mean it, I won't be responsible for my actions and that little tart of yours will get it as well.'

I hear the door slam and Shelly starts to cry. I go downstairs to make sure she's OK, but really I want to make sure Mike's not running off with Diane, the crazy slag. What if I never see him again? I don't even know where this Diane lives, what if it's not in Bridgeborough? Oh no, I might lose him. I couldn't bear that.

Later that day I make my way over to the club to see Jimmy, to see if he knows anything about this Diane and where she lives.

'Hello, Kate darling, are you OK? What are you doing at the club this early?'

'Nothing really, I wanted to see you. Thanks for shouting back at Mike yesterday for me.'

'It's OK, he shouldn't have taken that out on you, but he did find himself in a bit of a sticky situation.'

'Yeah, with that Diane girl. Who is she?'

'I don't know. She's sometimes in the club. I think they've known each other a while.'

'Shelly said she thinks it's been going on for a while. Has it?'

'I'm not sure. I think it's best we keep out of stuff like that. Seriously, don't even worry about it, let Mike and Shelly sort it out.'

'Why do adults cheat on each other?'

'I don't know to be honest.'

'You wouldn't cheat on Helen, would you?'

'You're kidding, aren't you, have you seen the girls around here? They're nowhere near as perfect as my Helen. If Kate Moss walked in here I still wouldn't cheat on my Helen.'

I believe Jimmy. I can tell he loves Helen so much.

Me and Jimmy start to check the dates of all the bottles in the fridge and in walks Mike. Jimmy looks at him and says, 'In the shit, are we?' while laughing at Mike. Mike looks at him and says, 'OK, Mr Perfect, don't you start on me as well. I'm getting it from all angles today.'

Jimmy walks into his office and I continue to check the bottles. I really don't want to talk to Mike after he shouted at me last night.

'Kate, are you OK? I never meant to snap at you last night, I was just panicking, with Shelly … and I never meant to call you a baby.'

'Why did you call me a baby? Is it because I'm not as grown-up as you and Jimmy?'

'No, not that, I don't know why, it's just sometimes you're a little younger in your years with certain things.'

'What certain things?'

'Oh, I don't know, can we forget about it, please?'

'No, I want to know why you think I'm a baby.'

'I don't. I just snapped, that's all.'

'But you've just said it there, in certain things. What do you mean?'

'I don't want to argue with you. I have enough going on. I'm back at my mum's now. Shelly has thrown me out.'

'Well, I'm not surprised. You cheated on her with Diane Thompson, the crazy slag.'

'Oh, your mum's been sticking her nose in, I see. Diane's not crazy. Don't say stuff like that, and don't judge people. Why don't you meet Diane? You might like her.'

'What, you mean you're actually going out with her?'

When Mike says that, my heart is breaking. Why on earth would he not want me and want that crazy slag instead? He really does think I'm a baby. Maybe I should have sex in the bushes like Jennie or let boys do things to me. It's not that I've never had the opportunity, boys do fancy me, but I only ever want him.

What Mike said about me being a baby is really playing on my mind. Why would he have said that? Of all the things he could have said, why that? As I walk in the house Mum is getting ready for work.

'Mum, can I ask you something please?'

'Is this about your dad again?'

'No, it's not about my dad, it's about me.'

'What about you, are you OK? Is everything all right?'

'Yes, everything is fine, but do you think I'm a baby?' She laughs, 'Of course you're a baby, Kate, you're my baby, you'll always be my baby.'

'But I'm not a baby, I'm a teenager, I'll be leaving college soon and heading off to university.'

'Don't try to grow up too fast, Kate, that was my problem. Stay young as long as you can.'

She starts to put her lipstick on, taking a look at her reflection in the mirror. 'I wish I looked a lot younger.'

It annoys me that she's yet again turned the conversation on to her thoughts and feelings instead of helping me with mine. Typical of her really. I don't even know why I bother.

Chapter 10 – Everything Has Changed

I can honestly say I'm as obsessed with the club as I am with Mike. Mike and Diane are still together. Shelly is also with someone else. He's called Brian, and they're trying for a baby. Mike looks after Billy where he can – he is his father, after all. My feelings for Mike are so strong I'm thinking of telling him on my eighteenth birthday. Well, I'll be an adult properly then and he should be OK about having sex with me. I think he always looked at me like I was a child before. Me, Jimmy and Mike have also carried out a few more robberies. We did the bank on Alderson Road and the post office again. It's easy when you know how. The police are still hunting for the sophisticated gang. Well, I suppose we are a gang now that Mike is carrying out the robberies with us. Not sure about the sophisticated part, mind.

I go running into Jimmy's office with the newspaper in my hand. 'Jimmy, look, look, I'm in the paper outside the club.'

'Jesus Christ, where? I can't have you in the papers outside the club. If I get caught with an underage drinker in here, I'll lose my club.'

'There I am, there, you're talking to that man and that's my hand.'

'Your hand, Kate… Jesus, I thought it was a full picture of you, give me a look.'

Jimmy snatches the paper from my hand. 'Why do they need to write that shite about me? All I'm doing is talking to that bloke, what is so interesting about that? Also, that's not even your hand.'

'Yes it is, I would recognise that hand anywhere.'

'It's not your hand. Do you know how I know it's not your hand?'

'How?'

'Because that hand is holding orange in the glass and you wouldn't drink orange juice, that's how I know.'

'Well, maybe I was holding it for someone.'

'Can you remember holding orange juice for someone? Why would someone ask you to hold their drink when they're just standing there?'

'I don't know, maybe they were fastening their shoelaces. I will get in the papers one day, there'll be a full write-up of me and you'll say, "Oh Kate, why don't they write about me any more, it's always about you." Then you'll be sorry.'

Jimmy laughs at me. 'Yes, it will probably be when you get that new club of yours, what's it called again? The name's on the tip of my tongue but I can't remember it. Was it Mike's Club or The Simpson Bar?' Jimmy starts to laugh and mock me again.

'Hey, you cheeky thing, it's Kate's Klub and, trust me, you will remember that name when it's open. You'll go to sleep crying that name.'

'Well, for now it's Jimmeez club and it's Jimmy in the paper, not Kate, so go put the kettle on.' Jimmy shoves me out of the door to put the kettle on while laughing at me again. 'I have no idea why you'd want to be in the papers anyway, it gets on your nerves after a while,' he shouts back at me.

As I walk back in with the tea Jimmy says, 'There's a club owners' get together tomorrow night. Helen doesn't want to come. Do you fancy it? You get lots of freebies, make-up and shit like that. I don't want it, you may as well have it.'

'Oh yeah, I quite fancy that. Plus, I'll be a club owner soon so it will give me a chance to meet the other owners. Pick me up tomorrow.'

It's the last day of college. I'm so pleased. I'm going to really enjoy my summer break starting with the club owners' get together with Jimmy tonight. Then my party, Jimmy says it's going to be the best party Bridgeborough has ever seen. Me and Jennie are going to have so much fun. She's been offered a job in the local salon as a junior hairdresser. I knew she'd do something with hair and make-up, she's always been into it.

As we get to the club owners' meeting there are lots of drinks promotions and things going on. I go to one of the desks and it's full of make-up. I bet Jennie would have loved it here. This stuff would be great for her new job.

'Excuse me, can I have two of these please? My friend Jennie would love one.'

If they won't give me two she can always have mine. They give me two and I'm over the moon. I might ask for two of everything to share with her. I can't even see Jimmy as he's mixing with the other owners. I go over to another desk and while I'm looking at the merchandise this man approaches me. He has blond hair and blue eyes, he has a scar going across his eyebrow which has no hair where it is. His suit is so crisp it looks expensive and his aftershave overwhelms me.

'Ah, I saw you come in with Jimmy the prick, and who might you be?' he says in such an awful tone. Yet it doesn't scare me, it angers me.

'What did you say there? You dickhead, Jimmy's not a prick.'

'So tell me who you are and why you don't think Jimmy's a prick.'

'He's my uncle, that's who he is. Why don't you piss off?'

'Tell me your name.'

'It's Kate Reilly, what the fuck is your name?'

I don't even know why I'm talking to him like that. I never swear and would never swear at an adult, but he was really mean about Jimmy. As I turn I see Jimmy storm over.

'What the fuck are you doing talking to her? Piss off now.' Jimmy grabs me by the hand and takes me away from him. 'Did you tell him who you were?' Jimmy is saying this in the kind of voice I haven't heard him use with me for a long time. Not since before we carried out the robbery. I'm a little nervous and I better not tell Jimmy that I did tell him who I was or that I said Jimmy was my uncle. I don't think he would like it.

'No, I never.'

Jimmy stays by my side for the rest of the event. After the event we drive home. 'Please tell me if you did tell that man who you were.'

'Honestly, I never, I swear, who was he anyway?'

'No one for you to know.'

I know who he was really because I heard him introduce himself to someone. He was Keith Nixon, that's the man who owns the Ocean Club. That's the club where I opened the safe for Jimmy and Mike when Roger got killed years ago.

'I know I keep saying it but please tell me if you did tell him who you were.'

It seems a little strange that Jimmy keeps asking me and it's making me feel a little nervous so I try to change the subject. 'Look what I've got in my bag. I asked for two of everything so I could share with Jennie. You don't think they'll think I'm greedy, do you?'

'Nah, course not, they're free anyway. I bet they get sick of looking at that stuff. They'll have boxes of it in a warehouse somewhere. They'd have given you three of everything if you asked.'

'Hey, I should have got Mike one of these lipsticks then. It looks like his colour.'

We giggle at each other and I start to get all my goodies out to show him. This has worked, I've changed the subject from Keith Nixon.

'So, then, are you looking forward to your eighteenth next week?'

'Yes, I can't wait, my party is going to be the best. Thanks for having it in the club. Jennie's dad got her a car for her eighteenth but I'd much prefer a party, it's much more fun than a stupid car. She can't even drive so what's the point in it?'

'Would you rather have a car?'

'What's the point? I can't drive either.'

'Well, I could teach you if you wanted?'

'There's no way I'd let you teach me how to drive.'

'Why not? I'm a good driver.'

'Yes, but you're not the most patient of men. You'd end up throwing me out of the car on the motorway. A party is fine, thanks.'

'Yeah, you're right there. I started teaching Helen once and I totally lost my temper. I gave up in the end and paid for lessons for her. I can't wait for you to be eighteen. You'll finally be legal to drink in my bar, which means I can start to relax a little bit now. I'm always on edge when you're in there in case I get caught serving underage drinkers.'

I can't wait either. But not for the same reasons as Jimmy. I'm going to ask Mike to have sex with me. I mean, I'll be an adult so he can't say no really.

Jimmy drops me off at home. 'Goodbye, Treas, I'll see you at your party. Be good now.'

I go back home and I completely forget about Keith Nixon. Jimmy looks like he would wipe the floor with him anyway.

It's here, my big birthday. I'm eighteen! I'm going to put my dress on, have a few vodkas with Jennie, build myself up and finally take the plunge to lose my virginity with Mike tonight. I can't wait. Jimmy has organised a party for me at 7pm but I'm going to get there early and catch Mike on his own. I head round to Jennie's in my tracksuit bottoms.

'Hey, I thought you had a dress to kill for tonight, and were making your move?'

'Yeah, well I will, but thought we'd have a couple of drinks first. You can do my hair and teach me how to be all seductive. Show me what do I do?'

'Well, flutter your eyelashes at him and wear bright red lipstick. When you talk to him, lick your lips all seductive, like this.'

Jennie starts to lick her lips and looks really sexy when she does this. I copy her but all I end up with is sloppy lips and smudged lipstick.

'Hmm, maybe don't do that, we don't want him thinking you're a shaggy dog.' We giggle like two naughty schoolgirls. 'What time you going to the club?' Jennie asks.

'About five-ish. I reckon it will be quiet until later on there, so at least we can be alone and I can turn on the charm. We'll be married this time next year.'

Jennie rolls her eyes. 'I really don't see what you see in him, you know, he's not even that fanciable.'

'Yes he is, he's gorgeous, and he looks after me.'

'I look after you, but you don't fancy me, do you?'

'Oh stop it, give me some tips. I've never even seen a dick never mind touched one.'

'Well, you do know that you should suck it, don't you?'

'Ugh, suck it? What if it's not clean?'

Jennie laughs at me. 'God, you're such a baby.'

'No, I'm not. I've just been saving myself for Mike, that's all.'

She finishes doing my hair. It's all tied up in little knots around my head, she's so skilled. Jennie is one of those girls who knows everything about hair, make-up and men. All I know about is how to open safes and run pretty quickly. Not very ladylike at all. She finishes my make-up and tells me to put my dress on. I do this and look in the mirror thinking, Wow, I don't even look like me, there's no way he's resisting me tonight.

'Right, go get 'em, girl. You look stunning. Ring me as soon as you're done and tell me how it goes, and don't forget to use a condom. God knows who he's been with and we don't want a pregnancy, do we? Take a swig of this.'

She passes me a red beaker and I take a drink of something that taste like vinegar.

'Yak. That's disgusting. Right, I'm off.'

I head towards the club with butterflies, but also a little excited. I can't wait until he kisses me. I wonder if he'll use his tongue.

I go round the back of the club as I know the door will be open. Mike will be there getting the bar ready for tonight. Once I'm inside I hear voices and see there are four men there. It's funny because I wasn't expecting anyone. Mike must have a bit of business or something. He takes one look at me and shouts, 'Get out, Kate, get out!'

One of the men comes running over and grabs me before I've even had a chance to leave or question Mike. Not that I would question Mike. I always find it's easier to stay out of his and Jimmy's business.

'Let's see how you like what we do to you, the little girl who needs to be taught a lesson.'

Mike starts shouting, 'If you hurt her I'll fucking kill you, I mean it, leave her alone!'

One of the men punches him full force in the face to shut him up. Yet he doesn't punch him back, just kicks out. 'I'm going to fucking kill you, I mean it.' Mike is shouting at them in a really angry way.

The men start passing me around in a circle. 'Look what we have here then, we've been waiting for you.'

'What do you mean, waiting for me? Why?'

I don't even know these men or recognise them. Mike is screaming in the background, 'Leave her alone!' I'm not even sure what they're going to do, maybe give me a slap or something.

'Oh, look what Jimmy's little angel is about to do.'

I wonder why they're saying that, what's it got to do with Jimmy? One of them slaps me so I push him back. I feel the other three grab me. Oh no, what's going to happen now? They push me to the floor and two of them grab an arm each and one has my leg. I still have a free leg and one of the men is standing over me and he starts opening up his trousers and bends down towards me. I can hear Mike screaming even louder. Yet he's still not coming over, why is he not coming over?

The man who opened his trousers has lifted up my dress. He grabs my knickers and pulls at them so hard he scratches my legs with his fingernails. I kick out at him as hard as I can screaming, 'Get off me, get the fuck off me!'

This eggs them on even more and they're all laughing. I shout, 'No, please, no, not that!'

But that seems to make him smile even more. He lies on top of my body and starts to penetrate me. I beg him, 'No, please, no! Stop, please stop!'

One of the men covers my mouth and the smell of his hand is repulsive, it's like he's never washed his hands for a long time. I'm still wriggling around like mad and the pain is unbelievable. Why would he do this to me, why? I can't think of one joke or trick that's going to get me out of this one. After what seems like ages he finally stops, gets off me and does his trousers up. I think I'm finally allowed to get up and I think they're going to leave, but he grabs my free leg and the man on my other leg gets up and opens his trousers. Oh no, not again, please. I don't want this, and Mike is still not coming over.

The first man says, 'Go on. Mind, she's not a virgin any more, look at the blood.'

The background noise is very echoey, it's like I'm in a dreamlike state. I'm still struggling like mad to get out of their grip, but I can't. I think I can hear Mike screaming, but with all the commotion I'm not sure. The second man starts to penetrate me. I'm still not giving in and I'm writhing around the floor but they're too strong. I'm crying and they don't even care. I'm not sure how but the third man is getting up from me, yet I can't remember him getting on me so I must have blacked out at some point, yet Mike is still not coming over. I can hear someone vomiting and I'm in such a state of shock I wonder if it's me, but it can't be me as my mouth is still being covered to stop the screaming. The last man is penetrating me and my thoughts are running wild thinking, They've all gone now so it will stop soon.

As he gets off me the first man climbs on again. I've stopped fighting, I'm just taking it. What's the point? I can't stop them. I'm lying on the floor, having been gang raped in front of a man

I'm totally in love with. How can things get any worse? Oh no, how long is this going to go on for? I want to go home. It's my eighteenth birthday and I never thought this was going to happen. They all finally let me go and pull their clothes right while laughing. Grabbing a bottle of whisky from the bar, they leave the club. I'm lying on the floor, my pretty dress all ripped and my hair all over. This is not what I wanted today. I lie there for a while. I wonder if Mike has left because I can't hear him. In fact, it's so quiet I think if a pin dropped I would hear it. I'm not sure what to do. I have no knickers on. Should I pick them up and put them on? I need to get home, I can't go home with no knickers on, what if people see me? But I'm in so much pain, I don't think I could put them on anyway. I finally manage to climb to my feet. The pain is all over me, not just in my vagina but my mouth, my arms and legs. I head towards Mike at the bar as I catch a glimpse of him. Why did he not come over? Why did he not help me? As I walk over there's vomit all over the floor where he's standing and he has tears streaming down his face, yet he's deadly silent.

I look up at him and the words, 'Are you OK?' come out of my mouth. How ironic – I've been gang raped, for what seemed like hours, yet the first thing I say is, 'Are you OK?' I look at his hands and they're chained to the bar. In another ironic twist, it's a bike lock they have chained Mike with. Exactly like the ones I used to break open for Mike when I was younger. Maybe I stole their bike, maybe that's what happened. I would have given them their bike back. I manage to open the lock for him.

'Gem, I...' He looks at me, not knowing what to say.

I'm standing there in disbelief, in a dreamlike state, when the door swings open and I think they're coming back for more so I quickly turn around. Jimmy is standing there with a present with a big bow on it.

'Treas, what the bloody hell is going on in here?' He can tell by the look of me that something is wrong, but I can't tell him what's happened, I don't want anyone to know. Mike is in a state of shock and pretty much as much use as me. Jimmy looks at my knickers on the floor. Before he can say anything else, I run out of the club. I run so quickly it feels like I've got home in three giant leaps. I run straight upstairs and into the bathroom where I vomit down the toilet. I can smell their dirty hands on my face. I run a shower and I stand there for what seems like hours, letting the water run down me. I can taste the salt from my tears mixed with the water.

How did this happen and why? I'm in so much pain it feels like every inch of my body is in agony. I climb out of the shower, my whole body shaking, and slowly pat myself dry with the towel. I'm in so much pain. I go to my bedroom and lie down on my bed and my head is spinning. Did that really happen? Am I dreaming? What on earth was Mike thinking? He saw me having sex with someone, not just someone, four people. He'll never want me now. Not that I want him any more, I never want to see him again. I can still smell their dirty hands, I can smell them all over me. I need another shower, I mustn't have cleaned myself properly the first time. I'll go in for longer this time.

I scrub my face so hard to get rid of the smell of their hands, then I climb out of the shower and I need to vomit again. Surely there's nothing left inside me to vomit. I lie back on my bed hoping if I fall asleep I'll wake up and it would have all been a nightmare. I hear the front door going and it's my mum, she's brought back another man. Oh no, Mum, please. I don't want to hear you talking to a man again. I hear the man's deep voice and panic sets in. He sounds like one of the rapists, it's definitely one, I can hear his voice. I recognise it. Actually, my mum also sounds like one of the rapists.

They're heading up the stairs. Please don't come into my room and disturb me. Thankfully, she goes straight into her room. I'm lying there sobbing and I can hear my mum having sex in the other room. God, this can't get any worse, somebody help me, get me out of this awful world. Maybe I could kill myself, that would help. I can still smell their dirty hands.

My mum has finally stopped having sex. Why would anyone want to do that for fun? There's nothing fun about that, it just hurts if you ask me. I think I'll shower again.

I lie on my bed, hair still soaking wet, just staring at the wall. Then I wake up. I must have dozed off for a couple of hours and the first thing on my mind is the fact that I can still smell their dirty hands. My mind is going over and over it, my whole body is aching, especially my neck. I can't understand it as it was my arms and legs they had, but my neck muscles are really hurting. It must have been because I was trying to pull myself up. The inside of my mouth is really sore. I must have been biting down on my gums as they had their hands over my mouth. Ugh, their hands, I can still smell them and I realise that it's my bed sheets that smell of their hands. I'll take them downstairs to wash.

As I start to put my bed sheets into the washer I hear my mum's voice behind me. 'Hey, what the hell happened last night in the club?'

'What?' Oh no, does everyone know what happened in the club? How can they know, has Jimmy told everyone, did he announce it at my party? I can't bear to turn around, what if I have 'I was raped last night' written all over my face? What if I look different? I'm so sore I'm sure my whole body is bruised. I cough a nervous cough.

'What do you mean, in the club, what happened?'

'Well, I went there about 9pm and there was a notice on the door. This club is closed until further notice due to electricity problems.'

'Oh yeah, there was a problem so we had to cancel my party.'

'Oh yeah, more like you, Mike and Jimmy had some business to attend to.'

'Whatever, Mum.'

I walk as quickly as I can out of that kitchen without even looking at her and back up to bed. It won't be so bad now I have clean sheets. I lie down thinking of what happened, I can *still* smell their dirty hands. Maybe I never washed myself properly, after all. I'll have another shower. Maybe I could pour antibacterial mouthwash all over me. That should take away any germs and smell. I go over and over the night for what seems like the millionth time and it hits me why this happened. Yes, of course, it was the tins, they're not in order. I knew there would be a logical explanation for it. I run to the cupboard and they all seem to be in order. I never ate anything that I shouldn't. I look at my phone and I have so many missed calls from Mike and Jimmy. I never want to see them again. Mike has texted several times asking if he can come over or for me to call him, but I can't face it.

There are a few missed calls from Jennie. How can I call her back? She'll be asking me all about it, and what can I say to her? She'll be wanting to know if I slept with Mike or not, and right now I can't even bear to think about sex. My phone is ringing again, it's Jennie. I'm not answering it. The phone finally stops ringing but flashes up as a left voicemail, I put the mobile close to my ear, I really don't want to hear what Jennie has to say but before I know it her excited voice starts coming through. 'Hello you, I'm assuming you're still in bed all shagged out, get up tell me everything.'

Oh God, I can't possibly talk to her about anything today. I want to die, never mind tell her about last night. I feel so dirty. I can smell their dirty hands again, maybe more mouthwash in the shower will do the trick. I only have mouthwash left as there's no soap or shower gel. I've used them all.

I start to think back to when I was at Jennie's and how excited I was. I looked so pretty, Jennie even gave me that drink as I was walking out of the door to calm my nerves. Oh no, the drink, what was it? I call her.

'Hey, you,' she says, 'what happened? I want all of the details and it must have been great because you even cancelled your party for it. Was Mr Simpson not annoyed, he went to so much trouble?'

'Never mind that, Jennie, you know the drink in that cup you passed me?'

'What cup, when?'

'Yesterday, as I was walking out of the door.'

'Oh, you mean my wine, hey, that's expensive wine that, you know.'

'I don't give a fuck how expensive it is, what colour was it?'

'Hey, what's eating you?'

'Nothing is eating me, I just want to know what colour the wine was.'

'Well, it was white. What difference does it make?'

'You know what, Jennie, you're a fucking bitch. Stay the hell away from me.'

I hang up the phone and realise that's it, it's all Jennie's fault. I can still smell their fucking dirty hands. I have no mouthwash left. The only other antibacterial thing I can find is a floor cleaner. That'll have to do. It's getting dark outside and I'm so annoyed with Jennie, it's all her fault. She's such a bitch and has everything her own way, she's such a spoilt brat, even that fucking precious car of hers. Well, I'll show her. With that, I go to Lawrence's old tool box he left for Mum and pick up the hammer. Then I make my way round to her house. It's pretty dark outside so no one will see me. I see that stupid car and I smash every window in it and start banging away at the bonnet. It's funny, I've been in agony all day yet I have built up the strength to smash my way through Jennie's precious new car.

I get back home and I can still smell their hands. So another floor-cleaner shower it is. I think I'll have some vodka. It might make me feel better. I'm sitting with my vodka and there's a knock at the door. I'm not answering it, they'll go away eventually.

'Kate, Kate, it's me, Mike. Look, I know you're in there, please let me in. I'm not going anywhere unless you let me in.'

He's not getting in here, no way is he getting in here. I can't ever let him see me again. I'm so ashamed. He shouts, 'If you don't let me in I'll kick down this door.' I don't care what he does, he's not getting in this house. I hear an almighty bang as he starts kicking at the door. I better let him in, I don't want the neighbours out. I open the door and he looks dreadful.

'Please, let me in. I need to see you.'

'What do you want, Mike?'

'I need to make sure that you're all right. Listen, I know what happened last night was bad, really bad, and they've paid for it today, trust me. Jimmy personally sorted it himself.'

'I don't care what you and Jimmy do. I never want to see the pair of you again. Just leave me alone.'

'Listen, Gem—'

'Don't call me that, don't ever call me that again. I'm not your gem, I'm dead to you, go away.' Mike reaches out and cups my face with his hands. 'Please talk to me. I want to help you. I love you, you know I do.'

'Don't.' I push his hands away from my face. 'Love me? You don't love me, you'd never have dragged me into any of your messes if you loved me.'

'I know and I'm sorry, I'm sorry that I dragged you into all that stuff. I can't get it off my mind, what happened to you last night.'

'Oh, that's funny, because the second I walked away from the club I completely forgot about it, silly me. Just get out. I mean it, and you can tell Jimmy he can stick his club up his arse. I'll never step foot in that place again.'

'But we've sorted it, me and Jimmy sorted them.'

'I don't care what you and Jimmy did, I told you. It was you and Jimmy doing something in the first place that got me into this. You know, how come you two give it the big talk, like you're something fucking special and I ended up paying for it? Piss off, and leave me alone.'

'Listen, you're upset, I can see that. I'm going to leave you, but I'll come back tomorrow and we can talk properly.'

'Don't bother coming back tomorrow, just go fuck yourself.'

I never swear – well, not really – but I can't stop doing it. My phone is going and it's Jennie, probably to tell me about her stupid car, like I give a shit about that.

'Are you not going to answer that?' Mike says.

'No, you fucking answer it. Why don't you answer it and tell Jennie all about my little party last night, tell her how much you enjoyed it. I bet you liked it, didn't you, eh, watching me?'

Mike slaps me. 'Don't you fucking dare ever say that to me again, I mean it. I know you're angry and upset but don't you ever fucking say that to me again.'

I'm shocked that he hit me. Aren't I in enough pain? He grabs me into him and holds me there. I sob into his arms and he strokes my hair, kissing me on the head, saying, 'It will be OK, we'll get through this.'

'I don't want to get through this, I just want to die.'

'Don't say that, please don't ever say that again.' Mike is crying. For such a big strong man this has certainly knocked him for six.

'Can you go, please? I'm tired.'

'Yeah, OK. I'll come back tomorrow. Do you want anything? I can get you anything you like.'

'Could you do some shopping for me?'

'Yeah, what do you need?'

'Mouthwash, shower gel and floor cleaner, the antibacterial stuff.'

'OK, I'll get it for you.'

Mike leaves and I can smell the dirty-hand smell again so I better have another shower before bed and maybe clean the bed sheets again.

I'm still not sleeping properly and I can still smell their hands. I would have thought three days of constant washing would have got rid of it. I've not seen Jennie or Jimmy. In fact, Jimmy has not even tried to contact me since he left the missed calls the night of the rape. Maybe I'm not his treasure any more, I'm just a dirty little girl who smells of dirty hands. The thought of sex is killing me. Yet I was so looking forward to having sex. Jennie seems to love it, so does my mum.

Dear Kate,

An adult at last, I can't believe it. I bet you got spoilt rotten off Mike and Jimmy. I was trying to get to your party, but work was so busy there is no way they would give me the time off. I hope you had a fantastic time. I sent you a present, I hope you got it in time as I missed the post office so couldn't send it until a day later. I heard you're off to university if you pass all your exams. Not that we need to worry about the results, I bet you passed every one with flying colours. I always knew you'd make it to university, you're such an intelligent girl.

Love Lawrence xx

I can't respond to Lawrence's letter. I love getting letters from him, but what can I even say? I'm so pleased he couldn't make my party. I couldn't bear him knowing what happened. Maybe I should write back and ask if I can live in London with him, that could be a way out. I can't even think about university at the moment. I don't want to go anywhere ever again.

Mike's been round every day, yet I feel like I'm treating him terribly when he comes round, but I can't help it. Even now he's at one end of the kitchen and I'm at the other and the only time I speak is to snap at him. But there's been something on my mind to ask him every day, but I'm not sure how to even go about asking him.

'Kate, are you OK?'

'Yeah, top of the world, how do you think I am?'

'I don't know, I don't even know what to say to you. Is there anything I can do?'

'Yes, there is actually.'

'What?'

'Will you sleep with me?'

'What?'

'You heard me, I want you to have sex with me.'

Mike looks at me with the most horrified look on his face. 'No, no way, I'm not doing that, what are you even talking about?'

'It's just I don't want to think of sex like that, not the way it happened and I think if I don't do it soon I won't ever do it. Please, Mike. You always said you'd do anything for me.'

'Yeah, I would, but not that. I can't have sex with you, no way on earth can I have sex with you.'

'Ah, thanks, am I that bad?'

'Don't be stupid, you're like my own. There's no way I could even think about having sex with you.'

'But you have sex all the time, surely it would be like that?'

'No, it wouldn't, it would never be like that with you, never. There's no way I can. I'm sorry, but no. I can't.'

'Do you think I wanted to have sex with those men? I had to have sex with four of them. I'm only asking you to have sex with one person. You either sleep with me or you leave me alone forever.'

'Don't be like that.'

'No, I mean it, I want you to go. Me and you, we're done here. Just get out.'

'You don't mean that, you're just upset.'

'Yes, I do mean it. Get out – now.'

Mike starts to walk backwards to the door. 'Gem, please, I can't bear this. It's been so hard for me this week, I can't stop thinking about you, please.'

'No, just go. I don't want to see you ever again.'

Mike walks out of the door. I'm so upset that he just walked away from me. All the things I've done for him and he just walked away.

I wake up the next morning and I'm still annoyed with Mike. He's so selfish. I think about packing my bags and leaving but I don't have anywhere to go. Mum has fixed me some breakfast but my appetite has completely disappeared.

'I made you some breakfast, we've got some good news.'

I stare at the food not even listening to what she has to say.

'The family's expanding. Shelly thinks she's pregnant. Well, she's hoping she is. They've been trying long enough. Hey, are you listening to me?'

'What? No, that's enough bacon for me, thanks.'

'Never mind the bacon, what about the baby?'

'What baby?'

'Shelly's baby, I've just told you. Are you OK?'

'Yes, I'm fine, why?'

'You've never been out in days, not even to the club. You can't just fester in here, you know. I know college has finished but you need to get out and do something?'

'Actually Mum, I've been thinking. I'm eighteen now so I really should know who my dad is. I have a right to know, I'm sick of you saying you don't know but you must know who he is.'

I'm desperate for her to tell me and the minute she does I'm packing a bag. I'll go and live with him and never return to Bridgeborough.

Mum snaps at me, 'Listen to me and listen good because I am sick of this. I keep telling you I don't know. You've been obsessed with finding out who he is your whole life. Do you think I would deliberately keep this from you if I knew?' I'm surprised she snapped at me as she normally puts her head down in shame, she never loses her temper.

'Yes, actually I do. It would be just like you to do something as selfish and nasty as that.'

'Go to hell, Kate. You want to stay indoors all the time and waste your life, you go ahead. I can't help you any more than I have. I'm wasting my time.'

Mum storms out of the house, slamming the door behind her. My head immediately hits the kitchen table and the sobbing starts again. When will this end?

I asked Mike to have sex with me five days ago and he's not been in touch at all. No phone call, no nothing. What's he thinking? Am I really that disgusting he couldn't sleep with me? Or maybe he doesn't want to sleep with a girl who had four men in one night. Either way, he couldn't even do the one thing I asked him to do.

I suppose I should ring Jennie and make sure she's OK.

'Hello, Jennie, listen, I know I was a bit off with you last week. I've been ill, had terrible flu, I could hardly even get out of bed. How's things?'

'Yeah, fine. I've missed you, I never knew what was going on, you were so nasty to me on the phone. Then you ignored my calls.'

'I'm sorry, I've not been feeling myself with this flu.'

'So come on then, tell me what happened on your birthday night?'

'Not much to be honest. I've been ill ever since.'

'So did you and Mike do it, then?'

'Yeah, we did, it was OK, but I won't be in a hurry to do it again. I've not really spoken to him since.'

'Maybe he doesn't know what he's doing. You should meet my new boyfriend, Paul. He's great in bed.'

'Listen, Jennie, I'm still not right, can we catch up later?'

'Yeah, OK, bye Kate.'

'Bye, Jennie.'

Well, that phone call made me feel worse, I must say. At least I've cleared the air and she must be head over heels, she never even mentioned her smashed-up car. Unless Daddy has fixed it up already for her.

There's a knock on my door. Who on earth is that, at this time? I open it and to my surprise I see Mike standing at the door.

'Hello, Gem, you OK?'

'Yes, what do you want?'

'Don't be like that, let me in?'

'Why?'

'You know why. Come on, then, if you want to do this.'

Mike walks through the door and grabs my hand.

I look at him, shocked, and say, 'What, you mean you will?'

'Yeah, yeah, I'll do it for you.' Mike seems a little drunk.

'Mike, you stink of booze.'

'Yes, of course I stink of booze, Kate, do you think this is easy for me?'

'Well, it's been a doddle for me so, yeah, I do.'

'OK, I've not come here to argue. I miss you. I'll do what you want.'

Oh my God, he's going through with it. As I lead him into the living room he pulls me back and says, 'Not in here, let's go up there,' and nods towards the upstairs bedrooms. We make our way into my room, my heart is pounding. 'Let's just lie on the bed first, Kate.'

We both get on the bed and as soon as I lie close to him I can smell the alcohol on his breath. He puts his arm around me and pulls me close. I look him in the eyes and say, 'Thank you for doing this.'

'Are you sure you want to do this? Once we've done it you can't take it back, you know. I don't know why you think this will make things better. You don't have to do this.'

'Yes, I want to. I have to.'

'No, you don't, you don't have to do anything until you're ready.'

'I want to do it now, please.'

'OK, but if you want me to stop you have to say so. I'm not a mind reader and I don't care how far we are, the second you say stop, I will.'

'OK.'

He holds my face and starts to kiss me. I've wanted to kiss Mike for so long yet, right now, I'm not feeling anything other than, do I really want this? Now it's happening, is it such a good idea?

His hand is down my knickers, why is he doing that? They never did that last week. He's touching me, yet I'm not entirely sure why. I'm too busy thinking about last week and thinking this whole sex malarkey is not for me. He's taking off my top, what is he thinking of my boobs, does he like them? Are they like Diane's? I bet she has better boobs than me. She must have, or why would Mike not fancy me more than her? He's pulling off my knickers and his head is heading towards my vagina. Oh my God, I quickly close my legs, I don't think that's a good idea. He comes back up and whispers in my ear, 'It's OK, darling, it's normal.'

He's never called me darling before. I wonder if that's what he says to all his girls.

'No, please, I don't want that. Just do it as quickly as you can.'

'No, I can't, you're not ready.'

'I am ready. I am.' I plead with him just to do it. He closes his eyes while kissing my hand. 'Trust me, Kate, you're not ready.' Then he makes his way back down and starts to lick me. I want him to stop doing that, I don't like it. I am ready, I know I am. What would he know, he's drunk. Drunken men never know what they're talking about. He tells me that in the club all the time. I'm not sure this is a good idea and I want to say 'Stop' but he'll think I'm stupid. I've not spoken to him in nearly a week because he wouldn't have sex with me, then he agrees and I don't want it any more. I close my eyes and just let it happen. He's heading back up.

'Are you OK, Kate? Do you want to carry on?'

Now's my chance to say, 'Actually, Mike, no.' But the words, 'Yeah, I want to carry on,' come out. He kisses me and I'm thinking about what he's just done and I'm not sure I want to be kissing my own vagina. He puts a hand on each of my bum cheeks and slowly enters me. It feels a little strange and uncomfortable. 'Is that OK?' he says and I want to say no. But I just say, 'Yes, it's fine.'

He starts to grind his hips slowly and kiss my neck gently. I can feel him rubbing inside of me and I hate it. I think back to the way the men were and even though it's not as rough as then it still hurts. My bruises may have cleared up on the outside but inside I feel every single one is still very much there and Mike is touching each one with every stroke. Mike was right, I wasn't ready. I'll never be ready. I don't get why people want to have sex for fun as this is not much fun at all. I'm screaming in my head, Stop, please stop! I don't want this any more.

He's been going for about ten minutes, and I wish he would just stop, even though I can tell he's trying to be as gentle as he can. When will he stop? is spinning in my head. I mean, how long does sex last for? An hour? I could be here all night. Oh – there's a funny noise, he's not made that noise before, he starts to breathe quite heavily. He seems to be getting harder and faster while the gentle neck kisses turn into tiny bites and his grasp against my bum cheeks is getting harder with each fast-paced breath he takes.

It's like he's lost in his own world then all of a sudden he pushes himself inside me, quite far, and lets out a moan. Ouch, that was a little too hard. He pulls himself out of me and rests his forehead on mine, holding my face, trying to catch his breath. I can feel the beads of sweat coming from him on my skin and the alcohol on his breath. After a few moments of us just staring into each other's eyes looking completely lost he says, 'I love you so much. I'd do anything for you, I want you to know that.' He lifts his body off mine and lies alongside me. We both lie in silence.

I wonder where I've gone. It's like Kate Reilly died. Where is she? Where has that lovable girl who tells jokes and does magic tricks gone. She's been murdered and replaced by this lifeless broken soul.

'Come here.' He pulls me in closer to him and kisses me on the head. 'Listen, I know you never really enjoyed that and I said you never had to do it, but sex can be good and fun with the right person. That, what we did there, is not the way sex should be and what happened last time is definitely not the way sex should be. But I promise you, when you meet the right person and the time is right, you will enjoy sex.'

'How will I know if he's the right person?'

'You'll know, Gem, you'll just know.'

He kisses me on the head again and we lie there in each other's arms.

'I've really missed you. Please don't let this be the end of our friendship. I hate what happened to you last week, I can't stop thinking about it, but those men, they've been dealt with. Make no mistake about that.'

'Do you mind if we never talk about that or them again?'

'No, I don't mind at all, but if you ever want to talk about it, at any time, you call me. I don't care where I am or what I'm doing, I'll drop it and be with you.'

Chapter 11 – In The Papers

I'm still thinking of the rape daily. Jennie and I are talking a lot more. She even came over for a drink yesterday. Still talking about her fabulous new boyfriend. I wanted to tell her about the rape. It was right there on the tip of my tongue, but I chickened out at the last minute. I've still not seen Jimmy but, to be honest, I don't think I ever want to see him again.

I'm sitting at home alone as per usual. I hope my mum doesn't bring a man back tonight. I really can't face it. In fact, I wish she would drop down dead. As I start to think about my mum dropping down dead I hear a knock at the door. Who can that be? It might be Jennie, she did say that she might pop round if Perfect Paul was going out with his friends.

I open the door and it's him, Jimmy. I can't exactly close it on him. I'll have to let him in. He walks in the door and bold as brass he says, 'Hello, Treas, are you OK?'

'Yeah, I'm fine.'

'I've not seen you at the club for a while. I was hoping you'd come round at the weekend, we're all missing you.'

'No thanks, I think I'll give it a miss if you don't mind. I'm thinking of staying away from the club.'

Jimmy comes right up to my face. 'I want you to listen to me very carefully. I want you to know that I know what happened to you and those men have been dealt with personally, by me, and put it this way – they suffered, by God did they suffer. But you've got to get over this, move on, show them that they can't break us.'

'But they have broken us, they broke me. They hurt me, they really hurt me. I never wanted that to happen, I never thought anything like that would happen. Where were you? Why weren't you there? It would never have happened if you'd have been there. I'm not blaming Mike, he couldn't do anything, but I really needed you, like I never needed you before.'

I look into Jimmy's eyes and he has tears in them. I've never seen him like that. This has devastated us all and I know Mike is distraught. I can see it every time he comes over.

'I can't get over this, there's no way that I can. I can never go back to that club, ever.'

'I need you, your Uncle Jimmy, he needs you. Who'll get me my tea? No one makes a cup of tea like you, and no one can tell a joke like you either. Listen to this one. Two blondes walking down the road, a guy says to them, "Hey, are you two sisters?" One says, "No, we're not even Catholic."'

I give Jimmy a half-hearted smile. He's trying, bless him. He holds my cheek and says, 'See, my jokes are shit. Come here, hug your Uncle Jimmy, he'll make it all go away.'

He pulls me in towards him and I sit there for what seems like hours. It's the safest I've felt since the rape. I must fall asleep on him or something because I wake up to his phone ringing. He answers, 'Hello? Listen, I'm busy, I'll call you back.' He switches off his phone and pulls me back in.

'I've been thinking it's about time I got rid of that club, anyway. I'm going to buy a new one, a better club, and you know what I'm going to call it? Kate's Klub, KK for short, would you like that? Instead of me working in your club, called Kate's Klub, and us breaking into the post office to fund it, I'm going to open the club for you. I'll make it the best club anyone has ever seen, I promise. And when you get back on your feet, I'll hand it over to you. It can be yours, all of it. Would you like me to do that?'

'I'm not sure, do what you like.'

'I would like to do that.' I'm not really interested in a new club or the old club for that matter. All I can think about these days is the rape. Thinking of that club kills me. I want to know why it happened, what did I do?

'Jimmy, why was I raped? What made them do that? I've never done anything to them. I've never even seen them before.'

'I think it was to get at me and Mike. You're our little angel and I think they thought a good way to get at us would be to clip our angel's wings, and that's exactly what happened.'

'But why would they want to get at you?'

Jimmy looks at the floor and then looks up at me and says, 'You know what, I'm going to level with you here. Have you got any idea who I am? And I don't mean Jimmy, your friend, I mean, do you know who I *actually* am?'

'I know people respect you. I don't know why, you're just you, Jimmy.'

'I know you think that, but I'm not the kind of man you mess with. My family were big round here a few years back and everyone in Bridgeborough knows who we are. My Uncle Davey used to run this town years ago and I'm pretty much the same now. If I tell someone to do something they do it, without question, and if they don't, they pay a very high price. But there's always someone out there who thinks they're tougher than me, like Keith Nixon. I could have taken him out because of what happened to you, but at least I know where I am with him. If I take him out there will always be some other monkey wanting to climb the tree. Men like me always think of a way to get at men like me, try to teach each other a lesson, like what happened to you last month. Can I ask you to be a grown-up and I can tell you what I did back to them, and it might make you understand exactly who I am?

'I want you to know that I personally dealt with each and every one of them. It broke my bloody heart, what they did, and mark my words not one of them will ever have sex again. Every one of them got beaten to a pulp the following day, and I mean fucking tortured when I say that. I was going to kill them but then I thought, you know, what would be worse than death? A man without a dick, that's what. They'll probably kill themselves anyway before long.

Well, one of them won't be able to kill himself, I made sure of that.'

'What do you mean?'

'I made sure that bastard was paralysed from the neck downwards.'

'Which bastard? Why?'

'The dirty bastard who took your virginity. I hate him for that, I made him pay more than any of them.' I put my head down, a little embarrassed. It's like my own father knowing what happened. Jimmy holds my head up, kisses me on the forehead and says, 'I love you very much, I want you to know that.'

'What would've happened when they went to hospital? The nurses would've asked questions. What if they told them you did it, then they told the nurses what they did to me. I couldn't bear that. I wish you had just left it. What if the nurses find out then they tell my mum.' My eyes start burning with tears at the thought of my mum knowing what happened, I never want her to know.

'Kate, please calm down, no one will find out what happened to you and there won't be any questions. Like I said, I have a way of making people do what I tell them to. Let's just say someone owes me a favour. He's a sergeant in the police force who, luckily for me, is married to a nurse at the hospital. So she will report it to him then it will all mysteriously disappear like most other things do. I'm nobody's fool, Kate, and the people of this town do what I tell them to do. That's all you need to know.'

We hug each other for a little while, not talking at all until Jimmy lifts my head to say, 'I made them deep throat each other before I cut their dicks off and posted them out to Keith Nixon's wife. That's who I am. I'm someone you should be scared of. Nobody ever messes with me or one of mine. I honestly think you're the only person in Bridgeborough who didn't know who I was, and I love that about you. I wish with all my heart I never had to tell you today who I was.'

Jimmy finally leaves. I'm pleased he came round. He never once looked at me like I was dirty. I was a little paranoid that maybe he could smell the dirty-hand smell – because I can still smell it. No matter how many times I shower or wash my face, it's still there. I'm a little worried that it was all because I told Keith Nixon I was Jimmy's niece at that club owners' event. That's why Jimmy kept asking me if I told him who I was. Maybe I should have told him that I did and he could have protected me.

It's been a while since the rape but I can't seem to get back into normal life. I shower at least six times a day. Even more if my mum's out. I'm trying to hide the fact I'm showering all the time so she doesn't ask any questions. All the showering is making my vagina very sore. Now everything in the cupboard has to be perfectly straight. I'm even measuring the distance between the tins with a ruler to be extra safe.

It's opening night at the new club, KK's, on Friday. I can't be bothered to go. Mike has been trying to get me to go all week, but I can't face it. He seems to think Jimmy will go mad if I don't go because he's arranged a big opening night. It's not for me, though, it's to show Keith Nixon that Jimmy's not afraid of him. I'm not getting involved in their little game. Jimmy can go to hell. I'm out from now on. I don't even feel like me any more. It's like I'm dead inside. I don't care about the club. I know Jimmy wants to start afresh, but I don't. I want to forget about Jimmy and Mike and move on.

It's Friday and it's opening night. I'm not going anywhere. I think I'll have a few drinks on my own tonight. Even Jennie is wondering why I'm not going. She really wants us to go but, again, it's not for me. She wants to show off to her adoring public that she's friends with Kate Reilly who is as thick as thieves with Mike Taylor and Jimmy Simpson. She even said she'll get dressed to go to the club on her own in case I change my mind. I know for a fact the press will be there, writing some crap about us. Even they think Jimmy and Mike are celebrities. They're often in the papers. Maybe I should tell them about the rape, that would give them a few double-page spreads.

I'm sitting in my dressing gown reading the TV magazine when I hear a knock at the door. Who the hell is that? I'm not expecting anyone. It better not be Mike forcing me to go to the opening night, I'm not interested. I open the door and it's Jimmy.

'Hello, Jimmy, are you OK?'

'No, Treas, I'm not. In fact, I'm a little pissed off. I was expecting you to be there this evening. I have two hundred and fifty people turning up at my club tonight and I wanted you to be there, considering I've named the club after you. Look at the fucking state of you. You're sick and you're getting worse.'

'What? No, I'm not.'

'Yes, you are. I mean, look at this.' Jimmy has opened the cupboard. 'I never wanted to say anything to you before, but last time I was here you washed your face ten times and straightened the tins in the cupboard six. I mean, it's fucking weird, Kate. Have you ever heard of a condition called OCD?'

'No.'

'Well, I suggest you get to the doctors and ask them about it and get some leaflets while you're there.'

He sweeps every tin out of the cupboard and on to the floor. He grabs me by the scruff of the neck and says, 'Sort your fucking self out before I do.'

'Who the fuck do you think you are? Coming in my house and throwing your weight around. Get out, I wish I'd never even met you, it's all your fucking fault. You and Mike, you can go to hell. You actually thought I was going to turn up at that fucking excuse of a nightclub? You never wanted to name that club after me, you did that out of guilt. You'll change it back in six months, once you think you've won me round. I never want to see you again, just leave me alone.'

I'm not sure what comes over me, but I start to hit him and push him. 'Get out, get out, leave me alone!'

I'm so angry and upset, my arms are swinging all over the place. The next thing I know, I'm on the floor. Jimmy has slapped me right across the face. I'm lying on my side. Ouch, that really hurt, that man can really slap someone. He bends down and grabs me by the hair.

'Get up, get the fuck up. Get dressed and get over to the club.' He drags me upstairs by my hair and into the bedroom. He pulls out a dress from my wardrobe. 'That will do, get it on.'

'No, I don't want to wear that, I need a shower, please.'

'No, you don't, you're cleaner than a bottle of bleach. Get the dress on, now.'

He looks terrifying but I can't bear to go to the club. He pulls my dressing gown off and starts to put my dress on.

'Hurry the fuck up cos we have people waiting for you to go and open that club. We'll get Caroline to paint you a smile, hurry up.' He can be such a prick at times and this is one of those times. He grabs me by the arm. 'Finished, let's go.' He drags me down the stairs and throws me into the car. As we head towards the club, Dave is there.

'Hello, Mr Simpson.' He nods my way saying, 'Kate.'

All I can think is, Does he know?

'No,' Jimmy says.

I look at him and say, 'What?'

'He doesn't know. I know that's what you're thinking, well he doesn't. Nobody does and anyone who finds out or mentions it will have their fucking heads chopped off by me personally, OK? Now, get in the club, put your best smile on, and stop fucking moping about.'

I make my way into the club. Caroline is there behind the bar.

'Wow, Kate, you look lovely, it's been a while. Have you been losing weight?'

I really want to say, 'Yes, Caroline, I've been throwing up religiously since I was held down and gang raped.' But I smile sweetly and say, 'Yes, I have. A new diet.'

'Caroline, fix Kate's face, will you?' Jimmy snaps at her. Then out of the corner of my eye I spot Mike walk in. Oh great, just what I need.

'Gem, you came.' He looks at Jimmy and says, 'How the hell?'

Jimmy gives him a funny look which stops Mike from asking any more questions. Jimmy shouts over, 'Get Kate a drink, Caroline, she wants an orange juice.'

Caroline shouts back, 'But she doesn't—'

Before she can finish Jimmy yells, 'Erm, I say what she likes and what she doesn't, get her one, now.'

I've never heard Jimmy talk to Caroline like that and I think even she's wondering what's going on. All of the club staff are there staring at me. Jimmy puts the drink in my hand and pushes it towards me. He's giving me the look that I know means I have to drink it. Why is he being so mean? Have I not been through enough?

He says, 'Drink your drink.' I take a sip, not enough to swallow it, I just place it on my lips. He pushes it right into my mouth, 'Swallow it, now.'

Everyone is looking at us and I feel a little embarrassed. I take a drink and swallow some.

'More than that.' Jimmy is starting to really lose his temper. I take another drink.

'For fuck's sake, will you just drink the fucking juice.' He pours the whole drink down my throat. I have tears in my eyes again. 'Get into the office.' We go into the office. 'Right, at 9pm I'm going to get up and speak. I'll say a few words about you and you can get up and speak.'

'Me? What on earth would I speak for? I don't want to do that, no. Please, I'll do anything.'

'Why don't you tell a few jokes or something, you're good at that. You'll then get up and cut the ribbon and the club will be officially open.'

'OK, I'll do it, but I'm going home after that, I mean it.'

'Whatever.' He opens the door and shouts, 'Caroline, get Kate a proper drink, something to relax her nerves. She's got a big night ahead of her.'

Everyone is turning up and smiling like it's the best party in the world. Jimmy thinks he's great. Even Helen is here. He's showing her round. It's meant to be my bloody club, not Helen's, why didn't he just call it Helen's Club? He's such an arsehole, I don't even want to be here.

Mike comes over, he's another arsehole.

'Hey, Gem, how's things? I'm glad you came. Being cooped up in that house isn't healthy, you know, and you look lovely by the way. I like the way Caroline has fixed your hair and make-up. You look really grown-up.'

'Do I? That's nice, I know things have been a bit weird between us lately, but how about you buy me a drink?'

'OK then, vodka is it? It'll do you good to relax.'

Mike heads towards the bar and as he does some drunken man grabs my behind. I get such a shock. I pick up an empty glass on the table next to me and the next thing I know I've turned around and smashed it into his face. Everyone is looking at me. Jimmy comes running over.

'What the fuck? Get in here,' and he drags me into the office. Mike soon follows. 'What the hell happened there, Kate? You can't go around glassing people.'

'That bastard grabbed my arse, Mike.'

Jimmy starts his shit again. 'Hey, it's a club, people get drunk and do silly things. You can't go around fucking glassing them. Mike, go outside, make sure he is all right, give him some money, give him anything to shut him up.'

Mike leaves the office.

'Shut him up? He grabbed my arse, Jimmy, who does he think he is?'

'Kate, I'm trying to help you here but, seriously, I can't keep trying. You either sort yourself out or, I mean it—'

'You mean what? What is it that you actually mean? You won't be my friend any more? Oh, boo fucking hoo.'

'I'm warning you, I've got a couple of hundred people outside and they've all seen you glass somebody. Are you fucking stupid?'

'Yeah, I am stupid. I must have been mad to have got involved with you two. I never even wanted to come here tonight, you knew I never, so why have you forced me? Why do you never listen to me, or anybody for that matter?'

'OK, I'm listening to you. I'm going to arrange a lift home for you and you know what? I'm not trying with you any more. I've got better things to do with my time. I've said I'm sorry about what happened and I've dealt with the people involved. I don't know what else I can do. Tell me what else I can do, because I'd love to know. If *you* can't come up with an answer, how the fuck can I?'

'Just let me go home.'

Mike walks back into the office with Jennie. Jennie looks at me.

'What the hell happened there, Kate? It's not like you to lash out at anyone. Has something happened?'

'No nothing, I just got a shock, he touched me somewhere he shouldn't have.'

'I'm sure it was an accident. Forget about whatever it is that's bothering you, we'll have a few drinks and a dance. I've been looking forward to the party all week. It'll be boring if you go. You have a club named after you, that's totally cool. I'm well jealous, please stay, because if you go I might as well go.' I look at Jennie and she seems so genuine that she wants me to stay. The thought of going back and sitting alone stewing about the rape is killing me. I'm just angry at the world. Maybe staying might not be such a bad idea.

'OK, Jennie, I'll stay for you.'

Jimmy gives me a smile and I feel like saying, 'Erm, I'm not staying for you. It's for Jennie.' But I walk out of the office, have a few drinks with Jennie and we actually don't have a bad night. I think I even stopped thinking of the rape for a little while.

At the end of the night Jimmy comes over to see me. 'See, I knew you'd have a good time once you had a few drinks. I'm sorry I was a dick, but you needed someone to give you a push and that someone had to be me, unfortunately. I hate seeing you this way, it's time to move on, darling. It's been three months, you're knocking yourself ill. Are you eating properly?'

'Not really, I don't even know what I'm doing or thinking. I'm sorry about what I did to that man but he touched me and I got such a fright.'

'It's OK, but you know you need to be careful with things like that. The police or anyone could get involved. If you ever feel the need to do anything like that you need to do it in private, not in full view of two hundred and fifty people. You should have come to me, I would have chopped his fucking hand off.' We giggle at each other but it's not really funny, that poor man will be scarred for life. 'Me and Helen were talking and you know Christmas gets a little bit lonely at times in our house. Do you fancy joining us?'

'Christmas is a couple of months away yet, but yeah, I would like that. My mum normally spends most of Christmas drunk anyway. That'll be nice, thanks.'

I think me and Jimmy might have started to build our bridges again. I hate the way I feel about him and Mike sometimes. I wish it could go back to the way it was.

It's Sunday morning and I've never been to see Mr and Mrs Richards on a Sunday since the rape and I really should because they'll be wondering where I've been. It might even make me feel better when I get there. For the first time in months, I get myself dressed and do my hair, getting ready to go out to do something normal for once. I make my way over to their house and knock on the door. Mr Richards opens it.

'Oh, Kate, sweetheart, where have you been? We've missed you. I see Mr Simpson has called his new club after you. I assumed you were far too – what's the word? – hip for us two now.'

'Mr Richards, I'd never be too hip for you.' I kiss Mr Richards on the cheek. I really have missed him. 'Elizabeth, come and see who's here.'

Mrs Richards comes into the living room. 'Kate, darling, I'm so pleased you're here. It's lamb today.'

Mr Richards says, 'We'll be in time for the car boot sale, if you want to go?'

'Yes, OK then, Mr Richards, let's go.'

I might even buy Jimmy something. He *has* named a club after me. As we make our way around the car boot sale I link my arm into Mr Richards. There are a lot of people here and I'm worried that one of the rapists might be here. I start to look around, worried that they might be looking at me.

'Mr Richards, I'm a little chilly, do you mind if we go home?'

'Are you cold, do you want my coat?'

'No, thanks, I just want to go, please. Can we?'

'OK, darling, not a problem, let's head back to the car and go.'

I started to panic there, I had to get away from the car boot sale. What have they done to me? They have changed my life. Being at the car boot sale was my favourite place to be and now I'm scared to be there. Am I going to be scared everywhere I go? Is it always going to be like this? We head back and Mrs Richards says, 'Oh, you two are back early, dinner's not ready yet.'

'It's OK, I don't mind. I've never seen you for a while. I missed you as well. It's not fair Mr Richards keeping me to himself.' And I give her a little hug.

'Oh, Kate, you've always been such a sweet girl.'

I pick at my dinner and make my way home. I run all the way there. I'm scared to be on my own outside of the house at any time.

I lie in bed that night and I'm so angry. It's not fair. Why did this happen to me? Why not Jennie or my mum, the girls who like to give it away, the good-time girls? Why me? I feel guilty that I'm having these thoughts. Maybe I should just stop thinking. I don't want to be scared, walking around. I want to be able to go places. I can fight. Mike showed me when I was ten how to fight and Jimmy has shown me a few more things over the years but when you're faced with four men it's a little difficult.

I need to get out, walk around properly. Maybe I'll call Jimmy in the morning and see if he will take me out.

The following morning I call Jimmy.

'Hello, Treas, what you doing calling me this early on a Monday morning?'

'Nothing really, I was bored and never got the chance to look around the club properly the other night with everything going on. I was wondering if I could come today?'

'Of course you can. I'd love you to come round today. What time shall I meet you there?'

'Would you pick me up?'

'Kate, it's only twenty minutes away. Just walk, you lazy thing.'

'Oh no, please come and get me. Will you knock on the door for me, don't wait outside in the car?'

'OK, if you like.'

'Thanks.'

Jimmy comes round and knocks on the door. 'Come on then, lazy bones.'

'Thanks, Jimmy.'

We head towards the club. The sign outside is fantastic, it's really trendy. It's a circle with 'Kate's' at the top, then a cocktail glass and 'Klub' underneath.

'Look at the sign. I always said Kate's Klub would be much better than Jimmeez.'

'Yes, you did, you're always right, I should have listened. When I switch on the lights the sign all glows up, it looks amazing.'

He opens the door and you can smell the newness of the carpets and the paint. As I walk in the door I'm faced with a few steps, then the main door. The bar is on my right-hand side and the dance floor is huge, I can see it from where I'm standing, and on my left-hand side is the DJ's stand. Straight in front of me is a little bar and the toilets. If you go behind the main bar there's another door. That's where Jimmy's office is.

'Come and have a proper look at it, it's really posh. I feel like a bit of a ponce in it.' We walk into Jimmy's office and there's a big wooden table with a huge leather seat. 'I even got a sofa put in over there for you and Mike to sit on.'

'More like for your afternoon naps, you mean.'

Jimmy smiles at me. 'Hey, nothing wrong with a sneaky bit of shut-eye.'

'I see you have a few other seats over there for your acquaintances.'

Jimmy says, 'Go and have a look out of the window, you can see the back streets of Bridgeborough through that window.' As I'm looking out of the window Jimmy says, 'Are you OK?'

'Yes. Why?'

'You've been holding my hand since you got out of the car and when you looked out of the window you grabbed my hand with both of your hands really tightly.' I look out of the window. I feel a little bit embarrassed. 'What is it? Tell me.'

'Nothing, really, I'm fine.'

'No, you're not.'

I look at Jimmy and say, 'I'm scared.'

'What do you mean, scared? Scared of what?'

'That.' And I nod towards the window, at the outside world.

'What are you scared of that for?'

'I don't know, I don't ever want to go outside again. I went to the car boot sale with Mr Richards yesterday and I panicked, I needed to get back to his house. I kept thinking that I was going to see the rapists and I don't know what I would do if I did see them. I'm scared of them.'

'Kate, come here.' Jimmy hugs me. 'You don't ever have to be scared. What happened to you was bad, really bad, I know it was, but something like that never happens twice.'

'How do you know it won't?'

'Because it was just an unfortunate thing, that's all. You're Jimmy Simpson's little treasure. Trust me, people should be scared of you.'

'What if I can never go back to the car boot sale or out again? I loved going to the car boot sale with Mr Richards, it was sometimes my favourite day, especially before I started coming to the club.'

'You still need to keep going, you can't stop going somewhere in case you bump into someone. Chances are they would never be at a car boot sale anyway. Who the hell goes to them? Only old people.'

'No, it's not old people. If it was for old people you would be there.'

'Hey, cheeky.' Me and Jimmy have a giggle. 'How about we go out for dinner today? We can go up to the high street and walk around a few shops. I'll be there right by your side and no one will come anywhere near you.'

'Would you?'

'Of course I will.'

'If you saw them, would you tell me, because I'm not even sure if I would recognise them.'

'I won't need to tell you, they will take one look at me and run, trust me. Come here, you silly thing.' Jimmy pulls me into him again. I feel so much better already.

Jimmy holds my face and says, 'Hey, I've got something to show you. I don't know how I forgot. Look, you're finally in the papers.' Jimmy hands me the newspaper. There's a full-page spread of me in the newspaper opening the club.

'No, I don't want to be in the papers, people will know where I am. Can you ring them and ask them to delete that and round up all of the sold newspapers? Please, I really don't want to be in the paper.'

'Don't be silly, that would be impossible, and why don't you want people to know where you are and that this is Kate's Klub? It's all you've ever wanted.'

'I know, but I've changed my mind, ever since my birthday. I don't want anyone knowing who I am, ever.'

'Kate, sweetheart, you have to stop this, please. It's happened, get over it, and get on with your life. Don't let those bastards change who you are.'

We head towards the high street and I spot the shop we bought the UV torch from. I start to laugh.

'Can you remember the first time we ever walked up this high street? We were about to break into the post office without a care in the world.'

'You never had a care in the world, Kate. Me, on the other hand,

I had the world on my shoulders. I was about to lose my club, I was worried sick, I'd hardly slept for months.'

'That was a good day, though, wasn't it?'

'Not at the time, no. I was never sure if: a) you could actually do it, or b) you would tell the police about it. I was shitting myself. Mind you, if you never managed it I would have just blown your head off.'

As we walk around I start to feel paranoid and wonder if the rapists are here. I wonder if Jimmy has seen them but doesn't want to tell me, 'Have you seen them yet?'

'No, I've not seen them.'

I point out a man who's walking his dog and say, 'Is that one?' I feel like I can see them all over the place.

'Kate, seriously, they're not here, please calm down. Let's go in here for dinner.'

He takes me into a cafe and I sit down while he orders the food. I sit looking around the cafe, wondering if the rapists are here. I wish he would hurry up at that counter and come back. He finally comes back and I pretend that I'm OK.

'Kate, I've been thinking about how you were due to go to university but with everything going on it was knocked on the head. Well, how about I teach you to be a club manager. If you come round the club on a night-time I'll teach you the basics. I'll pay you well for your troubles. After all, I wouldn't have any of it if you hadn't helped me.'

I don't really want to help out in the club but I do need the money. I need to get out of the house a bit more as well. 'OK, Jimmy, thanks I would like that.'

After lunch he drops me off back at home. I'm so glad to be back home, I feel safe here.

I've gone back to my old ways of staying indoors all day long, the only time I get out is to go to the club. I panic the entire time I'm there. Plus I think Jimmy is getting a bit annoyed having to pick me up and drop me off every day.

I've decided to try going out with Jennie. It might be better to go out shopping with a girl than going out alone or with an old man. Poor Mr Richards would have a heart attack if anyone started any trouble. Jimmy can't come everywhere with me. I don't want to become a burden to him. Plus, Jennie and I could go somewhere and have a few drinks. It might relax me a bit.

Jennie comes over. 'Are we ready, then?'

'Yes, come on, let's go.'

We start to make our way to the high street but the panic is setting in again and I'm not entirely sure this is a good idea after all. I keep looking at everyone, every man I see, I keep thinking they're one of the the rapists.

'Hey, Kate, how cool is the club?'

'Yeah, it's great. It's so much better than Jimmeez.'

'You're so lucky that Mr Simpson named a club after you.'

I want to say, 'Lucky, Jennie? Do you want to try being me?'

Speaking of Jimmy, where the hell is he? Because I'm feeling scared again. He should be here, with me, every second of every day to protect me, and Mike should be here as well, just in case we need back up. The more I'm drinking, the more angry I'm getting. I would never be feeling like this if it wasn't for them, or stupid Jennie giving me the white wine. Maybe I should go and trash the club. That might make me feel better. Smashing stupid Jennie's car made me feel better. She's another one I can't stand, come to think of it.

'I'm going to try and get Paul to come to the club. Have I told you about my new boyfriend?'

I want to say, Yes, you stupid spoilt bitch, you have told me about your stupid boyfriend, but who even gives a shit?

'Yes, you have, he sounds lovely. I'm not feeling very well, do you mind if we go?'

'No, not at all. Is everything OK? You've not been yourself for months. I was hoping to get some Christmas shopping in. We only have a couple of weeks left.'

Christmas is the last thing on my mind. Jimmy wanted me to go round there but if he can't even be bothered to protect me why should I go round there? He only wants me to go round because he feels guilty, not because he actually wants me to go, just like naming the club. He'll probably throw me out right after dinner and put the name back to Jimmeez. Why did Mike not ask me there for dinner with him and Diane and her son Gav? He'll be spoiling him rotten, I bet. He says he's dressing as Santa for him because he's only four. He never dressed as Santa for me. Santa? Mike has the cheek to call me a fucking baby.

I've managed to go out on my own a few times and, to be honest, it's not as bad as it used to be. I've even been Christmas shopping on my own.

My mobile phone starts to ring and I see Jimmy's name on the display. I'm having a bad day today and don't feel in the mood to speak to anyone, not even Jimmy.

'Treas, you're still coming over for Christmas, aren't you? Helen is really excited, she's even ordered a bigger turkey this year.'

'Yeah, I'm still coming. Do I need to bring anything?'

'No, just your pretty face.'

'OK, I'll be there for about eleven-ish, is that OK?'

'Yes. I can't wait, I love Christmas.'

'You don't wear a stupid Christmas jumper, do you?'

'What, me in a Christmas jumper, do you think I'm some kind of puff or something?' I put the phone down. Well, looks like I'm going for Christmas. Mind you, I don't normally see my mum till well after dinner time, once the hangover is settled ready for her to start drinking all day. We do normally go round to Mr and Mrs Richards but they're going to their son George's for Christmas dinner so it's probably a good thing I'm going to Jimmy's.

Chapter 12 – Heartburn

It's Christmas morning. I do like Christmas and I suppose it's nice of Jimmy and Helen to invite me over. I've never been to their house before. I wonder what their home looks like. I bet everything is in its place and perfect. Imagine if Helen had to call him Mr Simpson because it's Christmas, that would be quite funny. 'Mr Simpson, would you like stuffing with that turkey?'

The taxi drops me off and his house is huge. There's even a fountain in the garden. Bloody hell, who has a fountain in their garden? Well, Mr and Mrs Simpson would, wouldn't they?

'Ah, Treas, Merry Christmas.' Jimmy is more excitable than usual. He obviously likes Christmas. He kisses me sweetly on the cheek. 'Have you enjoyed your morning, then?'

'Yeah, fine.'

Like I've done anything all morning, I've not even seen my mum. Helen comes in and she looks so pretty, she's such a lucky woman living in a house like this. Jimmy spoils her rotten. Helen pours me a Buck's Fizz. Jimmy drinks his as quick as he can and swaps his empty glass with my full one so as not to upset Helen or confuse her with the whole, 'I can't drink orange juice or white wine, and mixing them together, Helen, what are you doing, trying to kill me?' thing.

We make our way into the living room and even the sofa is huge.

'Jimmy, I've brought you a present, open it.'

'I wasn't expecting anything.'

'It's nothing special, just a little something.'

He opens my present, takes one look at it, and says, 'Nothing special is right, I'm not wearing it. Thanks, but no thanks. Are you deliberately trying to wind me up?'

It's a Christmas jumper with Santa on the front. Helen giggles. 'Oh, put it on, humbug.'

'No, I'm not putting that stupid thing on.'

I give Helen her gift. It's a necklace and earring set.

'That's lovely. Look at this, Jimmy, what Kate has brought me.'

Jimmy rolls his eyes and says, 'Well, at least you get to fucking wear your present.'

Jimmy gives me a smile and a wink. Helen says, 'Thanks for coming, it's nice to have company on a day like today. Does your mum not mind?'

'No. To be honest, Helen, me and my mum don't have the best of relationships. Sometimes we find it best to keep out of each other's way.'

'That's a shame, you're such a lovely girl. If you were my daughter you'd be like my best friend. Wait till you see what Jimmy's bought you, you'll love it.'

'Oh, I wasn't expecting anything.'

'I've never known Jimmy spoil anyone the way he spoils you.'

I wonder if Helen knows he's not spoiling me, he's guilt-buying for me.

We all sit round the table having Christmas dinner and it reminds me of when I go over to Mr and Mrs Richards' for Sunday lunch. I half expect a car boot sale visit. They remind me of a younger version of the Richards.

'So, Jimmy, have you got any plans for your thirtieth? It's next year, isn't it?'

'Nah, I've not really thought about it. We talked about a holiday, but we'll see.'

'What, you're not having a big party? Oh, I see, it's just everyone else you like having a party for. Don't want the attention on you, eh? Well, we'll see about that. I'll try and get you something great.'

'Speaking of which, do you want to see your present?'

'Yeah, OK then, is it something for me to wear?' I say with a cheeky grin.

'Well, you have to come outside.'

'Outside, why?'

'Because, Brains of Britain, that's where your present is.'

'Have you got me a bloody bird table or something stupid like that?'

'A bird table would have been cheaper, put it that way.'

Jimmy takes me into the garden and points out a car. It's an electric blue Citroen Saxo and it has a private reg of 'Kate R' on it.

'What the hell is this, I can't even drive, are you crazy? Why have you bought me a car?'

'Because I'm fed up with arranging lifts everywhere for you. Mike bought the plates and he's going to teach you how to drive.'

'Is he? When?'

'Whenever you like.'

'Wow, Jimmy! I love it, I really love it, thank you! I wish I'd brought you something better than a Christmas jumper now.'

I jump into his arms and he hugs me really tightly. I think he secretly likes the fact he's put a smile on my face. How is it those two have a way of wrapping me round their little fingers? I better call Mike and thank him. I'm not even sure if he got to see Billy today. Since Shelly is five months pregnant with Brian's baby, it's a little awkward for him to go round their house.

'Mike, Merry Christmas! You got me a car, I can't believe you got me a car, what are you two like? When are you going to teach me to drive?'

'We can start tomorrow if you like.'

'Tomorrow, that soon? Wow, I can't believe it. Thanks.' I say in a soft voice, 'Mike.'

'Yes, Gem.'

'I love you, you know.'

'Yeah, I love you too. Merry Christmas, sweetheart.'

And that's that, those two have won me round by buying me a car. Why do they always know how to play me? I'm glad they do, though. I know Jimmy feels terrible about what happened and he would do anything to change things.

Mike has been teaching me how to drive and I'm quite good at it. Like everything else, it's something I can pick up really easily. He's even teaching me the basics of mechanics. I reckon he would be a good mechanic if he wasn't a gangster. We're out driving and the snow is really heavy outside.

'I can't drive any more. It's a blizzard out there, we'll have an accident.'

'Right, pull over.' We pull over and he says, 'Take off your coat.'

'Take off my coat, why?'

'Just do it, will you?' So I take off my coat. 'Right, get out of the car.'

'Are you crazy? I'm not getting out, it's a blizzard out there.'

'Get out. I want to show you something.' I get out of the car and he locks all the doors and says, 'Right, now, change the car tyre.'

'I'm not changing the car tyre here, no way.'

'Well, OK then, we can stay here all night if we have to, but you will change that car tyre.'

He is crazy at times, that man. What on earth does he want me to change the car tyre for? It's not even flat. I stand there for ten minutes and he's not breaking at all. I don't know why I thought he would because he never does with things like this. I give in and go to the boot to get out the jack and the spare tyre. I'm not sure if the nuts are seized up or if my hands are numb with the cold, but it takes me forever to get them off. I finally get the bolts off and change the tyre, put the stuff back into the boot and knock on the window.

'Let me in, you idiot.' He opens the doors. 'What the hell was that, Mike?'

'A lesson, that's what. No matter what the weather is like or what time of day it is, you know you can change a tyre. So if you ever get stuck and you're on your own, you know what to do.'

'You're crazy, you, why could we not have done this in the summer?'

'Cos that would have been too easy. Let's get you dry and warmed up.'

We get to my house and I run straight into the shower. I'm chilled to the bone. I lie in bed all night shivering. I hope Mike's pleased with himself. I'm probably going to die of pneumonia for a tyre that wasn't even flat. If I don't die of pneumonia it will be a heart attack. I seem to be getting heartburn constantly these days.

It's my driving test today. I feel so nervous. I can't wait to be able to drive all alone without Mike in the passenger seat. Jennie's not passed her test yet so it would be great to finally do something before her.

'Mike, I'm so nervous.'

'Don't worry, you'll pass, you're a brilliant driver. I'll be waiting for you when you get back and I'll take you out for lunch to celebrate.'

After my test I walk up to Mike with a sad look on my face.

'No way, how could you have failed? You're a great driver.'

I playfully slap him across the face with my passed paper. 'Ha! Failed, me? As if. Mike Taylor, how dare you even suggest such a thing. Come on, you can treat me to lunch.'

We head off out to lunch. Wait till I tell Jennie I've passed my test before her. It's probably the only thing I've ever done before her. Well, apart from break into a post office, a bank, have a club named after me and sleep with a gangster.

It's Thursday and Jennie's boyfriend has gone out with his friends. She wants me to keep her company and celebrate passing my test. But I think it's more the 'keep her company' angle than the test. I go round there, have a few drinks, and the conversation soon changes to the same thing it always changes to when Jennie's around – sex.

'Sex is not all bad, you know. And maybe Mike never knew what he was doing.'

If only she knew that it wasn't Mike, but four monsters. I'm desperate to tell her but I simply can't, no way can I tell her that. I know she'd never blame me, it wasn't my fault, but I still can't bring myself to talk about it. Jennie says, 'Sex is really good and you should learn to enjoy it. Paul, my boyfriend, is really good at it. Watch, I'll show you.' She leans in to kiss me and I laugh.

'What on earth are you doing?'

'Kate, don't be a baby, it's just a kiss.'

It's funny, I used to hate it when everyone called me a baby. What I wouldn't give to turn the clock back and go back to my baby days when everything was so easy. I don't want to kiss Jennie. I've only ever kissed Mike and, to be honest, it was the most uncomfortable feeling I'd ever had and I wanted to stop it as soon as it started. She leans in again, I can feel her lips on mine. I open my mouth, allowing her tongue to enter. She runs her hands down my back and grabs my bum. What on earth is she doing? I think she's really enjoying this. She's made her way round to the front of my jeans and starts to open them. Oh my God, I want to stop her. I'm wondering what she's even thinking, she's never done anything like this before. We've shared a bed countless times since we were kids and she's never once shown any sign that she might be into women. But then I think, Well, it's Jennie, she won't hurt me, she's been my best friend for years. I'm quite safe.

She puts her hand in my knickers while kissing my neck. She seems to be really enjoying it. I don't want her to think something is wrong or guess that I've been raped so I say, 'Oh Jennie, that feels really nice.' She stops and says, 'See, I told you that you would enjoy it. You do it to me now, go on.'

I'm a little nervous and fumbly when opening her trousers. I start to giggle. I think I should maybe tell a joke.

'How can you tell if a lesbian is butch? She kick-starts her vibrator and rolls her own tampons.'

'Just kiss me, Kate.'

'Hey, that's a film, isn't it?'

I pull her closer to me and kiss her the same way she did me. I'm probably not as tender as she was as I'm not really that confident when it comes to stuff like this. Put me in a room full of gangsters, I won't flinch. Put me in a room with someone who wants to have sex with me and I'm a wreck. I put my hands into her knickers and I'm fumbling a bit. She pulls away and quietly says, 'No, not like that, like this,' and she slows my hand down, directing it exactly where she wants it to go, and after a few minutes her breathing has changed and she's making a funny sound.

We stop and look at each other, giving each other a little smile.

'Did you enjoy that then?'

'Yeah, it was OK.'

'See, I told you sex could be enjoyed. You should have slept with a younger man anyway. What do older men know?'

'Nothing, they're too old for sex anyway.' I say this like I know what I'm talking about.

'Paul was saying he wanted to sleep with both of us.'

'What? What do you mean? I have sex with him, then the next day, you?'

'No, silly, we'll do it at the same time.'

'Well, how would that work?'

'Well, I'll do things to you, you do things to me, like we did just then, and Paul would do things to us both.'

'What, so I just have to put my hands down your trousers?'

'Yes, and you can use your tongue as well as your fingers.'

'What? My tongue? You actually want me to lick you down there? No way. I'm not doing that, that's disgusting.'

'No, it's not. Look, take off your jeans. I'll show you.'

'No, I'm not sure I want to.'

'You're not scared, are you? Take your trousers off.'

This is really uncomfortable. I never really liked it when Mike did it. But to have Jennie doing it as well… I think enough people have seen me with no knickers on, to be honest. But, then again, I don't want Jennie to think I'm scared either. She might start to work out what happened and I'd never want her knowing that. I take my trousers off and she tells me to lie down on the sofa. She kisses my neck and works her way down and puts her head between my legs. She's touching, kissing and licking me like she's loving it. After a few minutes she stops and says, 'See, it's easy, your turn now.'

She takes off her trousers and I make my way down there. I'm not sure what I'm doing and don't know if I'll even like this. I can see her vagina in full view. I'm not even sure where it is I'm supposed to lick. Before I know it my tongue is on her and I'm doing it, I'm actually doing it … yet it's not as bad as I thought it would be. It's kind of, a little bit of a hint of odour, but it's not a disgusting odour. It's just that: an odour. It soon turns extremely wet and Jennie is writhing around on the sofa and moaning with enjoyment. Afterwards we lie next to each other on the sofa. I'm so content lying in Jennie's arms. It's been such a long time since anyone actually held me. I wish it was like that with me and Mike all the time, yet just when I think it's going to be like that he asks for yet another favour.

'So you'll do it, then?'

'What?'

'Have sex with me and Paul. He's great in bed, really great.'

'Yeah, OK then, I will.'

'I'll tell him to come round tomorrow night, then.'

I make my way home and think about what a crazy night that's been. I hate sex and certainly never ever thought I'd be having sex with Jennie. I mean it wasn't awful, just not something I would have ever wanted to do. I don't understand why she's enjoying it so much more than I do.

It's Friday night and it's the night Jennie wants me to have sex with her and Paul. I'm a little worried and want to back out but I can't. If Jennie gets any idea about the rape I would be so ashamed. I have to not think about it and move on from it. Everyone around me likes sex – Mike likes it, my mum likes it and Jennie loves it. I have a few glasses of vodka before I go, to try and relax me. I make my way round to Jennie's. I'm half hoping that Paul can't make it. As soon as I get to Jennie's I head for the kitchen to pour another drink, still trying to calm the nerves. The doorbell rings, it must be Paul.

'Is she here, then?' I hear a masculine voice. 'I hope she's fit.'

'She is, she's gorgeous, and my best friend. I've told you,' says Jennie, all excited.

As he walks in I shriek, 'Oh my God, Jennie! You never said he was black.'

'What?' Jennie screams. 'What are you talking about?'

'Jesus, are you taking the piss or something?' poor Paul says.

'No, no, Paul. I'm sorry, I never meant anything, but you're black and a boy.'

'Is this a joke, Jennie? You said she was fit, not some racist.'

'I'm not racist, I'm just funny about colours. I can't possibly have sex with a black person who is a boy.'

'Jesus, Kate!' shouts Jennie. 'He's not a boy, he's a man.'

'Well, he's maroon then, which is still brown-ish in my book.'

'Right, Jennie, I'm off. I wouldn't touch her with a bargepole, anyway, she's fat. You said she was fit.'

Paul storms out and, to be honest, I'm quite pleased. At least I don't have to go through with it.

'Fat, me? Ha! What a cheek. How dare he say I'm fat. I have a good mind to knock him out for that.'

'Please, calm down. I never realised you had a thing against blacks.'

'I don't have a thing against blacks. I promise I don't. I'm not racist, I'm not.'

'It doesn't sound it.'

'He said I was fat. I'm not, am I?'

'Well, I have to admit you have put a little weight on the past few months, and your boobs are huge.'

'No, they're not.'

'Yeah, they are, they look the size of Shelly's and she's nearly seven months pregnant.'

Pregnant. My mind is racing. I can't be, please, no, I can't be. I would know, surely? I would be seven months, so I would know, of course I would.

'You're such a bitch, Jennie!' I scream at her, slap her across the face and run out of the house.

I can't be pregnant, not by those animals, this can't be happening. There's no way you wouldn't know that you're pregnant. Yes, I've had heartburn for a few months and never seen a sign of a period, but my periods have always been up and down. My stomach is a little larger than normal but not big enough for a baby, and my boobs have grown, but I'm a young woman, of course they would grow. That would naturally start happening with my weight gain. I never ate properly for a long time after the rape and lost a lot of weight. I thought the weight gain was because I'd started to eat again. Jennie is just being a bitch as usual and Paul called me fat because I knocked him back, that's all.

I get home and look in the mirror, pulling up my top. My belly does look very rounded. I run to the toilet and vomit down it. No, I can't be, please don't let me be pregnant. I'm praying to God I'm not pregnant. Why are you punishing me? What did I do today? All the tins are in order and I've not eaten anything I shouldn't have. I'm extra careful about this stuff since the rape.

I remember there's an all-night chemist on Alderson Road. I can't drive there, I've had vodka but I need a test really quickly so I put on my trainers and I run to it as fast as I can. It's raining outside, yet I have no coat on and don't even feel it. My whole body is just numb. I get to the shop and pick up the pregnancy test: ten quid. Bloody hell, are they kidding me with this? What, is there a mini doctor in the box and he pops out and says, 'Oo, you're pregnant, Miss Reilly,' and delivers the baby for you. Ten quid for a stick which will be urinated on and thrown in the bin? I reluctantly hand over my cash. I know if I wait another twelve hours the doctor's will be open and I could get a free one there. I can't tell the doctor I'm pregnant, though, no way can I tell the doctor, he knows me. I've gone to him my whole life. I'd be so ashamed.

I finally get home with my test. My fingers feel huge and I can hardly open the box. I think it's sheer panic. But it's OK, I'll take the test, it will say it's negative and I'll go on a diet tomorrow. Maybe Jennie's right, maybe I am just fat and probably should have looked after myself a bit. I wee on the stick and leave it in the bathroom. I sit at the top of the stairs to wait for the results. It feels more like three hours than three minutes. It's a waste of time anyway, I know I won't be pregnant. Everything will be fine in … one and a half minutes … I know it will.

The three minutes is finally up and I slowly go to the test.

Oh my God, I'm pregnant. There are two blue lines. I'm sure that means pregnant. I'll check again. I go over the instructions for the millionth time. Yes, it's definitely correct. I'm pregnant. I collapse in a heap on the floor. What shall I do?

I call Mike. 'Hello?'

'Mike, can you come over?'

'Why? What is it?'

'Can you just come.'

'Well, I'm busy at the club, can't it wait?'

'No, it can't bloody wait!' I scream at him. 'Get over here now.'

Mike puts down the phone and within ten minutes he's pulled up outside. As he comes in the door, he yells, 'What on earth is it?' He takes one look at me and can tell I've been crying. 'What is it?'

'Mike, I'm...'

'What, you're what? Kate, tell me what you are. What is it? You're scaring me.' I cry and fall into his arms. I can't stop crying. 'Please don't cry, you know I hate it when you cry. What is it?'

'I'm pregnant.'

'What, who by? I never knew you had a boyfriend. Who you seeing and since when?'

'No, Mike, you don't understand. I'm really pregnant, like, seven months pregnant.'

'You can't be, you have it wrong. You can't be seven months pregnant, you would know.'

'Well, that's what I thought as well, but apparently I don't know my own body as well as I think I do. You have to help me, get this thing out of me. I can't have a baby from a rapist. Can you kick me in the stomach as hard as you can, please?'

'I'm not doing that, no way, it's dangerous. No, we'll do it properly. Are you sure you're pregnant? How do you know?'

'Because Paul said I was fat.'

'Who the hell is Paul? I'll knock him out if he wants to start on you.'

'It's Jennie's boyfriend, we were going to have sex with him.'

'What? You were going to have sex with Jennie's boyfriend? You're not even making any sense here. Why would you go behind Jennie's back with her boyfriend? She's supposed to be your best friend.'

'No, he wasn't cheating, Jennie was going to be there.'

'Hang on, you were going to have sex with Jennie's boyfriend with Jennie there?'

'Something like that, yeah. Oh, please, can we focus on me being pregnant?'

'No, I want to know more about this pervert. Was he trying to trick you into having sex with him?'

'No, he wasn't. It was Jennie's idea.'

'Well, that Jennie is a tart if you ask me, and you'll do well to stay away from her. How many other men have there been?'

'No one, just those men and you.'

'Are you sure?' Mike has this look on his face and it looks like he wants to be sick. 'Kate, are you sure? Because if it was one of them, it means you're too far gone.'

'What do you mean, too far gone? Can't I just go to the doctors and have an abortion?'

'No, not after six months, you can't, it's illegal.'

'Oh no, well, that's even worse then. I can't have this baby, no way am I having this baby. It's all your fault, you got me into this mess, you better get me out of it.'

I start to hit Mike and hit him till I can't stop and he's not stopping me either. In fact, I think he's enjoying it as I know he has been feeling guilty about it all and maybe if I serve him some sort of punishment it might make him feel better. I finally stop hitting him and I'm crying in a heap on the floor. He's cuddles me in saying, 'It's OK. I'll sort this. I promise I will sort this. We'll get you straight to the doctors tomorrow and we'll get him to confirm that you're definitely pregnant. You can't always rely on those cheap tests.'

'Cheap!' I shout. 'Cheap! That cost me ten quid, that did.'

'What, ten quid for a stick you piss on and chuck in the bin?'

'Yeah, that's what *I* said.'

He kisses me and cuddles me in a little longer. 'I'm so sorry, I really am. I'll be with you every step of the way, I promise. Whatever you want, darling, whatever you want.'

There's that name, darling, again. He must be upset.

The following day Mike drives me out of town and to a doctor's there. We walk in the waiting room and I ask Mike, 'Will you do all the talking, please? I don't want to, I can't bear talking to anyone about this.'

'Yeah, course I will.'

I'm hoping the doctor will confirm what a terrible mistake it's been and that those expensive tests should be taken off the market with immediate effect. Not just for the fact every woman who thinks she maybe in trouble is now completely skint, but the fact they're giving everyone the wrong results.

Mike walks up to the receptionist and says to the girl, 'I rang up about my wife, we have an appointment.'

The receptionist asks, 'What's your wife's name, sir?'

'Jennifer Hart, she's called.' I can't believe he's booked me in under Jennie's name. 'Oh, yes, Jennifer is next. Have a seat and the doctor will be with you soon.'

Mike holds my hand the entire time we're here. He can be really sweet like that at times. I'm sitting here wishing I *was* his wife and pregnant with his baby. Instead, I'm not even speaking to Jennie since she called me fat and I racially abused her boyfriend and I'm pregnant with, probably, a monster inside of me. What a mess this has turned out to be. I wonder whether if I'd not drunk that white wine I would have spent the night with Mike and we would be living happily ever after now.

'Mrs Jennifer Hart to consulting room number two, please.'

Mike and I make our way over to the doctor's room and Mike still has my hand. He opens the door and shakes the doctor's hand.

'Hello, doctor, my wife thinks she's pregnant. I've been away for a while so if she's pregnant she's pretty far on and we'd like to know our options.'

I'm pleased Mike is saying all of this as my mouth seems to have stopped working.

'OK, Mrs Hart, can I ask you to go to the toilet and collect a sample in this?'

The doctor hands me over a little bottle with a blank white label on it. I make my way to the toilet and try to squeeze out a wee. I can wee quite easily as my belly feels so bloated anyway most of the time. There's wee going all over my fingers and it seems like it's everywhere but in the bottle. I start to wonder where your wee actually comes out of as it doesn't seem to be anywhere near the hole it's sprouting from, near the top end. I bet Jennie would know, Jennie knows a lot about the human body and where things go in and out. I'm sitting here thinking about her and feeling guilty for slapping her. I think I should call her as soon as I get out of here and for a split second I forget where I am. Oh dear, I better hurry, but there's wee all over the bottle and my hand now. How embarrassing. Mike is in there and he'll think I'm an idiot. Wee all over the place … look, that girl can't even wee in a bottle straight. I wash my hands and the outside of the bottle and go back into the doctor's surgery. It's pretty quiet in there and Mike's not saying a word, which is unusual for him. I think he's hoping I've made a mistake as much as I am. The doctor glides over to the other side of the room on his chair with wheels on and dips a stick into the pot. I wonder if he knows he might have droplets of my wee on his fingers.

'Yes, congratulations, you two. You're going to be parents.'

The tears start to roll down my face and the doctor looks at me and says, 'Not good news, I take it, Mrs Hart?'

Mike pipes up. 'Oh, we weren't expecting it, you know, it's not something we had planned. What are our options then, doctor? We think she's twenty-seven weeks pregnant. Well, actually, we *know* she is.'

'Well then, Mrs Hart, you have no option but to have the baby.'

I squeeze Mike's hand in panic and he gives my hand a little squeeze back, to let me know he's there.

'Listen, doctor, are you sure about this? Is there anyone we can go to, money is no object.'

'Mr Hart, it's too dangerous at this stage, not just for baby, but for mother as well. It can cause complications and mother may not make it out of the surgery. You have the option to have the baby adopted. I'll give you the number of someone who can help you.'

Mike takes the number and thanks the doctor for his time. We walk out of the surgery across the car park and into the car. We've not spoken or even looked at each other. We're both really shocked about it and wondering what to do for the best. I mean, what can we do, really? I don't want to die. The thought of having to go home and tell my mum... I can't bear that, no way.

'Mike, what am I going to do?'

'I don't know, I'm thinking.'

'I can't have this baby. I can't even look at it, ever, no way.'

'I know, I know.'

'If I go home and have the baby everyone will know about it and I can't bear that either.'

Mike thinks for a while and says, 'Listen, I'll take you somewhere. I'll get you a place and stay with you. Once the baby is born we'll come back and no one will be any the wiser. We never have to talk about this again and we can hand the baby straight over to social services but not local to us. We'll go miles out of the way, we'll pick somewhere really nice.'

'OK then, when shall we go?'

'I have a few things to sort out first and if you're twenty-seven weeks we still have about twelve weeks before the baby is due. It might come early, though, so we need to make sure you're settled in somewhere at least ten weeks before your due date, but if you get any bigger people will notice.' Mike points to my stomach. 'Where did that come from? I've never noticed it before.'

'No, me neither, until Jennie and Paul said.'

'Oh yes, speaking of which, do you want to explain to me what you were talking about last night, having sex with people's boyfriends? Don't you start getting mixed up in stuff like that, you're too nice a girl. I know what this Paul will get if I get my hands on him, the pervert.'

'Oh shut up, it was Jennie's idea, not Paul's.'

'Yeah, I bet Paul put her up to it, though. Get that Jennie as well, the dirty little minx. I knew she was trouble as a kid. I bet she gets it from her parents. They look like they would have those parties where you all put your keys in a bowl and all that. Mind you, I don't even think *that* would put a smile on her dad's face, the miserable old git.'

I give Mike a smile. He's doing that cute thing again. We head home and he tells me to start slowly packing up my bags to get ready. As soon as he has picked a place and got everything sorted we'll be off.

Three days go by and Mike calls me to say he's found the perfect place and he has arranged for us to move into a cottage. 'You'll love it, it's perfect.'

'I couldn't care less about the cottage to be honest with you, Mike. I want this kid out of me so I can get back to my life again. The sooner the better as well.'

'Listen, we'll go in around three weeks, so start getting sorted. Are you sure this is what you want because once you hand the baby over you can never go back for it. You can't change your mind with things like this so please think long and hard that this is what you want.'

'I don't need to think about it, I want this monster out of me.'

'As long as you're sure.'

I can't believe he would even question that. Why on earth would I want to look at that horrible thing on a daily basis.

Chapter 13 – The Cottage

Today is the day Mike and I are going to the cottage. I'm in a total mood and don't know why. Mike pulls up outside and I give him my bags to put into the boot.

'Bloody hell, what have you got, the kitchen sink? We're coming back, you know.'

'Yeah, I know, but I thought I better take enough. We could be there weeks for all I know.' We're driving down the road and I'm thirsty. 'Can we stop for a drink, please?'

'We've only just started, can't it wait?'

'Oh no, Mike, it can't bloody wait. I have a bad back, my boobs are swelling to the size of watermelons, this seat belt is killing me and I want a drink,' I snap at him.

'Jesus, OK moody-knickers, we'll stop for a drink. What's eating you?'

'Nothing, I feel anxious, that's all.'

'Well, you don't have to feel anxious when I'm around.'

He gets back into the car with the biggest bottle of water I've ever seen. I think he thought he better stock up in case I have another outburst.

We eventually get to the cottage and it's a lovely little place. There's a lovely garden with flower boxes under the window. It's the perfect setting for a lovely family holiday home. It even has a thatched roof. I love it before I've even set foot in the place. It's a pity that the circumstances are the way they are. I think I would have enjoyed staying here for a bit. We dump the bags and Mike suggests we go see the sights. He takes me to a nice little place for some food. I look at him and he looks like a little boy lost. I know he feels terrible. It makes me think of the time when I had my first period, when I was being eaten alive – or so I thought – and how he explained that I could get pregnant by someone. I bet he never banked on doing this with me six years later. What an absolute mess this has turned out to be. Why could I not have stayed innocent to it all, still thinking I was helping out his friends with their bikes and safes? I never in my life imagined I was part of such a violent bunch of people.

As the weeks go by, Mike and I are growing closer and I'm back to feeling obsessed with him again. I wish he was my husband and we lived here out of the way of everyone, just me and him forever. No Jimmy, or Mum, and definitely no Diane. It makes me hate her even more. I think to myself, Is this what it's like for them in the house all the time? Just those two, laughing and talking.

All of a sudden I feel such a pain. 'Ouch, Mike, I think today is the day.'

'Really?'

'Yeah, the pains have been coming and going for a while. Will you start to pack up my stuff to go home tomorrow?'

'What? You can't go home tomorrow if you have that baby today. You need to stay here and rest. Have you got any idea what you put your body through?'

'No, Mike, I want to go home. I don't want to be anywhere near this place once this baby is born. I want to get as far away as possible. You have to promise me that we can hand the baby straight over and don't even look at it.'

'OK, promise. But listen, when a woman has a baby it changes her.'

'What do you mean, it changes her?'

'Your hormones will be going crazy and you may feel like you want the baby back.'

'Don't be stupid, Mike, I'll never want this little bastard back.'

'I'm just telling you that you might, that's all. But if you do, it's perfectly normal.'

'Normal? There's nothing normal about any of this.'

Mike starts to pack up my belongings. The pains are stronger than ever before.

'Mike, please load up the car with our things. You'll have to take me to the hospital soon, the pain is getting really bad. I'm not sure how long I can stand it.'

We finally get to the hospital and they take us to the delivery suite.

Mike shouts, 'Can we get her some pain relief, please?' They come in with the gas and air and Mike says, 'This stuff will take the edge off, but it sometimes makes you feel sick.'

I hate the fact he knows all this and the reason he knows all this is because he was obviously there with Shelly when she had Billy. It was a nice happy time for them, having their baby, they would have been so excited because they would know that they were having a lovely little baby at the end to cuddle up with, a piece of both of them. What will I get at the end? A big fat nothing, like always.

The labour pains are really bad. I don't think I can take much more and I start to cry. Mike is holding me.

'I know it hurts, I know it does, but it will be over soon, I promise.'

The nurse has come in to check on me and says, 'Right, you, you're ready to push, on the next contraction I want you to push as hard as you can and your baby should be here soon.'

I push like there's no tomorrow. I need this baby out of me extremely quickly. After about forty minutes, that's it, the little bastard is out. I don't want to see it or look at it. It better stop fucking crying as well. The nurse goes to hand the baby to me and Mike jumps up.

'No, it's to be taken away, straight away, please.'

The nurse looks at us in the strangest of ways and says, 'As you wish.'

That's it, the baby is out of the room and gone out of my life forever, never to be seen again. Thank God for that. I'm exhausted and fall asleep soon afterwards. When I wake Mike is still sitting, waiting for me.

'Hello, Kate, how you feeling?'

'Sore and tired.'

'The doctor is coming round in the next hour or so and if he thinks you're OK, you can go home.'

'Great.'

I'm lying there thinking about the baby crying and where they have taken it. Is it in the next room? Has it been handed over to its new mother and father? What was the sex of the baby? All of these questions are running through my mind like there's no tomorrow. Maybe I should have looked at it. Maybe one cuddle from its mum might not have hurt it. It wasn't the baby's fault, after all. The doctor has finally come to see me.

'Well, Mrs Hart, everything is fine, there are no stitches and if your husband is happy for you to go home then so are we.'

The doctor leaves the room and Mike asks again, 'Are you sure you want to leave and go home today because I really think you should go back to the cottage?'

'No, please get me out of here quickly. I want to go home now.'

Mike packs up my belongings, I'm in so much pain and I know my baby is still in the building somewhere. We head out of the hospital and to the car. Mike puts my things in the boot and helps me into my seat. As we drive out of the car park my heart aches. That's it, I've left the hospital, I left it there just crying. It'll want its mum, all babies cry to be held by their mum when they're born, it's natural. I can't stop thinking of my baby. Where will it end up? Was it a boy or a girl? Will it have clothes? Will it have siblings? What if it ends up with a mother like mine? Oh no, what have I done? I instantly feel like I need to go back. It's not the baby's fault. It was Mike's really, if he wasn't such a wide boy none of this would have happened. Mike's been really quiet all the way home and I dare not say, 'Can we go back?' What will he think? But, then again, right now, I don't really care what he's thinking.

'Are you OK?' he says in a very soft voice.

'Not really, no. Did you look at the baby?'

'What?'

'The baby, did you look at it?'

'No, I never, I stayed with you the whole time, I never left your side.'

'I know, but you had time to look at it. What did it look like?'

'I don't know, I never looked at it.'

'Can we go back?'

'What?'

'Please, I need to go back, I need to get my baby back.'

'You can't do that, Kate, I told you once you handed over the baby that was it. But I said that you would feel like this as well. It's your hormones, that's all. You'll be fine in a few days, I promise. You can start to put this behind you and move on. I was thinking before – how about you look into doing that university course you wanted to do before all of this. You could be anything you wanted to be. An accountant, you're good with numbers. A science teacher, or you could do computer studies, you always loved mucking around on your computer. It's been such a long time since you did anything, don't let those men get the better of you. Start getting your life together.'

'But what about my baby, what kind of life will it have?'

'He'll have a great life, leave him where he is.'

'A boy? It was a boy?'

'Yes, it was a boy. Now please forget about it.'

It was a boy, my baby was a boy. We don't speak for the rest of the car journey.

We pull up outside my house and I have that awful feeling in my stomach that I have to face my mum. She probably hasn't even noticed I've gone anywhere, either that or she'll be devastated I'm back home. Mike pulls my bags from the car and asks if I want him to walk me in. I say no, it's OK. I'm feeling angry with him again, yet I don't know why. I go into the house and instantly hear my mum laughing with Shelly. I really can't be bothered with those two right now. I'm exhausted and sore. I want to go to my room and climb in my bed.

'Oh, hello stranger, decided to return, have we? And where might you have been? In prison, I bet.'

'No, Mum, I wanted to get a way for a while, me and Jennie had a falling out.'

'It was a boy, by the way!' she shouts. How on earth does she know that?

'What?' I say, shocked. Has Mike told them? Did he call Jimmy at the hospital? Does everyone know?

'The baby, it was a boy.'

I go all shaky and say, 'Whose, mine?'

'What? Yours, Kate, what are you talking about? You dozy beggar, it's Shelly, she had the baby, it's a boy. She called him David and he's a total sweetheart.' She nods towards a pram and says, 'Well, come in here and meet the new arrival.'

I hear a baby crying. Oh no, not now, anything but this.

'Mum, I'm tired, can I look later?' There's no way I can look at that baby, ever.

'No, you can't, and don't think you can sleep in your room. I'm renting it out. I never knew you were coming back. I thought you were gone for good.'

'What?'

'Yeah, Nick the glass collector from the bar is renting your room off me, so you'll have to sleep on the sofa for now, until he's gone.'

'The sofa. Bloody hell, Mum. Well I'm having a bath then and I don't want to be disturbed.'

I go upstairs and start to run a bath. I'm so sore and my boobs are getting harder by the second. I climb into the bathtub and my legs feels so shaky. I lie there for what seems like ages. I can't stop thinking of my baby. I want him back. He belongs to me, not some stranger. Maybe I should have gone back to the cottage tonight like Mike suggested, but I just wanted to be home. I finally get the energy to climb out of the bath and go downstairs. Shelly is still there. Oh God, I'm going to have to look at that baby. My mum shouts over, 'The baby was born three weeks ago today. Why don't you hold him?'

'No, I don't want to hold him. I'm tired, are you not going to work?'

'Yes, I'm going soon.'

'Well, go on then, and take Shelly and her brat with you.'

'Hey, there's no need for that.'

'Oh, whatever, Mum.'

I slam the living-room door and lie on the sofa. I wake up at 5am. I can't have slept all that time, it's been a solid ten hours. I must have needed it, but I'm in more pain than anything else. This is no good, I can't live on a sofa. Mike will have to get me somewhere. Again, this is all his fault so he'll have to sort it. I ring him and he slurringly says down the phone, 'Hello?' I must have woken him up. I can hear Diane in the background giving it all, 'Who the hell is that at this time of the morning?'

'Mike, it's me.'

'What's up, Gem?'

'Her again, what on earth does she want now?' Diane is still screaming in the background.

I'm so angry and I shout back down the phone, 'Does she want me to come over there and show her what I want? To punch her bloody face in is what I want.'

'Don't be like that, what is it?' Mike says.

'You'll have to get me a flat somewhere, my mum has moved someone from the bar into my room and I'm sleeping on the sofa. I'm not in any condition to sleep on the sofa, this needs sorting.'

'Look, I can't do anything at 5am in the morning, can I? I'll sort it first thing, I promise. Good night.'

He puts down the phone. God, I hate Diane, she's going to get it as soon as I'm on my feet.

Mike comes round first thing. 'Right, I've got you a flat, it's round the corner but you can't move in for four weeks.'

'Four weeks? Bloody hell, I could be dead by then. Have you got any idea how much pain I'm in?'

'I'm doing the best I can,' he snaps at me.

I know I've been hard work lately, but I'm in agony here and I still can't stop thinking about my baby.

'What did he look like?'

'I don't know, just a baby, they all look the same, don't they? I only got a quick look as he came out and they carted him straight off. Look, I said you would feel like this and if it doesn't go by next week we'll get you to the doctors. It's a big thing you've been through.' Mike pulls me into him and kisses me on the forehead.

Maybe Mike is right. 'Yeah, OK, tell me about this flat, then.'

'It's lovely, it's got a big open fire, it will be cosy in the winter. I'm getting it decorated for you now with new carpets and everything. I promise it will be lovely by the time I'm finished. Jimmy's been on the phone, he's missed us.'

'He doesn't know where we've been, does he? Tell me you've not told him, please.'

'No, I told you I wouldn't tell anyone. I told him I just took you away to clear your head, don't worry.'

He kisses me on the head. I want to hold him forever. I love the touch of him.

Mike leaves so I start to clear the kitchen. Some things never change, there are dirty cups all over the kitchen bench. I open the cupboard and notice that the tins are all in order. I smile at myself and think my mum must have missed me and was expecting me back really or she would've just put the tins in any old way. It doesn't take long before my thoughts turn back to my baby.

My mum finally comes down the stairs when Shelly walks in the back door with her brat. Great, just what I need.

'Julie, is there any chance you could get your Kate to babysit David? I need to go pay some bills. You could come, we'll get some dinner. I could do with a day without the kids. Mike's got Billy until tomorrow.'

Me, babysit? She better not even ask me, there's no way I'm looking after a baby today.

'Kate, watch the baby, will you?' my mum asks.

'No, I have things to do today.'

'What things? You never have anything to do. Stop being a selfish cow, and watch the baby. We're going out, and now.'

They get up and walk out of the door, leaving the baby in his pram. What on earth are they thinking? I've never looked after a baby before. I stand there staring at the pram for about half an hour thinking, You better not wake. Then he starts to cry.

'No, please, please go back to sleep, I'm begging you, I'll do anything if you go back to sleep.' But it's not working, nothing is getting this baby back to sleep. Well, certainly not standing in the doorway staring at it anyway.

I start to slowly walk towards the pram, taking a deep breath. 'Please go back to sleep, David, please.' He's not listening to me at all. I'm going to have to pick him up, his screams are getting unbearable. I look into the pram and the baby is all red-faced from screaming. 'Don't make me pick you up, please.'

I still stand there, staring. They've only been gone forty-five minutes, they won't be back for hours yet. I can't leave him in there screaming. I put my hands in the pram and pick him up. I'm still thinking of my own baby. I wonder if my baby felt this heavy. He's doing a cute gurgly noise, like he's really grateful I picked him up. I sit down with him, still unsure what to do, and he is crying again. It normally means a few things when babies cry – feeding, changing or winding. He's not eaten yet so it can't be wind. I can't smell anything in his nappy so it must mean he's hungry. He starts to open his mouth towards my breasts. My breasts are so sore and they're leaking a liquid. I've heard that if you have milk in your breasts a crying baby can do that. I'm looking at the baby and thinking about how sore my boobs are and if he was to have a little of the milk it would take the pain away. Don't be silly, Kate, you can't breastfeed someone else's baby. Can you? David starts crying a bit more, he's getting really agitated. I undo my top and before I know it David is quite happily suckling away on my breast. Ah, that feels so much better, it's like my boob is deflating in front of my eyes. I think I'll change breast to relieve the other one. I know this is wrong, totally wrong, but I'm in so much pain and it's helping. He's stopped crying. Everyone is a winner, really, aren't they? He's really cute. I wonder if I could just take him instead of my own baby. At least he wasn't born the same way my baby was. My baby. It leaves a terrible feeling in my stomach when I think of him – that baby was part of me, this one isn't. I better pour his milk down the sink. I don't want Shelly coming home and wondering why he's not eating.

He's done a poo, I can smell it. I'll have to change his nappy. I do it and it's like I just know what to do, like it's second nature to me straight away. I bet I would have been a good mother to that baby.

My mum and Shelly eventually come back. 'Oh, how was he? Mummy missed you.' She picks up David and gives him a kiss. I wish I could kiss my baby.

'He was no bother, Shelly. I'll tell you what, why don't you two go out tonight, let your hair down. I'll watch the baby.'

'What, all night?'

'Yeah, why not? If you two want to have a party, go to yours, Shelly. And Mum – me and David will take your room.'

'Have you had a personality transplant or something?' says my mum.

It's not a personality transplant I've had, I'm not letting this baby go, no way. They decide to go out for the night.

I have the whole house to myself with David, as even Nick is out working till the early hours. First step, a bath.

I lay David down on his bath mat and start to undress him. His skin is so soft. As I put my face closer to him I can smell the most unbelievable scent. That scent is overpowering. The scent of a baby, I wonder if my baby has that scent. Is someone smelling my baby? I can feel the tears stinging my eyes as I think about someone else laying my beautiful baby down on a mat and taking in his scent. It should be me taking that scent in. I take my face out of David's neck as I seem to have buried it there and I stroke his belly. His skin is the softest thing I've ever felt. I close my eyes and imagine it's my baby's belly I'm stroking. I gently kiss his belly. I have this overwhelming feeling of love. I can still feel the tears stinging my eyes. When will this stop? When does the aching stop? I think about what Mike said about it just being my hormones and he's right, maybe the feeling will go away soon. After bath time it's bedtime. I put David in his basket as close to Mum's bed as possible so I can hear his gentle breathing all night long. I nurse him a few more times. I like the way it relieves the tension in my boobs and they do say breast is best, so I'm doing him a favour, really.

The following morning I take David back home. Shelly is so hungover that I feel guilty leaving him there. I stay for a little while so I can just look at him. Billy soon comes back and I notice he's rocking David in his chair. It looks a little rough to me and Shelly isn't saying anything, just too busy popping headache tablets. I grab a hold of Billy's arm to stop him. 'Not too hard, Billy, you don't want to hurt him.'

'It's OK Kate, it normally gets him off to sleep then I can sleep.'

I'm so annoyed with Shelly. How can she think that is OK? Billy is so wild he's even throwing his cars around the living room, if one of them hits David I think I'll smack Billy's behind like he should have had years ago.

On my way back home I think about Jennie. I've actually missed her so I make my way round to her house and knock on the front door.

Jennie opens the door. 'Oh, hello you, where have you been? You've been gone ages.'

'I just fancied a bit of a break, clear my head. Can I come in, please?'

'Yeah, I suppose so. I've missed you. I hate it when we fight but lately I feel like no matter what I do it's the wrong thing. I know you spend a lot of time with Mr Simpson and Mike, but I feel like you've forgotten about me.'

'Don't be daft, you're my best friend. I can't talk to Jimmy and Mike about periods and sex, can I?' She giggles at me, so I know I've won her round. 'Listen, how about we go to the club on Friday and I swing us a few drinks?'

'Yeah, OK.'

That's the thing with Jennie. I can worm my way around her. Just the same way Jimmy and Mike can worm their way around me. Maybe I'm not so different from them after all.

The flat should be ready soon, at least that's giving me something to look forward to. I'm still feeding David daily. I've had to buy a breast pump to make sure my milk doesn't dry up. I really think it's helping David, he has such a glow about him. Breastfeeding is so much better than bottle feeding.

'Kate, your flat's ready today, want to come and have a look?' Mike says.

'Oh, yes, I can't wait.'

Mike takes me round the flat. It's fabulous, it smells gorgeous, all clean and nice with new carpets. It has a lounge which leads you to the kitchen. He even had a new kitchen fitted for me so everything is brand new. At the back of the kitchen is the bathroom. It's only got one bedroom so it means Jennie will have to stay in my room if she sleeps over. He's right, the open fire is beautiful. I've never seen anything like it.

'I love it, Mike, I really do.'

'You can move in now if you like, everything is there ready for you. I made sure you had a new sofa, bed. Even tea towels. All you need to bring is your clothes. I hope I've thought of everything, if I've forgotten anything let me know.'

'It's perfect Mike, thank you so much.' I kiss Mike on the cheek, he really has done well with the flat. He's even put flowers in a vase for me.

I rush home as quickly as I can, this is just what I need – a new start.

'Right, Mum, the flat's ready. I'm off!'

'Off where? What are you talking about?'

'I'm moving, I told you that.'

'I thought you were joking. Oh, Kate, please don't leave me again. I hate not having anyone in the house.'

'But I told you I was going. Mike has sorted a flat for me and I'll still visit.'

I pack up my stuff. Shelly and baby David are there. She pulls everything out of his bag saying, 'Jesus, that's the thing with kids, you have to carry everything, including the kitchen sink.'

I want to say, 'Hey, I don't, if you breastfeed you only need nappies and wipes.' She pulls out a yellow book and places it on the table. I open it and it has David's full name and date of birth. It also has dates of when he's been weighed. I wonder if my baby has one of these. Who will fill his out for him? 'What's that, Shelly?'

'Oh, that's David's yellow book, it's like his bible, everything he does is in there from his weights to when he smiled, everything.'

'Ah, that's clever.'

I pack up my stuff while my mum looks on in disbelief.

'Oh, you're really off, then?'

'Yes, I told you I was getting my own place.'

'Well, what am I supposed to do for money? I can't afford this place and you've even got your room back now Nick has left.'

'Look, Mum, there's some money and you know I'll give you money if you need it, I'm only round the bloody corner.'

I hand her fifty quid.

'Well, can I have a bit more than that? I want to go out Saturday.'

'Jesus, Mum. Here, have this.'

I hand her another fifty quid. That's the thing with my mum. I really don't like her but I always make sure she's OK. She's just vulnerable, that's all. I'd actually kill anyone who hurt her.

Shelly stands up and puts her cup in the sink. 'I'm going as well. David is due a feed soon and I have no bottles left. I'll pack his stuff up.'

She starts to put David's belongings into his bag, and then starts to search for something, pulling everything out of her bag again. 'Hey, have you seen his yellow book, it was right here?'

'Crikey, Shelly, you would forget your head if it wasn't screwed on. It'll turn up,' says my mum.

'I know, I'm terrible at the minute. Think I still have that baby brain.'

'Shelly, I'll leave with you. I want to get settled in the flat before it gets dark.'

My mum looks a bit sad that I'm going but I can't stay here any longer. I know I'm not in the right frame of mind for it.

I get to my new flat and Mike is already there. I start unpacking my bags. Mike helps me.

'You'll be well happy here, I can feel it. I've made sure it was done up really nice for you. I'll get us a Chinese takeaway for your first night.'

As we eat our Chinese I think back to when we were in the cottage and how nice it was. I love it when we spend time together, just me and him. I suddenly come back to reality as his phone starts to ring, bloody Diane again.

'Well, I'm not at the club, am I? I'm settling Kate in. Oh, shut up, Diane, so what, I'm helping her, that's all. Listen, I'll talk to you when I get back, OK?'

'Trouble?' I ask with a smile on my face.

'Ah, it's you two. I don't know why you two can't get on.'

'Hey, it's not me, I don't give a shit about Diane.'

'Exactly, and she's the same with you,' he says, shaking his head. Then he looks around the room. 'So what do you think of your new flat, then?'

'I love it, I really do, thanks for sorting it. I really do appreciate everything you do for me, you know.'

'Yeah, I know you do. How are you feeling these days, after giving birth?'

I don't want Mike to ask me about the baby. I don't want to talk about it at all so I shrug my shoulders. 'I'm fine, like you said it was my hormones.' He holds my face. 'Good girl.'

Mike finally goes and I get settled.

I reach into my handbag and pull out *my* baby's yellow book and start to fill it in. Date of birth: 8/4/99 ... that can go for a start – 30/4/99. David Mason, and that. Oo, what can my baby be called? Mike. Nah, that's stupid. Lee. Nah, don't like that either. Hmm... George, yes George Reilly, that's a nice name. It's the same name that Mr and Mrs Richards called their son and he grew up to be a doctor. I bet my George will have a good job when he grows older. Well then, George, you're a bit of a pudding, aren't you? Oo, look, David smiled last week so in two weeks' time George can have his first smile. There's three weeks between them, after all. My George and his little yellow book.

Chapter 14 – The MMR Injection

Seven weeks – baby George has learnt to push himself up, like a press-up. He's going to take after Uncle Jimmy. I can tell.

I'm totally settled into the flat. I've taken to it like a duck to water. Mind you, I was pretty much looking after myself at my mum's anyway. I've always been pretty independent. Well, I had no choice really. I've started to spend a lot of time with David so it feels like I have my baby close to me. I'm not missing those precious milestones. I seem to be catching them pretty well.

My phone starts to ring and it's Jennie.

'Hello, trouble.'

'Kate, could you come to the salon today at 1 o'clock please? I've had a cancellation and I need to have it filled or my boss will go mental.'

'Don't be silly, it's not your fault you've had a cancellation. Plus if I go to the salon I'll have to pay. Can't you just come round to my place and do my hair or I'll come to your house?'

'Oh no, please come here.'

'But it will cost me.'

'I'll give you the money back. Please, Kate, I'm begging you.'

'OK, if it means that much to you.'

'It does, thanks Kate, I owe you one.'

I wonder what that was all about, surely her boss understands that people can cancel appointments? It's not Jennie's fault.

As I make my way in the door I can hear someone talking in a really nasty tone. 'You have to wash the cups and sweep the floor properly. You've left hair over there. Are you blind or something?'

Then I hear Jennie. 'I'm so sorry, Sarah, I'll sweep it again, I promise I will. It's just I was busy washing Mrs Evans's hair and Mrs Coleman was sitting right there so I thought it was rude to start sweeping round her feet.'

Is that Jennie's boss speaking to her like that? Jennie turns round and sees me.

'Hello, Kate, come in, let me take your coat.' Jennie starts to pull my coat off me.

'Jesus, Jennie, I can take my own coat off you know.'

'I know, but it's my job to hang your coat up.' She passes me a black cape. 'Put this on.'

I put the cape on and she takes me to a seat near some sinks. 'Thanks for coming in. I'm so glad you're here.' She then turns to Sarah who was shouting at her and says, 'Sarah, this is Kate Reilly, have I told you she's my best friend? It's the same Kate who Mr Simpson named the club after. Mr Simpson loves her, he'd do anything for her.' What on earth is making Jennie say things like that? I mean, I know she likes to brag but she's practically pushing it into Sarah's face and I'm sure once Jennie called me Kate Reilly, Sarah would know who I was. Why go on about Jimmy?

Sarah smiles at me and says, 'Oh yes, I know who she is. Are you OK, Kate?' I get the feeling Jennie is saying this to make sure that Sarah really knows I'm her friend. I wonder if Sarah gives Jennie a hard time.

Jennie washes my hair then says, 'Come over to these seats.' She sits me down in front of the mirrors. Then Sarah says, 'Jennie, offer Miss Reilly a cup of tea at least. Honestly, you have no idea about customer services, do you?'

Jennie looks a bit embarrassed. 'Sorry, Kate, I was so excited about you being here I forgot, can I get you a cup of tea?'

I take one look at Sarah and say, 'You're kidding, her tea tastes like shit, you make me one.'

Sarah looks taken aback. 'I don't make the tea, it's Jennie's job.'

I give Sarah the don't-mess-with-Kate-Reilly look and say, 'Not today, it isn't. I'm asking you to do it.'

Sarah looks like she's about to shit herself and goes round the back to make me a cup of tea. I look in the mirror and Jennie mouths 'thanks' to me.

I wink over at her. I hate the fact that someone is treating her like that. No wonder she insisted on me coming to the salon. I'm angry that she feels this way. I know I've done some horrible things to Jennie but that's me, it's different. I won't let someone else do it. I also feel a little hurt that she never just came out and asked me to do something. Sarah comes back with the tea. I stare at her again and say, 'I hope you're treating Jennie well. She's a really hard worker and worth a lot more than just making tea and sweeping up.'

I don't think she knows what to say, but looks at Jennie and says, 'Of course I treat her well. In fact, I was thinking about splitting all the tips with her from now on.'

Jennie finishes my hair and I leave the salon but it's really played on my mind that someone is treating Jennie badly. I hate that.

Three months – George has noticed his hands this week and can open and close them, he looks so cute. Mummy's little angel.

I like this whole parenthood feeling. As an added bonus, with all the breastfeeding, I've got my figure back pretty quickly.

I still want my baby. We'll be together one day and I'll show him the book and pretend to him that he was here all the time. But when I don't have baby David with me, I get my stomach cramps back. I really need to start thinking of filling up my days with something else. It's all very well working in the club with Jimmy but that's only a few nights a week. I thought about a part-time job doing something else but with no experience I'm not sure anyone would give me a job. The only other thing I could think about was going to university. It would help me get out and meet other people. I don't want to do the management course that I said I would. I quite fancy a software degree and I've always been good with computers. Plus Jimmy keeps going on about me getting more involved in the club, but he is so much better at being a club owner than I would ever be. If I did the management course he'd push me into doing more.

I head into Jimmy's office with a cup of tea to try and sweeten him up.

'Jimmy.'

'Yes, Treas.'

'Listen, I've been thinking for a while now, I fancy going to university.'

'Uni, what on earth would you want to go there for? It will be full of ponces. I'll show you more than any of those stupid lecturers.'

'Yeah, but I fancy doing a computer course.'

'Computers, what the hell would you want to do on them? Just stay here and get more involved in the club.'

'I just want to meet younger people, some more girls my age would be nice.'

'OK, I hear what you're saying.'

I wasn't expecting that. I thought he would have said no and for me to start working more seriously in the club.

Four months – baby George has had his first solid meal this month, he likes it – not as much as breast milk, but he definitely likes it.

It's my first day at uni and I'm a little nervous. It's like going back to school only your best friend is not there with you. Jennie is lucky, she works at the hairdressers and is pretty sorted in life with her perfect boyfriend, a job. Me, I'm still trying to figure out what to do.

As I make my way into the classroom there's one seat left. Oh no, the person sitting in the seat next to that one seat is only Paul,

Jennie's boyfriend. I've not seen him since I racially abused him. Hopefully he won't recognise me. As I sit down, he stares at me.

'Oh, you're Jennie's friend, aren't you? Well, you've lost a bit of weight. Are you sure you're all right sitting here? I won't poison you with my touch or anything like that, will I?'

'Listen, Paul, about that – I'm really sorry. I'd had a lot to drink and shouldn't have said those things. I'm really sorry.'

'Yeah, Jennie did say that you weren't racist and well, to be honest, I can't say anything bad about you, she snaps my head off.'

Paul's actually not a bad-looking man. We even go to lunch together.

The lecturer says I'm really good with computers and I have a real talent. I've started hacking into his computer, not that he knows. Well, I couldn't tell him that, could I? I'll tell you something else I've done, really clever, I've hooked up CCTV outside Mike's house and at the club. It means I can watch them whenever I like and if they're ever in trouble I can rush to their aid. I probably shouldn't watch it all night long though, it gets a bit tiring.

Six months – baby George has cut his first tooth, it upset him a little and his little cheeks were all red. Mummy gave him a get-better-soon kiss and he soon perked up.

Friday night, I'm off to Jennie's. She can't be bothered with the club this weekend. Very unlike her, she loves going to the club. Especially now it's Kate's Klub, she makes sure she tells everyone that she's Kate's best friend.

'Hey, Jennie.'

'Hello, you, how's uni? Paul says you're quite the teacher's pet. You always were a swot.'

'It's not my fault I'm a smarty-pants. If you'd have listened more in school instead of thinking about boys the whole time you'd have been the teacher's pet.'

'Oo, speaking of which, Paul is coming round tonight. You don't mind, do you?'

'No, I like Paul, he's OK.'

'I'm glad you've said that. Listen, you know about a year ago when we were going to do the whole threesome thing?'

'Yeah.'

'Would you be up for it? Please, Paul really likes you.'

'Not really sure about that, Jennie, to be honest with you.'

'Oh, come on, Kate, when was the last time you even had sex?'

Come to think of it, it was with her. If I say no will she guess I was raped?

'Well, we'll have a few drinks and see what happens.'

'OK then, we'll see.'

We all start to drink vodka, I take a huge gulp in the hope that all my fears of Paul being a brown boy will disappear. I couldn't bear anything else happening to me. Paul suggests spin the bottle. So he'll spin the bottle and whoever it lands on has to kiss him, then it's Jennie's turn, then mine. He spins it first and it lands on Jennie. Thank God for that. They kiss, it's Jennie's turn to spin the bottle and – thank God, again – it lands on Paul, so they kiss again. Now it's my turn, bloody hell I hope it lands on Jennie, not sure I want to kiss Paul. Luckily it does. Me and Jennie kiss.

'Woo, look at you two sexy mothers out there,' shouts Paul excitedly. He's talking more gangstery than Mike and Jimmy. He grabs the bottle and spins it. Oh no, it's landed on me. I have to kiss him and he's brown and a boy. I'm worried sick, what if I die or get raped again. Come on Kate, don't be silly, nothing will happen to you. I don't even want to kiss anyone, never mind Paul. I've only ever kissed Mike and Jennie. I take another huge gulp of my vodka. He grabs my head and moves my face close to his and puts his lips on mine. Ugh, he stuck his tongue in. I wasn't expecting that.

'Oo, let's have a three way kiss,' he shouts out, so I go along with whatever they say. They know more about this stuff than me. I never even knew you touched someone in their intimate places until Mike did it. I nearly died when he did. We all kiss each other and they seem to be really enjoying it. Me, on the other hand, I wish I could fight him or something. I'd be OK then.

'Jennie, suck Kate's tits, go on,' says Paul. I can't let that happen, the milk will come out.

'No way. I'll suck Jennie's, I'm a better sucker then her.'

Well, that got me out of that, but now I have to suck Jennie's boobs. I start to suck Jennie's boobs. I'm not even sure what I'm supposed to suck so I just go for the nipple. How have I got myself in this mess? The next thing I know Paul pulls his trousers down and stands over Jennie. I get such a shock when I see his dick. It's quite big and I've never actually looked at one close up. During the rape I was screaming so I couldn't take much in. Then when me and Mike did it we were under covers. I feel so vulnerable looking at it. Yet Jennie is loving it, she giggles then places it in her mouth letting out a moan as she does. I watch for a little while and see Paul pull Jennie off him. He looks at her, then nods my way. Jennie then looks at me and says, 'Kate, you have a try.' Oh my God, she wants me to suck his dick. No way can I suck that. What on earth do I say? Before I know it he has shoved it in my mouth. I'm not even sure what to do with it. Should I hold it there? Paul says, 'Suck it harder, Kate.' Oh no, I don't want to suck it at all, never mind harder.

After a few moments he then pulls it out, thankfully, but then he starts to open my trousers. Jennie moves towards me and pulls down my trousers. She kisses my vagina through my knickers while slipping her fingers inside me. I then feel Paul's tongue inside of me. Then he moves his fingers inside and him and Jennie start to kiss. Paul grabs my knickers and pulls them off. 'That looks tasty.' He buries his face into me. Jennie comes towards me and starts to kiss me. She grabs my hand and places it inside her knickers. 'Put your finger in me, Kate.' I put my finger inside her. She then pulls Paul away from me saying, 'Don't forget about me,' so he starts to lick her out, while grabbing my boobs. Paul gets up and goes on his knees. 'Right, who's first?'

'Me, obviously,' says Jennie and she positions herself so she is on her knees but bending over. 'Come here, Kate, I'll pleasure you while he pleasures me.' I move my body towards her, lying on my back with my legs open ready for Jennie to 'pleasure' me. Little does she know I'm hating every minute of this.

I'm lying on my back and I dare not even look at the image of what is happening in front of me. I can hear those two moaning with pleasure and feel Jennie's tongue inside me. It feels like the more rough he is with her, the more rough she is with me. Like they are getting so turned on by each other. Yet I'm not turned on at all. I just want this to stop. I manage to open my eyes and look at them. He has this great big smile on his face. Jennie then comes up from licking me out and her smile is equally big. I wish I'd never looked now.

'Paul, give Kate some.' Oh no, why did you say that? I don't want any. Please, I really don't want anything. Jennie lies near my head and opens her legs. 'Lick me out, Kate.' She grabs my head and my whole body twists. She forces my head so my face is in her vagina. It feels so wet and has a much stronger odour today than last time. It tastes disgusting. I feel Paul grabbing me from behind to lift up my bum. Then I feel his dick go in me. I want it out, I hate this. He is pushing himself so hard inside me. Jennie then grabs my hair, pushing me into her vagina even harder while moaning, 'Oh Kate, that's nice.' I feel like I want to grab her hand off me and get myself up for some air. I can't breathe. Oh no, how can I stop this? Well, I can't really, can I?

'Jennie, I'm going to cum,' Paul shouts, which makes her pull me off her and she starts to laugh and says, 'Well wait for me.' The next thing I see is so disgusting it makes me feel sick. She sucks his dick and lets him cum in her mouth, she has saliva and cum dripping down her chin. 'Jennie turns to me and says, 'Eat it off my chin, Kate.'

There is no way I'm doing that, I'm drawing the line now. 'Don't be disgusting, Jennie, I'm not eating that.' Paul then says, 'It's only bodily fluids, baby face. I will.' Then he starts to eat it off her chin and they kiss each other like it's funny. Those two are disgusting. I don't care what anyone says, that's not normal. He's lucky I never punched him for calling me baby face.

'Did you enjoy that, Kate?' says Paul.

'Yeah, yeah, Paul, it was the best.'

God, what is Jennie doing with someone like that? It's like she wants to do anything to please him. But, to be honest, I'm no better. I did that to please Jennie.

Paul wants me to stay the night and we're fumbling around again in the bedroom. Goodness, do they not get sick of this? After a while I fall asleep.

I wake up and wonder where I am. It takes me a while to get my bearings and as I roll over in bed, Jennie is on top of Paul. They're like rabbits, those two.

'Don't worry, gorgeous, you can go after her,' Paul says in a really dirty voice, like I should think he's something special.

I give him the dirtiest look, get my clothes on and say, 'Jennie, I'll catch you later.' I go back and have a shower. Not only can I smell the dirty-hand smell on my face, I stink of sex now. Sex is disgusting. Especially the things they did to each other last night.

Seven months old – baby George is holding a two-handled cup now and he's been crawling. He's so clever.

I wake up and the first thing on my mind as usual is David. I might go over and see him later. As I make my way into the kitchen I see the dishes left over from last night in the sink and don't want the flat getting on top of me the way the house gets on top of Mum. I want to keep it nice and tidy. What's that phrase? Tidy house, tidy mind. Crickey, it would take every housemaid in the world to tidy my mind. I start to fill the sink with water and hear a knock on the door. Great, it's Mum, what does she want? Money, no doubt.

'Mum, I gave you fifty quid only yesterday, you can't have spent it already.'

'Don't be nasty, Kate, I've not come for money. I wanted to see you.'

'What for?'

'What do you mean, what for? You're my daughter, I wanted to see you. Why wouldn't I? Just let me in.'

She barges past me. I bet she does want money. She takes a seat in the living room. 'Wow, Kate, it's still really pretty in here. It even still smells all fresh and new. How are you finding living alone?'

'It's fine, I quite like it.'

'I get a bit lonely sometimes. Especially at night. I can lie awake for hours.'

'I sleep like a baby every night, my mattress is so soft.'

'Actually, Ronnie is going to buy me a new mattress. He says mine has springs sticking out of it.'

'Why is Ronnie doing that and how does he know what your mattress feels like?'

'Oh Kate, don't go on at me please.'

'Are you sleeping with Ronnie? Please don't say you are.'

'Kate, I've worked for him for years, he's good to me. He used to be really good to me when you were little. I'd always get extra shifts near your birthday or Christmas.'

'Yeah, but what did you have to do for those extra shifts? He's a married man and a pervert. Mum, please don't put yourself in a position where you sleep with him because you depend on his money. I'll give you money. Just ask.'

'Be careful there, Kate, I might start to think you care about me.' She gives me a little grin. Like she's joking.

'I do care, actually.'

'Well, you have a funny way of showing it. Plus I can't always keep asking you for money all the time. You're my daughter, it should be the other way around. Let's have a cup of tea and forget about it.'

I make us both a cup of tea. As I look at my mum sitting on the sofa she looks like a child. I hate the fact these men abuse her vulnerability in that way. I'll punch that Ronnie when I see him. My mum is the prettiest woman in Bridgeborough, how she couldn't find someone who would look after her and treat her like a princess I'll never know. Mind you, she probably did but cheated on them and they left her.

She leaves soon after and she didn't ask me for money. I wonder if she did just come round to see me, or thought better of it as I suppose I did bring it up the minute I opened the door to her.

I quickly finish the dishes and head over to see Shelly. 'Shelly, can I take David for the day tomorrow? It will give you a good break.'

'I would love that. I really appreciate all the help you give me with David. You forget how hard it is, especially with Billy.'

'Listen, why don't I take him for the weekend? That will give you loads of time to yourself.'

'Oh no, I can't expect you to do that.'

'No, you can, it's fine. I like spending time with David. Honestly, me and him will have a great time. Plus, I'm not being funny, but we could go on holiday and be charged baggage allowance for your eyes.'

'I know, David's not sleeping very well, then Billy wants to be up early. I never stop half the time.'

'Listen, I'll come over tomorrow to collect some of David's things. He's practically my nephew anyway. I'll even bring him back once you've dropped Billy off at school. I could even keep him some of Monday, if you like, then you can put your feet up all on your own.'

'You're amazing.' Shelly kisses me on the cheek.

So that's it then. I get to spend the whole weekend with my baby George. I'm going to have so much fun, I can't wait. I rush straight round to Shelly's the next morning, wanting to pick up my George.

'Look at him. He looks so cute in his bobble hat,' I say in my babyish voice that I seem to have acquired since spending so much time with David. I pick him up and kiss him on the cheek. His skin is so soft. I can smell him and he always greets me with a smile. I think he knows deep down I'm really his mum. Shelly passes me all of his things, even bottles. I feel like throwing them back in her face and saying, 'We won't be needing them, breastfed babies don't need bottles.'

I take him back over to my flat ready for breakfast. My boobs are going to explode if I don't get him fed soon. Expressing milk is never the same as breastfeeding.

'After breakfast let's take you to the park, my little angel.'

We make our way to the park and pass Mike on the way.

'Hey, where you off to?' He looks in the buggy. 'You got that baby again? She hung over again, I take it?'

'No, she needs a bit of a break, that's all. Maybe you should take your son once in a while and help her out. You know your Billy can be a bit of a handful.'

'Hey, I have Billy nearly every weekend, you know that.'

'Yeah, but it takes more than that to be a dad. Plus, you're at the club Friday and Saturday night so, in actual fact, *Diane* has Billy nearly every weekend. You should help out a bit more.'

'Oo, get you, Miss Mother of the Year.'

'You being funny?'

'No, shit, I'm sorry, I never meant that. I'm sorry, really.'

'Yeah, well, we're headed to the park, do you want to come? You can push me on the swings, if you like?'

'Nah, I've got to go over to the club, Jimmy wants something. Pop in on your way back if you like.'

'Yeah, I might do.'

As we make our way into the park there are some mothers sitting on the bench, chatting.

'No, I don't think I'll get it done. I mean, I don't want the baby having autism or anything like that,' one woman says. Then another one says, 'What? Both my kids had it and they're both fine.'

'What are you ladies chatting about?' I interrupt them.

'Oh, look at him, how cute is he? He looks just like Mummy as well,' one of the women says, looking at David in the buggy. The feeling I got when she said that…

'Yes, well, some people say he's like his dad. He has his temper, mind.'

One of the women asks, 'What's his name?'

'He's called George.'

'That's a lovely name. What are you going to do then?'

'About what?'

'The MMR injections.'

'Well, George has a couple of months to go before I start to think about that. Why? What's the problem with it?'

'Well, they say it brings on autism in kids, so I think I'll give it a miss.'

One of the women, who looks a little older than the others, says, 'Oh give over, you. Honestly, darling, both my kids had it and they're fine.'

I love all this talking to mothers in the local park, them saying George looks just like me. I could do this forever. I wonder what would happen if I took David away? I bet Shelly wouldn't even miss him. She's too tired to be bothered with him half the time. After a few goes on the swing and a few turns on the slide it's time to make our way back home. It'll be dinner time soon.

I get back to the flat and give David his dinner and his breast milk and he soon goes off for his afternoon nap. My mind starts to wonder whether this is what it's like. It's a total doddle, I could easily do this with my eyes closed. Shelly, indeed, what a bloody moron she is and maybe if she tried to discipline Billy once in a while he might settle down. I do hope George doesn't behave like him and get into trouble at school. He needs a proper mum, like me. David soon wakes up and there he is, smiling away at me from his travel cot. He loves me, I know he does.

'Hello, handsome, shall we take you to see Uncle Jimmy?' I take him round to the club and Jimmy is quite smitten with him. He's a little heartbreaker is my George.

'So you not coming to the club tonight then if you're babysitting?'

'Nah, thought I'd give it a miss, Shelly needs the break.'

'It won't be the same without you.'

'Hmm, you'll cope, I'm sure.'

'Anyway, get that baby out of here. It's no place for a baby in a club like this. Unless he wants one of my good-time girls that is. That'll put a smile on your face, young 'un,' Jimmy says while tickling David's belly.

'Oh, don't talk to him like that, he'll never have a good-time girl. He wants a wife, a proper one, to look after him.'

'Listen to you, getting all gooey-eyed over a baby. I hope you're not getting any ideas, young lady. You're far too young for a baby, Kate.'

'Don't be silly, I don't want a baby. Like you say, I'm far too young.' If only Jimmy knew. 'Right, I'm off, you behave tonight and no fighting.'

As I walk back over to my flat I keep thinking about the fact I have to give David back on Monday and I really don't want to. Shelly is a shit mother anyway. Mike's right, she's always hungover. I bet she'd not miss him if we went. We could get the train somewhere. Yes, that's a good idea.

'Does Georgie-Porgie want to go on the train with Mummy-whummy?'

I grab him and kiss him, taking in his scent again. I can't believe I'm missing all of this with my own baby. I'll never get it back again. It's all very well writing it in a yellow book, which isn't even my bloody book, it's Shelly's. I wish I could take him away or maybe if I even asked Shelly nicely she might give me him. No, don't be silly, Kate, she'd never do that.

The following morning David wakes up smiling over at me as usual and the thought of giving him up is killing me.

'Right, that's it, David. Me and you are going to live together forever. Would you like that? I know a lovely little cottage.'

I collect all of David's things. I pick him up and place him in his pushchair, kissing him on his cheek. 'We'll be together forever.' He gives me a laugh while tugging on my hair. 'Yes, forever, that's it. You like the idea of that too.' See, he wants to come, that's why he's laughing. I push his pushchair towards the train station. I'm shaking so much, it's a good job the chair is holding me up. I can't believe I'm doing this. I'm actually stealing someone else's baby.

Well, it's not really stealing, not if you're going to make a better life for him. I mean, that Shelly is a total moron, always has been. David loves me much more than he loves her and he wants to come, he smiled and pulled on my hair to prove it. We'll go to the cottage and one day we'll meet the real baby George and those two could be brothers. I get to the train station and go to the ticket office and the lady says, 'Good morning, madam, where are you off on your travels today?'

I stand there looking at her. I can't even say the words. They just won't come out. I shake my head and say, 'Nowhere, I'm fine thanks,' and walk away. That was a totally stupid idea. I'd be arrested for taking a baby without asking.

I go down to David's level and say, 'Not today David, maybe some other time.' He responds by laughing and tugging my hair. Hmm, maybe he never wanted to come, maybe he just likes laughing and tugging hair.

I take David home. I think I'll give Mike a call, see if he wants to go out on Friday night. I could do with some cheering up.

'Hey, Mike, you OK?'

'Yeah, what's happening?'

'Not much. Listen, fancy taking the night off from the club on Friday and coming out with me, have a few drinks, relax a bit?'

'Why? Not like you.'

'Ah, you know, I feel a little lonely once David goes home.'

'Kate, are you sure it's healthy you spending that much time with him? I mean, I know how you were after your baby and wanted to go back for him as we drove away from the hospital.'

'Yeah, I'm fine with all that. I want to help Shelly out, that's all.'

Chapter 15 – The Open Fire

After a long week at university, it's finally Friday night. I make my way over to the club in a dressed-to-kill outfit. I'm really going to let off some steam tonight. As I get there Mike has already had a few drinks and is on his merry way. He asks me if I want to dance with him. We've never done this for ages. Everything with us two has been so serious lately and it's nice for us to let our hair down a little. I quite like drunk Mike, I forget how funny he is.

At the end of the night, when everyone has left, we come running out of the club. Mike comes towards me and grabs me, putting his hand right across my cheek.

'God, Kate, you look gorgeous tonight.'

And then he kisses me. What is he doing? I'm kissing him back and it feels really nice. I have this funny feeling in my belly. Next thing I know, he's hitching up my dress and undoing his trousers. He's having sex with me against the wall. I've never seen him like this before. I liked the kissing but I don't like the feeling of sex so I close my eyes really tight in the hope it's over as quick as it started. He finally finishes and pulls up his trousers and kisses me again, saying, 'Come on, let's get you home.' He grabs my hand and we walk to the taxi rank.

Maybe the threesome has put a sparkle in my eyes or something.

'OK, then.' I'm not sure what else to say.

I wake up thinking about Mike and what we did last night. In my head, I've got us married. I mean, well, not straight away, he'll have to tell Diane first. Mike walks into my flat.

'God, my head, what on earth were we drinking last night?'

'God knows, but you were really necking them back.'

'Listen, Gem, can I talk to you?'

Oh yes! This is going to be it, he's finally going to propose, just what I've always hoped for.

'What is it?'

'About last night. I'm sorry. I should never have done that to you and especially in a back alley. I'm really sorry, can we forget about it?'

'Yeah, course we can.' I'm totally disheartened, but I'm not going to show him that. 'Listen, we were both drunk. Forget about it, yeah.'

'Thanks, is it breakfast time yet? I'm starving.'

I cook us both breakfast, but my mind is still wondering back to the sex last night. He must have fancied me to do that, surely?

It's been a month since me and Mike had sex. Things are back to normal with us. There's no embarrassment or anything, it's like it never happened. I wonder if he does that a lot. Has sex with girls then makes an excuse that he was pissed up.

I'm back at uni and sitting next to Paul. I'd like to say things are back to normal there, but that's not true. Me and him really got on before the threesome but since then I think of him in a different way. I wish I'd never done it. Sex always makes me go a little funny. Well, it's no surprise really, is it?

I'm tired today. I sat up all night watching Mike on the CCTV. I could watch him 24/7 and never get bored. Not that I can see much once he goes back into the house and switches the light off. As I sit at my seat and take off my coat, Paul seems in a jolly mood for some reason.

'Hello, Miss Reilly, what are you up tonight?'

'Nothing much, why?'

'Well, I would like to take you out.'

'What are you on about?'

'Me and you – let's go out.'

'What on earth do you mean, let's go out? What, you mean with Jennie?'

'No, me and you, like on a date.'

'I'm not going out on a date with you.'

'Why not?'

'Because I don't want to.'

'I'll make you breakfast,' Paul says in a really girly voice.

'Paul, I won't be needing breakfast off you, go away.'

'Why, what is it? Was it the sex?' He giggles.

'No, the sex was fine.'

'Oh no, it *was* the sex.'

'No, it wasn't.'

'Oh my God, it's the sex, do I give bad sex?' He's smiling and teasing me. 'Because, you know, if it was the sex, then as an independent woman it's your duty to teach me how to do it properly. Think of all the women you would be stopping from getting bad sex if you were to show me. You would be doing my future women a favour.' I giggle back at him, he's really quite funny. 'Come with me to that little Italian on the corner, I'll treat you to a nice romantic meal. Just once, that's all I'm asking.'

'No, Paul, absolutely not.'

What on earth is Paul's problem? I wonder if Jennie knows he's like that. Maybe I should tell her. Mind, she thinks he's so bloody perfect she's always rubbing it in my face, the things she has. Boyfriends and cars. I still have my moments with her. I sometimes wish my life was simple, like hers.

It's finally the weekend. I'm going to Jennie's as she is full of cold. She's upset because she can't come to the club tonight.

When she opens the door she looks like death warmed up. 'Here, I got you some oranges for Vitamin C and I never had any paracetomol so I grabbed some Calpol.'

'Calpol? I'm a grown woman, I don't have Calpol. Why have you even got Calpol in the house?'

'It's David's and he seems to like it.'

Jennie puts the Calpol on a spoon. 'Wow that brings back total memories, here have some.'

I put some on the spoon and take a sip. It's so funny how a little thing like a taste can take you back years and give you feelings you forgot about. It reminds me of being sick on the sofa and Mum taking care of me.

Once Jennie falls asleep I leave her there to make my way to the club. As soon as I get there I see Paul making a beeline for me.

'Hey, gorgeous, can I buy you a drink?'

'Yeah, OK then, if you must.'

'Jennie is still not well, she has a cold so I'm here all on my lonesome, so you'll have to take care of me.'

'I don't think you need anyone to take care of you, Paul. You're fine on your own.'

We have a few drinks and I feel a little tipsy by the end of the night.

'Kate, where is the best place round here for a kebab?'

'The one on the corner, come with me, I'm going anyway.'

Once we get our food I spot a taxi waiting outside so I get in it, the next thing I know he's jumped in with me. I try to push him out.

'No, Paul, you're not coming.'

'The least you can do is offer me a place to eat my kebab. I'll go home straight away, I promise.'

We get back to mine and he asks if I have anything else to drink. I do have some vodka and before I know it we've drunk half a bottle of that stuff. I can't remember much after that, but I wake up and we're both naked in my bed. Shit, I've drunkenly slept with my best friend's boyfriend. I don't know what's got into me lately, but I seem to be drinking more and this is a lot of sex I've had in a short space of time, especially to say I don't really care that much for it.

I practically throw Paul out of my flat. I feel so awful about myself but one thing that always cheers me up is David. I head straight over to Shelly's.

'Hey, Shelly, can I steal Precious for an hour or so?'

'Yeah, no bother, he loves his Auntie Kate. I'm shattered. Billy is having my life this morning.'

'I can have David overnight, if you like. I don't mind, it will give you a rest. I'll tell you what as well, I'll get on to Mike to have Billy tonight so you can refuel.'

'Oh thanks, you're a star.'

I get David home and snuggle him in on the sofa. I like the closeness of him near me when breastfeeding but, because of all the alcohol I drank last night I better not breastfeed him. I don't think I'll ever get sick of cuddling my baby. I love him.

'Baby George, that's who you are,' I whisper in his ear and pull him closer to me. We spend the whole night together. I wish George was here and I would never have to hand him over. I could cuddle him on the sofa as many times as I like.

It's Thursday and nearly time for the weekend again. I love the weekend. I do have to get through uni today first, though. As I get to class I see a note on the door telling us the lecturer is off sick so class has been rearranged for tomorrow. Paul has a good idea to hit the student bar round the corner.

'Great idea, Paul, let's go.'

That bar is so cheap, it's buy one get one free all day till 5pm, so we can get drunk on next to no money. I like the student life. Plus, I feel a lot more relaxed around Paul when I've had a drink. Maybe the drinking helps me to forget the things that have happened to me.

'So then, Paul, what's the secret to a good relationship? You seem to have Jennie wrapped around your little finger.'

'Well, it's a case of keeping them keen by treating them mean.'

'Ha! Liar, you must treat Jennie like a princess. She's always talking about you and how great you are.'

'Nah, I'm only kidding. I like Jennie. I like to spoil her with little gifts and things. Don't you have a boyfriend?'

'Me? No.'

'Before we slept together the other week I had you down as a lesbian and thought maybe I annoyed you because you fancied Jennie.'

'Ha! Me, fancy Jennie? You're kidding, aren't you? I think she fancies me, she's the one who convinced me to have the threesome. It's not even something I would have ever contemplated doing.'

'What about them two blokes you're always knocking around with?'

'What about them?'

'You seeing either of them? Ever had a threesome with them two?'

'Er, no way, I'd never sleep with Jimmy. I've slept with Mike a couple of times, but never Jimmy. It would be like sleeping with my dad, yak.'

'How the hell have you got in with them two?'

'I've known them since I was a kid really. It surprises me you don't know who they are. I thought everyone knew who they were.'

'I've heard about them but I never grew up in Bridgeborough so it's just gossip I've heard really. Isn't Mike a bit old for you?'

'He's only twenty-six which, yeah, I suppose that is a bit old but not *really* old, not like dead old. Jimmy, he's dead old, he's thirty. I mean, you may as well be dead if you're thirty.'

We carry on drinking and before I know it, it's happened again. I wake up in bed naked with my friend's boyfriend. What on earth is happening to me? I can't even remember the sex.

We sit at the kitchen table having breakfast.

'Sorry about the toast, Paul, it's a little burnt, but it's the only bread I've got left till I go shopping.'

'It's OK, I don't mind it burnt. It's a little bit like my skin, eh?'

'Yeah, just a little.' I giggle. 'Does it ever bother you that you're not white?'

'Not now it doesn't, but when I was younger it did. Kids at school, you know, you could get a lot of stick for it. One of the dinner ladies at our school said, "Hurry up and get outside, the sun is shining, you'll all have lovely brown skin after today." So me and my friends had a great idea that if they would turn brown then I would turn white so we decided to strip me naked and I sunbathed round the back of the school all dinner time thinking I would turn white like them. Imagine a little six-year-old Paul with his todger out.'

'Paul, you're so funny.' I start laughing at him again.

'Yeah, well, it's true and if you can't beat them, join them.'

I hear a key turning the lock in the door. Oh my God, it's Mike, what is he doing here? He comes in and sees Paul. I quickly stand up. I'm in my dressing gown and Paul is in his underwear. It doesn't take a genius to work out what has gone on. I'm expecting him to go back out of the door and have words with me later about sleeping with my best friend's boyfriend but he barges over to Paul and grabs him by the throat.

'Mike, what the hell are you doing?' I scream.

'What are you doing, you fucking pervert? Does Jennie know you're here? No, I bet she fucking doesn't!' Mike is yelling in Paul's face.

Paul panics. Knowing Mike's reputation I think anyone would panic when Mike Taylor has his hands around your throat. 'Listen, please, I'm going.'

'Oh, yeah, you're not wrong there, you dirty little bastard, you're going all right.'

I grab Mike's hands and shout, 'Oh, Mike, get off him!' The next thing I know Mike has punched Paul in the face. I'm screaming at the top of my voice, 'What the hell are you doing? Don't do that!'

Mike continues to punch him. I'm trying to pull him off Paul but he has that look in his eye, exactly how I remember it with Roger. He is punching and punching. I'm trying to push him off but nothing is working. It's almost like Mike is in another world and can't hear or feel anything. Paul has fallen to the ground and

Mike is stamping on his head.

'Get off him! I mean it, Mike, get off him, you're going to kill him.'

Mike is shoving me and going back for more with Paul.

'No, Mike, please, no!' I'm screaming at him to stop. 'Please leave him alone, leave him alone.'

Mike finally stops. I think it's because he's worn himself out. There's blood all over the place, including all over me and Mike and my walls. I look down at Paul and I can't believe what I'm seeing.

'You've killed him, you've fucking killed him.'

'Yeah, well, he was asking for it.' Mike is panting and he looks fierce.

'No, no, he wasn't asking for that, you've killed him. I don't believe it. Listen, we're going to have to call an ambulance, they might revive him.' I say this in a panicked voice.

'Don't be stupid, Kate, he's dead and I wouldn't want him revived anyway, he's a dirty little pervert.'

'How can you say that? He's dead, he's lying here in my flat, dead. We have to tell someone, we have to call the police. I'll just say I went to the shop and came back and he was there, dead.'

'You can't call the police, it won't take long before they put two and two together. Have you got a suitcase?'

'A suitcase? What for, are we leaving?'

'No, you silly cow, we're going to have to put him in it and dump the body.'

'What? I can't do that. No, we have to tell someone, please, let's call someone. Call Jimmy, ask him what to do.'

'We don't need Jimmy for this, now go and get a suitcase.'

I go into the bedroom and get a suitcase, shaking all the way. What has he done? Why did he do that? He's killed a man in my flat, not just any man – my best friend's boyfriend. Oh, Jennie, what on earth do I say to Jennie? As I come back out of the bedroom with the suitcase Mike has Paul's phone in his hand.

'Look, you weren't the only one, there was also a Debbie and a

Louise. He's a dirty bastard, who deserved everything he got.'

'Not that though, Mike, please let me call someone.'

Paul's body looks horrible, it's just lying there in a heap. Whenever you think of a dead body you think of it lying in a coffin, not lying all bloodied and battered in my front room. His face has a really frightened look on it. That's how he died, frightened to death. Well battered to death really, but by the look on his face I think it was mixed with shock.

Mike passes me Paul's mobile phone. 'Throw that in the fire, we don't want the phone traced to here.'

I throw the phone in the fire. There has been more evidence thrown into that bloody open fire than there has logs. I'm sure that's the only reason he bought the flat.

'Go get some black sacks, we'll have to line the suitcase in case any blood seeps out.'

'Blood seeps out? It's all over my flat, Mike. Please, I don't like looking at him, can we get rid of him?'

'Yeah, we will, but you'll have to clean the blood up first, go get some talcum powder and water in a bowl and make up a paste.'

'Why?'

'Because if we pour the talcum powder paste over the blood it lifts the stain when you scrub it.'

'What? How do you know what will clean up blood?'

'Don't ask me that, just fucking do it.'

'Don't swear at me. I never did it, you did.'

'The carpet will have to come up as well, you'll have to throw it into the fire. I'll get you a new one.'

I can't believe Mike is saying this. Does he not feel any guilt or remorse whatsoever? He's killed a man in cold blood. We both pick up Paul to lift him into the lined suitcase and I feel a mouth full of vomit. I want to scream at Mike, why did he do that? Why would someone kill another person and why is his body so heavy? Mike folds Paul's arm to stop it from sticking out of the case. But he can't fit it all the way in. He grabs Paul's arm and snaps it which makes me even more queasy. I zip up that case as quickly as I can and put it to one side while we clean up the blood. Mike tells me to go into the shower and take the bleach with me.

'Wash your face, it's covered in blood, and bleach your hands, scrub right under the nails with a scrubbing brush in case there's the tiniest speck under there.'

'What is happening here, Mike? How the hell are you so calm? How many people have you killed? Because you're taking this very lightly to say you've just beaten a man to death then, not content with that, you have to snap his arm for good measure. You scare me when you're like this.'

'Don't be scared of me, be scared of you. After all, you were the one shagging your best friend's bloke, not me. You've helped me load him into a suitcase and you've helped me clean up the mess. You're also the one to help me drop him into the river.'

'I'm not doing that, no way.'

'Yeah, you are, and think about this – all this, it's your mess so think on before you start shagging another pervert.'

'I knew I'd get the blame. I never asked you to come round. I never even wanted you to come round. Why do you turn everything around so it's me?'

'Look, Kate, I'm not arguing with you, just get in the shower will you, before I beat *you* to death.'

I go to the shower and scrub between my nails. My thoughts are going back out to Jennie, what the hell do I say to her? I keep having an image of Paul lying there. It was the worst thing I've ever seen, his eyeballs were as wide as anything, like a shocked cat. I always thought dead people's eyes should be closed. Maybe I should have closed them before I put him in the case. I also think about how heavy his body was. Pardon the pun, but it was a dead weight. Anyone who thinks they need bricks to weigh down the suitcase is totally wrong. If we went through an airport I'm sure it would have a 'Caution: Heavy' sticker stuck to it. God, how on earth am I supposed to help dump a body into a river? I get out of the shower and Mike jumps in.

'Go get me a T-shirt and trousers and burn these clothes.'

Fire's getting well fed today, what with mobile phones, carpet, and clothes. We wait until it starts to get dark outside so we have less chance of anyone seeing us. We drag the suitcase down the stairs and manage to lift it into the car. We're driving towards the river, not one of us having spoken to each other yet. I wonder what must be going on in Mike's head. If anything is going on, that is.

'We need to pick a spot where no one will be, so we'll drive further down by the valley. Cheer up, it could be worse – it could be you in that case.' Mike says this while giggling, as if this is totally normal.

'It's not bloody funny. What am I going to say to Jennie, eh? She's going to be devastated.'

'You're not going to say anything to Jennie, you just act like normal. She'll think he's gone off and left her. It's his mother we should be worried about, she'll report him missing and the police will want to know his whereabouts and who he was last with. So you better hope no one saw you in any pubs or clubs you two went to last night.'

'We never went anywhere last night, just to mine. We were in the student bar during the day but there were a few people there and it's pretty normal for students to sit in a student bar anyway.'

'Oh yeah, God forbid if the perv was to buy you a drink from a proper bar or show you a good time last night.'

'Oh, shut up, Mike, you're such a dick.'

'I'm a dick? Do you see me sharing my bed with my best friend's bird? No, even I've got standards, not like you.'

Mike stops the car, it's an area which is concealed by bushes. He points out a wooden bridge. 'If we walk halfway across the bridge the water is deeper there.'

I can't even bring myself to speak to Mike, never mind to help him decide poor Paul's final resting place. We grab the suitcase from the boot and wheel it over the bridge. It's so cold and dark I really feel I'm part of a horror story. I'm glad for the darkness, I couldn't bear to be seen by anyone. I still can't get over the weight of it. We throw the suitcase into the water and it bobs for a little while then starts to go down. I go to get back in the car and Mike pulls me back.

'Wait, we need to make sure it definitely stays down.'

I look at him as if to say, You have definitely done this before, I know you have. There's no way you would know that the suitcase might come back up, why would it? I get back into my flat and I can't believe what has happened. If only my lecturer had turned up at uni none of this would have happened. Paul is dead, gone, just like that. How can someone start a day off so normally to have it end in such a violent way? I start to think of the rape again and think *that* day started off normally and look what happened then. I think I better wash my face. I can smell their hands.

As I lie in bed I can't sleep a wink. I wonder what Jimmy's doing. I'll check the CCTV, see if I can see him. I can't see the point sometimes. I can't hear them, only see them entering or leaving the club. I finally stop watching at 4am and go to bed. No one is going to be going in or out of the club now, even Jimmy drove home an hour ago and he's normally last to leave. Even Mike's house is quiet, they went to bed half an hour ago. Sometimes I might catch one of them going to the toilet. I can tell they're going to the toilet because the light switches on.

I don't want to go back to bed. Everytime I close my eyes I see poor Paul's face. I think about his broken arm. I don't know why that is playing on my mind so much, his whole face was broken yet I really wish Mike hadn't broke his arm. Maybe it's guilt eating away at me for the fact I never stopped it. I just screamed at Mike. I should have grabbed him, hit him, broke his arm then he couldn't have hit him any more.

Morning has finally arrived and just as I'm getting angry at Mike he walks in the door.

'Morning, get the kettle on, Gem.'

'Get the kettle on, is that all you can say?'

'God, you're not still in a mood? Time of the month, is it?'

'Oh, yeah, yeah actually it is. I had time of the month all over there in the corner of the room, can you see where I had to lift the carpet?'

'Oh, speaking of which, I've got you a new piece in the car.'

'Is that all you can say, Mike? You killed a bloke yesterday and we dumped his body in the river, or have you forgotten that? I've had Jennie texting and calling me. I can't bear to pick up the phone.'

'Stop being a baby and listen to me. Take you out of the equation and Jennie finds out that he was shagging two other birds. She's come over here and says to you, "Aw, Kate, I can't believe it, he's broke my heart, I hate him," and what would you say to her?' I look down at the floor. 'Oh, sorry, what was that? Speak up, I never quite heard you.' Mike is holding his earlobe right in front of my face, waiting for my answer. 'Well, I'm waiting, what would you say?'

'I'd say to Jennie...'

'Yes, what would you say to Jennie?'

I mumble a half-hearted, 'I'll get Mike to sort him out.'

'Oo, give the girl a round of applause. Yes, she'd get Mike to sort him out. So take out the middle man, miss out the heartbroken Jennie and the fact that her best friend shagged her bloke behind her back and, hey presto, we get the same answer – Mike sorted him out.'

'Shut up, Mike, you're such a wind up.' But I do grin at him as I know he's right. He gives me that grin that I like so much and smacks me on the backside shouting, 'Kettle!'

That's that then, Paul is forgotten about. How could I have witnessed a murder and helped cover up the evidence and still be laughing and enjoying Mike's company? I don't recognise myself these days. Even sleeping around, what am I thinking?

Later that day, I'm sitting on my own and there's a knock at the door. Oh no, it's Jennie, what do I say to her? Do I mention it? I mean, do I ask how Paul is? Oo, are you going out with Paul tonight? Hey, how's Paul? Oo, Paul not with you, I thought you two were joined at the hip? No, it's best I let her mention him first. I pull my bobble out of my hair before I answer the door. I can try to hide my pretend-shocked face easier that way.

'Hello, Jennie, you OK?'

'Not really, Kate, no.'

'What's wrong?'

Oh my God, she knows, she knows he was here and that Mike killed him and that I put him in the suitcase. I'm going to prison. Oh no, I'm going to prison for a very long time. Jennie will hate me forever for this.

'It's Paul.' Oh my God, she does know.

'What about Paul?'

'Well, I think he's seeing someone else.'

'Really, what makes you say that?'

'Well, a few weeks ago I had a cold and I'm convinced he went out and slept with some slag.'

'No, I don't think so, are you sure?'

That was me. Oh no, I'm a slag. I'm a slagidy slag-slag. A slagidy slag-slag that doesn't even like sex, that's the worst kind of slag.

'Well, I couldn't contact him all the next day and when I finally did contact him he wasn't in the mood for sex. Why would he not want to have sex with me, he loves sex? Then today, I've been trying to call him since Thursday afternoon and his phone is switched off. I have a funny feeling it's someone at uni. I don't know why, I just do. You've not noticed anything, have you?'

'Me? No nothing, are you sure you're not being paranoid? You know what men are like, they like to go out, get pissed, and forget about us women. We're pains in the arses to them. Honestly, give him a couple of days. He'll come back with his tail between his legs and begging for your forgiveness, and your sex.'

'Do you think so?'

'Yeah, I know so. Listen, he's in a huff for some reason, let's go out tonight, me and you in the club, forget about him.'

'But I love him. We even talked about marriage and kids, eventually. Well, it was more me talking, but he never said no.'

'Well, there you go then, you know he was the type of bloke to say what he was thinking so he must have wanted to marry you.'

Oh my God, I'm talking in past tense, do you think she knows something? Plus, marriage – he was never going to marry her, there were about four of us, Mike was right, he was a pervert. Bastard probably deserved it. Well, maybe not that. That's the thing with Mike and Jimmy, these awful things seem to happen to people and they go about their business like it's never happened and I'm being dragged into it. Sleeping with my best friend's boyfriend, he was murdered in front of me and I helped to dispose of his body and clean up the mess ... anyone else would need counselling and what do I do? Treat my friend to a night at the club.

Me and Jennie head over to the club and I spot Mike serving drinks at the bar. He winks over at me as if to say, You sorted it then. Why should I keep sorting his messes? I wonder if he would ever sort my mess. Well, I suppose he did with the baby, but it was his mess in the first place. I wonder why I love him so much sometimes. I can't help it.

Eleven months – how clever, one month before baby George's first birthday, he just got up and walked. I missed it, I was at the shops but Uncle Brian never missed it.

Paul's mum did call the police but so far they have not found any evidence that Paul is dead so the file is a left-open case. They're assuming that he's run away, they say it's very common in men of his age to want to go out there and find themselves. Jennie's not even thought about the possibility that Paul's dead. I really am lucky she's just a dumb blonde.

Chapter 16 – A Baby For Someone Else

Twelve months – George said his first word today. I'm so excited. It was Mama, I can't believe it. I got butterflies when he said it. Mind, he looked at Auntie Shelly when he said it. I think I better take him for an eye test.

It's George's first birthday today, what shall I get him? I bet he's having a great day. I might even drive up to where the cottage was, have a look around, see if I can see someone who may resemble me. Don't be silly, Kate, you never even looked at the baby, how on earth would you know if he resembled you or not?

I'll go round and see David. It might help me think of something other than George's birthday.

'Hi, Shelly, I was wondering if I could have David for the day.'

'Yes, course you can, it will give me a chance to pack.'

'Pack? Why? Where you going?'

'Oh, Brian has decided we all need a holiday so we're having a two-week break.'

'What? When?'

'We leave on Tuesday.'

'No, you can't, what about David?'

'Well, he'll be coming.'

'What, for two weeks? Is he not a bit young for a holiday?'

'No, don't be silly, he'll have a great time.'

I rush home quickly and cry my heart out. I can't not see David for two weeks, no way. I've never gone a couple of days without seeing him. My boobs will go hard and dry up in two weeks. Expressing is never the same as breastfeeding, what on earth am I going to do? Maybe I should have gone back to the cottage and looked for George or taken David on the train when I wanted to.

David's been on holiday for five days now. My boobs are getting sore and going hard. I wonder if I should let my milk dry up. He's over a year old now, maybe it's time he stopped breastfeeding anyway. I hate this, how can Shelly take him on holiday? He's my baby, he belongs to me. I have this constant pain in my stomach.

I'll go over to the club, see what's happening, it might take my mind off things a bit.

'Hello, Mike.'

'All right, Gem, what you up to?'

'Nothing much. David's gone on holiday. I really miss him.'

'He'll be back before you know it. I did say you were spending far too much time with him and I know how you kind of…'

'Kind of what?'

'Well, obsess with things.' What on earth does Mike mean? I'm angry at him for that remark. I snap, 'What the hell do you mean? Obsess with things. I don't get obsessed with things.'

'OK, calm down, I never meant it like that. How about I take you out tonight to that posh little restaurant that's just opened up?'

Mike hugs me and it feels a little better, but it's still not the same as David. As I pull away from Mike, he gives me a funny look and points towards my boob. 'Hey, Kate, what's that?'

'What?'

'There's liquid coming from your tits. Is that milk?'

'No, I don't know what it is.'

'Jesus, I know what milk out of tits looks like and your milk should have well dried up by now, you gave birth over a year ago. What have you been doing?'

'Nothing. Fuck off, I've been doing nothing, maybe it was the sinks back-splashing me when I went to the toilets.'

'Please tell me that all this time you've been spending with David, you've not been breastfeeding him.'

'Don't be stupid, that's insane.'

'Yes, *I* know it's insane, but do *you*? This is what I mean about you being a bit, erm ... you act fucking crazy at times.'

'Piss off, leave me alone. I've got one of my headaches coming on.'

'Kate, look me in the eyes, and tell me you've not been breastfeeding that kid.'

I look at the floor. What on earth do I say? He knows it's milk coming out.

'Oh, I don't know, leave me alone.'

'Why have you not told me about this? And what the hell were you thinking?'

'I don't know, maybe I'm upset about George.'

'George? Who the hell is George in all of this?'

'Forget it, some guy at university.'

'Oh, a boyfriend?'

'Yeah, well not any more, he went off with another girl at uni. You won't tell anyone about this? It's just my boobs were so sore after I had the baby and it relieved them, that's all. I know I shouldn't have done it, but I couldn't help it. You won't tell Shelly, will you?'

'No, I won't, but I want you to stay away from David and I mean it. If you go anywhere near him I'll tell Shelly. Let's get you out of here, change your top and I'll meet you later for a drink. Fucking hell, Kate, I honestly don't know what gets into you at times.'

Mike takes me out to tell me how silly I've been. We have a couple of bottles of wine and Mike ends up a little merry. We go back to my flat. 'I worry about you sometimes,' Mike says as he sweeps my hair away from my face and moves towards me, placing his lips on mine. My heart skips a beat, he's actually kissing me because he wants to not because I'm forcing him to. He grabs my skirt and pulls it up exposing my underwear. He wants to have sex with me again, yet I'm not sure I want to have sex with him. I've never enjoyed it, but I do want him close to me. I also know if I want him to leave Diane I need to start enjoying sex, so in a weird way I don't want to stop him. He places his hand inside my knickers and grabs my hand towards the zip on his trousers, wanting me to open them. I unzip his trousers and put my hand inside his underwear. I don't even need to touch his dick to make it hard, it's almost throbbing in my hand which makes my nerves kick in even more. He lies me on the bed, kissing my neck and whispers in my ear, 'I want to make you cum.' Then he works his way down my body till he eventually gets to my vagina. He starts to caress my clitoris with his tongue. I'm not enjoying this at all, I want him to stop and cuddle me. That would be nice. He works his way back up my body, pulling his trousers down so they are at his knees and tells me to turn over with my knees on the bed. He then enters me from behind and lets out a moan as he does. He is penetrating me hard and fast while moaning, 'Kate.' I like the way he says my name but I'm not liking the feeling of him inside me. He's getting very rough, then with one big push, he lets out a heavy breath and says, 'Sorry Kate, I was quick then. I wanted you to enjoy it this time, but I understand.'

I want to ask him what he means. Understand? What is it that he understands? 'Come on, let's get dressed,' he says while pulling up his trousers. 'Oh no, Mike, can't we stay here for a while? Take your clothes off, we can lie in bed.' He looks at me as if I'm a little silly, but then gives me a pity look and says, 'OK, Kate.'

We lie in bed and I have my head buried into his chest, the smell of him is amazing. I could inhale his scent all day long and never get bored. I can feel his breathing is getting slower as my head is going up and down with every breath he takes. Before I know it he's fallen asleep. I gently lift up my head to take in his beautiful face. I start to fantasise about us two living together. Especially once he ditches that stupid Diane. With each breath he takes I notice his lips gently shake on his exhale, even more so on the third exhale. I know that because I counted them. I look at my clock and it says

3am. It can't be 3am, surely not, we came to bed at 10pm, I've not been watching him all that time. He starts to move and it looks like he might wake up so I snuggle in bed in case he spots me staring at him. False alarm, his lips are now doing the movement on his exhale again. I sit back up to stare at him. I wonder if he would wake if I was to gently kiss his lips. I think back to last night when we kissed and made love. I know most people wouldn't exactly call it making love as there was no cuddling involved but it was making love in my mind. The next thing I know Mike wakes up and says, 'Shit Kate, what time is it? I need to go.'

'It's only 6.30am, go back to sleep.' I snuggle back into his chest again.

He gets out of bed quickly, putting his clothes on. 'Jesus, Diane is going to go mental. I'll have to go, I'll see you later.' He kisses me on the forehead and runs out of the flat. I can't believe it's 6.30am, that means I've watched him sleep the entire night. Mind you, I'd rather watch him in real life than through the CCTV any day. I hope he's going to tell Diane he's leaving her now.

It's been two months since I spent any time with David. I miss him like crazy. I've not been able to write anything in my yellow book because I don't know anything. Mike was probably right anyway. It's getting easier but it means I've been watching Jimmy and Mike more and more on the CCTV. Mike's not left Diane yet, he's not even mentioned it, but we have slept together a few more times.

Mike pops over and he looks like he's furious. Something is going on.

'Hey, Mike, what you up to?'

'Nothing much. Bloody Diane, she's getting right on my nerves. She wanted me to take her out again this weekend. She knows I have to work most Saturday nights at the club, it doesn't run itself.'

'Aw, cheer up, here, have a vodka. I've told you to ignore her, she's far too needy for you anyway.'

'She's OK through the week. It's at the weekend when she acts like this. What does she think I'm going to do at work?'

I roll my eyes at him. 'I dread to think.'

'Leave it out.'

'Hey, you came round here for a moan, what do you expect me to say? Yeah, that bloody Diane, what a bitch. I mean, it's not like you've never cheated on her before or anything, is it?'

'What you on about now?'

'Me and you, that's what I'm on about, you have sex with me.'

'Yeah, but that's different, it's not cheating.'

'Ha! Not cheating? Look up cheating in the dictionary, Mike. I think you'll find it says something along the lines of – having sex with another person while in a relationship.'

'Yeah, but it's different with you.'

'Ah, thanks. What, it wasn't like real sex, was it not?'

'Nah, you know what I mean, well, it's you.'

'What about, well it's me? What, so you have sex with me but it doesn't count? Why?'

'Why do you always have to cause an argument?'

'No, I don't, you've come round here to have a moan about your girlfriend thinking you're cheating on her with a girl you've cheated on her with. I'm asking you to explain yourself, that's all. Maybe if you didn't cheat, Diane wouldn't get so uptight, would she? Don't even try to make out like I'm the only one, because I know there have been more. That little brunette bird with the big nose who comes into the club with her daft friend every week is all over you. Don't tell me you've not been there.'

'I haven't,' Mike says with that look he has when he lies.

'Yeah, you have, I can tell by your face you have. That's the thing with you. If me and you were together, I would know straight away if you'd cheated because your face gives it away.'

'Oh, shut up. Are you here to cheer me up or make me depressed?'

'Neither. I'm here to be honest with you. Don't come whingeing on to me for sympathy when you're doing exactly what Diane is accusing you of. I don't even know what you're doing in a relationship. You clearly can't keep it in your trousers, can you?'

'Whatever, listen to you anyway, you shagged your friend's bloke. I'd never do that.'

'Yeah, and I paid a high price for it as well.'

'So, it's official then – we're both as bad as each other.'

'Not really, don't try to make yourself feel better by dragging me into it. Here, have another vodka. Who gives a shit anyway? Dump Diane and get on with it.' I pass Mike a glass of vodka, he takes a huge gulp and says, 'I can't.'

'Why not?'

'Look, I wasn't going to say anything, but the longer us two have been going out, the more I realise how unstable she is.'

'What do you mean, unstable?'

'Well, I don't know, she scares me sometimes.'

'What do you mean, she scares you sometimes?'

'It's her mind, she's not like normal birds. She really is needy. She's told me she'll swallow a load of pills if I don't stay in this weekend. What am I supposed to do? She's even asked me to stay away from you. We have so many arguments about you, she's convinced something is going on between us.'

'Is she now? Well, you know what I'd do?'

'What?'

'Go to the chemist, get a shit-load of pills, and go out partying all weekend. That would get rid of the little bitch, ha!'

'You're terrible, you. Plus, she has a kid, I couldn't do that. Look, I never wanted to say anything and I know it will upset you but…'

'But what?' Mike puts his head down and starts to look all nervous. What on earth is he going to say? 'What, Mike? What don't you want to tell me?'

'Well, erm...'

'Well, erm, what? Spit it out.'

'I'm sorry, I never meant for it to happen, but Diane is pregnant.'

'Pregnant! How could you let this happen? You know how

much I miss my baby. How can you do this to me? *Pregnant?* You're having another one, what about mine, Mike? Get out, leave me alone.'

'No, please. I'm sorry, it was an accident.'

'An accident? No, you spill a cup of coffee, it's an accident. You get someone pregnant, it's more than an accident.'

I have tears rolling down my face. What about my baby, what about George? How can he do this to me? He knows how close I got to David, he stopped me from seeing him, and now he's going to have another one of his own. I really hate Mike sometimes. I feel like he deliberately hurts me.

'Look, here, have another drink. Please don't cry. I'm sorry. I never meant to hurt you.' Mike pours me a drink and holds me.

'Well, how come you walk in here and tell me having sex with me is not like real sex? Have you got any idea how that makes me feel?'

'I'm sorry, I never meant it like that. You know I think the world of you.'

He puts both his hands around my face and says, 'Come here.' He starts to kiss me. I wonder if he's only doing it to make me feel better, but I don't care. I need something to take the pain away. How can he be having a baby? I kiss him back. We end up in the bedroom having sex again and it does make me feel better, I suppose. But then I know he has to leave me to go back to Diane and her perfectly growing baby. Why does this hurt me so much? It's like some sort of punishment. I really hate myself and my shit life.

I wake up the next morning with the instant thought of Diane and her baby. I turn to Mike who's stretching as he's also woken up. 'Morning. How was the not-so-real sex then?'

'You're such a wind up. Get the breakfast on.'

'Cheeky,' I say as I make my way into the kitchen with a smile on my face because that was nice to have him in my bed all night, holding me. Maybe he will leave Diane after all. Maybe me and Mike could have our own baby. That would be great. All I need to do is get rid of Diane. Maybe I should send her some pills in the post. Oh, I am wicked sometimes. Mike comes out of the bedroom buttoning up his shirt.

'Bloody hell, Diane's called me several times. I better ring her back. Shh.' He puts his finger on his lips to make sure I don't speak. 'Hello, Diane, me and Jimmy got totally pissed up last night. I had to crash at his. Helen's not best pleased. She's making me breakfast now, so I'll be home after that. Don't be stupid, I'm not putting him on the phone, he'll think I'm daft. I've told you, you're paranoid. I'll be home soon. We'll pop to that pram shop you wanted to go to.' What is he thinking, saying that in front of me? He puts down his phone and I give him that look. 'Ah, come on, what else could I say? Tell her I'm here?'

'Whatever, do what you like, I couldn't give a shit any more.' I turn my back on Mike. I can't bear to look at him sometimes. He grabs me and turns me round placing his hand on my chin to lift my head up. 'Don't be like that. We had a good time last night.'

'No, Mike, you had a good time. Me, on the other hand, had pretend sex with someone.'

'Oh, come here, you.' He grabs me closer to him and kisses me. We have sex again on the kitchen table.

It's been five days since Mike told me about the baby. I still can't believe it. I wonder if Jennie fancies spending the day with me. She's never been the same since Paul's sudden disappearance.

I call her up. 'Hey, Jennie, fancy doing something really fun today?'

'Yeah, like what?'

'I don't know, anything to get away from here for a little while.'

'Well, they do trips over to Amsterdam on the boat. Fancy that? We'll have a right laugh.'

'Yeah, OK, let's do it.'

I quickly call Jimmy. 'Jimmy, me and Jennie are heading off for a couple of days to Amsterdam.'

'Hey, stay away from those peep shows, mind. You'll go blind.'

'Want me to bring you anything back? What about a dildo?

'Piss off. I don't need help in that department. I'm enough for Helen, thank you.'

'I meant for you, and ya big tight ass.'

'Shut it, madam. Enjoy yourself.'

I'm looking forward to spending some time with Jennie. I've been avoiding her since the whole Paul incident. We do have the odd night in the club, but it's not the same. I sometimes wonder if we're just growing apart.

We get on the boat. We're so excited, we've even brought our own drink as Jimmy said it can get pretty pricy on that boat. The conversation soon changes to Paul.

'I'm still upset about Paul going off like that. Do you think he's dead?'

That's the first time she's ever asked me if I think he's dead. Maybe she realises now that he isn't coming back. Or, knowing Jennie, she would probably be thinking, 'There's no way anyone could leave me, I'm bloody perfect.'

'I'm not really sure. I know in uni he used to say stuff like, "I wish I could leave this place. I fancy going abroad where no one knows where I am." Maybe he did just that. I'll tell you what, he might be in Amsterdam. When we get there, we'll keep an eye out for him. Failing that, we'll get you the biggest dildo they do, eh?'

'Ha ha! Thanks, but I'm not sure a battery-operated toy will replace my boyfriend. I hate the fact he may have gone off. Maybe he has killed himself. Who knows.'

'Forget him, cos either way – running off or killing yourself – it still makes him a selfish prick. Speaking of which, Diane is pregnant.'

'Oh, really? I'm so sorry. I take it Mike's still not succumbed to your charms.'

'Nah, we've slept together a few more times, but I don't think he wants me like that. Not sure why. I don't know how I can be good enough to sleep with yet not good enough to be with.'

'Well, I hope he's got better at the whole sex thing.'

'Yeah, he has. Maybe Paul taught me a thing or two and I showed Mike,' I say with a smile.

'Yeah, Paul was good in bed, wasn't he?'

'Yeah, he was Jennie, you were lucky to have him.'

'Mind, you weren't bad in bed either. Who knows, this could turn into a dirty weekend if you play your cards right.'

Jennie winks at me. I do hope she's not serious. I still don't like the whole sex thing. I don't get why she does. Maybe me coming to Amsterdam was a stupid idea. I should have suggested St Paul's Cathedral.

The following day we finally get off the boat and the bus driver tells us where to get back on the bus for taking us back to the ferry. We walk around, trying to find our way and getting lost everywhere. I mean, how can you walk up to a local saying, 'Excuse me, sir, can you tell me where the red-light district is?'

Jennie suggests going to a little shop to buy a map. We get the map and it's huge. It takes both of us to hold it and we still can't figure out where we're headed. Then Jennie shouts, 'Is there not a bit that says "you are here"?'

I start to giggle uncontrollably. 'Jennie, I thought I did the jokes around here. Do you honestly think every little shop in Amsterdam has its own map to point out that you are standing outside that shop? Give it here.' I manage to find out where we are and say, 'Look, we need to head that way.'

Off we go to the red-light district. It's a really strange place and I hate it. You have women standing in the glass windows banging on them for you to come in. I wonder if they're happy. I think my mum and Jennie could do a job like that, they love sex so much.

'Hey, Kate, we should buy one.'

'What, a prostitute? Yuk, no way. Could you imagine the amount of people who have been with those girls? They will be riddled with diseases. We could see if we could take one home for Mike and Jimmy, though. I think Jimmy would have a fit and probably beat her to death. These girls are definitely good-time girls. Let's go to a cafe. We could get one of those space cakes.' We've never been ones for drugs. We like our drink, but drugs is a different matter.

For a start, Jimmy would kill me. We settle into the cafe and the guy comes over with rolled up joints.

'You want one of these, madam?' There are so many to choose from and we don't even smoke.

'No, just a cake, thanks.'

We buy one cake and halve it but, to be honest, we're both far too scared to eat it so we end up binning the cake. Yeah, definitely should have been St Paul's Cathedral.

We manage to find our way back to the bus with our big map. Back to the ferry, safe and sound. It's been nice to get away from Mike for a while, but I definitely see the cracks between me and Jennie. We never had half the fun we would normally have had. We went all the way to Amsterdam, never tried any of the drugs or the prostitutes. Maybe she really is upset about Paul or maybe I'm not the same person any more. Maybe deep down I know my problems are because of her giving me the white wine. Who knows what the reason is, but there definitely is a divide growing.

Well, after a two-day break it's time to get back to the norm and head over to the club. Jimmy is on holiday for his birthday. He wanted a quiet one for him and Helen. Funny how he wants a party for everyone else. As I get to the bar I see Caroline grinning and she has a twinkle in her eye.

'All right, Caroline, what you grinning at?'

'Nothing.'

'Hey, it's something, I've not seen anyone grin like that since I watched *Alice in Wonderland* with that bloody cat. It's one of two things with a woman, it's a man or men.'

'Oh no, please, I can't say, it's a secret.'

'What do you mean, a secret? How big a secret?'

'Evening, ladies.' In comes Dave and winks at Caroline. She goes all giddy. Dave grabs a drink and walks back out of the bar.

'What the hell was that?'

'What?'

'Don't "what" me. That, that, what just happened there. Dave walked in here and you turned into a giggly teenager. Have you got something to tell me, missy?'

'Oh, please don't say anything, I don't want Jimmy knowing, he'll start to wind Dave up.'

'Are you telling me something is going on?'

'Yeah, we've been on a couple of dates, I really like him. It gets a bit awkward me working here every weekend and on my night off he seems to be working.'

'Well, is he working tonight?'

'No, but I am.'

'Well, here, I'll cover for you. I can work a bar, it's easy, surely?'

'No way, Jimmy would go mad if you worked the bar, you know he hates you working the bar, all those drunken men getting shirty.'

'Hey, Jimmy is not here, is he?'

'No.'

'Well then.'

'But if he finds out I might get sacked.'

'Don't be silly, Caroline, he'd never sack you. Now out, before I change my mind.'

'Are you sure?'

'Yes, on one condition.'

'What?'

'You call me tomorrow with all the details.' I squeeze her bum in a playful fashion. I'd hate anyone to hurt Caroline. I've always liked her. 'You tell Dave I'll have his bollocks on a plate if he breaks your heart, mind.'

She kisses me on the cheek. 'Oh, Kate, you're a total angel. Thank you, thank you, thank you.'

I start to get the bar ready for the hustle and bustle and in walks Mike. He takes one look at me behind the bar and says, 'Erm, what are you doing behind that bar like you're working?'

'Working, what are you doing not behind the bar working?'

'You're not working the bar. Where's Caroline?'

'She's sick, very sick, she's full of cold, so I gave her the night off. You're going to have to help me here and keep me right and, whatever you do, do not tell Jimmy I'm working the bar. He'll blow my head off.' I wink and grin.

Working the bar is much harder than I thought. I'm sure I'm deaf. I've never had a problem with my hearing before but I couldn't understand a word anyone was saying. So I gave everyone a bottle of beer, doesn't matter what they asked for, and no one dared to complain. Can I have a gin and tonic, please? What, a bottle of Becks, yeah, coming right up.

Finally everyone goes and it's a case of clearing up the bottles. There's only me and Mike left.

'I'm knackered. This is not what I thought good-time girls did. I definitely don't want to be a good-time girl, no way, there was nothing good about that.'

'Yeah, well, why do you think Jimmy keeps saying you're not to be one?'

We giggle at each other and probably at Jimmy, the way he is he acts like a little old granddad. You wouldn't think he was only thirty-two.

'Kate.'

'Yes.'

'Can I ask a huge favour?'

'Yeah, what?

'It's about Diane.'

'What about Diane? You want me to bump her off? OK then, when? Soon, please let it be soon.' I giggle while saying this and prodding him in the belly.

'Stop it, not that.'

'Well, what then?'

'I don't know why, you know what she's like, but she's stolen some money from work.'

'What?'

'Yeah, I can't even understand it myself, she's crazy, she knows she can have anything she wants. I think she did it for attention. Well, she's the only one who knows the number for the safe, so they know it's her.'

'What's this got to do with me? Stupid bitch is an idiot if you ask me. Hey, you should have asked her to steal us some while she was there.'

'I have something to ask you and it's serious. I don't even know how to ask you this, but would you say that you did it?'

'What?'

'She's looking at serving time. I can't have my baby being born in prison. I wouldn't ask but—'

'Jesus fucking Christ, Mike, are you taking the piss? You walk in here all nicey nicey and ask me something like that. No, absolutely not, no way.'

'Please, I'll pay you. You'll only do about six months, it was just a petty theft, we won't even say you broke into the safe, we'll say Diane drunkenly told you the number.'

'No way, how can you even ask me that? Prison? I'm not going to prison.'

'But Diane hasn't got the right frame of mind for prison.'

'Oh, but I bloody well have? What are you trying to say?'

'Nothing, I don't mean it like that. It's just, well, you're harder than Diane and I wouldn't ask, it's just the baby, you know. I don't want it being born in there, prison is no place for a baby.'

'Prison is no place for me. Now please don't ask me again.'

'OK, I'm sorry. You're right, I should have thought. I'll think of something else.'

'Yeah, you're damn right you will. You really take the piss sometimes. I'm off. You can lock up. I've got things to do tomorrow. Going to prison is not one of them.'

I'm so angry with him. Fancy him choosing to stay with Diane more than me.

I'm twenty-one next week and that's as far as my plans have

gone. Except not leaving the house. Think I'll lock myself away that day.

Chapter 17 – Prison CCTV

I don't like celebrating my birthday. It reminds me of some terrible things. I'm missing David like crazy. I've still not been anywhere near him. Jimmy's back from holiday today. No doubt he'll want to show off his holiday snaps.

I take Jimmy a nice cup of tea to his office.

'Morning, Jimmy, how was the holiday?'

'Great, here, I've got my snaps.'

We look through over one hundred holiday snaps, all of him and Helen with the same expression on their faces, just with a different background. How boring, but you can't tell Jimmy that, you have to look really interested as you get your blow-by-blow account.

'Hey, have I told you what Mike's asked me to do?'

'No, what's he asked you to do?'

'That crazy bitch girlfriend of his has only been caught stealing money from the safe at work. She's the only one who knows the code and the police are involved. She's looking at doing time. Mike has only asked me if I would do her time for her. Can you believe the cheek of him?'

'What's he asked you to do that for? Can't she do her own fucking time? Cheeky twats.'

'Yeah, that's what I thought. But he doesn't want the baby being born in prison or some shit like that. With a mother like her anyway, you can wrap that baby up in cotton wool, it will still end up a little shit when it's older. I was so angry with him. I mean prison, imagine *me* going to prison. I think I'd be a bit scared.'

'What, you scared? You're not scared of anything, you. Christ, you're not even scared of me half the time. I've seen you cart a few people out of this club, men and women, you're like a little Rottweiler when you get going.'

'Yeah, but not hard enough for prison.'

'Nah, it would only be a low-security prison, not a high-risk one.'

'What, so no Kray twins? I could have got their autographs.'

'You'd have a hard job anyway, unless you've grown a dick overnight and you're not telling me. They don't put men and women together, Treas. Imagine if they all started breeding, the up-and-coming generation would be something to be bloody scared of. Anyway, what we doing for your birthday next week? I've booked the DJ, the really good one as well, what's his face. I've done two hundred and fifty tickets for the door because it's a ticket-only event. It's five pound a ticket as well, you're quite the little star. Even the press will want to be there.'

'What are you talking about?'

'You, you're twenty-one next week, it's your birthday party.'

Jimmy is organising a party. No, there's no way I can have a party. I couldn't bear it, not after my eighteenth party in the club. How can he even think that's OK? How can he and Mike be so selfish at times?

'I'm not having a fucking birthday party. No.'

'Yes, you are, this is your club and you need to take a bit of interest in it.'

'It's not my club, it's only named after me. You don't want this party for me, you want it for you, so everyone thinks you're great. Oo, look at great Mr Simpson hosting a party like he's something special. You don't even like me, you just tolerate me. But you know what? I don't care about that, cos I hate you.'

Jimmy is getting up out of his seat. 'You hate me, do you? Come here.'

He grabs me by the arm and drags me into the bar area of the club. The girls are bottling up and the doormen are having a few drinks before their shift. Great, he's going to beat me in front of everyone.

'Hey, you!' Jimmy shouts over at one of the girls. 'Blondie, how long have you been working for me?'

'Erm, a year, Mr Simpson.' This girl is really nervous and wondering what is going to happen to her. 'What is your name, then?' he snaps.

'It's Donna, Mr Simpson.'

He looks over at the doorman. 'You over there, with the tash, what's your fucking name?'

'I'm Mark, Mr Simpson.'

'And how long have you worked for me?'

'Four years, I worked for you over at the other club.'

He grabs me by the arm again and drags me back into the office.

'Did you hear that? They have both worked for me for God knows how long and I never even knew their names. They knew mine, though, didn't they, and do you know why that is? Because I couldn't give a fuck about them in there. Do you know why I couldn't give a fuck?'

'No.'

'Because I tolerate them, that's why, they come in here day after day. Without people like them working for me I wouldn't even have a club. So I have to tolerate them. I don't give a shit about them, so I tolerate them. Do you know how many underage drinkers have got through my door in all the years I've had a club?'

'No.'

'Two. That's how many. Do you know who they are? You and your stupid friend. You heard those people in there call me Mr Simpson. There are only a handful of people call me Jimmy outside of my own family and one of them is you, so don't you dare say I fucking tolerate you. I love you like you're my own. I've even had you round my family table at Christmas, do you think I would do all that for someone I tolerate? You come in here and tell me you hate me. Well, I'll tell you what, get out of my club and don't you ever come back. Me and you, we're done and, from now on, IF I let you acknowledge me in the street, you're to call me Mr Simpson, no more Jimmy. Now fuck off out of my club.'

I head towards the door. I walk through the bar and think, No, I'm not walking away like this. I'm going to tell him why I hate him. At least then he'll have an explanation. He'll probably smack me one as he was really angry in there but I don't care. If I'm going, I'll go with a bang. I make my way back into the office. Jimmy has poured himself a whisky and he actually looks a bit sad. Maybe he does care about me after all.

'Do you know why I hate you, Jimmy?'

'No, and it's Mr fucking Simpson. Like I said.'

'It's because I'm jealous of you.'

'What?'

'You heard me. I'm jealous. You tell people to do things once and they do them, you tell them to stop once and they stop.'

'Not everybody, Kate. You bloody don't. I told you to get out.'

'I hate that you can do that. If I could do that, I could have stopped them raping me.'

Jimmy raises his head and gives me a shocked look. 'What?'

'You heard me. I asked them to stop. I begged them to stop, but they wouldn't, they wouldn't stop.' Before I know it I have tears rolling down my face. 'I never wanted them to rape me. I wanted you to be there, you could've told them to stop and they would've.'

'I'm sorry I wasn't there. I made them pay, believe me, I made them pay.'

I don't know why, but I feel like I need to tell him about George. I'm not sure I could bear him looking at me in disgust. I want to be his treasure but somedays I don't feel like a treasure. I cover my face with my hands and cry, 'I've had a baby.'

'What?'

'I had a baby, they got me pregnant. It was too late for an abortion when I realised I was pregnant.'

'Jesus Christ, why have you never told me this?'

'Because I was ashamed.' I start sobbing. I can't believe I'm finally telling someone but it's like I need to get it all out. Someone needs to help me. 'Mike took me away and we put him up for adoption. It was a boy.'

'Kate, sit down here, have a drink of this.' He passes me the whisky he's been drinking. 'I can't believe you've not told me this before.'

'I've been obsessed with Shelly's little boy, David, ever since he was born. I even nursed him for over a year. I breastfed someone else's baby and I couldn't stop.' I snuggle closer to Jimmy's chest and I can hear his heart, it's beating so fast. 'I'm crazy, I know that and I want to get better, I do. I wash my face all the time because when they held me down and raped me they put their hands over my mouth and I can smell those hands on my face every day. It doesn't matter how many times I wash my face it's still there, the smell. I'm talking to you now and I think you can smell their hands on me. Please help me, don't make me leave this club. You're all I've got.'

'Bloody hell, why have you not come to me before? Who else knows about the baby?'

'No one, just me and Mike, I can't talk to anyone about this. My mum isn't interested in anyone but herself. I've asked her a million times who my father is and she keeps telling me she doesn't know. She was pissed up, but surely she knows, she has to know. After the rape, I wanted to find him, get away. I can't tell Jennie. I'm so ashamed.'

'Hey, you've got nothing to be ashamed about, nothing.'

'I can't talk to Mike. You know why I can't talk to him? Because you were right. I do have that condition, OCD. It's not just about washing my face, or checking the cupboard, or Shelly's boy, it's Mike as well. I have an obsession with him. I've been in love with him since I was ten years old. At first I wanted him to be my dad but the older I got the more I wanted him in other ways. Do you know we're sleeping together?'

'What? You and Mike are sleeping together?' Jimmy looks shocked.

'Yeah, I don't even know how it started, but I wish I could stop.'

Jimmy rubs his forehead. 'Jesus, this is a total mess. Is there anything else? Any other crazy things?'

'The reason I don't want a party in here is because every time I celebrate a birthday something terrible happens. It started the day me and you had an argument in here. I got drunk the night before the prison visit and spewed and slept the whole day and missed the phone calls. You slapped me.'

'I remember that day, that was the start of me being intrigued by you. I thought, The cheeky little swine, telling me she's not doing something.' Jimmy gives me a smile and moves his thumb across my face to wipe away my tears. 'See, you've always done it. You know you called me a cartoon character?'

'Ha ha! Yes, I remember. Homer Simpson. You got up out of your seat and smacked me one. You're the first person to ever smack me. I never knew whether to smack you back or crawl into a ball and cry. So I just got up and walked away thinking, What a wanker.'

'I thought to myself then, She's got balls of steel, that girl, I'm telling you. I thought you'd never come back yet you walked back into that club without a care in the world like it never even happened and you told me that joke about the handjob in a bar. I still laugh at that joke now. You're something special to me, and you know what? Seeing you like this is breaking my heart.'

'I can't stand it, I need help, I know I do. You won't tell anyone, will you, or even tell Mike that I told you we're sleeping together?'

'No, of course I won't. What you tell me stays with me, I promise. Come here.' He pulls me into him again. 'You know what I think you should do?'

'What?'

'Do Diane's time.'

'What?'

'Go do her time, it will give you a few months' break from everything. I'll have a word with the right people and we'll get a doctor to look at you and get some counselling when you're inside. I'll help you, you'll be like a new person when you come out.'

'But I'm scared, I don't know if I could do prison. But staying out here is scaring the shit out of me as well.' I think for a while and say, 'I'll do Diane's time, you're right, it's for the best. I'm sorry about the way I spoke to you before. I don't hate you, not really. I just hate that I'm not you, that's all.'

'You should have told me about this before. I could have helped you. You know you can always come to me, don't you? If ever you're feeling down please talk to me. I am human, you know. Now, blow your nose and make a bucket list of things to do. You don't have long before we cart you off to prison AKA the funny farm, you crazy thing.'

'I better have Sunday lunch with Mr and Mrs Richards on Sunday. It might be a long while before I get any meat again.'

'What do you mean?'

'Well, in prison they only feed you porridge.'

'Porridge? You watch too much TV, you. It's three square meals and a warm bed. It'll be like Butlins in your low-security prison.'

'What should I say to them?'

'Who?'

'Mr and Mrs Richards. They'll be so disappointed in the way I've turned out.'

'Oi, madam, there's nothing wrong with the way you've turned out, you've just hit a bit of a stumbling block, that's all. You still have a heart of gold, Kate. When you get to their house just waltz in and say, "I hope I'm not late for the mad hatter's tea party."'

'Jimmy, don't, it's not funny.' I giggle, yet still have tears rolling down my face.

'We must have a party for you though, please. Listen, these things don't happen because the tins aren't straight or because you celebrated your birthday. It's just coincidence. Like me yesterday, I dropped the TV remote and it smashed. I couldn't watch my favourite TV programme because I couldn't be arsed to get up out of my seat. Do you think that happened because I never brushed my teeth in a circular motion? It's ridiculous when you hear it out loud, isn't it?'

'Not in my head, it isn't, no.'

'Well, it is in my head. You're going to have the best party this place has ever seen, and then I'll get you sorted, and I promise I'll visit you every week.'

So that's it, I have my party and nothing bad happens, well apart from Diane turned up, even pregnant. Stupid little cow. Mike was all over her. Can I get you this, Diane? Can I get you that, Diane? I'll get you something, Diane – bloody arsenic.

She was all over me. 'Oo, happy birthday, Kate.' Like she wanted my birthday to be happy, she hates me. She was just glad that someone was going to do her time for her. So she steals money, gets to keep it and gets rid of me in the process. I must be bloody mad.

Everything happened exactly like Mike and Jimmy said it would. I was a little surprised I was so nervous. I thought I had 'Diane did it' written all over my face when it came to the cross-examination. It took so long for the case to even get to court I was hoping they had forgotten about us. But I eventually ended up in prison. I think I'm going to enjoy the break, to be honest. I can clear my head in here at least. As I get to my cell there's a girl there and she looks like a frightened rabbit.

'Oh, hello, Kate, I heard you were coming in. It was in the papers.You don't recognise me, do you?' says the girl.

'Nope, I have no idea who you are.'

'It's me, Rebecca Bradshaw, we went to primary school together.'

Oh my God, it can't be, it's her, she's totally changed. Well, her clothes fit her now, at least. She has long brown hair, longer than I've ever seen before. I'm quite pleased to see her really. After all, I did hide behind her for years. I wonder what she would think if I ever told her that.

'Here, I'll help you make your bed.'

'Oh, you don't have to do that, Rebecca, honestly, I'm fine.'

'No, here, let me help. I'm glad of a friendly face, to be honest. Being in this place reminds me of school, all the girls picking on me.'

What, she still gets picked on, even now? How awful. I feel sorry for her in a way and wonder what my life would be like if Mike had not helped me stand up to Jennie. Well, I wouldn't be in this shithole for a start. That Diane has a lot to answer for.

As I make my bed I hear the ringing of a bell. 'Oh, that's the lunchtime bell, I'll take you and show you around.'

As we get to the canteen, I spot her – Jacquie bloody Nixon. That's Keith Nixon's wife. I never even knew she was in here. Not that she scares me. I'm going to just do my time, keep my head down and get out.

'The food's not great, but it's OK, I guess.'

We get our food and sit at the table. No one seems to be coming anywhere near me, yet they're all having a good look. 'So, don't you have any friends in here, Rebecca?'

'Not really. I keep myself to myself. I try to spend as much time in the library as possible and keep out of people's way.'

'I take it you're not getting on very well in here, then?'

Rebecca almost looks unsure how to answer the question. I can tell she's very shy and worried about what others think of her. I suppose that comes with years of childhood bullying. 'It's not that really, it's just, well, I don't know. I don't get on with people, that's all. Ever since I was a kid I've never really been a people person. I did have a friend once, her name was Lucy. I think you met her, when you and Jennie saw us in town and Jennie picked on us a bit. I was so scared that day. I thought you two were going to beat us up.'

I feel guilty that she thinks I was part of that. I never even wanted Jennie to approach those two back then. Maybe I should show her not everyone hates her and try and help her. Crickey, what am I thinking, I'll need my tissues at this rate. I'm supposed to be in here to get my head clear. I'm not the doctor. I'm the sickest patient they have in here. Even Jimmy has started calling me 'the mad hatter who smiles like the Cheshire cat.' Cheeky pig. Aw, I think I might even miss Jimmy. He did say he'd come and visit every week. He says Mike's not allowed to visit, though. He can write if he wants, but not visit.

'Well, don't worry, Rebecca, you have a friend in here now. I'll take care of you.'

Oh, there goes another bell which means lunchtime must be over. We make our way back to our cells.

'God, is it always this boring? What are we supposed to do around here?'

As I look at the door three women appear and Rebecca jumps out of her skin.

'Oi, Cousin It, Jacquie Nixon wants her cigarettes, have you got them?'

They look at Rebecca and she goes to her pillow, gets out a box of cigarettes, and is about to hand them over. I don't bloody well think so. I'll see to this. I'm not scared of that lot. I quickly grab the cigarettes and say, 'You tell Jacquie Nixon that Rebecca has stopped smoking, but I've started. She can have them if she likes, but she's to come for them herself.' They just smile at me and walk out.

'Oh no, you should've let me give her them, there will be trouble now. It's part of the prison rules, see. Jacquie Nixon is top dog and everyone has to give her something out of their weekly supplies. If you don't, well ... well, actually, I don't know what happens because no one has ever not given her anything.'

'Really, Rebecca? Well, that was until now, you won't be giving her anything any more, and I certainly won't. Me handing something over to a Nixon? Jimmy would have my eyes out.'

I can't believe how boring prison is. 'Are there any computers here, Rebecca?'

'Yeah, we have a computer room, but you have to be a prisoner who is on special benefits for that.'

'What do you mean?'

'Well, they can't just let anyone use them, can they? Who knows what people could get up to. We're criminals, after all.' We smile at each other.

'Yeah,' I giggle. 'You're right there, bunch of bloody crims. Bet you can't trust anyone round here.' I'm enjoying my first day. Prison is nothing like you would think it would be. It's like a little holiday.

It's my first visit and it's Jimmy.

'Hello, Jimmy, how's things? Come here, give me a hug. I'm missing you.'

'Are you? I miss you too, how they treating you? Did you get your cocktails on arrival?'

'Yeah, and my caviar. Mind, I don't like caviar much, so I settled for sausage and mash.'

'Yeah, I don't blame you, that stuff tastes like shit. Have you seen the doctor yet?'

'No, I've got my psychoanalysis tomorrow. I think they'll just opt for electrocuting me an hour after the appointment, to be honest with you.'

'Yeah, it might knock some sense into you.'

'Hey, you'll never guess who's here?'

'Who?'

'Jacquie Nixon, Keith's wife. Throws her weight around a bit as well.'

'She giving you any hassle?'

'Nah, she tried to take some stuff off my cellmate and I put a stop to it, but I've not seen her since.'

'Be careful there, she's not a one to be messed with.'

'Yeah, I know, they reckon she's top dog around here and that's fine, but she's not taking any of my weekly allowance off me. No way, I don't care who she is.'

'Yeah, you're right there, don't give the little bitch nothing.'

'So what's been going on, then, since I've been away?'

'Nothing, really. Dave and Caroline are shagging.'

'Yeah, I know.'

'How the hell do you know that in here?'

'She told me, they've been at it for ages. He's quite sweet with her. I hope you're not winding him up about it.'

'Me? As if I would,' Jimmy says while giving me a naughty grin.

'You would, you.'

'Listen, I'm sending you some stuff in tomorrow. Is there anything you want or need?'

'Nah, not really. Some chocolate wouldn't go amiss. Oh, is there any chance you could have a word in the right ear and get me in the computer suite? They reckon you have to be a prisoner on special benefits for it and, well, you know I like to mess around on computers.'

'Leave it with me. I'll get it sorted today for you.'

'Thanks, Jimmy.'

Jimmy is gone an hour and a half and one of the guards comes to my cell. 'Reilly, you have been assigned to the computer suite tomorrow. A guard will collect you at 10.30am.'

Good old Jimmy...

It's 10.30am and the guard has come to collect me to take me to the computer suite. As we walk down the corridor you could cut the atmosphere with a knife. It's almost like the guard is annoyed because I'm allowed on the computers, yet I'm not a prisoner with special benefits. I sit right at the back. I don't want them seeing what I'm looking at, but I must see Mike. I'm missing him like crazy. I log on to the computer and go on to a few websites, like Sky News, the normal ones you would look at. I then have to make sure I bypass the prison security. I'm assuming they have a main server that reports back what websites are being logged on to using the prison IP address, but I'm too smart to not realise this. I log on to the CCTV and he's not there, it's just an empty street. Mind you, it has only just gone 11am. No one will be at the club yet either. Oh well, this is boring. What to do now? I wonder if I could log on to the prison CCTV? That might be cool. I try a few things and, bingo, I'm in. Oh look, there's reception and the kitchen. What we having for lunch then? I zoom into the pots and pans in the oven. Oo, curry. Oh, the guard is coming over, better change the screen. I smile sweetly at the guard, like butter wouldn't melt. I log back into Mike's street camera. Ah, there he is. I like that jumper he is wearing. I got him that for his birthday last year. I wonder what he would think if he knew I could see him. Oh, there's Diane, the silly little cow. Damn, there's the lunchtime bell. Surely it can't be already.

As everyone sits having their lunch my table, all of a sudden, feels crowded. It was just me and Rebecca yesterday. Why is everyone now sitting here? Rebecca looks petrified but she needn't be scared. I won't let anyone touch her.

'So, Rebecca, what have you been doing today?' I say to try and occupy her mind.

'Oh, I was in the mail room today.'

'Really, what do you do in there all day?'

'I sort through the mail for everyone, you have had something through the post today.'

'Did I?'

'Yeah, it'll be delivered later.'

'Great, something to look forward to.'

One woman shouts, 'Hey, I had dog shit through my door once,' and everyone starts to laugh.

Jacquie Nixon shouts, 'You'll never guess what I had through my door once.'

'What?' says one of her friends.

'Four dicks.'

'Jesus, four dicks, ha! I'd love just one dick through my door,' replies her friend.

'What I couldn't do with a dick right now.'

Everyone is laughing. Yet I know why she got the four dicks. I wonder if she does. I raise my head and look her in the eye. You can normally tell if someone is talking in general terms or trying to have a dig and she's not really looking at me. She's involving everyone in the conversation, so I'm guessing she doesn't know.

'What did you do with them, then?' shouts one of the girls.

'Keith had been a wanker all day so I chopped them up and put them in his tea, the little bastard.'

So that's what eventually happened to their dicks, then. The bell goes and it's back to our cells for another hour. Then at 2.30pm I can go back to the computer suite. I'm liking all this. Jimmy's right, it is like Butlins.

It's 4.30pm. 'Reilly, doctor is here to see you.'

'Great, does he have his red-hot poker to stab me with if I don't give him the right answers?'

I make my way into his office and he's a little man with a small frame, grey hair and glasses.

'Hello, Miss Reilly. I'm Doctor Cavendish. Today is just an introduction to each other. I can even show you some breathing techniques which may help with your anxieties.'

What? Who the hell has told him that?

'I don't have anxiety.'

'Don't worry about anything that gets said in this room, it's totally confidential. Mr Simpson has explained a little bit to me. I'm here to help you, nothing else.'

'I don't get anxious about anything.'

'What about the kitchen cupboard?'

'What about it?'

'Why would you feel that something would happen to you if the tins aren't straight?'

I shrug my shoulders and it's not that I'm being uncooperative, I just don't have the answer.

'Tell me about your relationship with Michael Taylor.'

'What? Jesus Christ. What has that got to do with anything? Why would he even be mentioned in here today? He's my friend, nothing else.'

'Why are you getting angry, Miss Reilly? It's a simple question.'

This doctor has one tone and one tone only. He's like a machine.

'I'm not getting angry. I just don't see what Mike has to do with anything.'

'Have you always been in love with him?' For God's sake, Jimmy, what on earth are you telling the doctor that for? I'm a little embarrassed. I put my head down in shame.

'No, not always. I wanted him to be my dad for a little while and as I grew older my feelings towards him changed, that's all.'

'Who are your parents and what role do they play in your life?'

'I don't have any parents, doctor. Mr Simpson and Mr Taylor invented me in their back garden in the 80s.' I give him a cheeky grin. I can see this is going to be a waste of time.

'Do you often tell jokes to get yourself out of uncomfortable situations? Is that how you deal with difficult problems, by making a joke out of them?' Bloody doctor, what does he know? 'What are your feelings on your father?'

'I don't have a dad. I've never known who my dad is so I don't have any feelings on him. Are we finished here?'

'Why are you so eager to get out? I'm here to help you, we still have plenty of time.'

'No, I don't want to spend any more time with you. Is that OK, doctor?'

'OK, Miss Reilly, I can see we're not going to get anywhere today. Maybe next week you will be in a better mood.'

Cheeky bastard, and wait till I see Jimmy. What the hell did he tell him all that for? Like I want people to know that I'm in love with Mike. Imagine if he found out.

I rush straight to the phones to call Jimmy and I don't care who's using them, I'm furious with him. Someone is on the phone so I grab it from her hands and hang up on her caller.

'Erm, I think you've been long enough, don't you? Let others have a turn.'

She's not impressed. 'Hey, you cheeky bitch, wait till I tell Jacquie.'

'Jacquie indeed, like I give a shit about her.'

She was probably talking to no one anyway. Actually, it might have been her kid. Aw, what about my kid, poor George? Wait till I see Jimmy.

'Jimmy.'

'Ah, Treas, have you seen the doctor yet?'

'Seen the doctor? I'll bloody doctor you, what the hell have you been saying to him?'

'Nothing, I told him what I know and I know that you need

help and he's going to help you. Don't blame me, it's not my fault you're fucking nuts, is it?' He laughs down the phone.

'There's nothing funny about this.'

'What did he say? Did he say you're crazy, like that mad hatter?'

'Oh, certifiably, he got the certificate out in front of me, but he got a sudden bump on the head before he could sign it.' We giggle. I suppose it is a little funny. 'But you told him about Mike. I was so embarrassed. I never knew where to put my face.'

'Oi, listen, you've got nothing to be embarrassed about, especially in front of me. You tell that doctor everything and I mean it, you need help. I know we laugh and joke about it but you do, you're not well.'

'I know, I'll be better next week and open up to him a bit more. Do you think I should talk about my eighteenth to him?'

'Yeah, I think you should, you need to talk to someone about it. I should have taken you straight away to speak to someone. But only if you feel comfortable, but it's probably best to get everything out of the way.'

'Yeah, maybe. See you, Jimmy.'

'Yeah, see you, Treas.'

I hang up the phone and go back to my cell.

As I'm lying on my bed lost in my own thoughts of what the doctor was saying about my anxiety the bell goes. That's all that seems to happen in here, bells.

'Oo, come on Kate, I've heard it's apple crumble for pudding today.' Rebecca is so childish in that way, she gets excited over the littlest of things. I like it, I think she's cute. We make our way into the dining room and sit down to our dinner, my table seems full again. Jacquie decides to sit next to me.

'So, Rebecca, what shall we do tonight, then? Fancy coming to my club? We'll have a right laugh. I'll introduce you to Jimmy and the boys.'

Rebecca looks too frightened to answer. I think these people intimidate her and they shouldn't really, they're just loud-mouthed bitches with nothing else to do.

Jacquie turns to me and says, 'Hey, Treas. How's your dinner?'

I look up at her. What a cheeky bitch, only Jimmy calls me Treas.

'It's OK, Jacquie, it's a meal anyway.'

'How's the mince?' she says. As I move my fork around the mince, I see there's a ton of salt in it. Really, is that the best she gets? A bit of salt in my dinner, oo, I'm quaking in my boots. I turn to her and say, 'I'll tell you what, Jacquie, since my mince is so nice, why don't I share?' and I tip my whole dinner over hers.

I get up from the table and walk away. She doesn't follow me or say anything else. It's normally the case with people like that – you show them you're scared, they take the piss. You answer back and they're unsure as to how far you'll go. After all, if I beat her in a fight she'd lose her status in here and can she really afford that? It means a lot to her, whereas me, I'm not bothered. I've got enough of my own problems. I want to do my time and go home.

I get back to my cell and the guard is there.

'Reilly, post.'

She throws me a letter. They've opened it and read it first, mind, cheeky things.

Hey Kate,

I can't believe you're in prison, are you not scared? Have you seen Myra Hindley yet?

I'm going on holiday next month, I can't wait, Turkey. I'll be a bronzed babe by the time I get back. You could have come if you weren't in prison. I've been promoted at the salon too. I miss you like crazy though. Six months can't come quick enough. We'll go on holiday when you get out, somewhere really nice. They reckon Ayia Napa is the place to go – party central.

Love Jennie x

Oo, Jennie's had a promotion, good for her. Jennie the spoilt little bitch is going on holiday. I hope customs stop you for having too much fake tan and a big head. Bloody salon, who gives a shit about the salon? You'd still be getting picked on and made to sweep the floor and make the tea if it wasn't for me.

Hey Jennie,

Wow, a holiday... You're so lucky and we definitely need to try that Ayia Napa when I get out. I can't believe you've been promoted. I always said you were too good to be a junior. You're going to turn the men wild when you're on holiday, you always suit a tan.

Myra Hindley is not in here, it's a low-security prison. But I'll tell you who is. That Rebecca from our primary school. We share a cell, believe it or not. She's not changed much. She's finally found cardigans to fit her and her hair is so long, she's obsessed with it. Mind, it's lovely. You'd love to get your hands on it, especially now you're not a junior, you could style it for her when she gets out.

I'm not scared in here. It's a bit like a holiday, really.

Love Kate x

I put Jennie's letter in the envelope. I sometimes wonder what they would say if I wrote down all the things I actually do think. I glance over at Rebecca and she's brushing her hair. It goes down right past her bum. I've never seen an adult with hair that long before. I thought it was a given that when you get to a certain age you have your hair cut. I walk over to her and hold her hair in my hands. It takes both my hands to grab it all as it's really thick. 'Can I brush your hair, please?'

'Yeah, course you can.' She hands me the brush and I start to brush it. It makes me think about Jennie. Imagine this being your life, just brushing hair all day long. Is that all she has to think about? Well, I suppose not, she does cut hair as well. But still her life is so much easier compared to mine. Ever since we were kids she had it all. Boys always fancied her. Perfect mum and dad, perfect clothes. Even being able to do hair and make-up. It's a perfect girl's world compared to my life.

Rebecca pulls away from my brushing and turns to me. 'Kate, I'm so pleased you're here. Ever since you came in no one has said anything unkind to me. I think they're secretly a little scared of you. Thank you.'

'You don't have to thank me Rebecca, we're friends.'

'Are we?'

'Well, of course we are.'

Rebecca has a smile on her face which looks like it's taking over the room. 'It's nice to have a friend, isn't it?' Rebecca then turns her head. 'Please brush my hair again. I like it.'

Rebecca really is pleased to have someone. I bet she's gone her entire life like a loner with no one. I return to the brushing. I want to say, 'Actually, Rebecca, if I had no friends I would have had a perfect life. You're better off staying the way you are.'

Dear Kate,

I spoke to Mike last week and he told me the situation. You're a good girl, you always have been. I've had a few friends over the years who've been in prison and it's not as bad as you think. Especially the prison you're in. You'll probably enjoy the peace and quiet. I'm sending you in a few good books to read, to help pass the time away. If they offer you any courses, take them. You really need something to occupy your mind in a place like that.

Love Lawrence x x

My favourite thing to read. I always love getting his letters. I wonder what my life would have been like if he'd stayed in Bridgeborough.

Dear Lawrence,

Thank you for your letter I always love reading them. There is a knitting course being offered so I might take them up on it and knit you a jumper. The image I have of you in my head wearing a pink jumper is enough to keep anyone going. When I get out I'm going to look at coming to London. I know I keep saying it but this time I mean it.

Thank you for the books. I gave one to my cellmate. I hope you don't mind.

Love Kate x x

Well, that's my first week over with and I'm pleased to say I've not been in any fights or felt a need to obsess about anything. Well, apart from looking after Rebecca. But that's normal. I suppose she did look after me all the time when I was younger, without her knowledge, obviously. Oh, and the CCTV. But that's not an obsession, it's just I like looking at Mike and Jimmy. It's more a hobby than an obsession.

I can't believe Rebecca is in prison, she doesn't seem the type.

'Rebecca, what on earth are you in prison for?'

'Well, I lived with my grandmother from being a little girl. My mother died when I was five.'

Oh my God, her mother died, no wonder she dressed like a nana. What an awful thing to happen. 'I never knew that. How awful, how did she die?'

'She died of cancer. My dad left us when I was three, so my grandmother raised me. She ended up in a care home, she got a little too much for me to handle, really. Anyway, I never really felt like they were looking after her, they said I was being a bit picky. How picky can you be when you're taking care of a loved one? My grandmother deserved the best, she'd always looked after me. I hated the manager in the care home. I'm sure she used to deliberately try and upset me. Anyway, when my grandmother died, I was so upset I went back to the care home and set it on fire. I knew there was nobody there, they were all on a day trip. So I'm in here for arson. Well, I was lucky it wasn't murder, really. Mind, the old folks are happy as Larry. They all got transferred over to the new home half a mile up the road. They say it's luxury, some of them still write to me now.'

Goodness me, Reckless Rebecca setting free the old folks. I can imagine the scene: all running in, I want the penthouse suite, I'll hit you with my walking stick you even think about taking it off me.

'So how long did you get, then?'

'Two years. I've only done nine months so still got a while to go. Not that I have anything to get out for.'

'When you get out of here Rebecca, you make sure that you find me. I'll give you something to get out for. I could even get you a job at the club.' Just then a guard interrupts us.

'Reilly. Visitor.'

Great, Jimmy is here. I'm missing him loads in here. I make my way to the visiting suite and can't believe who it is when I get there. Oh God, it's her, why is she visiting me in here? She can't even stand looking at me on the outside, never mind in here.

'Hello, darling. How are you? I've been worried about you.'

'Have you?'

'Yeah, I mean fancy you being in here. It's no place for a girl.'

'Well, that's funny, Mum, cos I reckon there's enough of us girls in here so it must be a place for girls.'

'Kate, I'm so embarrassed. I mean, prison, really? I know you think knocking about with Jimmy and Mike makes you look cool, but this is not cool. Why can't you just get a job in a salon, like Jennie? I bumped into her mum last week and she was asking about you. I was so embarrassed. She was bragging about Jennie.'

'Yeah, well, Jennie is wonderful, isn't she?'

'You couldn't speak to Mike and ask him to give me some money, could you? It's just, well, you know, it's hard for me sometimes.'

'You know what? Doctor Cavendish would really like to meet you. He thinks I make you up.'

'Doctor Cavendish, who is he?'

'It's my doctor.'

'What on earth are you seeing a doctor for?'

'It's a weekly thing. The guards in here don't think this is a place for girls so we must all be ill in some way, so it's compulsory to have a doctor check you over on a weekly basis.'

Mum leaves, we even manage a half-hearted hug before she goes. Probably because I said I would get her some money.

Dear Gem,

How's things? I'm missing you. Jimmy has said it would be best if I didn't visit you. I'm not sure what's going on with you two but if Jimmy is telling me not to visit I think it's best I don't. Jennie was in the club on Friday with a new bloke. So looks like she's finally over Paul. Wink wink.

Your mum says she might visit you so I thought I better give you the heads up so you can start planning your escape. Oops, probably shouldn't write that, the bastards will intercept the letter and probably bin it thinking you're a mastermind criminal and planning on escaping. IT'S A JOKE, YOU FUCKING TWATS.

By the way, Diane had a little boy. Thanks for doing this, you know you mean the world to me. When you get out we'll have the biggest party Bridgeborough has ever seen.

Love Mike x

Oh, how very nice. Diane having a little boy. What about my boy, my baby George? Bastards. It's OK for you two, having everything you want. Thanks for doing this? I ain't doing this for you two. It's for my own sanity, not to help that bitch of yours out. If you were any kind of friend, no matter what Jimmy said, you'd be visiting me on the sly. I would if it was you. You're a selfish bastard, Mike.

Dear Mike,

I'm really happy for you and Diane, give the baby a kiss from Auntie Kate. I'll buy him the biggest present when I get out. Hope Diane is feeling better.

Yeah, don't visit, Jimmy's here enough and even that's doing my head in. Six months will fly by. I'm already one month in. It's more like a holiday camp than prison. Can't wait for the party. Bit late for the heads up, Mum's already been. Could you sort her out some money? You know what she's like. Please take care of her till I get out. I do worry about her sometimes.

Love Kate x

PS Really pleased Jennie is over Paul, wink wink.

The breakfast bell's just gone. Rebecca just lies on her bed which is unusual for her, she's normally excited, trying to guess what we are having.

'Hey, Rebecca, you coming to breakfast?'

'No thanks, I feel a bit sick, if I'm honest. I think I'll just rest in my bed all day, it must have been something I ate.'

'Do you want me to tell a guard?'

'Nah, you're OK, it will pass. I'm sure it's a twenty-four hour thing.'

It's funny how, when I was younger, I used to pray she'd not get ill. Now I'm doing the same. Poor Rebecca. I make my way to breakfast and sit on my own. I'm a little like Rebecca and don't get on too well in here. Well, I think it's partly that, and partly the girls are scared that if they talk to me they will get in trouble off Jacquie Nixon. It's almost like they expect us to have some big kick-off. Probably because Jimmy and Keith would kill each other if they were in the same prison but it doesn't mean that we would do the same. That's the bell gone, it's time to make my way to the computer suite.

I log on as usual and check out Mike's place. I might catch a glimpse of the baby. I'm still not sure what they've called it. Jimmy is due tomorrow, I must ask him. Nah, no sign of them in the street. They're probably not even dressed yet. I'll have to just look at the prison goings-on again. Why I find it so intriguing to look at a place where I live all the time is beyond me. As I'm looking at the CCTV, I see Jacquie and the girls walking the corridor. Where are they going at this time? Hey, they're heading to my cell, what the hell are they up to? I zoom in on them and to my shock I see the top of a pair of scissors poking out of Jacquie's pocket. I click off the computer and jump up from my seat.

'Hey, guard, I feel ill, can I go back to my cell, please?'

'No, you can't. There's no one to take you. You will have to wait.'

'Hey, I'm going to shit myself here. Where do you think I'm going to go?'

'For God's sake, Reilly, do you think this prison revolves around you? If you need to shit yourself, well, just do it then.'

What a cow. I need to get back. What is going on in that cell? Rebecca wasn't well this morning. She's in there. If they have touched her I'll kill them. The guard finally lets me go and I rush as quickly as I can to my cell. I have this awful vision in my mind that Rebecca will be dead on the bed when I get there, covered in blood. I finally get back to my cell and Rebecca is in bed, not moving. I take a huge gulp of air and walk slowly towards her bed.

'Rebecca, are you OK? You coming to lunch?'

'No, please just go away.' The minute she speaks I jump out of my skin, I thought she was dead.

'Hey, what is it? What's wrong?'

'Nothing, leave me alone.'

I walk over to her and playfully tug on her hair. She has it in a plait today. 'Come on, miserable chops, the food's not that bad, is it?'

As I tug her plait the whole thing comes off in my hand. They've chopped her hair off, the fucking bitches. I'm going to kill them. I stand up and without thinking about anything other than Rebecca I storm over to the dining room. I'm going to kill her, I mean it. I walk in and Jacquie is laughing like a hyena. I storm over to her and nut her square in the face.

Before I know it, I'm punching and kicking her. I can't seem to stop. I can hear the guards milling around but the anger inside of me is too much for me to even comprehend what they're saying to me. Even the girls are in uproar. There's a lot of commotion going on around me. Then all of a sudden… What the hell is that? What has happened? I'm lying on the floor. Oh God, I'm a dead weight. I can't move. What's that? Jesus, I've pissed myself. They've shot me with a stun gun, the bastards have shot me.

As I'm lying there, I see Jacquie lying beside me. Ugh, fucking hell, she looks like Roger and Paul. Tell me I've not killed her. Please, someone tell me I've not killed her. Several guards come towards me and grab a piece of me each and drag me to a cell with only a bed and a toilet in there. I'm lying on the bed, still piss-stained, yet

I don't have the strength to get up.

I've just killed Jacquie Nixon. SHIT.

Chapter 18 – Doctor Cavendish

It feels like I've been in here for years, never mind months. Surely I've done my time now. They can't leave me here. But at least I've been allowed to shower and change my piss-stained trousers. I start to think of the fact I'm never going home. I'm a murderer, I've actually killed someone. Then I hear the rattling of the locks and a guard comes in.

'What's going on? You can't leave me here.'

'We can do what we like, Reilly. You think your Mr Simpson can get you out of this one?'

'I've been stuck in here for months. Surely this is against my human rights?'

'Ha! Months, Reilly? It's only been three days. Anyone who violently attacks another person is sent to solitary until we think they can control their temper.'

'What, three days, is that all? I need to make a phone call. I've got to speak to Jimmy.'

'A phone call, Miss Reilly? Of course you can. I'll get an escort to take you to the telephones as soon as the butler has served you your lunch. Anything else, Miss Reilly? Can I plump your cushions for you? This is solitary, you don't get phone calls or privileges in here and your Mr Simpson won't be visiting you for a while.'

What the hell will I say to Jimmy? He'll go mental. He sent me in here to sort myself out. Another fine mess I've got myself into. It wasn't even my fault, she cut Rebecca's hair off. What else was I supposed to do? Well, probably not kill her.

I'm not sure how much time goes by, but it feels like years.

'Reilly, I'm here to take you to see Doctor Cavendish.'

Oh great, the freak show begins then. At least I can get out of here. As I walk into the office he's sitting there looking at me like I really am crazy.

'Miss Reilly, do you want to explain to me what happened this week?'

'No, and it's Kate, you can call me Kate. Miss Reilly is far too formal. Have you spoken to Jimmy? Because I know you two talk.'

'Yes, I have.'

'Well, what's he saying?'

'He wants you to tell me exactly what went on. There has been trouble with Keith Nixon as well. He thought Mr Simpson had put you up to it.'

'What? Jesus Christ, is Jimmy OK?'

'Yes, he's fine, which is more than I can say about Keith. Remind me never to cross you two. Listen, I'm not bothered about turf wars or anything like that. I want to keep out of stuff like that. Mr Simpson is paying me to take care of you and that's all I'm doing. So let's start again. What happened last week?'

'Listen, Doctor Cavendish, do you have a telephone, can I use it, please? I'll be really quick.'

'You better be.' He hands me the phone.

'Jimmy, Jimmy, it's me.'

'What the fuck have you done, Kate? You do realise if she dies you'll be in there forever, don't you? I sent you in there to sort yourself out. Why do you have to take the piss every time?'

'What? She's not dead? Bloody hell, why have they not told me? It wasn't me, it was her. She started following me around the prison, sitting next to me.'

'Oh, bloody hell, Treas, why did you not say that before, if she sat next to you she deserved to be put on a life support machine, you should have said earlier. I'll tell you what, the prosecution won't have a case against you with that one.'

'No, I don't mean that. I mean, well she was sabotaging my meals, winding me up. They went into my cell with a pair of scissors, they cut off my cellmate's hair. I swear if I'd have been in that cell I would have been stabbed. Yeah, I lost my temper, and I should have thought – but, it could have been me.'

'Listen, Kate, you better hope to God she pulls through. I can't help you if you go down for murder, but I'll get you the best solicitor money can buy to get you the least amount of time. Even attempted murder you're looking at years.'

Years… I'm only supposed to be doing six months and it's not even my crime.

Dear Gem,

I went round to see your mum again yesterday and sorted her some money. Don't worry, I'll take care of her.

Not sure what happened with Jacquie Nixon but keep your nose clean. I miss you. I want you home soon. Caroline and Dave are getting wed, can you believe that? I hope they hang on so you can come. Jack is getting massive now, he can't wait to see his Auntie Kate. The bastards treating you OK? Yes, I mean you twats reading this. Having a good look, are we?

Mike x

Caroline and Dave are getting wed. That's nice. I like Caroline and he makes her happy. I'll be upset if I miss their wedding. I can't believe I'm stuck in here for something I never even did. I hope Jimmy is not winding them up. Oo, his baby is getting big. What about my baby, what about George?

Dear Mike,

Thanks for sorting out my mum. You know what she's like, she needs looking after sometimes. The whole Jacquie Nixon thing was a total misunderstanding.

I can't wait to see the baby when I get out, if I get out. Will you get Dave and Caroline a really good present from me if I miss the wedding? I'd have loved to be bridesmaid. Hey, maybe they could give me day release in here. It's not like I'm a criminal or anything. Well, not a real one like that Myra Hindley.

I miss you too.

Gem x

Jacquie Nixon pulled through eventually and has been transferred to another prison. The guards think maybe it's best if us two are kept apart. She's also decided not to press charges. I think Jimmy and Keith may have helped her come to that decision. The prison authorities have said that it must be a punishable offence. I'm not sure what strings Jimmy is pulling on the outside as it should be attempted murder regardless of whether Jacquie presses charges or not, but they have decided to just add three months on to my sentence. It was classed as inciting a riot. Ha! As if.

The girls keep asking me to be top dog. They feel like they need some direction or instruction but I don't have time for that. I've got enough problems. Baby George is pining for me. So is Mike.

Hey Gem,

How's things? I got married last week. I can't believe you missed it, but Diane was getting a bit shirty about it. Especially since Jack has been born. She did say it would be better that you weren't there anyway and I suppose she does have a point. You two are a nightmare together.

Hey, only four months and you'll be out. I can't wait. Baby Jack is dying to meet you. If only I could visit. I could have brought him in to see you. The boys at the club are missing you, it's not the same without your shit jokes.

Love Mike xx

Married! He got married without me. No, no, how could he get married without me even being there or writing to me to tell me first? He knows what he's doing, he does this all the time, waits until events are past before he mentions them to me because he knows what my reaction will be. I cry all night into my pillow.

How could he get married without me being there? I can't even write back to that, what on earth do I even say? God, I hate him. I'm stuck in here for that fucking bitch Diane, doing her time, and she gets it all, everything I have ever wanted – a baby, Mike as her husband. What has she got that I don't? I'm going to kill her when I get out. That's it, I'm going to kill the fucking bitch.

I'm so angry right now. Why do nice things happen to everyone else yet I get the shit? I walk towards the visiting suite as Jimmy is here to see me. Right now I don't want to see him. It's all his fault, he told me to come in here. He said he would help me get my head sorted out yet he arranges for the shitest doctor in the world to see me.

'Hello, Jimmy, you OK?'

'Yeah, what's the matter? You don't seem your happy self.'

'Ah, nothing. I'm fed up now, I want to go home.'

'Yeah, well, you would have been home by now if you weren't playing the fucking hero.'

'Yeah, I know.'

'Are you still seeing the doctor? He says you're not really talking to him much and that you've become quite withdrawn. Are you sure you're OK?'

'Yeah, listen, I have a headache, do you mind if we cut the visiting short today?'

'Are you sure you're OK? I've not seen you like this before.'

'Yeah, I'm fine, honest. I'm just headachy. It's my period, you know what I get like.'

'OK then.'

I walk out of the visiting suite and don't even look back. I never want to see Jimmy again. When I get out of here, I'm not even going to tell them. I'm going to get my George back. I don't need those two.

Hey Gem,

I never got a response to my last letter. I wonder if the bastards put it in the bin. Yes, you fucking twats reading this letter. Give us a break. I hope everything's OK. I'm counting down the days before you come out. I really miss you. Your flat is fine. I've been going over making sure all the time and I sorted your mum out with some more money.

Jack is crawling now, can you believe it? He'll be drinking cider by the time you come out of there, so you better hurry up.

Love Mike xx

How can he write to me like everything is OK? Surely he knows how hurt I would be. I scrumple up his letter and throw it against the wall. I don't want any more letters from him. I want nothing from him.

Just then I hear, 'Reilly. Visitor.'

'Tell them I'm sick.'

'Are you sure? Because we can't be coming back, you can't change your mind in half an hour, you know.'

'Tell them I'm sick. I'm fucking sick of them.'

I'm not going to see Jimmy any more, or that stupid doctor of his. I don't even know why he bothered getting him, he was shit. I could be a doctor if that's all they do, sit and talk to you about your childhood.

I still watch Mike and Jimmy on CCTV. I can't give them up completely, my stomach cramps would start again.

I might go back and kill Jacquie Nixon. I don't even mind being in prison. It's a lot easier than being on the outside, wondering who to argue with next or get annoyed with. Plus, there's no cupboard for me to keep track of in here. Mind, the dirty-hand smell is still in the prison.

Gem,

You're worrying me now. Jimmy said you refused his visit, is everything OK? Can I come to see you, please? If it's something I have done or Jimmy has done, please let us help. Jimmy said you've not been well. You won't be in there much longer and when you come out we'll have a huge party. We were even thinking of upgrading your car.

Love Mike xx

Yeah, I bet you were thinking of upgrading my car. What's wrong, your little angel not falling into line any more? Why don't you just fucking die, Mike? Let me get on with my life.

I don't even want to leave prison now. I think I would happily stay here forever. I don't want any more letters or visits from anyone.

Rebecca is sitting on the edge of my bed. 'Are you OK, Kate? You seem really upset about something.'

'I'm fine honestly. It's just the longer I stay in here the more I don't want to leave.' We get interrupted by one of the guards. 'Reilly, your weekly appointment with Doctor Cavendish is now, so come on.'

'No, I don't want to see the doctor any more. I've decided to train as a doctor, so you tell him I've been to the library to get some medical books and I've cured myself and I wasn't even as sick as he thought, so maybe he needs to go back to university and resit his exams. He's clearly a shit doctor.'

'Reilly, do you think I have time to waste coming to tell you that you have visitors that you don't want to see, or doctors that you don't want to see? This is not a hotel. I wonder if there's anyone you *would* like to see.'

'I don't want to see you right now, so be gone before someone drops a house on you.'

Treas,

Why are you refusing to see me or write back to Mike? You know I get pissed off when you do this. I hope everything's OK and you're not back in solitary. You've not done something else stupid, have you? You'll be out soon. I'm signing the club over to you. It's yours, Treas, every piece of it, just like you've always wanted.

Love Jimmy xx

You know what, Jimmy? When I get out, if I ever get out, I might take a match to your stupid club. You won't be so clever then, will you?

I lie on my bed just staring at the ceiling and wonder why it all went so wrong. What did I do to deserve any of this? I always thought I was a nice person. Well I *was*, before the rape. Just then I feel someone sit on my bed. As I turn my head I see Rebecca. She touches my hand.

'Kate, are you OK?'

'Yes, Rebecca, I'm fine.'

'It's just, you seem to have gone all depressed the last few months and it's not the same in here. You used to be good fun. I've never seen you smile for ages.'

'Really, I'm fine. I just want to get out of here now. Hey, your hair's growing back at least.'

'Yeah, thank God. I looked like a boy before, ha!'

'Ha! Yeah, you did a little.'

'Listen me and the girls have managed to get some booze in here. We're thinking of having a party later. Why don't you join us? We'll have a laugh. It would be nice to let our hair down. Ha! Get that? Can you believe she cut my hair off?'

'Oh, I'm glad you can see the funny side of it.'

'You looked after me for months. I've never had anyone look after me before and I wanted to say thanks. Please say you'll get drunk with us.'

'OK then, you're on, let's get drunk.'

I don't know how they got the booze into the prison but they did. We drink an absolute skinful. Rebecca even kissed one of the other girls, the little minx, as Mike would say. Mike, the dirty bastard, I drunkenly slur to myself. I'm going to respond to his letters, yes, drunkenly respond to his letters, and Jimmy's. This is such a good idea in my drunken stupor and don't even try to talk me out of this.

Dear Mike,

You're a fucking wanker and so is your fat bitch wife. You

know what, as well? I wish that worm had eaten you alive. I was hoping you would have a big hole in your belly. It would be a better sight than what's there now. Dickhead. And another thing, I never enjoyed sex with you, it was shit every time. A young student was better in bed than you. That's because you're old and old people shouldn't have sex. What does Diane even see in you? Speaking of which, did I ever tell you that Diane looks like a cross between a bulldog and a bumblebee? Not to mention that baby of yours. I heard it won the ugliest baby competition – must take after its dickheaded cunty dad then.

Love Gem xx

PS Don't bother writing back, you won't get a response. In fact, if you do write back make sure it's on soft paper because I would only use it to wipe my arse on.

Dear Jimmy,

Have I ever told you that you're a fat wanker with wanky hands? In fact, someone once said he caught you wanking in the office. You're a dirty wanker who is only good enough for wanking. Don't visit me any more, oh, and another thing – that half a million pounds, I want my half or I'm telling everyone you wanked in the office.

Love Treas xx

My head is ringing the next day. I don't normally suffer hangovers but this is terrible.

'Morning, Rebecca. God, that booze, what the hell was it?'

'It was home brew, they've been brewing it in the garden.'

'Jesus, I've never had booze like that in my life. I could bottle that up and sell it in the club. One glass of that and you're off your head all night.'

'It was a good night, though, wasn't it, Kate? Can you remember you and Lucy swapping clothes? I think you even swapped bras at one point.'

'Really?'

'Yeah, look on the floor, they're her clothes.'

'How the hell did fat Lucy fit in my clothes? Look at them, they're like a circus tent.' I pick up these huge black tracksuit bottoms and they could honestly fit two people in. 'Ugh. I bet they stink of Lucy's big fat arse.'

My head is thumping. If I wasn't so ill, I'd rub the sweaty crotch in Rebecca's face for a laugh.

At the breakfast table I can't even look at the food without vomiting in my own mouth. The sooner I can go back to my cell and lie down the better.

I finally get back to my cell. I think I'll sleep off this hangover. I can't even make my way to the computer suite today so I must be bad.

The following day I still can't make it to the computer suite or even the dining room for lunch. I'm sure I must have picked up a bug, a hangover can't last this long, surely. Maybe it's because I haven't drunk for so long that it effected me more. I'm having the most terrible flashbacks. I remember dancing on the table for all the other girls. I start to think about dancing in the club. I really miss the club. My stomach cramps are coming back as I think about the club and the people in it. Especially Mike and Jimmy. When is it going to be my turn, when is something nice going to happen to me?

As I lie on my bed thinking of nice things that could happen to me I turn my head and notice there is a letter waiting for me.

Dear Gem,

I'm not really sure what has got into you but me and Jimmy got some extremely strange letters from you. I can only assume someone else wrote them as they weren't in your handwriting, it was more like a child's scribblings than your neat writing. Mind you, it is something you would say when you get into one of your furies. Never mind, I wish you would write back or allow us to visit, please respond. Oh, and I used soft paper in case you wanted to wipe your arse on it.

By the way, Jimmy says he has never wanked in his office and if he finds out who told you that he will shoot their dicks off :)

Love Mike xx

PS Calling a baby ugly. Really, Kate.

Holy shit, I seem to have some vague memory of writing a letter to Jimmy about wanking. Oh my God, I hope they don't realise it was me while drunk. Imagine the shame. I'm going to have to let them visit now. God, they'll think I'm crazy. Well, I am crazy. What on earth would even make me write that stuff? Kate Reilly, another fine mess you've got yourself into. He is right as well, calling a baby ugly, how cruel. No one better call my George ugly, I'll kick their faces in.

I better give Jimmy a ring, I suppose, and try and make amends. I'll never get his club or my upgraded car.

'Hello, Jimmy, it's me, Kate.'

'Treas, you're alive! Where the bloody hell have you been and what was the big idea of those letters?'

'Listen, Jimmy, it wasn't me.'

'Well who the hell was it? And how did they know about the half a million pounds, then?'

'Well, yeah, it *was* me, but it wasn't me, if you know what I mean.'

'I can't imagine anyone in the world ever knows what you mean.'

'Doctor Cavendish suggested I try an exercise, said it will help me. I had to ignore you both, not even respond to your letters or visits, then write you both a note with the cruellest things I could think of and, well, wanking was the worst thing.'

'Hey, I've never wanked in my office.'

'Yeah, I know that, but what else could I put?'

'Did you have to mention the half a million pounds? You could have had people asking questions.'

'I'm sorry, don't get at me, tell the doctor. You know he says I'm sick and need help so I'm doing everything he asked me to. I never wanted to do that, you know.'

'OK then, whatever. Can me and Mike visit you? We've been missing you.'

'I'm thinking maybe you should leave it. I'll be out soon anyway.'

I have two weeks before I'm out of this hellhole. I'm still undecided if I should get Jimmy to pick me up or leave and go to the cottage without a trace. Mind you, even if I got there I'd not know what to do, who to even ask for. Imagine me going up to the locals. Hey, you've not seen a baby, have you? He's about three now. I think he answers to the name of George, but I'm not 100 per cent sure. Oh well, that's decided then.

'Jimmy.'

'Treas, it's you, long time no speak. You heard when you're getting out yet?'

'Yeah, the twenty-eighth. Will you pick me up, please?'

'Yeah, course I will, me and Mike will be there.'

'No, not Mike, just you, please.'

'If that's what you want, but you know running away from him is not going to solve these problems?'

'Yeah, I know, I want to get my head clear, that's all. Please come on your own. Will you do me a favour and not even say I'm getting out that day? Last thing I want is my mum and Jennie round fussing. I fancy a night in my flat on my own.'

'Anything you like, Treas.'

It's my last day in here today. I think I might actually miss Rebecca a little. I wonder if my life would have worked out differently if me and her had stuck together, rather than me and Jennie. Well, I bet she wouldn't pass me white wine and send me to the wolves like Jennie did.

'Kate, I've made you this card. I'm really going to miss you. Can I come and see you when I get out?'

'Of course you can, Rebecca, you're always welcome at the club. You call me beforehand, I might even fix you up with a fella if you like – or a woman. I saw you kissing Louise again.'

'Oh, I just get lonely, that's all.'

I kiss Rebecca on the cheek. I really hope she does look me up. I think we could really help each other.

As I start walking through the gates, I spot this car with 'KATE R' on the plate. What has he brought me?

'Look at this, a nice new set of wheels. Call it a coming-out present.'

I mean, really, who on earth gets a present for coming out of prison? Kate bloody Reilly, that's who. I'm glad I never went to that cottage.

'Jimmy, it's you.' I grab a hold of him, it's been that long I forgot what it was like to have a friendly hug off someone. 'Hey, I'm out, can you believe it? There was a time I thought I was never getting out of there. The whole Jacquie Nixon business…'

'Yeah, I think we'll forget about the Nixons for now.' Jimmy says as he throws me the car keys. 'Holiday's over, you can drive.' As we make our way back to Bridgeborough Jimmy says, 'Doctor Cavendish says you've not even been seeing him. What happened there? I thought you were OK with the whole doctor thing, you said it was a good idea.'

'Well, yeah, it was, but to be honest with you, he talked a load of crap. I could be a doctor if that's all they do. Asking me questions about my childhood, how is that going to help me now I'm nearly twenty-two years old? What I did when I was ten is totally irrelevant.'

'Can't you give him one more chance? You probably should talk about what happened on your eighteenth and what happened with that baby and things. It might help you. I mean, you scared me when you ignored us in there. I didn't know what was going on. Doctor Cavendish also said he never got you to write those letters. I'm not annoyed or anything, I don't know what gets into you sometimes. Wish I was a head doctor, then I would know.'

'I'm sorry. I was so annoyed with Mike and Diane. He was writing to me and bragging about the baby and the wedding. I mean, I was stuck in there doing that bitch's time and they're out having parties. It sticks in the throat a little.'

'Yeah, I know what you mean, but you're out now. *We* can have a party.'

'Not another party. Honestly, if someone fell off a chair you'd hold a party, unless it was you that fell off the chair. You won't have one for you.'

We eventually get back into my flat. It looks bigger than I remember.

'Mike's put you some flowers in there, ready for tomorrow, and a bottle of vodka. You can relax on your own for tonight, but please promise me that you two will get sorted tomorrow. Honestly, you'll probably see him tomorrow and wonder what all the fuss was about. I'm much better looking than him. Why can't you fancy me instead?'

'Leave it out, you could never handle me.'

'You're right there, Treas, one woman is enough for me. I've been trying to work Helen out for years. I reckon I would work out a hundred Rubik's cubes before I worked you out. Oh, and I've got Doctor Cavendish ringing you tomorrow, so make sure you answer and speak to him.'

'OK, you're such a pain.'

Jimmy finally leaves and I'm fit to drop, so I go straight to bed. Ah, this is nice, back in my own bed. I start to drift off and I'm sure I can hear the girls crying through the night and the guards doing their checks.

I wake up and it takes me a while to work out where I am. Oh, it's my flat, my lovely flat. I stick the kettle on and make me some breakfast. I think I'll enjoy the peace and quiet before Mike, Jennie and my mum start to pretend-fuss around me. None of them actually gives a shit. My mum will be on the bum for money, Jennie will want to brag about something and Mike, well, where do we even start with that one?

As my toast pops out of the toaster the door opens. 'Gem, you're already here? You must have got out early this morning.'

'I got out yesterday. I just wanted some peace and quiet.'

'Come here, then, give me a hug. I would have brought Jack round if I'd known you were here. Ah, Gem, I missed you so much. I can't believe what you've missed. Me becoming a dad again, getting married. Dave and Caroline getting hitched.'

'Yeah, I'll have to see the pictures. I'll go over to see Dave and Caroline later.'

'We've got a new lad on the doors, Dan. You'll love him, he's so funny and, get this, his jokes are better than yours.'

'Get lost, no one has better jokes than me.' Mike holds my face and stares into my eyes. 'I can't believe you're actually here. I thought I was never going to see you again. You look different.'

'Do I? How?'

'I don't know, you just do.'

Then before I can even say stop he starts to kiss me and the next thing I know we've ended up in bed together. Great! I lasted all of five minutes of staying away from him.

'Can I hang around here most of the day? I've been worried sick about you.'

'Yeah, whatever, if you like.' We sit and watch a few movies together and it's like I've never even been away. Mike's phone starts to ring. One guess, it's Diane.

'Hello, babe. Don't be stupid, I'm not at Kate's, she doesn't get out till later on this afternoon. I'm at the club. Listen, I'm busy, I'll call you later.'

I've only been out one day and he's lying to his wife already, not a good start to a marriage, is it? Not at Kate's indeed, she should have been round with a thank you present, the stupid bitch. The next thing I know my phone rings with an unidentified number.

'Oh look, it's Diane, what shall I say?' I pick up my phone. 'Hello, this is Kate Reilly here. I can't get to the phone right now. I'm too busy sucking Mike Taylor's cock. Please leave a message after the tone.'

'Hello, Kate.' Oh, Jesus, it's Doctor Cavendish.

'Oh, Doctor Cavendish, I'm so sorry, I thought it was my friend Jennie mucking around, I'm so sorry.' Mike is laughing in the background, like it's funny. 'Yes, I'll come to see you tomorrow, 3pm, I'll be there. I'm so sorry once again, Doctor Cavendish.' I hang up the phone. 'Jesus, that was Doctor Cavendish. I have to see him tomorrow, bloody hell.'

'Ha! That's what you get for trying to wind up my wife.' We giggle in unison and it's like the last nine months never even happened. 'What you seeing a doctor for anyway?'

'Nothing, I was given a course of antibiotics inside and he wants to check me over.'

I never do make it to Doctor Cavendish's office. I'm busy washing my hair. Tell you what, though, I'm having the most strangest of thoughts about Diane. I'd like to break her arm and fold her dead body in a suitcase.

Chapter 19 – The Bubbles

It's my party tonight. I dress up to the nines. I look really stunning. I'm glad I got out of that hellhole eventually. Good job Jacquie Nixon never died, I'd still be in there. Everyone is going to be there tonight, even Jennie. Diane is going as well, mind, which I'm not happy about. If it wasn't for her there would be no need for a party. As I stand at the bar looking out at everyone, I see Diane making a total beeline for me.

'Hello, Kate.'

'Hi, Diane, are you OK?'

'Yeah, I'm great, thanks. Listen, I've never really had the chance to thank you properly for going to prison for me.'

'It's OK, it was better for you to stay at home with Mike, with you being pregnant. How is Jack by the way? Mike brought him round the other day, he's gorgeous.'

'Yeah, he is, he's no bother at all either. I wanted to say how pretty you looked tonight and, well, sorry, really.'

'Sorry, what for?'

'Well, I used to get so jealous of you before all of this. I don't know if it was my pregnancy hormones or what, but I used to hate how Mike was with you. I used to get paranoid that something was going on between you two and when you were away he explained it to me, that he likes to look after you. Plus, you being away, he was still out every weekend and I realised that it was just Mike being Mike and had nothing to do with you. It's just when your boyfriend is hanging around a really pretty girl who seems to have him and

Jimmy Simpson wrapped around her finger, I suppose anyone would worry. Even Dan, Mike's new best friend, has been asking after you. You must have something really special. The way they look after you and love you, you're a very lucky girl.'

Lucky? If only she knew. Lucky would be for me to have just grown up in a normal life, having a husband who goes out to work doing a normal job and me and the kids being at home. Not me going to prison, fighting, hiding murders and rapes. There's nothing lucky about the way my life has turned out. I look at Diane like she's the lucky one and lucky it wasn't her being gang-raped. I have a funny feeling Jimmy has made her come over to me and say all this shite.

'Speaking of which, Diane, Mike told me you two got hitched when I was inside.'

'Yes, we did, you want to see my ring?'

'Yeah.' She flashes me her ring with the stupidest grin on her face. 'Wow, Diane, that's really pretty. It seems you're the lucky girl, not me. I must go now, my friend Jennie is over there and I've missed her. I'll see you soon.'

Bloody Diane, and her ring is awful, stupid cow.

I make my way over to Jennie. 'Jennie, look at you! You look gorgeous. How have you been?'

'Oh, Kate, come here.' She grabs me. 'I've really missed you.' She kisses me on the cheek.

We make our way to the bar and order a couple of cocktails.

'What was prison like then?'

'It was fine.'

'What on earth was that Rebecca like? Is she still a freak?'

'Nah, she was all right, she's quiet, a little bit socially unaccepted, if you know what I mean.'

'Yes, I know exactly what you mean. Freak is what you mean.'

'Jennie, you're so awful.' But we look at each other and giggle. I have missed Jennie.

As I turn around I'm greeted by a man with dark hair and dark brown eyes. He smiles and says, 'Hello Kate, I'm Dan. How was prison?'

'It was OK, I enjoyed the break actually.'

'You and Jimmy seem pretty close. I bet he's glad you're back to help him cover a few things up.'

'What do you mean by that? Cover what up? What has Jimmy got to do with you?'

'Oh nothing, I was just saying that's all. Just making conversation.'

'Well, go and make it somewhere else.'

'OK, I'm sorry, I didn't mean any offence.' He heads over to Mike and I see him put his arm around him like they are two teenage boys at school. Mike smiles at him like he's in awe of him. Why would he be questioning me about Jimmy?

My party is a great night and Jimmy gave me an envelope with the deeds to the club in it. I'm not sure why. I think he wants me to get a little more involved in things or focus on something other than my so-called obsessions.

It's funny how life just seems to go on. I've been out of prison three months and everyone is still the same. I'm still thinking daily about Diane and how to get rid of her, as me and Mike are sleeping together practically on a daily basis now.

There's only one way to get rid of Diane – if she really is as unstable as Mike says she is, let's push her further over the edge. I get dressed quickly and put on as much perfume as I possibly can. I go round to Mike's and there's no sign of Diane. Only one thing for it. I grab Mike.

'Kiss me.'

'Jesus, what, are you on heat or something?'

'Maybe. Just do it.'

We start to kiss and I pull him towards the bedroom. Oo, naughty Mike, even in his marital bed. After we finish having sex Mike says, 'We better get up, she could be back any minute.'

I start to get myself dressed and as he walks out of the room I grab my earring out of my ear and throw it on Diane's side of the bed. Then I grab her pillow and rub it on my neck so my perfume transfers on to it. She'll spot that and know he's had a woman in here. If she's already paranoid about it, imagine her fury.

I leave Mike's house and head towards my mum's. She'll need some money, no doubt.

'Hello, Mum, are you OK today?'

'Yeah, I'm fine. I'm glad you're here actually. I wanted to ask—'

Before she finishes her sentence I take some money from my pocket. 'Here.'

'Oh thanks, Kate, I'll get the kettle on.'

'Not for me, thanks. I have to get home. I'm going out with Mike and Jimmy tonight and have to get ready.'

I go home and get ready, waiting for Jimmy and Mike to pick me up for our night out. As we get to the pub I notice there's a karaoke competition and the winner gets a trophy.

'I want that trophy, Mike, will you get it for me?'

'What? You can't sing,' says Jimmy.

'Yes, I can, and I'll win that trophy. Won't I, Mike?'

'Yes, of course you'll win that trophy,' Mike says with a grin. Mike gets up and talks to the guy in charge of the competition. 'Right, I've put your name down.'

'Great.'

As we sit there drinking our drinks it's my turn to get up and sing. I've never really been the best singer. I'm a better dancer than I am a singer, but I get up anyway. After all, it's for a trophy. I sing my song and make my way back to the table.

'Was I good then, boys?'

Mike puts his arm around me and says, 'Yeah, you were the best, you're definitely winning that trophy.'

'Really?'

'Yes, really.'

Then I look at Jimmy and say, 'Well, was I the best?' Jimmy raises his eyebrows and says, 'Hardly, that girl who's on now is a pub singer, she even has a band and gets gigs and shit. You got up there and you may as well have had your hairbrush in your hand.'

'Hey, you cheeky thing. You'll not be saying that when I win.'

'No, I will, because you won't be winning. In fact, you've actually given me a headache with that cats' choir you've just orchestrated.'

The winner is about to get announced and Mike is on his feet waiting for the name.

'Let's put our hands together, ladies and gentlemen, for tonight's winner, Kate Reilly!'

Yeah! I jump up and kiss Mike on the cheek and give Jimmy a look that says, See, told you I was the best. I get my trophy and say, 'I would like to thank my fans over there in the corner, without them I wouldn't be who I am today, thank you very much you two, especially Mr Simpson who said he knew all the time I was a good singer and I should have a band and do gigs and shit.' As I go back to the table I say, 'See, Jimmy, I told you I was the best.'

'Treas, you weren't the best. Mike threatened him to make sure you got that trophy, that doesn't mean that you won.'

'You're just jealous of my trophy, you. In fact, you know what? I was going to let you put this trophy in the cabinet in the club. You're not now. In fact, I'm going to get myself a bus and call it a bar bus, Kate's Bar Bus, and have a cabinet and put my trophy in it. You're not getting on the bus. Mike, you can come on the bus, do you want to come on my bus?'

'Yeah, I do. Hey, I'll even be your manager. Jimmy's not going to be your manager.'

'Pack it in, you two, you're like a couple of kids the way you two go on,' Jimmy says while shaking his head.

This makes me poke more fun at Jimmy. 'Oh, Jimmy is going to cry, look, cos he's not allowed on the bus. Hey, I'll get my face put up on the side of the bus. Mike, do you want your face on the other side?'

'Yeah, I'd love my face on Kate's Bar Bus. Jimmy's not getting his face on the bus. Jimmy is not even looking at the bus.'

'Pack it in, you two, I don't even want to look at the stupid fucking trophy or the bus. I'm going to go home in a minute if you two don't stop fucking about.'

'Aw, Jimmy, here, do you want the trophy? You should have sung, you might have won.'

Me and Mike are laughing totally at Jimmy's expense. He gets a bit huffy like that when me and Mike act silly. My happy moment doesn't last too long once Mike looks up.

'Hello, babe, what you doing here?'

Great. Diane is here, I hope she's going to shout at him for the perfume and the earrings. He gets up and kisses her and she smiles as they go to the bar. My face must drop as he does this because Jimmy puts his arm around me and kisses me on the head.

'Come on, then, show me this trophy. You were the best really. I was only joking.'

'No, I wasn't, Jimmy. Mike threatened that guy. I told him to.'

Jimmy gives me a little smile. 'I'll walk you home, you don't want to be sitting with them two, you can tell me all about this bus you're getting.'

'Yeah, OK then.' We walk over to the bar where Mike and Diane are and I say, 'Mike, we're heading off, OK? See you tomorrow.'

'Diane, you OK?' says Jimmy. I can't even be bothered to speak to Diane. I'm feeling worse and worse about her.

As we walk home, Jimmy puts his arm around me and pulls me into him and says, 'You are getting better about the whole Mike thing, aren't you?'

'Yeah, much better. I hardly think of him in that way now.'

'Are you sure? I was thinking maybe you should speak to Doctor Cavendish again.'

'No, honestly, I'm fine.'

'OK then, if you're sure.'

Jimmy sees me to my door and flags down a taxi. Jimmy always tries to look after me, bless him. But fancy that Diane ruining my moment tonight. I should have smashed that trophy over her head.

Jimmy has a little bit of a drinks promotion going on today

with a new fruity cider that's just come out. As I'm looking over the flavours I feel someone standing behind me. I turn round and I'm met by those big brown eyes of Dan's. 'What are you doing sneaking up on people?'

'I wasn't sneaking up. I'm waiting for Mike.'

'Well, go wait somewhere else.' He starts to walk backwards while pointing at me and says, 'What's the difference between a tuna, a piano and a pot of glue?'

I roll my eyes and don't even ask what the difference is, why would I care.

'You can tuna piano, but you can't piano a tuna. Then he laughs his head off.

I tut at him and say, 'That's not even funny, what about the glue?'

He winks at me and says, 'I knew you'd get stuck on that one.' I notice Jimmy has now joined us. I say, 'Do you find him funny, Jimmy, because I find him weird.'

'Never mind that, what's your thoughts on this cider?'

I look at Jimmy and snap, 'It tastes like shit.' Then I leave the club and go home. I hate Dan. Mike thinks he's marvelous. His jokes are rubbish compared to mine. Piano a tuna? What a stupid thing to even say.

I left Diane her little present over a week ago. Mike's not even mentioned the perfume or earrings. What can I do next? I'll ponder on this, something will come up to get rid of the little bitch.

I go back round to Mike's when I know Diane is at mother-and-toddler group. I grab a hold of him. 'Hey, you, come here.'

'What is it with you? You can't leave me alone in here.'

'Yeah, I know, I like it, please, she won't come back, you know she won't.'

'OK, then, if you say so, come here.'

How can he take me into his marital bed all these times? He must feel something for me. Once I get rid of Diane we'll be together, I'm sure of it. After we've finished, I think, What can I possibly do? She obviously never spotted the earring or the perfume so I shove my knickers under her pillow. Any woman who doesn't react to that must be crazy if you ask me.

A few days later, Mike comes over to see me.

'Kate, I'm so excited, our Lawrence is back for a couple of weeks. It's been ages since I saw him. He's staying at my mum and dad's, he said he'll meet us at the club later.'

'Wow, Lawrence, hey. He was nearly my stepdad before my mum cheated.'

'Yeah, I could have been your uncle. Not sure if what we do would have been legal if I was your uncle.'

'Nah, it would only have been through marriage not blood, so we're perfectly safe.'

'Great, let's do it now, then.'

The next thing I know me and Mike are kissing and heading to the bedroom. As we lie on the bed together afterwards, I look at his face and take in the image. I can't wait for him and Diane to split up so I can have him all to myself.

'What you staring at?' Mike says.

'Nothing, I'm just looking at you. Am I not allowed to?'

'No, you've got me paranoid. I'm wondering if I have something on my face or something.'

'No, you've not, I was just looking. How's baby Jack getting on these days, then?'

'Yeah, he's great, just a baby, really. It's not until my sons get older that I'll have real fun with them. I can't wait for them to start working in the club.'

'I never thought of that, imagine them hanging around the club. We'll be too old to hang around the club by then.'

'Nah, we'll never be too old for the club.'

Later that day I make my way over to the club and Lawrence is there with Mike. He takes one look at me and says, 'Kate, look at you, you're a total sight for sore eyes, you're a pretty little thing, aren't you?'

'Hello, Lawrence, come here, give me a kiss.' Lawrence picks me up and swings me around in his arms. 'Let's do dinner together. I'll cook for you on Tuesday. We can sit and watch the TV, like we used to. They were great days.'

When I think about it, they actually were – before the rape and all the bad things that have happened since.

Tuesday comes and we have dinner.

'Right, I'll do the dishes, you can dry.' I start to wash the dishes. 'Oh, Lawrence, it's great to see you again. I've really missed you. How's that London, then?'

'Not all it's cracked up to be. I should have stayed round here. It costs a fortune sometimes. Even for a packet of chips you could be spending two pounds fifty.'

'What, two pounds fifty for a packet of chips? I'm in the wrong business. I should tell Jimmy we're branching out to a chip van in London.'

'Hey, imagine Jimmy serving chips in his little chef's hat and apron.' Me and Lawrence giggle at the thought of Jimmy. 'I have met a woman who I think is pretty special, though, and things are going really well between us.'

'What, you mean you're not marrying the queen?'

Lawrence laughs. 'Nah, she asked me but I said, "Hey, I'm too posh to be going out with you."' As Lawrence dries the dishes he stops what he's doing and asks in a very concerned voice, 'Kate, are you OK?'

'Am I OK? Of course I'm OK, why do you ask that?'

'Well, it's just you seem to be washing your face all the time.'

'What? When?'

'You've just done it, you even still the have bubbles on your face. You did it a few times when you were cooking as well.'

Oh my God, I never even realised I was doing that. I look at my hands and they're full of bubbles. I've become so obsessed with washing my face I don't even know I'm doing it. I should tell him everything. Maybe I could move to London with him. He could help me get George back. We'd live happily ever after, I know we would. I dry the bubbles from my face and hands.

'Sit down, Lawrence, I have something to tell you.' He takes a seat and looks really concerned. 'It was Jennie's fault, she gave me the white wine and it spiralled out of control from there and I wanted to stop it, I swear I did, but I couldn't. I don't know what it is.'

'What do you mean, what is it?'

At this moment I could fall into his arms and cry like a baby. He would help me, I know he would. He would never judge me, it wasn't my fault. I never asked to be raped. Then I come back to earth. I can't possibly tell Lawrence. He'd know then that I'd slept with four men all on the same night, he would think I was a slag.

'Oh, it's this new make-up Jennie is trying on me from the salon, it stinks like white wine. I keep smelling it all day, no matter how much I wash.'

'Bloody hell, you had me worried there.'

We continue to do the dishes. Lawrence soon leaves and I lie in bed really scared, thinking, I really am crazy, I'm not even sure when I'm washing my face.

The following day at the club I make Jimmy a nice cup of tea. As I walk into his office he looks up and says, 'Hello, Treas. Could you do me a favour and watch the club tonight?'

'Why?'

'Because Lawrence is here and we're all going out, it's a lads' night out.'

'Well, can't I come?'

'No.'

'Why not?'

'Because I already said, it's a lads' night out.'

'I always go to lads' nights out.'

'Not this one, you're not.'

'Why not?'

'Because I said so, that's why not.'

'I'm coming, I'll follow you.'

'No, you won't.'

'Why not? I always come.'

'Because where we're going is not the kind of place for young girls. Now, shut up.'

'What kind of place?'

'Bloody hell, Treas, what is this, twenty questions? Never mind what place.'

'Are you going to a strip joint?'

Jimmy grins. 'No, we're not, don't be so disgusting.'

'You are, I can tell by your face you are. Why?'

'Never mind why. Lawrence wants to go.'

'I never knew you liked places like that. Does Helen know you're going?'

'Of course Helen knows. I can be trusted, you know, and I don't like places like that. I'd rather be here than somewhere like that. Bunch of pervs eyeing up good-time girls. They better not even try to approach me, I'll blow their heads off.'

Me and Jimmy smile at each other. I know Jimmy won't be looking at the girls and probably will blow their heads off if they go anywhere near him. But I bet Mike will be looking at them and I bet they're all prettier than me. Well, they have to be with a job like that. Bloody Lawrence, asking to go there, he should be next on my hit list. Hopefully they will all be so petrified when they see Jimmy walk in there they won't go anywhere near them.

I reluctantly look after the club, but I can't get Mike off my mind. What if he gets a private dance? I've heard you can go into a booth if you pay extra for the dancers. I hope he hasn't but knowing him he will have. What if Diane leaves him and the dancer muscles in, all my hard work has been for nothing. Maybe I should become a dancer.

I can't concentrate all that night wondering if Mike has gone off with someone. When I get home I check the CCTV to see if I can see them coming back. They may even be back by now, who knows. I sit there till 5am and see him and Lawrence stumbling up the pathway. He's home and they're on their own. Thank God for that. Mind, they could hardly take them back to Diane's.

The following morning I go straight round to the club to get the gossip from the night before. There's no sign of Mike.

'Well then, Jimmy, did you get a dance?'

'No, I bloody never.'

'Did they try to approach you?'

'Never mind, you, I've told you – don't ask me shit like that.'

'You did get a dance, didn't you?'

'No, I've said I never.'

'Did Lawrence then?'

'Yeah, Lawrence did.'

'Did Mike?'

'Jesus, yes he did, he even ordered a shag on the side.'

'What?'

'You have to stop thinking about him. What answer would you like me to give you right now? A yes or a no? What answer is going to make you feel better because, either way, you'll think I'm lying anyway. I'm getting less grief off Helen for going than I am off you. Get your coat, let's go and get some dinner. That will cheer you up. Plus, I'm a bit rough. That Lawrence can drink some.'

Me and Jimmy go for dinner and he tells me he got home for 2am, so what were Mike and Lawrence doing till 5am? I can't even question it or they will know that I watch them. That Lawrence is leading Mike astray.

Chapter 20 – Call The Funeral Director

I can't stop thinking about Diane and the fact nothing's been mentioned. It's been three weeks since I left her a little present. Surely she has to react to it? Unless Mike is not telling me. Maybe he knows what I did. Oh, shit. Nah, he would have said, surely? I think it's so strange she's not reacted. I'm going to have to come up with something really good next time, and quick. Luckily for me I spot Mike's phone on the side. I'll text her from Mike's phone.

Come to the club at 5pm I've got something to show you!

She replies back.

OK.

I delete both messages and put his phone back where I found it. So at quarter to five, I get on my knees and start to give Mike a blow job.

'Bloody hell, what is going on with you lately? You like your sex, don't you?'

I climb on to the table and we have sex. In walks Diane bang on cue. I take one look at her in the mirror with the biggest smile on my face. She's going to go crazy here, it's bound to split them up. Yet she looks at me, and walks out again. What the hell? She really is crazy. I would have scratched my eyes out for that. Mike finally finishes and says, 'Fancy going out for something to eat, I'm starving?'

We head out for something to eat and I can't stop thinking of Diane and the text message. I bet by the time we get back her clothes are packed up and she's gone.

After the meal I tell Mike I'll pop into his for a coffee. I'm hoping to have some sort of showdown with Diane if she's still there.

We walk into Mike's house. 'I'm bursting for the toilet. I'll just pop upstairs.' I run as quickly as I can up the stairs to check if Diane has packed up her things. As I go into the bedroom I see her and think all my prayers have been answered. Diane is lying on the bed with an empty bottle of pills at her side. I better not shout Mike in straight away. I'll make sure she's dead first, even though I know she is cos she has that dead look. I've seen a few dead bodies in my time and, yeah, that's definitely one. I feel for a pulse and there isn't one, so I walk slowly down the stairs, into the living room and say, 'Oh, better ring a hearse for your wife.'

'What?'

'She's topped herself on the bed. Hey, we could keep her there and if you ever want to remember what she looks like you just walk into the bedroom. We could call her a memory-foam topper.'

'What you on about, you idiot?'

'Your bitch wife has topped herself up there. Go check if you don't believe me.'

I never liked Diane anyway so it's no hardship to me. Mike runs up the stairs into the bedroom and with panic in his voice he grabs a hold of Diane's lifeless body and screams, 'Aw, you stupid cow, what have you gone and done? Kate, call an ambulance!' He starts screaming down the stairs.

I look up the stairs and walk into the kitchen to pour myself a drink.

'Hang on, I'm pouring a drink. She's gone now anyway.'

Mike runs down the stairs and grabs me by the throat.

'Fuck me, Kate, are you mad or something?'

'OK! OK, jeez, I'll call one, calm down.'

I grab the phone and dial 999 and start to make my way back up the stairs to join Mike. The operator says, 'Emergency services, which service is it you require?'

'Well, a hearse really, but he's making me ring an ambulance, but I can confirm she's dead, topped herself, there's an empty pill bottle there and she's definitely dead so no point in CPR and I wouldn't put my lips on hers anyway. You might want to send an ambulance for him, though, he's going to have a heart attack if he doesn't stop bouncing round like the Duracell bunny.'

Mike is hysterical in the background. 'You stupid fucking bitch, you have kids, what am I supposed to do? Why did you go and do this, Diane, why?'

I'm just standing sipping my vodka and do you know what scares me more than anything? I'm not even bothered, little bitch can rot in hell for all I care. Yet if you asked me if she'd ever done anything untoward to me the answer would be no. I just don't like her, simple as that.

The private ambulance soon leaves with Diane's body in the back and it brings a smile to my face. Mike is sitting staring into space, even Jimmy is a little shocked when he gets here. He keeps trying to give him whisky for his nerves or something stupid like that. What on earth would he even be nervous about?

I'll take the kids to mine for a few days so Mike can get on with the funeral arrangements. The sooner this is sorted, the sooner I can move in. We can get rid of that bed, though.

I've been taking care of the kids for a few days now. I'm hoping they will start to call me Mummy soon.

I really should go and see Diane at the chapel of rest, say my last goodbyes to her.

I walk into the chapel of rest and there she is, Diane Taylor. It's like I've been given the golden throne. Long live the queen. I don't feel one ounce of guilt. I walk slowly over to the coffin. I can tell there has been no expense spared. Mike has put some of her things in the coffin.

'Aw, that's nice, isn't it, Diane? Look at Mike playing the dutiful husband. Mind, I think he was a bit upset. That annoyed me a bit. I bet you wondered what he saw in me. Shall I show you what he saw in me?'

I take off my knickers and open her mouth. I put the underwear in her mouth, at the side of her cheek. She looks like a little hamster. I close her mouth and whisper in her ear, 'Well, now you can taste what he tastes every day for eternity, you fucking bitch.'

And I walk out of the chapel of rest and make my way to the club.

As I walk into Jimmy's office he looks like he's worried about something as he hardly even raised his head when I walked in.

'Hey, Jimmy, you OK?'

'Not really, I'm a little worried about Mike – with Diane, you know. You've got to keep an eye on people when they lose someone close. They can become withdrawn and depressed.'

'Why would he be depressed over Diane? I'm not being funny but she was a total moron anyway, always paranoid about him going out. He's better off without her.'

'Don't be silly, they loved each other, she was his wife, the mother of his son. He's left on his own with that baby, not to mention her older kid, he'll have to take that one on. He probably won't be hanging around the club much or going out, he won't have time. Being a dad is hard work.'

'Oh no, I never thought of that. Can't he just have the kids adopted, like I did with my baby?'

'No, Kate, this is totally different to what happened to you. You never even knew your baby. You can't give kids up like that. No, he's going to need a lot of help and support. I might see if he wants to move into ours for a bit.'

'That's nice, Jimmy. You really like Mike, don't you?'

'Well, course I do. I've known him years.'

'How did you two meet?'

'Well, he was best friends with my younger brother, Stephen.'

'You have a brother?'

'Well, I did, he died when he was sixteen. Him and Mike decided to go joyriding. They stole a car while drunk, our Stephen was driving and he died instantly. Mike was lucky, he walked away with only a few scrapes. I said then he had a guardian angel looking down on him, he was lucky to be alive.'

'I never knew any of that.'

'Well, we never really talk about it. Mike and Stephen were inseparable as kids, bit like you and your friend, what's her face. My mother was heartbroken when our Stephen died. She's still not over it really.'

'You have a mum?'

'Well, of course I do, what did you think, I'd been hatched out of an egg? I've got a mum and a dad, they live a few miles away from here. I try to get up to see them as often as I can but it's hard when you're so busy. When our Stephen died they couldn't stay round here. My mum thought people were looking at her funny or would cross the street when she passed them, people she'd known for years. I suppose it's because people don't know what to say, really. But at the time I got really pissed off with people. Like they had disrespected my family. Disrespected the Simpsons – and no one disrespects us. My dad always drummed that into us as kids. That's when I decided everyone would call me Mr Simpson, to make sure no one ever disrespects the Simpsons again or forgets us. It sounds a little silly now but I was so angry back then. My family had lived round here for years, my mother was devastated when she had to leave that house.'

'I never realised that Mike's best friend who died was your brother. You must have been devastated.'

'Yeah, I was in a bad place for a little while. Mike used to wear this friendship bracelet for years, it was our Stephen's. Come to think of it, I've never seen it for years. He must have thought it got too old.'

'Yeah, I remember that friendship bracelet, he used to wear it every day. It was plaited on his left wrist for years. I bet it was left for love as well. I'm sorry to hear about your brother, and you're right – I think Mike will need us.'

It's the first time I've thought about Diane dying hurting Mike and her kids. What on earth have I done? I don't even know why I did that. I was so jealous of her, yet I don't even know why now. How is it that people can be wiped out of someone's life so quickly and easily and yet we all go about our business like it never happened? Maybe I should go over and see Mike, see if the kids need anything. I never even knew all that stuff about Jimmy. I thought I knew everything about those two but it seems I don't, just what they want me to know. Again, it goes back to secrets and lies. Do any of us three ever say what we actually think? It scares me to think of the relationship us three have because I realise how fucked up it actually is.

I make my way over to Mike's.

'Hello, Mike, are you OK?'

'Yeah, I'm fine. Come in, sorry about the mess, I've not really done much since the funeral.'

'Don't worry about it. Here, let me help. I'll clean the house for you.'

'No, it's fine, you don't have to do that.'

'No, I do, I will.'

I clean the house from top to bottom. Mike's not said much, he's been so quiet. I've never seen him like this before. I'm starting to feel guilty about Diane. Maybe I shouldn't have hidden my knickers under her pillow or sent that text. Even then, I still went to the chapel of rest and shoved my knickers in her mouth, what on earth was I thinking? I get these crazy thoughts in my head at times and no one or nothing can stop me. I'm starting to get completely out of control and I know I am. I might start seeing Doctor Cavendish again, once I've sorted Mike out. I'll do it properly this time, though, I'll make sure I do exactly what he asks me to do. That's a good idea, get better, stop these awful thoughts.

'Right, what do you boys want for tea?' I look in the cupboards and there's nothing there, poor Mike. 'Listen, I'm going to go shopping. I'll be an hour. How about I take Jack with me?'

'Whatever, Kate.' Mike is staring into thin air.

'Come on, Jack, let's get your coat.'

Me and Jack make our way to the supermarket and I put him in the trolley and start to pick the groceries. As I put them into the trolley I catch a glimpse of Jack and he looks like his mum. He has a sadness in his eyes. Then he starts repeating, 'Mummy, Mummy, Mummy.'

This little boy is aching for his mummy, just like my George is probably aching for me or like I ache for George. I pick him out of the trolley and I hold him in the shop. I start to cry as I don't know what else to do. This is all my fault, I've broken this little boy's heart. He will never know who his mummy is and it's all my fault. What on earth was I thinking? I put him back in the trolley after I've managed to compose myself and get some more shopping. This woman approaches us. I don't know who she is and she asks, 'Is that Jack? Diane and Mike's little boy?'

'Yes, it is.'

'How is Mike?'

'He's fine, bearing up, you know.'

'Poor Diane, she must have been in a terrible place to have done what she did. It's this little one we have to look out for now.' And she grabs Jack's hand and shakes it a bit.

'Yeah, well, we must get on,' I say, while pushing her hand away from his, and start to walk away. I have no idea who that woman was but it certainly is not up to her to be looking after this little one and she needn't even bother thinking Mike needs her help. They've got me, that's all they need. Stupid bitch, does she want to feel the wrath of Kate Reilly? Because trust me, darling, it ain't pretty.

Back at Mike's he's still sitting in the same seat I left him in.

'You have to eat something. Open these curtains. Get up, you can help.'

'No, piss off, what are you even doing here? Just piss off. You never even liked Diane, so what the fuck are you doing here?'

'Don't talk to me like that. You're right, I never liked Diane, but I like you and you're in a bad place. I'm helping you whether you like it or not. Now, open those curtains. You have Jack and Gavin to think of, get up.'

Mike stands up and holds Jack like he's never letting him go. He whispers, 'I'm sorry,' in his ear. Maybe he feels guilty about something as well.

'You got to get yourself back on your feet. Kitchen, now. What we having?'

We decide on chicken casserole. Jack and Gavin could do with some goodness in their systems. As we sit at the table no one has spoken for ages. Gavin won't eat his tea. Mike yells, 'Eat your tea, Gavin, now!'

'No, I won't. I don't want my tea. You eat yours.'

The next thing I know Mike is yelling in his face, 'Eat your fucking tea, you little bastard.'

Gavin runs out of the kitchen and Jack's crying and the next thing I know Mike has his head on the table and he is crying like a baby. Oh my God, I never expected this to happen. I never thought this far ahead. I pick Jack up and give him a hug to see if I can ease his pain, but it's not me he wants, it's Diane. I look at Mike and it's not me he wants, it's Diane. I go to see Gavin and sit down next to him.

'Listen, Mike doesn't mean to be like that, he's just upset, that's all.'

'Where's my mum?'

'What?'

'Well, where is she? Where do you go when you die? I know she's dead, but what if she wakes up in the coffin and no one is there to help her? What if she wasn't really dead?'

I put Jack down at this point, this little boy needs someone to talk to him, explain things. 'Look, Gavin, sweetheart. Your mum, she's definitely dead, darling. When you die and you go to hospital, the doctors, they do lots of tests and they open up your body and take out your heart and lungs, all your major organs, and they give them away so people who need them can have them and that's what happened to your mum. The doctor said your mum had the biggest heart they have ever seen, they wanted to put her in the *Guinness Book of Records* it was that big. So she won't be waking up in the coffin, I can promise you that, sweetheart. When people die they go to a place called heaven. It's far, far away from here and your mum, she would have turned into an angel and she's allowed to come down and see you, but we can't see her. She's watching you all the time. She's probably watching you thinking, Why is Gavin not eating his tea? I bet she would be smiling if you went in there and ate your tea. Maybe you should say sorry to Mike as well because, between me and you, I think Diane is watching you more than Mike, and deep down he knows that and that's why he's so upset. She loved you and Jack more than anyone.'

'Do you think so? Do you really think she's watching us?'

'Of course she is. Now, back in the kitchen everyone.'

I pick Jack up and take him back into the kitchen. Mike gives me a half-hearted 'thanks' smile. Yet if only he knew what I'd done, he'd knock me into next week. I certainly wouldn't be given any angel wings from the Lord above, not the way I behave sometimes.

I settle the kids into bed and sit with Mike for a while. I pour him a glass of red wine, not white, I still have the whole colour–food thing going on, even now. I don't think that will ever go.

'Listen, Mike, I know how upset you are. I want you to know that I'm here. I won't leave you. I'll even stay the night, so I can get the kids sorted in the morning.'

'Thanks, Kate, you're a real friend, you know.' He gives me a hug, so at least I know I'm not in the bad books. We finally climb into bed and I hold Mike all night. I don't even think he realised I was there. I never thought it would be like this. I thought once the doctor confirmed Diane was dead, he would drop to his knees with a ring and a proposal. Maybe I'm wrong, after all, about the way Mike feels about me.

Chapter 21 – Euphoric Dancing

I've still not had my proposal from Mike yet and it's been three months since he buried Diane. I still feel the need to watch the CCTV constantly. Last night, I saw Dave and Lee, the doormen, selling drugs and handing over the money to Keith Nixon. I do hope Caroline is not involved. I never thought Dave would do that, ever.

I head straight over to see Jimmy to tell him. 'Jimmy, I hate to tell you this, but it's Dave and Lee, I think they've been selling drugs on your door for Keith Nixon.'

'What?'

'Yeah, I saw them, I'm sure they are. I just wanted you to know so you can keep an eye on it, that's all.'

'How do you know that?'

'I saw them meet up with Keith last night, after everyone had left the club, and they handed over some money to him and he handed them a bag. I can only assume it was drugs in that bag.'

'Bloody hell, Treas, are you sure?'

'Yeah, positive. I would never have said anything if I wasn't. I know how fond you are of Dave.'

'Jesus, Dave? Are you sure? You're definitely sure it was Keith Nixon?'

'Yeah, it was him, plain as day, I know it was.'

'When?'

'Last night, I said.'

'What time?'

'About 3.30am.'

'Well, what were you doing round here at 3.30am?'

'Hey, never mind that, a girl has a private life, you know.'

'Oo, boyfriend, is it?'

'Something like that. Listen, I'm not sure what you want to do about it, but that's what I know.'

'I'll keep an eye on it.' I make my way out of his office. 'Treas?'

'Yes, Jimmy.'

'I appreciate your loyality, you know.'

'Yeah, I know you do.' We both smile at each other.

I walk out of that office not even feeling guilty about what I've told Jimmy. I know for a fact there will be repercussions for Dave and Lee but, to be honest with you, I couldn't give a shit. I wonder what has happened to me sometimes. I never used to be like this. I would have normally kept my mouth shut and hoped that it would go away. I like Dave, and Caroline loves him, but I can't have him taking the piss out of Jimmy like that.

Later that day Mike calls me. 'Hey, Gem, I was talking to Jimmy earlier and he reckons that Dave and Lee have been doing dodgy dealings with Keith Nixon. They've been selling drugs for him on Jimmy's door. I wouldn't want to be them two when Jimmy gets his hands on them.'

'Really, how do you know that?'

'Not sure how he knew. I reckon Jimmy must have caught them. But however he found out, there will be trouble. You coming to watch the showdown? It's happening in the next hour or so.'

'OK, see you soon.'

I hang up the phone. I'm pleased Jimmy never told Mike that it was me. He'd only question how I know and Mike has a way of getting things out of me. Imagine he found out I watched them on CCTV, there would be hell on.

I finally get to the office. I sit down in the seat facing Jimmy's right side. Lee sits beside me. Dave is standing behind Lee and Mike is sitting at the other side of Lee.

'So, Lee, they tell me you've been doing a bit of business with Keith?'

'What, Jimmy?' Lee is shaking and it's a funny sight to see as he is twice the size of Jimmy. 'No, Jimmy, I would never do that, you know I wouldn't.'

Before Lee can say anything else Jimmy opens his drawer, takes out a gun, and blows off his head, right there and then. He doesn't even flinch. You can always tell when Jimmy doesn't want to kill someone but knows he has to, because he uses a weapon. It's quicker. If he just tolerates the person, it's normally with fists and with suffering. Funny thing is, me and Mike don't flinch either. Dave is shaking as he knows he's next. He's waiting for someone to say something so I take it upon myself to say it, as I want this to be over. I can feel Lee's brains and blood all over my face. Have you ever smelt human blood in a heavy dose? It's all metallicy and the smell of the human brain is like dirty cardboard. So the smell of those two mixed up and still being warm across my face is not making me feel overclever, but I won't show Jimmy and Mike that I'm bothered.

'Jimmy, I heard Dave was doing the same thing. He was seen in the Ocean Club on Wednesday.'

'Nah, Jimmy. Nah, she has it wrong, I swear.'

'You calling my treasure a liar, you little bastard?'

'No, no, I'm not saying that, just that's she's mistaken.'

'Treas, are you mistaken?'

'No, Jimmy, I'm quite sure.'

Jimmy pulls the gun out again and, in an instant, blows off Dave's head. Great, two blown-off heads in the space of ten minutes. Jimmy throws me a towel and says, 'Get cleaned up, Treas, you've got Lee's only brain cell on your cheek.'

'Mike, get one of the lads who we can trust to help you take their bodies. There are some skips at the school with all those refurb works going on. Put them in there and set fire to them. I'll make sure it's covered up when the police are called.'

'OK, I will do, are we still all going out for drinks tonight? I've told Dan to meet us.'

This annoys me. I don't want Dan there. Mike seems to hang on his every word.

I leave the club and get showered. I feel disgusting after being splattered with blood. I pick out a few outfits for tonight and finally settle on one.

As I head into the bar, those three are there earlier than me. How do men do that? Throw on a pair of jeans and a shirt and Bob's your uncle. By the time I've done my hair, put my make-up on, changed my outfit several times, I'm always the last to make it.

'All right, boys, what we having then?' I say to them all before I head to the bar. Jimmy stands up looking a little bit on the merry side.

'Here, Treas, sit down. I'll get them.'

Jimmy makes his way to the bar. I look at Mike and say, 'I can tell he's had a few.'

Mike rolls his eyes and says, 'Yeah, he has. I think that Dave business bothered him a little today. Mind, Dan's being a bit boring.'

Oh, Dan's being boring, this is swinging in my favour. Hopefully they will realise that he's not up to much and ditch him.

'Where is he anyway?' I say, looking around the room for him.

'He's gone to the toilet, but don't worry, he'll soon perk up when he gets back and drinks his drink,' Mike says with a shifty look.

'Why's that?' I question Mike.

'Because I've dropped a little party pill in it for him.' Mike says this while grinning away like a naughty schoolboy.

'What? Why on earth would you do that?'

It's not like Mike to do that. We've never been ones for drugs. I think Mike and Jimmy dabble in them to sell them. But even then I think that's more so they know what is being sold on their door. They don't like the reputation that the Ocean Club has for the number of ODs that happen in there. So if they sell drugs on KK's doors, at least they know it's the real deal as they only buy from reliable suppliers. Dan comes out of the toilet and heads towards us.

Mike gets up from his seat and says, 'Right, I'm going for a slash.' And winks at me.

'All right, Kate?'

'Yeah fine, thanks, Dan. You?'

'Yeah, great.'

I never really know what to say to Dan. He's someone that I always feel shouldn't be here. Jimmy and Mike are *my* friends.

'Here you go, Treas, there's your drink. Oo, whisky chaser, thank you very much.'

Jimmy says this and picks up Dan's drink and necks it. Oh dear, he's just necked a party pill. This should be fun. Mike comes back from the toilet.

'Right, what we talking about?'

'We're not talking about anything yet, Mike, but you might want to buy Dan another whisky chaser. Jimmy has downed it in one.'

I look at Mike with a huge smile on my face and wink over. Mike's face is a total picture. He jumps up and says, 'Right, I'll go to the bar, you can help me, Kate.' He grabs me by the arm and drags me to the bar. 'Shit, the bloody pill was in there.'

'Yeah, I know,' I laugh at him. 'This is going to be fun.'

'You can't say anything, he'll kill me.' Even Mike is laughing at this while saying, 'Jesus, he's already on his way, he'll be off his head in about half an hour.'

'Right, lads, here we go.' Mike places some more whisky chasers down for us. I better stay a little sober for this. Jimmy is going to be off his head before long.

'Hey, I'll tell you who I was talking to last week,' Jimmy says. 'Remember that bloke who used to work the door, can't remember his fucking name, but he had a tash. Well, him, turns out his brother was shagging his missus while he was doing the nights in our club. That's why he had to pack it in.'

'Yeah, we know, Jimmy,' me and Mike say in unison.

'How the hell did you two know?'

'Everybody knew, bloody hell, where you been?' I roll my eyes at Jimmy.

'I don't know, Treas, but is it just me or is it fucking hot in here?'

I look at Jimmy and the sweat is pouring off him. 'I better get you some water.'

I go to the bar and get a jug of iced water. I take it back to the table and Jimmy picks up the whole thing and drinks from it, pouring water all over his shirt. Jesus Christ, if he finds out what Mike has done he'll go mad. He starts to slump forwards towards me and Mike. 'You know what I love about you two?'

'What, Jimmy?'

'Everything, you're my favourite people in the whole wide world, you two. I love you both. I love nights like this and I love this pub.'

'It's just a pub.'

'Yeah, but have you noticed the wallpaper though? That's proper wallpaper, that.'

I roll my eyes. 'Is it?'

'Yeah, let's go somewhere else, though, somewhere with a bit of music. I fancy a dance.'

Jimmy dancing? I don't think I've seen Jimmy dance, ever. Maybe once with Helen when Mike and Shelly got married, but I think she had to bully him into it.

'OK, Jimmy, let's go somewhere else. Mike can show you how to dance.' Mike gives me that look as if to say, You're making this worse, please don't wind up the situation.

'I know this little rave bar that should be fun.'

'Not a rave bar, Kate.' Mike is really panicking.

'Nah, I reckon I quite fancy a rave bar, let's go there.' He looks over at Mike and Dan.

We get up and start to head over to the rave bar. I'm giggling all the way. Once I get Jimmy in there, it'll be wild. Mike will be shrinking into himself by the time I've finished with him. That's what he gets. As we walk to the bar Jimmy stops.

'Hey, listen to that music. Let's go in there.'

He starts to walk down the alleyway. Holy shit, he's only on his way to the Ocean Club, Keith Nixon's bar. This is not going to be fun.

'No, Jimmy, we can't go in there.'

'Yeah, we can, have I ever told you that I actually like Keith Nixon? I'll check out his bar and I think I'll buy the bloke a drink. I mean this whole club-owning business, fighting on and that, it's all a pantomime really.'

The doormen all stand shoulder to shoulder. They think we've come for trouble. I have this awful feeling it's going to kick off here.

I grab Mike's arm. 'Do something.'

'Ha ha! I don't know what to do, he's off his tits.'

'Hello, lads!' Jimmy shouts at the doormen. 'Where's Keith? I fancied a night out in his bar, is he in?' They shout for Keith Nixon on the walkie-talkies and he walks through the door. Jimmy goes straight over to him. 'Keith, lad, how are you? I was walking past and said to this lot, "Hey, this looks like a good bar." Do you mind if us lot come in for a drink?'

I'm not sure what Keith is thinking but he looks like he's shitting himself a little bit. 'Erm yeah, yeah, Mr Simpson, come in.'

Mike looks at Keith and nods. 'All right, Keith.'

We might even get jumped on once we get in there and Jimmy is not going to be much use. I'm hoping Dan can fight as well as Jimmy and Mike say he can because we might need him.

We get in there and the music is like dance rave music. Next thing I know, Jimmy is on the dance floor looking like, what can only be described as, an uncle Bobby dancing at a wedding.

'No wonder he never dances,' I say turning my head towards Mike. It's only then that I notice how funny Mike thinks this is, he has tears rolling down his face and is in fits of laughter. 'What are you laughing at? You did this to him, it's not even funny. Jimmy will go crazy when he finds out he's been bobbing around like a vibrator in Keith Nixon's bar.' I look at Mike and we both start to giggle uncontrollably. 'What on earth are we going to say tomorrow? He'll go mad.'

'Well, he can't know it was me. I'm depressed, my wife recently killed herself.'

'Yeah, well, he can't think it was me. I'm a psycho, things like this could push me over the edge. There's only one thing for it.' We both say in unison, 'Dan did it.' We start to giggle again.

'Hey, Treas, get over here. It's euphoric this, euphoric.'

I look over at Jimmy and he's all over this poor young girl. She looks like she's going to die of fright. 'We can't let him pull some tart, he'll blow her head off in the morning. Ha ha! Somebody stop him.' I search the dance floor to see if I can see Dan. 'Where is Dan, anyway?'

Mike points him out. 'He's over there with some bird.'

'You're joking, that's a bloke, that is. I'm telling you, that's no bird.' Tonight is actually turning out to be a lot of fun.

'Hey, Keith!' Jimmy shouts over to Keith Nixon. 'It's euphoric in here, isn't it? Bloody euphoric.'

I think even Keith is secretly laughing at Jimmy. Dan comes over with his new-found bloke – cough – bird.

'Hello, Dan, who's this then?'

'This is, erm, what's your name again?'

The girl says in a really shy voice, 'Shirley.' I look at Mike and cough, 'Burly, more like,' in his ear. Mike literally can't take any more, he's hanging over the bar still laughing at Jimmy and Dan with his bloke–bird thing.

'Am I the only normal one in here tonight?'

Jimmy comes over. 'Get the drinks in, all this euphoric dancing has got me thirsty.'

'Mike, get him water. Jesus, he's going to overheat in a minute if he doesn't stop all this *euphoric* dancing.'

After about three hours of dancing like your grandad, we decide it's time Jimmy went home.

'We can't let him go home to Helen in that state, she'll freak,' I say to Mike and Dan. 'He's not coming to mine. He'll be up talking shit all night,' Mike says.

'He's not coming to mine. Shirely is coming back to mine, he'll frighten her off.'

I look at Dan and roll my eyes. 'Dan, I don't think Frank Bruno would frighten her off.'

'Kate, you'll have to take him.' Mike is *still* laughing at this situation.

'I'm not taking him, no way.'

Mike points over at him. 'Look, go get him off the dance floor. We'll discuss it then.'

I go over to get Jimmy from this poor woman he's draping himself over.

'You're euphoric, you, darling, you really are.'

Is that Jimmy's best pulling line? I've never even heard the word euphoric before and won't be pleased to hear it again. I finally manage to get Jimmy away and take him back over to where we were sitting. Oh, great, those bastards have left! They have left me with Jimmy so he's going to have to come back to mine. Well, this is great. 'Jimmy, you'll have to come back with me.'

It takes me an hour and a half to get Jimmy back to my flat. It's normally only a twenty-minute walk. If I have to stop and look at the workmanship of another wall, I'm going to bang my head against it.

I finally manage to get him into my flat. 'Jimmy, drink some water.' As I'm in the kitchen, I call Helen, she'll be worried. 'Hi, Helen, it's Kate. Listen, Jimmy is in a drunken stupor on my sofa. I just wanted to ring you and tell you in case you worried about him. I'll call you in the morning when he's awake.'

'Jimmy's drunk? Not like him, he can always make his way home.'

'Yeah, I know, I've never seen him like this either. He's enjoyed himself, mind, Helen.'

'Thanks for taking care of him.'

'If he's sick he'll be cleaning it up himself.' We giggle. 'Goodnight, Helen.'

'Goodnight, Kate.'

I go back into the living room and Jimmy still can't keep still.

'Have I ever told you how pretty you are? You're special to me, you know, I love you.'

'Yeah, I love you too. Here, have a drink of this.' I pass him some more water to make sure he keeps hydrated. I'm going to kill Mike tomorrow.

'Do you like me?'

'Of course I like you, bloody hell, what a stupid thing to say.'

'Well, it's just, I fancy you.'

'What? You're drunk.'

'I'm not drunk. I only had a few, I do fancy you, not as much as I fancy my Helen, but I do fancy you. Do you fancy a shag?'

'Jimmy, no. You need to sleep this off.'

'Nah, I don't want to sleep, I want to dance, do you want to dance?'

'No, it's late, please go to sleep.'

Crikey, imagine me and Jimmy having sex, especially him being all euphoric and sweating all over me. No thanks, sex is bad enough.

'Right, I'm off to bed.'

'No, stay up, we're having a good night.'

'Bloody hell, no, I'm tired.'

'Come on, stay up with me.'

'OK, just for a little while. Here, have one of these.'

I give him a chewing gum as his mouth is making some really funny shapes. We end up talking crap till six in the morning. I really am going to kill Mike but, then again, he did have a really good night and I suppose after the whole Diane episode I can't be too angry with him.

We finally wake up at 10am, only because Mike and Dan have turned up.

'Come in, you two. What the hell happened to you? Have you any idea how hard it was for me to get him home on my own? It took well over an hour, and if I'd heard one more story about his builder because we kept walking past walls...'

Mike is still laughing. 'Got any pop, my mouth is like a birdcage.' He makes his way over to the fridge. 'Good night, though, I really enjoyed it. Keith Nixon's bar wasn't up to much, mind. KK's kicks that bar's arse. Did you see his face? I don't know what he was more shocked at, the fact we never kicked off or the fact we were even there in the first place.'

'Don't you dare tell Jimmy we were in there, he'll go mental. You're right, though, it's not up to much. I can't believe we were actually handing money over to him.'

'Speaking of Jimmy, where is the little euphoric pill-popper?'

'He's in the shower. Hey, he tried it on with me last night. I could kill you two.'

Dan opens up his arms and shouts, 'Well, you should have taken him up on it, Treas, it would have been euphoric.'

We all start laughing again. Jimmy then opens the door. 'All right, boys, what you doing here? And what would have been euphoric?'

Dan quickly says, 'Nothing, Jimmy. Kate going shopping today.'

'You're right about him, Treas, he is weird. Euphoric. What kind of word is bloody euphoric, anyway?'

I pipe up with, 'Hey, Jimmy, Dan pulled a bloke last night.'

'What, a bloke? Never knew you batted for the other team, Dan.'

'Hey, she wasn't a bloke. I should know, I took her home.'

Jimmy nods over and says, 'Let you tickle her bollocks, did she?'

'You lot are such wind-ups. I pulled, which is more than I can say for Mike and Kate last night.'

'Yeah well, bloke or bird, who cares? Get out of my flat, you three. I've got things to do. I'm doing a spot of euphoric shopping. Now out.'

They all leave my flat. I'm shattered. Raving all night with some drugged-up gangster was definitely not on my agenda this weekend. We did have a good time, though. I do agree with Mike on that one.

Chapter 22 – Not Every Girl Is A Good-Time Girl

Helen is in the club today, which is strange. Helen never comes in the club, but it's lovely to see her.

'Hello, Kate, how are you?' She kisses me on the cheek. She always kisses me on the cheek. 'Is he in, then?'

'Yeah, go in. Knock first, I think he's with someone.'

Leon, one of Jimmy's acquaintances, comes out of the office. As I'm walking past it sounds like Jimmy and Helen are having words. Yet, it's not like them. I don't think I've ever heard them have cross words. Helen storms out of the office, slamming the door shut. What on earth is going on with them? I hope it's nothing serious.

Me and Mike go into the office and Jimmy doesn't look right at all today. Leon soon joins us and we're all sitting there talking about the Nixon lads and the trouble that went on in the Ocean Club last week. Another drugs overdose. Jimmy turns round to Leon and says, 'Hey, you've been looking at my fucking wife?'

'What? No, Mr Simpson, not me.'

'Yeah, you were, I fucking saw you.' Next thing I know Jimmy is on his feet, he punches Leon in the face and screams, 'You know what? You'll never look at my wife again, or anyone else's for that matter.' He bends down and starts to pull out Leon's eyeballs. What is he doing? Leon is on the floor squealing like a pig, the noise is echoing right through me. I've not heard anything like that in my life. I dare not look at Mike as Mike doesn't seem to be flinching. Jimmy gets up and goes to the drawer to wipe his hands on a towel.

He throws the eyeballs into the bin. Leon has crawled to the door and is squealing outside the office. Jimmy shouts, 'Mark, get rid of that fucking prick, will you?'

Mike says, 'Bloody hell, Jimmy, he was squealing like a pig there.' And again my nerves kick in and I say, 'Speaking of which, a little boy goes running into the farm house and says, "Hey, Daddy, no wonder that mummy pig is so fat, all those baby pigs are out there blowing up her belly."'

Mike rolls his eyes and says, 'God, Kate, your jokes get worse.' He gets up and walks out of the room. This has got me feeling so squeamish I could be sick.

'Jimmy, are you OK?'

'Yes, why?'

'I really don't think he was looking at Helen. Do you want to talk about it?'

He snaps at me, 'Not really, no, what the fuck has it got to do with you?' Yes, he's definitely in one of his moods and I'm unsure if I want to push it. I'd hate him to pull out my eyeballs and you can never be too sure with Jimmy. 'Nothing, I'm just saying. Hey, it's me, you know, you can tell me. I tell you allsorts.'

'Ah, nothing, it's fine, piss off.'

I think maybe I should piss off but I wouldn't be me if I wasn't insistent and there's definitely something wrong. I pull up a chair and sit beside him. I grab his hand and hold him the way he would normally hold me if I had something on my mind.

'You know, you can't always be strong. Some people do have problems and like you keep saying to me you should never be ashamed of anything, especially not in front of me. Please tell me.'

'Nothing, Treas, it's just...'

'Just what?'

'It's Helen. Me and her, you know.'

'What?'

'Well, we're having a few problems.'

'You and Helen? I thought everything was perfect with you two, what's the problem?'

'I can't seem to do right for doing wrong. We've been trying for a baby, and, well, it's not working. Helen is devastated. We had our last try of IVF last month and it never worked. Helen came in here to tell me this morning.'

'I'm sorry. Helen must be so sad, if anyone knows what it's like to want a baby, it's me. I never knew you two were trying. Goodness, imagine a little Jimmy running round, ha!'

'You could've been his godmother.'

'It will happen for you two, I'm sure it will. I've heard once you stop trying you can sometimes fall, sometimes it's the stress of trying. How about I go round and see Helen, make sure she's OK.'

'Would you? It's just, I'm trying with her but, if I clear the dishes away, I'm taking over. I ask her if she wants to go out for a meal, I'm fussing. If I sit there and don't say anything, I'm in a mood.'

'Oh, Jimmy, what am I going to do with you? Come here.'

I hug Jimmy and kiss him on the cheek. I hate the way he's feeling. I've never really seen him like this. Well, apart from when I was raped but I never really see him being weak and emotional with his own private thoughts. You sometimes forget that Jimmy Simpson is human, like us all.

I go to the toilets to wash my hands and I can see the image of Jimmy ripping out Leon's eyeballs and the noise was the worst noise I've ever heard and he really did that for nothing. I hate them sometimes. I go to the toilet and vomit. I flush it away. Sometimes I daydream I can flush myself away.

I drive to Jimmy's and knock on the door.

'Hello, Helen, how are you?'

'I'm fine, Kate, how are you?'

'Yeah, good. I was wondering if you fancied going for lunch today?'

'Not really, I wanted to just relax.'

'I know it's none of my business but you and Jimmy seemed a little tense today. I hope you two are OK.'

'Yeah, we are. Come in, we can have lunch here. Like I say, I don't fancy going out.'

'OK then, whatever you like.'

Helen makes us some dinner. I think they would make great parents. It might even calm Jimmy down a bit.

'Helen, are you sure you're OK? You seem a little distant.'

'What do you mean?'

'You just don't seem quite with it.'

'Well, it's just me and Jimmy, we've been trying for a baby and it's not working.' She starts to cry.

I grab Helen in my arms. 'Oh, come here.'

I want to hold Helen to make her feel better because I know exactly what it's like to have that feeling of longing for a child and just not being able to reach it. At least she's never had to feel what it's like to carry one inside her, give birth and have to give it up. Give it away like an old toy or something, that's the hardest thing. Had I been in time for an abortion I would know there's nothing I could do, but to know that there's a child out there walking around that might look like me, who would love me unconditionally… Helen and Jimmy could've been his auntie and uncle. They would have spoilt George rotten, I know they would have. I would love to tell Helen all about George, but I'm supposed to be here for her, not me. I think if I started to talk about him I would never stop.

'You know, just because you haven't fell pregnant doesn't mean you can't be a mum, there are loads of other options, have you ever thought about adoption?'

'Jimmy would never adopt. He has this idea that all girls who give up their babies are drug addicts or alcoholics, good-time girls, you know what he's like.'

I feel this wave of anger come over me and snap, 'That's not always true, sometimes it's girls who got themselves into a little bit of trouble and they may regret giving them up, may even want their babies back. It doesn't mean they don't love them. They do love the baby, it's just the circumstances they might have found themselves in. That's a really unfair comment of Jimmy to make.'

'Hey, calm down. Anyone would think you've given up a baby or something. You're very maternal all of a sudden, maybe you should adopt a child.'

'Nah, I'm too young for a baby. I'm saying Jimmy shouldn't always be so judgemental, that's all.'

I'm angry at Jimmy for making that comment, he knows I gave up my son. I'm not a drug addict or an alcoholic. Yes, the baby wasn't born in the best circumstances but it was still a baby nonetheless and wherever he is, his mother still loves him. I bet I love him more than my mother ever loved me. I bet if I told Helen everything she would help me find him.

I start to cough.

'Oo, that sounds like a bad cough.'

'Yes, I've been feeling a bit off all day. I think I'm coming down with something.'

Me and Helen have lunch and I make my way home. I'm feeling worse as the minutes pass.

I've been in bed for the past five days. I've had a really bad cold. That's the thing with me, I never get poorly but I get a really bad cold once in a while where I end up bedridden for days. I finally get up and I can't be bothered to go to the club, that cold really knocked me for six. I wonder how they're getting on, though. I open up the laptop and hook into the CCTV. It's early yet so I won't be seeing much going on. There's Dan. Mike is so far up his arse these days it annoys me. I don't really know why it annoys me. Hey, who's he talking to? That looks like that copper I spoke to at the station when I handed myself in over Diane stealing from work. It bloody well *is* that copper. What's he just handed him? Is he a copper too? Is that what Dan is up to? I knew he unsettled me a bit but I wasn't expecting that. Wait till I tell Mike and Jimmy what he's been up to. I think I'll ring Dan and see what he has to say for himself.

'Dan.'

'Hello, Kate, you coming to the club tonight? We've not seen you all week. Mike says you've got a cold. Is everything OK?'

'Yeah, it is with me, but what about you?'

'What do you mean?'

'Who are you really and don't even give me that bullshit of being a doorman with a wife who won't let him see his kid. I bet you're not even called Dan. You're a copper, aren't you?'

'What? Don't be daft. That's crazy. I know Mike said you can be crazy at times, but this—'

'Hey, don't you start that shit with me. I'll be telling Mike and Jimmy and they can judge for themselves who's crazy or not.'

I hang up the phone and switch it off. Last thing I can be bothered with is a million call-backs. I'll let Jimmy deal with him.

As I glance back at the laptop I see two figures come out of the bar, a man and a woman. They look like they're having fun. He's hitching up her skirt. Oo-er, he's giving her a right go there. Hang on, that's Mike. Who's he with, then? As I zoom in on the camera I see her. I don't believe it. It's Caroline, that cheeky fucking cow. I'll kill her and him. What are they playing at? Is he seeing her? How long's that been going on?

I head straight over to the bar. I'll teach her not to mess with Kate Reilly.

'Hey, Caroline, how are you today?'

'Not so great, I can't get Dave out of my head, you know. He was my husband and now he's just gone, dead, never to be seen again.'

It looked like she was over him earlier on, the stupid cow.

'Listen, fancy coming out for a drink?'

'I can't, I have to work.'

'Well, I'll speak to Jimmy, get you the night off. It'll do you good, there's a little cocktail bar round the corner, we could go there. A little girly company could be what you need.'

'Jimmy would never give me the night off, it's Saturday, one of the busiest days of the week.'

'Wait there, I'll go and see him.'

'Jimmy!' I yell at him. 'How about you give Caroline the night off tonight? I want to take her for a drink.'

'What, on a Saturday? You're kidding, aren't you? No way, never.'

'But she's upset about Dave and, let's face it, we both know how he ended up dead in that skip. The least you could do is let Caroline let her hair down tonight before she starts asking questions, go on.'

'Go on, then. Here, take this.' Jimmy hands me some money. 'Listen, just make sure she doesn't ask any more questions.'

'OK, Jimmy, I will do.'

'Caroline, you have the night off and look at this.' I wave money in her face. 'Jimmy's treat.'

We make our way to the cocktail bar round the corner and I can't help being annoyed with her. I keep seeing the image of her with Mike on the CCTV. What a stupid bitch. I sit down with our drinks and I'm still not exactly right with her but I'll play along. 'So then, Caroline, how are you?'

'I don't know. I just don't understand why anyone would want to hurt Dave, he was so soft underneath once you got to know him.'

'Listen, Caroline, I never wanted to say before but I heard a rumour, some of the other doormen talking, I don't even know how true it is, but I think he was involved with Keith Nixon's lads somehow. Maybe it was one of them, you never know, do you?'

'What, Keith Nixon? No way. Dave hated Keith Nixon, he would never have done that to Jimmy.'

Like you would never do that to me with Mike either. God, I get so angry when I think of the two of them together. I grab my glass, ready for the plan to take hold, smash Caroline's face in and make sure the shards of glass blind both eyes so she could never look at Mike again.

'Kate, are you OK?'

'Yeah, why do you ask? What's wrong?'

'Nothing, it's just you've got a funny look on your face.'

'What look?'

'Like an angry look and you're holding that glass pretty tightly.'

'Am I?'

That's it. One more word from her, she's getting it smashed

right across her face. My phone starts to ring and it's Dan. I better answer this. I'll get back to that cow in a minute.

'Hello, what do you want?'

'Just to talk to you, explain.'

'Yeah, well, you can explain it to Mike and Jimmy because I'll be telling them, you know. And how long do you think you'll last then once I tell them?'

'Please don't tell them, listen I can help you.'

'What? You help me? I don't think so. You're the one who needs help, you will do when Jimmy gets his hands on you.'

'No, Kate, listen, I need to see you.'

'No, you don't, you'll see me when I go to meet my maker too, so keep my angel wings polished for me, won't you?'

'I can get you something, something you want.'

'There's nothing I want, Dan, piss off, I'm busy.'

'I can get you your baby. Your son back.'

'What?' Did I hear Dan correctly there, did he say he could get me George?

'You heard me.'

'How the hell do you know about that?'

'Mike told me.'

'What?'

'He told me one night when we were pissed up. You help me and I'll get you your son back. Meet me in half an hour.'

Jesus Christ, George, my baby George, this is it, I can finally get him back.

'OK. I'll meet you at the train station in half an hour.'

I put the phone down and wonder if that conversation actually happened. Did he really say what I think he said? I look over at Caroline and say, 'Listen, Caroline, I have to go, you take care of yourself though, OK?'

I kiss her on the cheek, completely forgetting what I was actually there for. I run to the train station to meet Dan. George, I'm coming, Mummy is coming to get you.

Chapter 23 – The Final Countdown

Holy shit, I'm so annoyed with Mike. I catch him like that with Caroline and now I find out he's told Dan about my son. What would make him even tell anyone about that, regardless of how pissed up he was? If I can no longer trust Mike, I have nothing left. We've always trusted each other with everything. I would never tell anyone any of his secrets. I can't believe he's told Dan about George.

I finally get to the train station and Dan is there.

'Kate, thanks for coming.'

'Just talk to me, I don't need your bullshit, what do you want and I'll do it. I know you're trying to get Jimmy but I can tell you now you're fighting a losing battle. There's no way I'm giving you him. I can give you something else, though.'

'What?'

'Mike Taylor.'

'Mike is not really who we've been watching, it's Jimmy we want.'

'Yeah, well, Mike Taylor is the best you're getting. There's no way I'm giving you Jimmy. I take it you've not found anything out about him yet or you would have made your move by now.'

'We would've come up with something before long. I just needed a little bit more time. Jimmy and Mike keep their cards close to their chest. I was hoping I may have broken you.'

'Well, looks like you were wrong and your time has run out, so you take Mike Taylor or you take nothing.'

'What have you got on Mike Taylor, then?'

'I've got nothing, but you could have him for bank robbery.'

'That's not enough, my boss will go mad if I go back with that.'

'Well, you're going to go back with nothing if I tell them what you're up to. As an added bonus I could get him to hold a loaded gun.'

'How could I be sure that this would even work?'

'It would work because I'll make sure it does.'

'How do I know I can even trust you?'

'Have I gone to Jimmy or Mike yet? No, well then, you can trust me so far and at the end of the day you've nothing left to lose really, have you?'

'What, so Mike would go to rob a bank on his own and then you give us the time and the place? How do we even know he'll be there? Do you have any idea how much these undercover operations actually cost?'

'No and I don't care how much they cost. It'll be a total waste of time anyway if I go and tell Mike and Jimmy what you're up to. He'll be there because I'll be with him.'

'But then you'd have to get caught.'

'Not if I die, I won't.'

'What?'

'You heard me. I've heard of these witness protection programmes you run. Me and Mike carry out the bank job, he'll be armed, I'll make sure he believes the place is on fire. I get caught up in it and don't come out alive. It's the only way this would work because if I ever did come out alive and they found out I'd set him up then they would kill me, so I may as well be dead. It's the only way, but you have to promise me my son.'

'I'm not sure, I would need to run this by my boss. How do I even know you could pull it off?'

'I can, you'll have to trust me. I know that bank inside out. We've carried out a robbery on it before so I can work the electrics, I know I can.'

'Like I say, I'll speak to my boss tomorrow and I'll meet you Monday morning at my office and we'll discuss it further.'

All weekend, all I can think of is George. I'm so close to him now that I can actually smell him. What if Dan's boss says no, what will I do then? His boss can't say no, he just can't.

I get to Dan's office and he introduces me to his boss, Linda. I was expecting a man for some reason. I shake Linda's hand. She seems a straight-up woman who will say it how it is. She wants every criminal off the street and will stop at nothing to get it. I have a gut feeling she's going to say yes, I know she is.

'Listen, Miss Reilly, I don't have to tell you that this needs to be thought out properly. Once you go ahead with this and you walk out of that building, there's no going back. You have to leave everyone behind, your mother, your friends. How will you feel leaving Mr Simpson and Mike? Don't you run to them every time you've got a problem?'

'I'll be fine with it. It's about time I started standing on my own feet anyway. I can make this work, I know I can, but you have to promise me my son. I need you to promise me, that I get my son at the end of this.'

'Yes, we can promise you that. We have tracked your son down and it seems he was never adopted out.'

'What, you've tracked him down, well, where is he? When can I see him?'

'It won't be a case of you walking out of that building and claiming back your son. It takes time, we need to make sure that it's in the best interests of the child.'

'Why was he not adopted out?'

'We can't discuss this any further with you. We need to arrange what is happening with Michael Taylor first. You have to come up with the goods you are promising us, or you will never get your son back.'

Linda says this like some schoolteacher or something.

'OK, this is what will happen. As I explained to Dan, I make sure Mike thinks the place is on fire. I'll trip the switches when I'm in there. That bank on Alderson Road is an old bank and when you trip the switches, metal gates will close. I'll make sure Mike is on one side of the gates, trapped in the building with no escape, and I'll make sure I'm on the other side. I'll also make sure he's armed, he will spend years in prison for being armed. You'll have to get a smoke machine arranged so it looks believable for Mike, with him being on the other side of the room it won't be too hard to do.'

'Well, Miss Reilly, you're more intelligent than we thought.'

'Yeah, don't underestimate me, Linda, I'm nobody's fool. So don't even think about double-crossing me either. I want to do this soon, though, so next Friday it has to be.'

'What? We can't arrange that in two weeks.'

'Yes, you can, it's two weeks or nothing.'

I say that because if it's any longer I'll be afraid that I may change my mind and not be able to go through with this.

'OK, we'll see what we can do.'

As I walk away from that office I'm shaking like a leaf. I'm going to get him, my baby George. After all this time, I'm finally going to get him. The only thing is, though, to get him I have to hurt my best friend, my love, my everything. Oh God, it's just hit me what I actually have to do. Can I do this? Can I trick Mike into this? How will I feel? Maybe I should sit him and Jimmy down and tell them what is happening. Maybe they would help me get my baby back if I asked them nicely.

I make my way over to the club. My heart is still pounding from the visit and Mike is there.

'Hey, where've you been? I've been trying to call you.'

'Ah, sorry, Mike. I was busy shopping. I never heard my phone.'

'Well, it must have been a bloody good shopping trip then. What did you get?'

'Nothing much. Listen, I don't quite know how to say this, but you know my baby?'

'Your what, Kate?'

'My baby, the one we gave up, I was thinking of maybe seeing if I could track him down and get him back. I know it's a total long shot, but would you help me?'

I look at Mike and he laughs in my face, he actually laughs.

'You think they would hand a baby over to you? You're fucking nuts, even Jimmy has told you that. No. I said when we were coming back from the hospital to leave him where he was. You'd be doing him a favour.'

'Erm, all right, no need for nastiness, I was just asking.'

'Well, don't ask. Help me sort the fridges out, and no more hare-brained schemes. Crikey, woman, you nearly gave me a heart attack there.'

So that's it then, I'm definitely on. Mike has no idea what he's just done there.

Linda calls me. 'Right Kate, we're OK for Friday. We'll have everything arranged for you. Are you sure you can do it? If it all goes wrong, heads are going to roll.'

'Yes, I'm sure. Can you definitely get me my son, though? If I go through all of this for nothing heads *will* fucking roll, I'm warning you.'

'Yes, we have looked into it and spoken to social services. Do you need a gun?'

'No, I'll sort that. I just need the smoke machine and entrance to the bank after closing time one night this week so I can look at the electrics and how to trip them. This needs to be done properly. I can't get this wrong. If I get caught my life won't be worth living.'

'Yes, I know, mine neither if this goes wrong. I need you to be sure that you can do this and you can cope with it.'

'Yes, I can. I'm a strong person, a lot stronger than you think.'

'OK, then. I'll get you access to the bank after closing hours on Tuesday.'

'Thanks.'

I go back over to Mike and say, 'Mike, do you fancy carrying out a bank job with me next Friday?'

'What on earth do you want to carry out a bank job for? What do you need money for?'

'I was going to see if I could buy a house, instead of living in the poky flat. I quite fancy a garden.'

'I don't know if I can be bothered, Kate, I thought we were past all this now.'

I can't believe he's not said yes straight away. I never thought about him saying no. What will I do now? I grab a hold of his arm.

'Please, Mike, I really need some money. Look at all the times I've helped you, when have I ever said no?'

'Can't you just ask Jimmy for some dividends out of the club or something? What do you want a house for anyway? The flat's a good size just for you.'

'I don't want to ask Jimmy for any money. I think they've used all of the money on IVF, or at least most of it. Hey, we could surprise him and pay for another shot for them. He'd be so happy if we did that.'

'Go on then, you've twisted my arm.'

I jump up and shout, 'Yes!'

'Steady on, Kate, I can't believe I've let you talk me into this.' Mike kisses me on the cheek. I bet he wouldn't be kissing me if he knew what I was planning. That's it, then. It's all arranged. It's actually going to happen.

It's my last Sunday in Bridgeborough. I go to Mr and Mrs Richards and I say, 'Mrs Richards, will you come to the car boot sale with us today?'

'Me, what on earth for? I never come, it's always yours and Graham's day.'

'I know, but I would like you to come.'

'But what about the dinner?'

'Well, we'll have a late lunch. I'd like to stay with you two all day today, if that's OK?'

'Kate, you can stay as long as you like. Graham, will you be OK with that, a late lunch?'

Mr Richards winks over at me and says, 'Of course I will, Elizabeth.'

We make our way to the car boot sale and I say to them both, 'I'll tell you what, why don't we all buy each other something just to remember us all by.'

Mrs Richards laughs and says, 'Goodness me, do you think we're about to die? I'm not quite ready to go yet.'

'No, but it would be nice if we could buy each other something. Get me something that I can wear and think of you two, like a brooch or something.' I want something to remember those two by. I won't be able to take any of my possessions with me. Imagine me showing up for a robbery with a suitcase full of memories. Mike would get suspicious. Mind you, that idiot would think it was empty ready to fill up with cash. When I start my new life the only thing I'll have left of Kate Reilly will be something from my two favourite people. I should have just lived at their house my entire life. I would have been cared for and loved unconditionally.

I buy Mrs Richards some lovely earrings and Mr Richards an old war medal. They buy me a bracelet. We head back home and as I'm sitting eating my dinner I look at them and think, I can't believe I'll never see you two again. I'm quite sad. Will I even ever go to another car boot sale again? How will they take my death? They're getting older by the day, what if one of them has a heart attack or dies with shock? I'd never forgive myself.

'You do know that I love you two, don't you?'

'Oh, of course we do. We love you too,' says Mrs Richards.

'I've always thought of you two as grandparents, you know. I've never found out who my father was but at least I've had grandparents. I'll never forget these days, ever.'

'You can be so sweet at times. I think we would be lost without you.'

As I leave their house, I give them both an extra squeeze.

Tuesday comes and I make my way to the bank to look at the electrics. It's not like I've not been here after hours before. Me, Jimmy and Mike broke in here a couple of years ago. I start to think back to that night and remember that as we walked in the door Jimmy slipped. Me and Mike laughed so hard that night, even driving home. I don't even think we needed to start the car, we were bumping it down the road by the sheer fits of giggles. Jimmy got annoyed in the end and told us both to fuck off. Which made us laugh even more. He stormed out of the car and said he'd walk home. I had tears rolling down my cheeks that night. Even back in my flat, lying in bed, I was still laughing away to myself.

I'll miss times like that with those two. I start to think of all the fun times we've had over the years. Like when it was Mike's birthday at a curry house and we dared him to eat the hottest curry they serve. Jimmy told the waiter to make it double the strength. He did and Mike vomited all over the table. It stunk of chewed-up curry mixed with beer, the whole restaurant emptied. Jimmy had to pay them a full night's takings in compensation for the loss. I realise that not everything over the past few years has been bad and I do love those two. Before I know it, I have tears rolling down my cheeks. I don't think I'm strong enough, after all, for this. I can't leave them, they're all I know. I need them, both of them, in different ways. I start to feel an ache in my stomach like the ache I feel for George. No, come on, Kate, stay strong – your son, he's waiting for you. You only have three days to get through. Try and focus on Mike and Jimmy's negatives.

I have three days left to see all the people I know and love, and say my goodbyes. I'll start with Shelly and David, one last look at him before I go.

'Hello, Shelly.'

'Hello, Kate. How you doing, stranger? We hardly see you these days.'

'Yeah, I know, I get so busy and so tired. How's David?'

'He's fine, he's started nursery, he loves it.' David comes running into the room. 'Look at him, he's so big.'

I look at him and realise how big George will be when I finally get to meet him. He's running around with a toy car in his hand, him and Billy are playing together. That's amazing, how big he is. I've seen him now and then, but since Mike told me to stay away, I couldn't see him too often. Not that I care, I'll be dead in a few days. I grab David and kiss him.

'Goodbye, David, goodbye, Billy.'

I grab a hold of Shelly so hard. This is it. I've known her my whole life, she practically helped my mum bring me up.

'Hey, what's up with you? Have you gone soft on us all of a sudden?'

'Yeah, something like that. You will always take care of my mum, won't you?'

'What, are you kidding? She takes care of me.'

'Yeah, you're right there, she does as well. I remember her telling you to stay away from those Taylor brothers and did you listen? Did you heck and look what happened.'

I wink at Shelly and walk out of the door.

Next stop Jennie. How on earth do I say goodbye to Jennie? I have tears rolling down my eyes even thinking of saying goodbye to her. All the nasty things I've done to her, I blamed her for this whole mess and I suppose it's because I needed someone to blame. It was just one of those things. I wish I could go back and do things differently with Jennie, she really is a big regret of mine. I would sometimes get so annoyed with her. I wish I could explain it to her and say I'm sorry for everything. I really do love her, she's my best friend. Can I live without a best friend? I've slept with her, I've nursed her when she was bad, she's nursed me when I was bad. This is all a lot harder than I thought it would ever be. Maybe I'm not strong enough for this, maybe I should have spoken to Jimmy more about my son, spoken to Doctor Cavendish, got someone to help me.

As I approach Jennie's house I need to dry my eyes. I need to keep it together. If any of this gets out, Mike will kill me.

'Hello, Jennie.'

'I was just thinking about you.'

'Oh, really, why?'

'I was sorting through some stuff and I picked up that jewellery box you got me for my thirteenth birthday. Can you remember yours, and we were sick all over your mum's hallway?'

'Ha! Yeah, I remember that, my mum was so angry with me the next day and I noticed how you slunk off home and I had to clean up after both of us.'

'That was such a good time.'

'I miss those days, come here, give me a hug.'

'Oi, not like you to get sentimental.'

'Jennie.'

'Yeah.'

'Will you sleep with me again?'

'What! Why?'

'I don't know why. I just want you to.'

Me and Jennie end up in the bedroom. I kiss her so gently. I want this to last forever, I want to take in the taste of her so I remember it. Afterwards, I lie in her arms. I wish I could stay here forever. Maybe Jennie could help me get my baby back. Me and her could move away together, maybe I could tell her what I was planning, she could get on the witness protection plan with me. Nah, that's stupid. It has to be like this, it just has to.

'Jennie, I need to go. Please don't ever forget the good times.'

'Kate, what on earth has got into you?'

'Nothing, you just enjoy the rest of your day.'

I should go and see my mum, but I can't face that today. Maybe tomorrow.

It's Thursday. I have one full day left in Bridgeborough for the rest of my life. After tomorrow, that's it. I'll go and see my mum, make sure she's OK with money and things before I go.

I turn up and the place is a mess.

'God, Mum, don't you ever clean up after yourself?'

'Oh, I don't have time to clean. I work most nights.'

'Yes, but not most mornings.'

'Why are you always moaning on at me? You're so ungrateful, you've always hated me.'

'No, I haven't, what on earth are you even saying that for?' I feel like maybe she has that maternal feeling and she knows tomorrow is the day I die. 'Here is some money.'

I give her ten thousand pounds in an envelope. It's all the savings I have as Linda says they'll get me a job and give me a little money once this is all over. But I'm not to take anything of Kate's as she'll be a dead girl.

'Jesus, Kate, you been robbing bloody banks or something?'

How ironic. 'No, I've got some savings, I just wanted you to have them. I'm going to clean this place for you so it's nice. Will you promise that you will spend that money wisely and take care of yourself?'

'What on earth are you on about? Anyone would think you were emigrating or something. I'll see you tomorrow night in the club anyway.'

'Yeah, you will.'

If only she knew that she won't see me in the club tomorrow or anywhere ever again come to think of it. I think I'll even miss her in my own way. I clean the house from top to bottom. As I make my way round the house I go into my bedroom and think of all the things that have happened to me in this house. I think back to the night I met Mike and Lawrence in here. We had so much fun. I used to show off with all those stupid magic trick sets I had, they loved them. When Mike showed me the card trick with Shelly, when I would place my hand over the cards and he would take a drink to show me which card was hers… We still do it to people, it winds Jimmy up something rotten, he really doesn't know how I do it.

I think I'll go round and see Mike. Spend one last night with him.

'Hello, gorgeous, what you up to?' he says as he greets me with a smile.

'Not much, I just thought I would come round to see you.'

'You getting sorted for tomorrow?'

'Nah, I don't need to get sorted, you know I'm good at carrying out bank jobs. We're professionals at it now.'

'Yeah, I suppose you're right.'

'How about we stay in tonight, have a bottle of wine and a takeaway and chill out, have a laugh?'

'OK, if you want, what do you fancy?'

'Anything, gentleman's choice.'

'Gentleman, bloody hell, it's been a while since someone called me that.'

'Yeah, slip of the tongue there.'

We sit with our wine and I find myself looking at him, taking in his face, what he looks like, what his scent is like. I better take it all in now because by tomorrow my heart will be racing. I can't imagine I'll be taking much in at all. It's going to have to be precise and done properly. I can't afford any mistakes. This is not just some straight forward bank job, it's a death, it's an end to me, and to Mike and Jimmy forever, our little group. Those two will never be the same after tomorrow, their little angel will be gone, never to be seen again.

I think about how much they worried about me when I was in prison and think they will be out of their minds tomorrow. What on earth will they say? I wonder if Mike will be as upset about me as he was with Diane? Who will be there to take care of him? I took care of him after Diane. I have that feeling in my throat again, like it's closing up, like I'm going to have a panic attack. I jump up.

'I can't do it, Mike.'

'What?'

'Tomorrow, it's off, it's all off, I'm not doing it.'

'Don't be stupid, Kate, it's all arranged. We're doing it and that's that.'

'No, no, I'm not, you can't make me do it. I'm not doing it.'

'You asked me to do it. I told Jimmy I was going to get him

some money. He wants to invest in the club, in *your* fucking club. So stop being a fucking pussy and pick your arse back up.'

Why is he being such a dick today? I'm trying to get out of dying.

'Whatever, Mike, OK, but it's the last time I ever do a job with you, that's it.'

I storm out and slam the door behind me. Right, we will go ahead with it. I might even get the shotgun and blow his head off.

Well, today is the day, I'm finally on with my next journey. I wonder what George will look like? Will he even want to come and live with me? I mean, he's four now. What on earth are four-year-olds even into these days? Or any days, come to think of it. Maybe I should get him a present. I really need to see Jimmy today. I'm not sure if I'm strong enough for that yet. I think I'll miss him a little more than Mike. Mike has hurt me so much over the years, but Jimmy has always taken care of me. I can tell Jimmy anything. I sometimes wish I was Helen and he was my husband. I can have babies. I could be what he wanted and he could be what I wanted. Not sure if I could ever have sex with Jimmy. Mind you, give me a bit of booze and who knows? As I make my way over to the club, I'm walking as slowly as I can to try and prolong it. I really don't think I can cope with this any more, my head has been banging all week with the thoughts that are running through my mind.

'Treas.'

Oh, my heart melts when he says that. It will be the last time I ever hear those words coming out of his mouth. Treas and Gem, that's who I am, no one will ever call me either name ever again. Or Kate, come to think of it. I wonder what my name will be.

'Wow, you look extra handsome today.'

'You all set for tonight?'

'Yeah, you know me. Listen, Jimmy, I just wanted you to know how much I love you and appreciate everything you've ever done for me.'

'What? Are you going soft on me again?'

'No, I'm just saying. How's things with you and Helen now?'

'Great, I've just booked a cruise for us, she reckons only old people go on cruises.'

'They do, bloody hell, it'll be like a pensioners' picnic on there.'

'Nah, they have pools and cinemas on those ships now.'

'Have they? That's amazing, that.'

'Hey, how about I book you on? You could come with us, we'll have a right laugh. I'll see if Mike wants to come.'

'Yeah maybe, don't book just yet though, leave it a couple of weeks, make sure I can definitely make it. I think Jennie was going to book us two somewhere so I better check the date first. Do you fancy some lunch today, spend a few hours together?'

Jimmy's phone starts to ring. He picks it up and moves the phone away from his ear. 'Listen, Kate, this is important. I'll catch you later, yeah? We'll do lunch another day. I'm mad busy today. Could you shut the door on your way out?'

'OK, then.'

I have to leave his office. Oh no, I never got my hug, he never hugged me. I never got to take in Jimmy's scent. Why did that phone have to ring then? I want to spend some more time with him, I'm not ready. I'm not ready to leave him. I've been able to say a proper goodbye to everyone, yet one of the most important people in my life was too busy, too busy to even give me a couple of hours. That's all I needed, that's all I wanted. It's happening tonight, I can't delay this, but how can I do this without saying goodbye to Jimmy properly? I run to the toilet and I can hardly breathe, my breathing seems to have stopped and I feel a little lightheaded. I splash my face with water and take in deep breaths. Calm down, Kate, calm down. You'll be OK, think of George, keep thinking of George. He's out there with no one to love him, he needs you more than Jimmy and Mike need you. My breathing returns to a normal pace. I make my way out of the club, taking one last look at the place. I'm going to miss this club so much. It's my club, Jimmy gave me this club, it has my name in lights above the door. People talk about me in their wedding speeches, just like Jimmy told me they talked about Jimmeez when it was called that. How can I do this? I'm so scared. I want to run back into Jimmy's office and hang up on that caller and tell Jimmy everything. I don't think I can leave him, not like this, it's not how I wanted it to end with Jimmy.

It's time, today has flown over, and Mike is outside in the car waiting for me. My legs are like jelly as I make my way over.

'Hello, miserable,' Mike says.

'What?'

'You heard me, what was all that about last night?'

'All what? What are you going on about?'

'You, on one again, wanting to pull out, you're such a scaredy-cat, Miss Reilly.'

'No, I'm not, leave me alone.'

'Come on, cheer up. I'll tell you what, when we get out of here tonight, how about I take you to that restaurant we went to years ago with Rusco, when you first told me about your eating phobia?'

'Hey, it wasn't a phobia, leave me alone.'

We giggle as we drive away, it's almost like I believe I'm actually going to go to that restaurant.

Yet I know I'm not.

As we make our way to the bank my mind is racing with all the things I need to do.

'You got the gun?'

'Yes, but I don't know why, we've never taken a gun before.'

'Yeah, but you never know, we might need it. We won't use it. Is it loaded?'

'Yeah, it's got a couple of bullets in.'

We get to the entrance of the bank and Mike breaks open the door with a wrench. As we get inside the smell hits me and all my memories come flooding back of when I was younger and we broke in here. I wish I could back out but I need to do this for George. If only Linda had told me he'd been adopted out years ago there would be nothing I could do, so I could back out. But as it stands I have to do this. 'Come on, Kate, you're standing there like an idiot, move along.'

'Sorry, Mike, I was miles away there.'

'Yes, so I noticed. What do you want me to do?'

'You go over there, as soon as I work the alarm, go into the open door.'

He starts to walk over to the other side of the bank. I watch him as he does and it breaks my heart I won't ever see him again. As soon as he is in the open doorway, I head towards the alarm panel. Just like Tuesday night, I trip the switches and a loud bang happens and the door he is standing in front of closes, locking him in the other side of the bank. He has the gun, that's exactly how they wanted him. The gate in front of me also locks so we're both locked behind gates. There's an emergency exit over at his side, which is where the police are going to bust the door open and get him. My side is where the illusion of the fire will be. Now it's up to me to make sure that I do my bit right.

'Bloody hell, Kate, what the fuck happened there? I'm locked in.'

'Shit, I'm sorry. I've tripped the electrics, wait there, I'll try and sort it.'

I run over to the other side of the bank where the front door is. The smoke machine is there waiting for me. I put it on the reception desk and switch on the power button. Nothing happens. What the hell has happened, have they not even tested the smoke machine? I click the switch a few times and nothing happens. I can feel the tears stinging my eyes. I'm so angry I punch the wall.

'Ahh, it's all gone wrong!' I screech at the top of my lungs.

'What's gone wrong, Kate? What is it?'

'Erm nothing, Mike, it's fine.'

I wipe the tears from my eyes. I don't want him to start to guess anything is wrong. Then I think to myself, This could be a sign that I'm not supposed to have George, maybe it's for the best he stays wherever he is. Then out of nowhere a memory springs to my mind and I'm lying in the hospital and I can hear George crying, plain as day. Then I remember why I'm actually here, it's for him. I look at the socket on the wall and realise it's not even plugged in. I plug it in, flick the switch and the smoke comes billowing out. It even makes me cough. I mean, I've heard of dramatic effect but this is going a little too far. I head over to the fire alarm and turn the key making the sirens whirl out. They nearly deafen me. I go running back to the main room where Mike is still locked behind his gate.

'Shit, it's on fire, the place is on fire.'

'What do you mean it's on fire? How the hell is it on fire? What's happened?'

'I don't know. I went to trip the alarm and it's done something to the wiring, it must have been dodgy electrics. But worse than that there's only one way out! It's on your side, because the fire is on this side.'

'What the fuck are you saying?'

'I'm locked in, there is no way out for me. I'm going to die.'

'No, you have to get out, try and open the gates, go and get an extinguisher. Quickly!'

'I've already looked, there isn't one.'

'Don't be stupid, there has to be an extinguisher at the entrance to a bank. Health and Safety would make sure there was.'

'There isn't, I looked, it's too late the smoke is too thick, it's on it's way over to me, look.' I point towards the smoke as it is now slowy billowing towards me.

He starts to scream. 'No! No! Please do something.' He shakes the gates so hard I think they might open.

With all of the commotion coming from Mike, the smoke machine and the alarm that's ringing in my head, I have images of my mum in my face saying, 'You have no right to know who your father is, he wouldn't want a little bitch like you.' Jennie then pops up. 'Want some white wine, Kate?' With an evil laugh, she hands me a bottle of white wine. My mind has started to go all hazy. Jimmy is now in my mind saying, 'Your burnt body will be in the skip next, Kate.'

I'm not sure if I'm strong enough to do this. How do I know they will even give me George back? I could be going through all of this for nothing. How do I know it wasn't me that Dan was watching? Everyone I've ever loved has tricked me into something, one way or another. Maybe this is a trick, maybe it's me who's going to be arrested. It did seem funny that Dan was there as soon as I got out of prison and I kept telling Jimmy and Mike that there was something about him, but they kept shrugging it off. Maybe they knew all the time who he was. Maybe they sent him here because they want rid of me. It's not right that Mike would have told him about George. I've always trusted Mike, why all of a sudden has he started to betray me? Maybe he found out what I did to Diane, maybe that's why this is.

'Kate, please, please, try and get out.'

'Throw me the gun.'

'What?'

'The gun, throw me it.'

'Why?'

'I'll try and shoot this lock off and come over your side. I'll have a better chance of getting out, pass me the gun.'

He slides the gun over to my side.

'Hurry, Kate. Please hurry, I don't want you to die, please.' I wipe his prints from the gun. 'What are you doing?'

'I can't do this any more. I'm so sorry.'

'What? What can't you do? Stop fucking about, and get over here, now. The fire, it's getting nearer.' He starts to shake the gates again.

'No, I'm tired.'

'What are you on about, tired of what? Please just come over here. I'll let you sleep for a week. I'll do anything.'

Mike is hysterical over there, he is really panicking. He's panicking more than when he found Diane.

'No, that's it. I'm sick of running, I'm sick of everything, that fire is coming for me, but I'm not going to die like that. One shot, Mike, that's all it's going to take.'

'What? Stop it, you're scaring me. Please don't fuck about, get over here, now. I promise, I'll do anything you want.'

'You've never done anything I want. It's always been about you. You have used me my entire life and I'm tired of it. All I ever did was love you and you never loved me back.'

'Of course I love you, I've always loved you, what would make you even say that?'

'You never loved me enough to marry me. I'm in love with you, really in love with you and all I ever wanted was for you to tell me that you loved me and you wanted to have babies with me but you never said those words. I wanted you to take me back to my baby and you never even cared.'

'I explained to you before you handed the baby over you can't change your mind. I asked you so many times if you were sure and you said yes. I'll marry you if you want, please don't do this.' Mike starts to cry.

'No, I have to, I'm tired. Have you tricked me?'

'Of course not. What are you even on about, tricking you? There's a fucking fire, get over here, we don't have time for your craziness, please.'

'You did, you told Dan about George.'

'Who the fuck is George? Can we discuss this later? Please get over here.'

'No, I see it now, you and Jimmy tricking me into this.'

'But this was *your* idea. Listen to me, OK? I want you to listen to me properly, look at me and think straight. You're panicking, the place is on fire and you're panicking. Look at me, I'm not tricking you. I love you, you're my best friend, my soulmate. I've practically brought you up. I've known you since you were this crazy little girl, showing me all your tricks. I knew then I was going to know you for the rest of your life and kill anyone who tried to hurt you and I did, I protected you from Roger and Paul. Please come over here, I need you, I really need you.'

'Why did you tell Dan about my baby? I always thought I could trust you. I feel like you and Jimmy have twisted my mind so much that I don't even recognise myself these days. I've had enough. I love you, I've always loved you, and I know you love me, just not in the way that I wanted you to. I saw you with Caroline and realised then that you think of me the same as any other little tart.'

'I'm sorry I had sex with Caroline. I can't even remember telling Dan about your baby. I must have been really drunk and it must have been in the back of my mind. Don't think that I don't think about that baby sometimes, it was part of you, Kate. I don't hate that baby, I never did, and if you'd wanted to keep it back then I would have stood by you, helped you, but I did what you wanted. You can't just give up a baby and go back the next day for it, that's not fair on anyone. I bet he's having a lovely life now. I'll tell you what, we'll track him down, if that's what you want, what you really want. I'll help you.'

'I asked you to help me last week and you laughed in my face. Please tell Jimmy that I love him and, Mike, I'm really sorry it has ended like this. I love you so much. Probably a little too much.'

I head out of view towards the smoke machine. Mike is really hysterical, he's screaming at me.

'No! Please, come here, please come back! I need you, I love you, Kate, please.'

I can't go back. I've really had enough. The pain in my heart is too much to take. I pull the trigger and that's it. One bang.

Kathryn Reilly. Aged twenty-three. May she rest in peace.

17 October 2003.

ABOUT THE AUTHOR

S.M. Hope released her debut novel *Tainted Jewel* through the BNBS crowdfunding campaign for pre-orders. The campaign exceeded all expectation and took only 18 days to be 100% funded. S.M. Hope was still getting enquiries of *Tainted Jewel* even after the campaign had ended.

In the real world away from thoughts of gangsters and who to kill off next, she manages the day-to-day running of a busy engineering company – or tries to keep up to date with her teenage son and his capers – while they decide who's turn it is to take their two pet dogs for a walk.

Writing is one of her many hobbies as well as arts and crafts which means her dining room table is normally split between the laptop and glitter/glasses. Maybe when she retires she may get to eat a meal from the table, but until that time, glitter flavoured casserole it is.